THE HEART OF THE FAMILY

Also by Elizabeth Goudge

Novels
ISLAND MAGIC
A CITY OF BELLS
TOWERS IN THE MIST
THE MIDDLE WINDOW
A BIRD IN THE TREE
THE CASTLE ON THE HILL
GREEN DOLPHIN COUNTRY
THE HERB OF GRACE
THE HEART OF THE FAMILY
GENTIAN HILL
THE ROSEMARY TREE
THE WHITE WITCH
THE DEAN'S WATCH
THE SCENT OF WATER
THE CHILD FROM THE SEA

Omnibus
THE ELIOTS OF DAMEROSEHAY
THREE CITIES OF BELLS

Anthology
AT THE SIGN OF THE DOLPHIN
A BOOK OF COMFORT
A CHRISTMANS BOOK
THE TEN GIFTS

Non-fiction
GOD SO LOVED THE WORLD
ST. FRANCIS OF ASSISI
A DIARY OF PRAYER

THE CHRISTCHURCH EDITION

ELIZABETH GOUDGE

The Heart of the Family

HODDER AND STOUGHTON
LONDON SYDNEY AUCKLAND TORONTO

Copyright 1953 by Elizabeth Goudge. First printed 1953. This edition 1974.
ISBN 0 340 18152 4. All rights reserved. No part of this publication may be
reproduced or transmitted in any form or by any means, electronic or mechanical,
including photocopy, recording, or any information storage and retrieval system,
without permission in writing from the publisher. Printed in Great Britain for
Hodder and Stoughton Limited, St. Paul's House, Warwick Lane, London EC4P
4AH by Richard Clay (The Chaucer Press), Ltd., Bungay, Suffolk.

There lives the dearest freshness deep down things;
And though the last lights off the black West went
Oh, morning, at the brown brink eastward, springs—
Because the Holy Ghost over the bent
World broods with warm breast and with ah! bright wings.

GERARD MANLEY HOPKINS

CHAPTER I

MEG, wearing mackintosh boots and a red mackintosh, and with a red sou'wester tied beneath her chin, splashed down the drive, and under the dripping oak-trees, in a state of happiness deeper and more perfect than any other she was likely to know while she lived in this world. Had she known that she would never be happy in quite this way again she would not have been so happy, but she did not know. She was four years old, and much beloved, and regarded happiness as the normal state of everybody. She was not happy when her tummy ached or she had a cold in her head, or when her mother or father went away and left her, or when the black beast pounced; at such times the depth of her misery was quite appalling; but those awful times did not come very often, and in between were these long stretches of shining joy.

She thought it was a gloriously squelchy day. The drive was in a deplorable state, full of ruts and holes, and pools of rain-water brimmed them all. Meg zigzagged from one to the other, planting a booted foot firmly in the middle of each, so that fountains of water shot up into the air to descend again upon her head, together with rain-drops dripping from the oak-trees, in a perfect deluge of sun-shot gleaming silveriness. Every time this happened she chuckled softly, and Mouse, running at her heels, barked joyously. Mouse, a microscopic grey cairn, was two years old. She had been given to Meg by her father when Robin, Meg's brother, had been born, so that Meg as well as her mother should have a tiny thing to care for. She had a minute pointed face, very long whiskers and a small dainty head with only two ideas in it—Meg and dinner. Of these two ideas Meg was the predominant one. She loved Meg with a love that was out of all proportion to the size of her body. She went where Meg went, loved whoever and whatever Meg loved; and as Meg loved nearly everybody, she loved nearly everybody, too. She had no life apart from Meg and would gladly have died for her. Because Meg liked splashing in the wet she liked it, too, and because Meg gloried in this day she also thought it a gift for the two of them sent straight out of heaven.

And it was a good day. The sun and the rain were flying and the whole world was washed in silver and drenched with the scents of wet earth and grass and flowers, the smell of the sea and the aromatic pungent smell of the herby things that grew in the sea-marshes beyond the oak-wood. Over her head the bits of sky that Meg could see between the wet leaves were thrilling: a patch of bright blue here, a bit of inky storm-cloud there, a bit of a rainbow somewhere else. The cry of the gulls was wild and high and excited, and within the walled garden there was a blackbird singing.

Meg looked ridiculous. Mackintoshes being the price they were, her splashing outfit had been bought large enough to allow for growth. The bottom of her mackintosh descended to her ankles and the sleeves to the tips of her fingers. The brim of her poppy hat, weighted with water, flapped to her nose in front and descended over her ears each side. There was nothing to be seen of her except a small pointed sunburnt chin with water-drops trickling off it, and yet a keen observer hidden behind the oak-trees would have known quite a lot about Meg just by watching her progress down the drive. The sheer ecstasy with which her booted feet came down in each puddle told of the depth of her capacity for happiness. And yet her chuckle was without undue excitement and devoid of squeak. It would seem she knew already, with subconscious knowledge, that restraint is estimable in women, and would love it and exercise it all her life. And she was game. It was obvious that she would not cry if she tripped over the hem of her ridiculous mackintosh and fell headlong, for not even that ungainly flapping garment could hide the trim gallantry of her little figure. She was determined, too. Though she zigzagged from puddle to puddle, she was never deflected from her determined progress down the drive. She knew where she was going and what she was going to do when she got there.

She was down! There had been treacherous foothold in one of the puddles and the toe of one boot had caught on a shifting stone. It could not have been a nastier fall. She went down flat, with her poppy hat flying off her head and her face against the stones of the drive. Yet she was up again in a moment, with no outcry. But she stood still now, unable to go on, one small brown hand, with the fingers spread out starfish-wise, pressed against her excoriated little face.

The observer who had been hidden behind the oak-trees was beside her in two strides, had picked her up and carried her to the bench just inside the gate that led from the oak-wood to the village, the marshes and the sea. He set her down and sat beside her. Mouse lay down on his feet to comfort him. She would have lain on Meg's had they been available, but Meg's did not reach the ground. Mouse always lay on people's feet when she felt they needed comfort. She did not know why with her mind, but her instinct told her that in times of desolation the extremities should always be kept warm. To make up for the lack of ideas in her head, Mouse's instincts were very highly developed.

" That was a bad fall, wasn't it? " said the man who had picked Meg up. " Might I see your nose? "

Meg, her starfish hand still flat against her face, shook her head. This person was a stranger to her, and she had her dignity. She could feel the blood running down from inside her nose and she knew she must look a mess. She did not like to be looked at by a strange man when she was a mess. But she felt very desolate, and had an awful feeling that the black beast was just round the corner somewhere, waiting to pounce. Her father and mother were not home yet, and the French Mademoiselle who helped her mother look after her and Robin was cross today. Mrs. Wilkes, who came up each day from the village to help with the cooking and cleaning and washing-up, was not cross, because she never was, but she was in that rather difficult mood which very good people get into when if they were not so good they would be very cross indeed. She did not feel a bit nice, and there was no one to help her to bear it. A small strangled sob broke from her, but was instantly repressed, for she had her pride as well as her dignity.

The stranger produced a large pocket handkerchief. " I must mop up your nose," he said firmly. " If you please."

Meg had been trained to obedience, and she recognised the voice of authority as well as the note of repressed exasperation to which she was well accustomed in the voices of grown-ups. They were always in such a hurry, and arguments that delayed them in their perpetual rush from one task to another could bring that edge even to her mother's warm and pretty voice, as she ran from the washing-up to the butcher waiting to be paid at the back door, and from the butcher to Daddy, who had lost his spectacles again, and from Daddy to Robin, who had fallen out of the pram and was dangling by the straps. She removed her hand.

" Bluggy," she said.

" A merely temporary affliction," said the stranger, and he mopped her up expertly but with such quick jerky movements that she felt like a kitten with its fur stroked backwards.

"You're in a hurry," she said, a rather sad little statement of fact that made him feel oddly reproached. He put his handkerchief back in his pocket and tried to relax. He took off his hat and held it between his knees. Then, catching sight of his thin nervous hands clenched on the hat, as though he were clinging to a lifebelt, he gave an impatient exclamation and dropped it on the ground, letting his hands dangle.

" I'm not in a hurry," he said gently.

" I'm not either," said Meg.

He smiled down at the top of her head. " You seemed to be, coming down the drive."

" I wasn't in a hurry," said Meg. " I was just going somewhere. I was going to look at the gulls at the harbour. I needn't."

" Then we'll stay here for a bit, shall we? "

" Yes," whispered Meg. She felt a little shy, and still shaken, and would have liked to go back to the house to Zelle, but she wanted to oblige.

The warm sun of the stormy August day was out again and it beat down upon them. Here in the sheltered drive, with the rampart of the oak-trees between them and the marshes, they did not feel the wind from the sea. Through the wrought-iron gate in the wall the man could see the golden and orange glow of autumn flowers, the tall and gracious trees of an old and matured garden, and, beyond, the irregular roof of the house. To ease his restlessness he had chosen to walk from the station instead of taking a taxi. He had asked his way in Radford and taken the coast road through the marshes carrying his bag, a thing the doctor had forbidden him to do, but the beauty of the walk had made him forget the weight of it. To his right the marshes had been splashed with colour like a painter's palette; to his left, just at the corner of the lane that led down from the high-road, there had been a cornfield bending beneath the wind. On the horizon he had seen the silver line of the sea and the estuary, with the cliffs of the Island beyond, at one moment half hidden in mists of driving rain, remote and far away, at the next leaping out under the sun in such clear distinctness that they looked like the longed-for Celestial Mountains at the end of the unending way. Then he had reached the harbour, with wild sea-asters growing beside the harbour wall and fishing-boats and yachts rocking peacefully at anchor. Clustered about it, the small grey houses of the village, their gardens bright with tamarisk trees and fuchsia bushes, had had a look of weatherbeaten enduring strength that had brought him ease. A swan had flown overhead, the rhythmic beating of its wings adding to the note of strength, and everywhere, in the wind and sun and rain, the gulls had been flying and calling. He had asked an old salt seated upon the harbour wall the way to Dame-rosehay, and a pipe-stem had been jerked towards the broken gate propped open by a stone, leading into the oak-wood. He had gone through the gate, and the trees had taken possession of him.

It had been a queer experience. He knew little of rural England and he had not realised that the pools of country quiet that still existed, wedged in between the din of towns and factories and the bungaloid growth of seaside resorts, had such intense individuality. To turn down the lane from the high-road had been to enter a new world, quiet in spite of momentary turmoils of wind and water, clean and immensely invigorating, holding within it a sort of leaping up of heavenly freshness from depths that were older than time and yet forever new. And then, when the storm-twisted oak-trees took hold of him, it had been different again. Nothing primeval now, but a sense almost of home-coming that deepened when he saw a child running to meet him. He remembered just in time that this was not his home, and never would be. He was coming here to work for a short time for a man he disliked, and he was not expected by this child, who would merely be repelled by his ugly face. He had turned aside into the trees so as not to startle her.

And here they were sitting companionably together on a seat in the sunshine, taking for the moment no notice of each other. Sebastian was glad to sit still. Though he had enjoyed it, that walk from the station carrying his bag had been a crazy undertaking for a man in his state of health, and his heart was banging about most uncomfortably inside him. He breathed quickly while the familiar hot waves and cold douches broke over him, then impatiently detached his mind from his detested body and looked down at the child beside him.

Though her gallant little figure had so stirred him, the poppy hat had prevented him from seeing anything of her face except her pointed chin, and now when he looked down at her he saw only the top of a smooth fair head. Her hair, cut short, was fine and soft as silk, of a shining almost silvery pale gold. David Eliot, his employer, had hair of the same colour, and in Eliot it was a source of profound exasperation to him, for he rated it high amongst those many levers to fame which the man possessed entirely by fortunate accident, and yet carried with such an intolerable air of courtly arrogance. Was this child Eliot's child? He couldn't believe it. He couldn't reconcile this child with David Eliot, any more than he could realise that this was Eliot's home. He couldn't see Eliot's lacquered smartness in this fairy wood, or visualise him with a muddy little child in his arms. Yet he had been told that he had children.

Meg suddenly looked up, and she was very like her father. She had his blue eyes, very deeply set and a little disconcerting in their steady appraising glance, his broad low forehead and beautifully modelled cheek-bones. But there the resemblance ended, for her bloodied button nose, her soft little mouth and tiny pointed chin bore no resemblance to her father's much-photographed classic profile. Then she smiled, and when Meg smiled it was obvious that she was somebody very special. It was not the smile that her father bestowed on strangers, charming but a little wary, as though, taught by troublesome experience, he deliberately withheld himself, but a smile of such all-embracing warmth that the smiled upon were taken captive for ever. Sebastian was no exception to the rule and capitulated on the spot.

Meg laid her hand, fingers still spread wide, upon his knee. It was an exceedingly dirty hand, but delightfully dimpled over the knuckles, with minute nails like sea-shells, of a shade of pink that blended quite perfectly with the golden sunburn of her skin. She would have been pale but for the sunburn, and in spite of the dimples she was too thin, but the little hollows at wrists and temples, and below the cheekbones, gave added beauty to the play of light and shadow that is so exquisite upon the perfect texture of a child's clear skin. It was so long since he had looked with normal attention upon a lovely happy child that she seemed

like a vision from another world. He had seen many
children since the war had ended, but in the early years
they had been mostly travesties of childhood, heart-breaking
to look upon, and then when in America he had seen normal
children again he had seen each one always with his small
son Josef standing beside him, and had clenched his hands
that he might not strike a fist against the rosy mouth that
had always had all the food it wanted. But Meg's mouth
was not rosy, it was pale and in spite of her happiness a
little poignant, and he looked at her now without bitterness, seeing only herself. Or was it that this wood had
done something to him? Had the shining leaves and the
glancing sunlight momentarily come down like a curtain
between him and that bitterness?

In any case, for the first time in a long while, a child
was not afraid of him. But, then, this was the first time in a
long while that he had been able to look at a thing of
beauty with no emotion at all but that of humble reverence.

" Did you come on the twelve-five? " asked Meg.

" Yes, I came on the twelve-five," said Sebastian.

" And did you walk from the station? "

" Yes, I walked from the station."

" Dinner," said Meg briefly, and levered herself forward
on the seat, lowering her mackintosh boots towards the
ground. On her feet again, she picked up the poppy hat
and put it on, so that she was once more obliterated. She
did this with great absorption, and no hurry, and, unhurried
himself for the first time in months, Sebastian replaced his
own hat with slow deliberation, tipped Mouse gently off his
feet and picked up his suit-case. Hand in hand, preceded
by Mouse, they strolled slowly towards the house.

" Have you come to stay? " asked Meg.

" I have," said Sebastian. " Do you object at all? "

" No," Meg assured him equably. " Do you like cod? "

" Not very much," said Sebastian.

" It's for dinner," Meg warned him. " But with baked
apples after, Zelle said, to make it nicer. We don't have

cod when Daddy is here because he won't eat it. He'd
sooner starve, he says."

" There he deceives himself," said Sebastian grimly, yet
his face twisted into the grimace which did duty with him
for a smile, for this mutual dislike of cod was a point of
contact with David Eliot, and as such it had its value.

" My Daddy has been in America," said Meg.

Sebastian's smile faded and his expression took on its
customary aridity, for he knew that only too well. He had
been with her father in America.

" My Daddy is an actor," said Meg.

Sebastian remained silent. This also, to his cost, he knew.

" Mummy went in the car to meet the big boat," said Meg.
" They'll be home for tea."

The impact of this glorious fact suddenly smote her
afresh, as it had been doing at intervals throughout the day.
The first long parting that she and her father had ever
known was over and he would be home today. Each time
she remembered this it was as though a wave made not of
water but of light broke over her head. She was drenched
in light, and it had a glowing warmth that reached even
to her toes. She looked at the world through it, too, and
the world shone and sparkled as though God had suddenly
bent down and put a fresh polish upon it just to please her.
When this happened she had to stand still for a moment
because the light and the glow seemed to hold her so.

The stillness took Sebastian by surprise, for he had expected the suddenly jump sideways and the swinging on his
hand that he had once been accustomed to in an excited
child; he had even braced his gaunt body to hold firm as she
swung. He stopped, too, and for a brief and extraordinary
moment there came again that freshness, this time within
himself, welling up from that fountain down at the roots of
things. What sort of a place was this to which he had come
with such reluctance, and yet which twice in an hour had
made him feel again this emotion of renewal? He supposed
he had once known it, because there was a feeling of
familiarity about it, but he had utterly forgotten it.

They had come out from the trees to an open sweep of gravel in front of the house.   Here they could feel the wind again, sweeping across the marshes from the sea.   Sebastian put down his suit-case and, taking off his hat, faced it for a moment, feeling its cleanliness reaching through his clothes to the sick body that he carried about with him with such extreme distaste wherever he went.   The wind was not cold, only fresh and invigorating.   The reeds and rushes of the marsh swept up as far as the stream that bordered the strip of grass edging the drive, and rustled beneath the wind.

He turned round again to look at the house.   The trees of the walled garden hid the length of it, and what he saw was only the gabled east end, yet that attracted him immensely. Damerosehay was an eighteenth-century house, but its irregular roof and grey stone walls were so battered by the gales of a couple of centuries that it looked older.   At this end of it Virginia creeper veiled the battered stone, each green leaf already touched with fire, and a climbing rose ran riot over the old porch.   There were seats inside the porch and a wide front door with an old-fashioned brass handle.   Over the porch was a window, slightly open and with a gay curtain fluttering out from it.   Sebastian looked up for a moment.   From that window a man would look out over the bending rushes to the silver line of the estuary, with the Island beyond.   He would see the ships passing, and the gulls beating up into the wind, and the great skies that are the glory of the flat and marshy lands.   He liked that window.

But Meg was inside the porch, struggling with the door-handle, and he went to help her.   He turned it and, preceded by Mouse, they went in together.   Meg went straight to the stairs, sat down on the bottom step and began struggling with her boots.   " Zelle," she called into the shadows of the house.   " Please, Zelle, my boots, and there's a man."

Sebastian did not help with the boots, for he doubted his efficiency, and he could not at the moment attend to any-

thing but the house. Hat in hand, he stood and attended
to it. He was aware at once of that sense of depth and
strength that all old houses have. The wide staircase rose
only gradually, with shallow worn uncarpeted stairs that
gave the impression that they would take you very deeply
in to withdrawn and peaceful places. The hall was dark,
velvety with shadow and cosily warm. Beneath his feet,
under the shabby rug, he could feel uneven flagstones.
Meg's soft voice, calling for Zelle, and the sound of Mouse
lapping water from a bowl marked DOG no more affected
the deep silence of the house than Meg's glowing little
figure disturbed the shadows. There was an old settle
against the dark-panelled wall and a pot of flowers on a
table. The house smelled of flowers, furniture polish,
baked apples, dog and tobacco. Somewhere in the shadows
a grandfather clock struck one, and a cuckoo clock far away
upstairs made the same remark.

Then the silence was broken by the light steps of a girl
running down to them, and the roars of an angry baby left in
the lurch upstairs. A door opened at the back of the hall,
letting in light, and a woman came through it, a country
body of immense size and immense charm. She advanced
with a stately swaying motion, shifting her great weight
from one foot to the other with a patient humorous determination that did not quite mask her fatigue. Her
white apron billowed before her, and her bright pink
knitted cardigan, buttoned up over her bosom to her chin,
strained at all its buttons with desperation but success,
holding fast, but showing spotless white petticoat at all the
interstices. Her scanty grey hair was strained back as
tightly as possible and skewered with a couple of hairpins
at the back of her head. Her face was round and red and
shone with selflessness and lathered soap; for Mrs. Wilkes,
when she washed anything, including herself, washed with
a sort of religious devotion that could be satisfied by nothing
less than a really supreme lather. Her sleeves were rolled
to the elbow, and her large red capable hands, with the
wedding-ring nearly imbedded in flesh on the left one, were

slightly flecked with lather now. She dried them on her apron as she considered Sebastian.

Zelle, expertly peeling Meg, also considered him. Zelle was twenty-six years old, petite and dainty in her gay flowered overall. With her thin face and sallow skin she was not strictly pretty, but her little head, covered with short dark curls, was beautifully shaped, and she had a fine air of distinction. Just at the moment she was both tired and cross, but that she was one of those women born to care for children was obvious in her handling of Meg. Buttons flew in and out of their appropriate holes at the touch of her fingers, and when she removed the obliterating hat and saw Meg's nose her loving outcry had a tenderness that made Sebastian wince. And there was something else about her that made him wince: a tautness across the cheekbones, and a hard sadness in the eyes, that he had seen so often in the faces of the young who have suffered much at an age when they should have known nothing but joy.

" Mon petit chou, quel dommage ! "

Meg made no complaint. Upon her face had dawned that look of placid peace that children's faces wear when they give themselves into hands whose skill they know and trust. Her nose no longer mattered. Zelle would see to it.

" It's not so bad as it looks, Mademoiselle," Sebastian reassured her. " The child tripped in a puddle and fell and bumped it and it bled a little. That's all." He spoke hesitantly, for the roars of the angry baby upstairs, who was apparently being murdered but to whom neither woman paid the slightest attention, were confusing him a little.

" I'll take 'er upstairs and put some Dettol on it," said Zelle. Her English was good, and charming, with its foreign inflection, and she spoke French in moments of emotion only.

" Now wait, Zelle," said Mrs. Wilkes. " The gentleman —'e can't be left stood there. Yes, Sir ? "

Zelle turned round, Meg's hand in hers, and once more considered Sebastian, this time with the astonishment and slight dismay to which he was only too well accustomed.

" You're not expecting me? " he asked.

Both women shook their heads.

Sebastian, suddenly exhausted beyond endurance, sat down on the settle. Now once again he would have to explain himself. He was always explaining himself. In fresh situations, always difficult, to new people, mostly without understanding, he was perpetually explaining himself. What a senseless affair it all was! Why did God, if there was a God, demand the continued existence in time and space of such disconnected items as himself? There should be a celestial bonfire once a year to burn up all extraneous humanity. War should do it, but did not. War only created more of the rubbish. And here they were preparing for a new war with the remaining heaps of it left over from the last war not yet sorted out. Abruptly he pulled himself together to explain himself yet once again.

" I am Mr. Eliot's secretary," he said.

" Mr. Collins? " enquired Zelle.

" No, not Collins. He left Mr. Eliot in America and went to Hollywood. I took his place. I gather Mr. Eliot's secretaries follow each other in rather quick succession."

The moment the words were out of his mouth he could have kicked himself for the bitterness with which he had spoken. Eliot had, according to his lights, been kind. What sort of creature had he become, that he could not even be loyal in the presence of his servants to a man who employed him? No, servants was the wrong word, for servants had vanished now, like loyalty. He had last visited England in the days of nannies and butlers. The little French girl and the enormous kindly soul were, he supposed, the modern equivalents, but he did not know how to describe them. Yet whatever they were they were loyal, for he could feel the disapproval that his remark had immediately brought into their consideration of himself.

" I am wrong. It's not dead yet," he said.

The disapproval faded into bewilderment.

" Loyalty," he said.

Bewilderment became apprehension. Even Meg, who had at first accepted him with equanimity, had her thumb in her mouth. He supposed he was talking to himself again. They must think him mad. So he probably still was at times. He pulled himself together once more.

" My name is Sebastian Weber," he said; and even now there was a ghost of pride hovering somewhere in the tone of his voice, the wraith of that full-bodied thing that had made him so sure of himself in the days when the announcement of a well-known name, in a man's own country, could command immediate respect. " Mr. Eliot wanted me to come down here to do some work for him. He said he would telephone and tell you to expect me."

This was a familiar situation, and apprehension vanished as tolerant smiles appeared upon both women's faces.

" There now, that's Mr. Eliot all over! " said Mrs. Wilkes. " 'E never done it. A wonderful memory for all the nonsense 'e talks on the stage, so they tell me, but none at all for anything useful."

" It's a wonder Mrs. Eliot didn't give us a ring," said Zelle.

" Likely 'e never told 'er," said Mrs. Wilkes. " She'll be took aback, same as us. Now then, Sir, gimme your bag. I'll take you upstairs and see you comfortable."

Mrs. Wilkes had a way of saying comfortable, stressing the solidity of the word and softly rolling the ' r ', that made it a word of infinite reassurance. Resisting his effort to carry his own bag, she took Sebastian firmly into her kindly charge. It was obvious that she was as expert with men as Zelle with small children. As the little procession wound its way upstairs, Zelle going first with Meg and Mouse and Mrs. Wilkes following with Sebastian, his face for a brief moment had a look that was almost a reflection of Meg's expression of placid peace. Mrs. Wilkes saw the look, recognised it, sighed and accepted the burden. She already had five men—a husband and four sons—dependent upon her for their every comfort, and now here was another, making a half-dozen. Well, she'd always had a fancy for an even number.

"That poor child!" ejaculated Sebastian, for the roars of the angry baby increased in volume as they reached the top of the stairs.

"Master Robin," said Mrs. Wilkes placidly. "Creating. Proper temper 'e 'as. This way, Sir. Mind, now. This 'ouse is all steps up and steps down, for no reason, as you might say."

But the abrupt little flight of steps that led down into the quiet room added to its charm, seeming to cut it off more completely from the rest of the house. With the door shut one could no longer hear the angry baby. The window-curtains stirred in the breeze, and the cool sound of the rushes was like the sound of distant water. It was the room over the porch that Sebastian had noticed from outside.

"Mr. Eliot's room before 'e married," said Mrs. Wilkes. "All swept and dusted. I've only to make the bed up. Don't you unpack your bag now; I'll see to that later. You'd best 'ave a tray of lunch up 'ere in peace and quiet. Now sit down and make yourself comfortable."

She spoke with the same patient humorous determination with which she moved, unconsciously forcing her voice to rise above the tones of weariness to a kindly command that allowed no disobedience. She had been a publican's wife for many years, sobriety had not been among her husband's virtues and her sons took after him. To her way of thinking if a man was not drunk at the moment, he soon would be, and she had long ago left off suiting her manner to the variations of his state; from sheer fatigue she had adopted now for good and all the one that was most in use. Yet Mrs. Wilkes liked men, always had and always would. There was no resentment in her manner, for acceptance and not resentment was the essence of her, and it was never resented; indeed the sober among her sons sometimes wished they were drunk just for the sheer comfort of being shepherded to bed by Mrs. Wilkes.

Sebastian found himself sitting in a comfortable little

arm-chair by the window. He had been taken out of his mackintosh by Mrs. Wilkes and placed there almost without his own knowledge, for in spite of her weight and bulk she had the gift of sure touch and noiseless movement. Sebastian, with the sensitiveness of the ill to the hidden qualities of those about them, was aware of a depth of quietness in her. A well of quiet, he thought, akin to the primeval freshness of the village beyond the fairy wood.

But the next moment it was of the room that he was thinking. He was not looking at it, for he had relaxed in his chair and shut his eyes, and it seemed that a century of time had passed over him, but he was aware of it; gentle in colour, with its quietness only accentuated by the rustle of the reeds and the sheets that Mrs. Wilkes was spreading on the bed. The creak of the door, when she left the room and came back again, had seemed to come from miles away, but her acceptance of the tasks that his arrival had imposed on her was so close that it seemed a part of him. That was one of the queer things about illness: things seemed now near, now far, so that the sense of distance, as of time, was revealed as mere illusion. But acceptance was not illusion. It was salvation. This time the sudden click of the door, as Mrs. Wilkes went away again, came as a physical shock that set his pulses hammering and sent a fiery thread of pain along the track of an old bullet-wound that went through his body.

He opened his eyes and looked about him. So this had been David Eliot's room before he married. Yet Eliot's restlessness, that at times rasped Sebastian's nerves almost beyond endurance, had left the peace of it unscathed. The spirit of this house was obviously a strong tough spirit, that would always be greater now than any human turmoil that its quietness would enclose. Yet in the beginning the spirit of a house is made by those who live in it, and he wondered who had lived here during two centuries, and what they had suffered. Mrs. Wilkes was obviously the heir to their fortitude. He thought of fortitude as being not endurance only but endurance with added to it that quietness and acceptance that he had felt in her.

The walls of this small room were painted a pale silver-grey, and it was filled with the clear silvery light that in his romantic boyhood he had described to himself as sanctuary light. Tracts of land enclosed by water, as these sea-marshes were almost enclosed by sea and estuary, were bathed in it on the clear and windswept days. In his youth islands had always given him a feeling of sanctuary, and he could still recognise the light. The few pieces of furniture in the room were old and beautiful, and so was the blue-green model of a horse that stood upon the chest of drawers. He fancied it must be a sea-horse, for there seemed a swirl of water about the galloping hoofs and a hint of spray in the flying mane. Over the bed hung a reproduction of Van Gogh's painting of the lark singing and tossing over the wind-blown corn. He remembered the thrill of delight the picture had given him when he had first seen it, and he remembered naturally and easily. That was odd, for he had lived for so long with shutters in his mind closed against all memory of past happiness. He had himself put up the shutters and almost exhausted his will with the effort of holding them shut; yet the memory of the light, and of the lark, had slipped through quite easily and brought no pain.

Mrs. Wilkes entered with lunch daintily set on a tray and put it down beside him on the little table in the window. " Poached egg, a glass of sherry and a nice baked apple," she said encouragingly. " There's a nice bit of cod, but from Mr. Eliot I know the feelings of gentlemen with regard to cod. Very fussy about his food, Mr. Eliot is."

She spoke the word " gentlemen " with archaic respect. Evidently she had not moved with the times. And how came she to apply the title to him? He knew what he looked like.

" A weak stomach," continued Mrs. Wilkes with kindly tolerance. " And Meg the same. I'll unpack your bag, Sir, while you eat your lunch. Yes, Sir, I'd like to do it. I'm in a better state of 'ealth than what you are."

Sebastian smiled. "How do you know that, Mrs. Wilkes?"

"I've been laying out the dead in this village for close on forty years," said Mrs. Wilkes placidly.

Sebastian laughed outright, and the sound of his genuine mirth startled him more than it did Mrs. Wilkes, used as she was to the peculiar sense of humour of those whom she still called the gentry. There was never no knowing what they'd laugh at and what they wouldn't, she would say to Wilkes, any more than there was any telling what crazy thing they'd do next. Like children, they were. A body who looked after them through all their vagaries had to be prepared for anything.

Mrs. Wilkes unpacked quietly and efficiently, and Sebastian did not mind in the least that she should see how meagre and shabby his possessions were. Her mind, he felt, was too weary for comment, and her loyalty to those she cared for too deep for gossip. Eliot paid him a good salary, but in the bitter world of today he had something better to do with it than the buying of comforts and luxuries for himself.

"There now," said Mrs. Wilkes when she had finished. "Coming on to rain again. Bad for the 'arvest, and I'll never get me washing dry. But there it is. There's One Above and there's the weather, and it ain't no good fighting either on 'em. If you've finished I'll take your tray. Like a cupper tea?"

"I'm not English," said Sebastian. "I've no great passion for tea."

"Well, there, it mightn't mix with the sherry," said Mrs. Wilkes. "Seeing it's raining, you might 'ave a nice lay down."

It was a command. Obediently Sebastian removed his shoes while Mrs. Wilkes folded up the quilt. Then, to his astonishment, he found himself flat on the bed with the eiderdown over him, yet without any clear idea as to how he had got there. Had the excellent sherry gone to his head? His face twisted with a spasm of amusement, for evidently

Mrs. Wilkes had thought so. She had applied that swift steerage movement, that abrupt lift below the elbow, whereby the intoxicated are landed in a place of safety.

"There now," said Mrs. Wilkes, departing with the tray. "Out of 'arm's way."

CHAPTER II

I

LUCILLA ELIOT was ninety-one years old.

"Most extraordinary!" she said aloud. She talked to herself a good deal nowadays, but so softly that those who heard her murmuring voice did not hear what she said. It was like overhearing a small child in its cot telling itself stories, a soft bee-hum of reminiscence that had little to do with the stark reality of day-to-day life as they themselves lived it. The small children and the very old, with the stuff of life hardly yet grasped or perforce nearly relinquished, were protected and secure and could enjoy their dreams and illusions immune from the daily wear and tear. And how lucky they were! . . . Lucilla knew that was the thought in the minds of those who came in and out of her room, attending most kindly to her wants and reading to her only those extracts from the daily papers which they considered suitable. They did not say so, of course, but Lucilla had the clairvoyance of the very old and she knew what was in their minds.

There were times when she wished very much that she did not. It could be most uncomfortable; and disillusioning, too, when she discovered the thoughts in the minds of those she loved to be not so invariably excellent as she had hitherto imagined. But, on the other hand, she was aware now of honest thinking and humble charity in inarticulate non-entities that turned all her previous judgements of them upside down; and that was excellent, like picking what you thought was a scentless flower and finding it smelt good after all. At first this growing clairvoyance of hers had frightened her. Did all old people have it? She could not remember in her younger days that any old people had told her about it; but, then, she was not telling her children about it: it would have made them too uncomfortable. Probably

26

her experience was the normal one and nothing to be surprised at. At her age one was already beginning to live a
little in the life to come and to know as they know who are
set free from all the deceptions and disguises of existence in
the body.

" Most extraordinary ! " she said again, and then laughed,
remembering that that had been one of the favourite ex-
clamations of Queen Victoria in her old age. Doubtless
it was the favourite exclamation of many old people, for the
state was full of surprises, not the least of them being that
one's body could be so incredibly antique while deep
inside one felt so young. Well, of course, one was young.
The Old Masters had known that. She could remember
a painting of Fra Angelico's that she had seen once. In the
foreground a corpse lay on its bier, and behind the bier
stood God holding a child in His arms. She had puzzled
over the picture for a long time before she had realised that
the child was the soul. She had been young then, just grown
up, and had felt extremely mature. Now, being so old and
feeling so young, she would have felt no puzzlement. She
could remember as though it were yesterday the blue sunny
day when she had seen that picture. She had worn a white
spotted muslin dress and a leghorn hat with a pink rose in it.
She moved her hands a little, feeling not the rug over knees
but the crisp feel of the muslin. A sudden gust of rain was
pattering against the window, but just for the moment she
felt only the warmth of that sunny day. The joy of memory
was one of her chief joys now ; only the memories were so
vivid that they could scarcely be called memories. It
was more as though her life had come round full circle and
the beginning was with her at the end as actual experience
that would pass her on, like all experience, to an enriched
existence beyond. And so anticipation was merged in
memory and it was hard to know at times which was
which.

There was for her no longer any bitterness in remembered
experience. It was a curious fact that as she looked back
over her life she thanked God for its happiness, while at the

time she had thought it to be largely made up of grief and pain. A loveless marriage and the bearing of children whom at the time she had not wanted. At the beginning of it all how bitter it had been! Yet now the fact that in the end she had made a success of her marriage, in the end had loved her children, somehow acted retrospectively to sweeten the whole experience. Then that parting from the man for whom she had almost left her husband and children. For duty's sake she had denied herself what she had described at the time, with Edwardian magnificence, as the one great love of her life, and the immensity of the sacrifice had, she had thought at the time, nearly killed her. And yet now that memory, out of all her memories, was the only one that had grown not vivid to the point of present reality but dim as a dream. She could scarcely remember now what the man had looked like, and yet at the time he who was now a dream had seemed her very life. Yet she was grateful to that dream-figure of a lover because he had been all that is most lovable, and her love of his lovableness, and sacrifice of it, had both gone to the making of the child she had borne to her husband after she had returned to her wifely duties. Maurice, that child, had had a charm and beauty that none of her other children had possessed, and a spark of that heavenly genius that springs only somewhere, somehow, from a true denial, and she had loved him with what she thought now was in truth the great love of her life. When he had died in the First World War it had seemed like the death of her own soul; and yet now he was with her more constantly than the sons and daughter who still lived with her in this world.

That silence of the world of light, that can seem so heavenly when for a moment or two it hushes with its peace the tumult of material things and yet so terrible when it takes to itself the souls of the freed, had lasted from the day of his death until now. He had seemed to vanish so utterly that she had been tempted to doubt the truth of the immortality of the soul. She had felt at times that he lived only in the qualities he had handed on to his son, her grandson David, and that David had handed on to his daughter Meg; and for that reason David and his Meg were loved by her with an intensity considered by the rest of the family to be extremely bad for the characters of both.

And yet now, after a lifetime of absence, here was Maurice back again, returned from the great distance and the deep silence with an ease that suggested that they were neither so deep nor so great as she had thought. He had made himself known to her as an enfolding of warm joy, as though her small soul was held within his, that was so much greater. It was almost, she thought shyly, as though his adult soul was carrying her childish one to a new birth, as once through nine long months her body had carried his. She never mentioned his presence to anyone except very occasionally to Meg, or to her eldest son Hilary. How could she? How explain to men and women fixed extremely firmly in their mortal bodies the existence of someone who could be neither heard nor seen, and yet was there? You had to be slightly loose in your body before you could understand. Extreme old age had loosened Lucilla, and his lifetime of austerity would have caused the sword that was Hilary to rattle in the scabbard of his body, had he not been so fat. As to Meg, her flower-like body had scarcely had time to close its petals over and about her and she was very loose indeed.

"And so, with you so constantly here, Maurice," said Lucilla aloud, "my lifelong grief for you seems slightly foolish. If I had my time over again I would weep for nothing but sin."

"Did you speak, Mother?" asked Margaret Eliot, Lucilla's daughter, from the door.

"Not to you, dear," said Lucilla with a touch of asperity. "But if you are there you can come in and light this fire. It's laid."

"But it's only August," objected Margaret, coming in.

"An English August," said Lucilla. "Cold as January. And David comes home today. He'll be in to see me, perhaps."

"Tomorrow, I expect," said Margaret. She was aware

that Lucilla was waiting for David with an intensity of expectation that was likely to wear her out if it went on too long. " There will scarcely be time for him to come today. Don't start expecting him before tomorrow, Mother."

" The matches," said Lucilla, " are behind the clock."

" Shall we have the electric stove? " suggested Margaret with a forced brightness.

" I dislike it intensely," said Lucilla. " It makes my head hot and leaves my feet exactly what they were before the thing was lit. Don't argue, dear Margaret. Do as you are told."

" It's the coal," explained Margaret. " They say it will be very short next winter."

" Why bother with next winter? " asked Lucilla. " What I am bothering about is cold feet now."

Margaret laughed and knelt down to light the fire. She gloried, as did all the family, in Lucilla's moods of asperity, for they were as sparks flying up from the vivid and glowing vitality that had warmed them all their lives long and was still their life and their delight. For even at ninety-one there was no dying down of Lucilla's vital fire. Her body was weakened with age and rheumatism, so that she moved very slowly, and she could no longer read small print even with her spectacles on, but her deafness only troubled her when she chose that it should, and her mind was as keen and alert as ever. And she was still a delight to look at, her white hair growing vitally from her low forehead and her blue eyes seeming only more lovely because they were so deeply sunken in their shadowed sockets. The fine bones of her face showed more clearly than they used to beneath the delicately wrinkled skin, and her hands had lost some of their shapeliness, but she had kept her grace and air of distinction.

" I am extremely fortunate, Margaret," she said.

" What about, Mother? " asked Margaret, pushing her untidy short grey hair back from her face with one of those quick nervous gestures that betray the overworked. There had been some coal-dust on her fingers and it left little streaks of black on her temples.

Lucilla flushed a delicate pink, for she had not known that she had spoken aloud. She had been thinking that she was fortunate still to retain her beauty at ninety-one, while Margaret at only sixty-nine looked more deplorable than words could say. But she was not going to lie about what was in her mind. This new knowledge of the thoughts of others that had come to her in old age had given her an almost fantastic horror of the life of half-unconscious deception which almost everybody seemed to lead. Of course to a certain extent one had to build from the outside in, one had to act with a willed charity, however unloving the thoughts in one's mind, on and on till feeling came to heel and followed action, but that was a creative thing, utterly different from the hypocrisy of the easy flattery and the easier platitude that were just a floating with the tide. The word integrity was one which she had come to love almost the best of the words in the dictionary; though she recognised that the union of charity with honesty was dreadfully difficult; one was sure to be lopsided one way or the other.

"That I was born beautiful and that my beauty has not left me," she said to Margaret. "It will not be counted unto me for righteousness, but it has eased my way. Even as a little girl, Margaret, you were never pretty, and that has made a hard life harder. Could you sit down for a moment?"

Margaret drew up a low chair to the fire and held out her work-roughened hands to its warmth. "I should be ironing your handkerchiefs," she said guiltily.

"I wish your love for me did not take the form of disliking the laundry," said Lucilla. "If I could see you rested I'd joyfully blow my nose on torn handkerchiefs."

"If it was our own torn handkerchiefs that came back, I should not mind so much," said Margaret, "but it's other people's."

"To see you sitting down and doing nothing I should not

care whose handkerchief I used," said Lucilla. "That was one of the reasons why I wanted to leave Damerosehay, but I believe this is the first time in five years that I have seen you do it."

"Have we really been in Lavender Cottage five years?" marvelled Margaret.

"Five years," said Lucilla. "Which reminds me that it is the anniversary of David's and Sally's wedding on Wednesday, and there is to be the usual party. I mustn't forget."

"You're not likely to forget, Mother," said Margaret. "You love family parties."

Lucilla flushed again. Here *she* was, now, expressing her thoughts with a certain measure of deception. For weeks she had been counting the days to the party, and yet she must needs imply that she was so above such things that she was likely to forget them.

"I own I have been counting the days," she said with steady truthfulness. "I own I have thought a good deal about that new black silk dress, for it suits me, and I like to be admired."

"Mother, you're adorable!" laughed Margaret.

"They say that humility is so important," sighed Lucilla, "but I'll never learn it, not in this world, if all my children and grandchildren persist to the very end in adoring even my faults. Now then, Margaret, sit down!"

"Even if I don't iron the handkerchiefs there are still the beans for supper," said Margaret, half in and half out of her chair. "Shall I do them here with you?"

"Don't do them at all," said Lucilla. "Why be a slave to beans? There are moments when I wish we had no garden. It's such a worry trying not to waste the things in it. Put some logs on and then lean back and sit quite still for half an hour. We said to each other, when we left Damerosehay for Lavender Cottage, that now we would make our souls, but so far as I know neither of us has made the slightest attempt to do it."

"Yes, we did say that," thought Margaret, leaning back

with her hands tightly folded in her lap and her rough grey
head unwillingly propped against a patchwork cushion.
" Though I'm sure I don't know what we meant by it."

She and Lucilla had lived at the family home of Damerosehay for nearly thirty years. It was Lucilla, house-
hunting after the First World War, who had found it, and
had seen in it not just an old house for sale but a sanctuary
for battered Eliots for ever. She had lost another son as well
as Maurice in that war, and, clear-sighted in her grief, had
had no faith in the era of perfection that its vileness was
supposed to usher in. Instead she had seen in it but the
beginning of sorrows for her children and grandchildren and
great-grandchildren, each in their turn and in their generation. But she had vowed that they should have something
of beauty and security in their lives, a home where they could
come and be refreshed physically and mentally when the
world had been too much for them. She had thought of
Damerosehay much as a man thinks of that quietness within
the soul to which it is possible to escape if he can but learn
the way to get there. She had even hoped that the physical
withdrawal might help them to the spiritual one. Perhaps
it had and did. She did not know. In any case she and
Margaret, with little leisure for spiritual withdrawals of their
own, had given all their strength for thirty years to Damerosehay, Lucilla the strength of her spirit and Margaret
the strength of her toiling body, and had not left it until
David had married Sally and gone to live there in their
place.

David was the most vital and successful of the Eliots,
the natural head of the family after Lucilla, and Sally had
in her character that union of warmth and selflessness that
in the mistress of it can make a house always welcoming.
Lucilla and Margaret had felt their life's work safe in the
keeping of those two when they left Little Village, wind
blown and washed with light in the marshes by the sea, for
Big Village, cupped in the sheltered lanes and fields a mile
inland, to live in peace and quiet and make their souls.

" Which we have not done," repeated Lucilla. " We go

B

on behaving here exactly as we used to behave at Dame-rosehay. I go on worrying about the family and trying not to tell them what they ought to do, and you go on cooking meals we don't need, and washing clothes we can quite afford to send to the laundry, because overworking the body is the only way of life of which you have experience. We still have no time to make our souls."

" Even if we stopped worrying and overworking, would the emptiness that would leave do us any good? " asked Margaret. " People always think that if they lived in a different place, in a different way, they would be different sorts of people, but they never are."

"You are most depressing, Margaret," said Lucilla.

" I know," said Margaret. " I always was, and I can't change now. I must do something about those handker-chiefs, Mother. I left them soaking in salt and water."

" She's right," thought Lucilla when Margaret had gone. " I talk a lot of nonsense. But, all the same, if we can't stop worrying and overworking we ought to worry and over-work in a different sort of way. That's the sort of change that should be possible. What a problem! I'll ask Hilary."

It was warm and cosy with the fire lighted, and she slept a little, lightly and fitfully, very much aware of Maurice. The awareness increased and became a sense of patient wait-ing on the part of the other. This she had not known before, for those in the world of light who waited for her had no need of patience. It could not even be said that they waited, for waiting, like patience, implied imprisonment in time. They were just there. She opened her eyes and it was not Maurice who stood beside her but his son David.

They smiled at each other, and then he said, " Are you all right, Grandmother? "

" Yes, David," she said. " Are you? "

Ever since his school days they had given each other this greeting when he came home. As a boy he had considered this form of words adequate and informative without being sloppy, but now he did not care whether he was sloppy or not and he kneeled down like a child beside her, his folded arms on the arm of her chair and his face buried in them. It was a ridiculous attitude for a middle-aged man, an attitude both extravagant and sentimental, but he was both extravagant and sentimental, and when he was with Lucilla he did not care. He loved her more than anyone else in the world excepting only his daughter Meg.

Lucilla gently touched his silvery fair hair. Then she withdrew her hand and waited. With his face still hidden he wondered if when she was dead he would feel that touch occasionally or whether he would have to do without it. Probably he would have to do without it. Lucilla, aware of what he was thinking, knew he would, for it is not in such ways that the dead make their presence known. It would do him no harm to do without it, for he had done without very little in his life. Though he and Meg were, she believed, her best beloved in this world, she was now a little more critical of him than she had been. This new clairvoyance of hers had given her new insight into his mind and she found it most alarmingly egocentric. Even now, though genuine feeling had put him where he was, she knew that self-dramatisation kept him there. He was well aware how charming they both looked in the flickering firelight.

" Get up, David," she said sharply.

He got up, laughing, for like Margaret he enjoyed the reassuring tang of her occasional sharpness. Then he sat down beside her, took her face in his hands and kissed her. In the past she had enjoyed the caresses that her beauty called down upon her, but she was not now so fond of them as she had been. She wondered if Meg liked being perpetually kissed; she had sometimes fancied that she had seen an expression of patience on her small face. She believed that the very old and the very young are less fond of caresses than their admirers imagine. She fancied that at the extremes of life, when one was either coming or going, one felt a certain detachment from the possessiveness of the time between.

Yet her love for David was not less because she saw his faults more plainly and was a little fatigued by his emotions.

She loved him more, if possible. Pity for human frailty grew with knowledge of it, and in the case of one's children and grandchildren, through heredity and upbringing, one was responsible for so much of it. Would David, whom she suspected of being increasingly unhappy as he revolved upon himself in alternations of self-dramatisation and self-hatred, have been a healthier man if she had spoilt him less as a child? Would Ben, the grandson who came next in her love, be so tormented now by indecision if she had not always made up his mind for him when he was a small boy? As her earthly life drew to its ending it was not only the sins of others that she saw with such clarity, it was her own even more, especially those that had harmed the children. " Is it well with the child? " was the question that often kept her awake at nights. There were only two of the children towards whom she could bear herself without a sense of guilt: her eldest son Hilary, whose sanctity in his old age had the quality of light, life-giving but untarnishable, and her grandson Tommy, a magnificent young savage who at the opposite end of the scale had a polished marble hardness that had always seemed impervious to any influence whatever, good or bad.

" Are you all right, David? " she asked again.

" You've asked that twice, Grandmother. That's never been in the game."

" You've been away so long. Five months."

" Without you or Sally or Meg to keep me on the rails. More than likely to get in the devil of a mess, you think? "

He spoke with a charming airiness, meeting her eyes with that straight, keen glance that Meg had inherited from him, but he did not deceive Lucilla. He was in some sort of trouble, as usual. She hoped not emotional this time, for surely he had left that sort of mess behind him when he married Sally. Economic, of course, but that was habitual with him. Something else. Something that went deeper than falling in love or inability to pay his super tax. She told herself she would do her best not to try to find out what it was, remembering that when she came to Lavender

Cottage to make her soul (whatever she had meant by that) she had laid down the burden of Damerosehay and David. Sally carried it now.

"Where is Sally?" she asked.

"Outside in the car. She wouldn't come in. We're on the way home."

"You've not seen Damerosehay yet? You've not seen Meg?"

"Not yet. You first, Grandmother."

"I don't know why you should be so good to me," she said humbly. Nor did she. The days when she had taken her children's and grandchildren's devotion for granted had long gone by. Nowadays she took nothing for granted. Her slow relinquishment of earthly life had taught her that nothing was truly hers but the love of God.

"You had a good tour in the States?" she asked.

"I had what newspaper jargon calls a magnificent triumph," said David wearily.

"I'm sorry," said Lucilla simply, and reflected that fame was most peculiar. Men worked themselves to death for it, yet when they had the thing it seemed to go sour on them.

She took his hand gently. It was a fine hand, very like his father's, supple and with a strength in it that was lacking in his body. Hands, she believed, were indicative of character. She thought there was a hidden strength in David that had not yet been fully tested, not even by the gruelling experience of war. Her hand in his felt light and brittle as an autumn leaf, and a pang went through him. How would it be possible to live without Lucilla?

"There's Sally," she answered him. "Go and fetch her, David. It's not right to leave that darling child alone out there."

"She wanted to rest," said David. "Tired to death. This new little varmint that's on the way is wearing her out."

He could not quite hide his exasperation. He had not wanted a third baby. Meg and Robin, especially Robin, were enough. But Sally was an incorrigible mother, and obstinate in it. But for young Christopher (Sally said he was Christopher) he would have come home to the comfort of a wife instead of a weary woman near her time. Lucilla was undisturbed by his exasperation. David was much older than Sally and they had their inevitable difficulties, but she knew that whatever their surface agitations all was well with their roots.

Lucilla had difficulty these days in remembering the ages of her children and grandchildren. She had managed to grasp the almost incredible facts that her eldest son was over seventy and that Ben and Tommy had both had their twenty-first birthdays, but there she stopped. How old was David now? She supposed he must be nearly forty, but she hardly liked to ask, for he had had spectacular good looks and she realised that he would not find it easy to relinquish them. Not that they were leaving him yet. The height and grace that he had inherited from her he would never entirely lose, any more than she had, and there was not much grey in his smooth gold hair, but his skin was far too lined for his age and the hard lines of cheekbone and jaw showed too clearly. In the light of the fire his face seemed full of almost fantastic contrasts, sharp highlights and pits of shadow. The little hollows in Meg's face caused a gentle and friendly play of light and shade, but in her father's it was as though one fought with the other. Though he held his body relaxed and still in the chair beside her, Lucilla knew it was only with an effort of will. His restlessness, so rigidly controlled, was giving her almost a sense of suffocation; a faint echo, she supposed, of the torment it was to him.

" And yet you have everything in the world to make you happy," she said.

" Grandmother, you've always told me it's not the things in the world that do make you happy," he said lightly.

" Are not Sally and Meg and Damerosehay in the world? " she asked him.

" Yes," he said, and smiled. " And yet not the part of them that matters, and I can't find my way to the roots.

Is not that the trouble with most people? The surface is arid, and we do not find our way to where the freshness is."

"I suggest that you need a good dinner, darling," said Lucilla. "And a good night's rest."

He laughed, suddenly grateful for her refusal to be deflected from trivialities. They were best at first, while one found one's footing afresh in the place and among the people who were the same and yet not the same, because after long absence one was not the same oneself, and neither were they. The surface shifted perpetually, like sand, and bedrock could not be found.

He wrenched his thought back from the unattainable thing and with a glance at his watch ("Twenty minutes," Sally had said) set himself to talk amusingly for the ten that were left. The gift of being entertaining at will he had inherited from Lucilla, and she seconded him ably; yet all the time her mind knew with eagerness that somewhere in what he had said there lay the solution of her own problem.

2

Sally gave a sigh of relief. She was at ease again and the fears had vanished. "Just leave me alone for twenty minutes and I'll be all right," she had said to David. And he had done what she asked. Another man would have refused to leave her alone in the car, feeling faint and sick after the long drive. He would have made her come in and lie down on Margaret's bed and be driven distracted by Margaret's fussing. But not David. He had an intuitive knowledge of how to treat the suffering; if just feeling sick and frightened could be dignified by the name of suffering.

"It can't," said Sally to herself. "Nothing that I ever suffer can really be called suffering. I don't know the meaning of the word. I've always had everything. I have everything now."

It was quite true. She had been Sally Adair, the only child of John Adair, a fashionable portrait painter and wealthy man who had delighted to give her everything she

wanted, and now she was Sally Eliot, the much-loved and
indulged young wife of a man equally famous and equally
prosperous. She had a beautiful home and two enchanting
children and would soon have a third. She looked younger
than her twenty-six years, and in spite of haphazard features,
and a body too tall and muscular for grace, she was good to
look at, with her red-brown curls, white skin and courageous
golden eyes. Her unselfconsciousness, her complete lack
of pose, gave her a sort of grace, while her humility made her
appear not quite so tall as she really was. She had a deep
voice, with the Scotch lilt in it—a singer's voice. Her big
hands were clumsy with her needle and with washing up but
wonderfully skilful with children and sick animals. She
was a comforting sort of woman, warm and glowing when
she was in health, serene and strong. She looked born to be
what she was, a loyal and selfless wife and mother in whom
intensity of loving managed to co-exist with steady common
sense.

Yet it was just here, in her vocation of wife and mother,
that she suffered and was afraid. She knew that David did
not love her as much as she loved him, that he never had and
never would, but that she had accepted with a humility
that robbed her knowledge of bitterness. It was not in
hurt pride that her trouble lay, but in the fact that after
five years of marriage he showed her so little of himself. He
had been a sick man when she married him, for upon his
highly strung temperament the war had borne hardly, and
in the first years of their marriage she had rested him and
given him ease. But there it had stopped. He had seemed
to move beyond her then. Loving each other, they yet
seemed alone, he in new and hard experience that he could
not share with her, and she in her fear that she was incapable
of sharing it. What could she ever know of the peculiar
torments of a nervous and highly gifted man? She seemed
not to have a nerve in her body and, apart from bathing
babies and singing in tune, her gifts were nil.

And merely physical pain, that so frightened her, was
something he had not experienced. But even had he known

what it was like she could not, for very shame of what she considered her cowardice, have talked to him about her fear of it; for shame and because if he had known how child-birth terrified her Robin would have been their last baby. And she wanted others. Her longing for children, her un-reasoning conviction that it was right to have them, was stronger than her fear. And her fear was a double one, because her children seemed to her an integral part of her-self, the most precious part, and she shrank from pain for them more than for herself. And what sort of world was this into which to bring children? That was a question that David had asked her with bitterness when she had wanted Christopher, and she had answered steadily that even with the world as it was she still believed it was right to have children. Had they not immortal souls? But even while she spoke of their souls, and smiled at David, the thought of the pain of their bodies had gone through her like a sword.

She wondered often why it was that she, who had never ailed in her life, should suffer so much in bearing children. Everyone, including herself, had expected her to have them easily, and instead of that the whole process was for her as difficult and humiliating as it could be. She had worked too hard and too long in the Land Army in the war, her doctor said, but sometimes she thought there was more in it than that, some reason that for want of a better word she called a psychological reason. And certainly the fact that she who was naturally courageous shrank from pain with such dread seemed always demanding an explanation that she could not give. It was not like her, either, to question bewildering fears in loneliness. Until David went away from her into his private wilderness it had not been her habit to question anything, and she had thought about herself as little as it is possible for a human being to do.

But still came the wonderful moments, as now, when her body was suddenly at ease and her fears fell away from her and she knew, instinctively, that below the deserts hidden waters run to far green pastures. She rested a moment in the thought of them and then turned gladly to the beauty outside herself in which she had always found her joy.

A fuchsia hedge grew just inside Grandmother's low garden fence and burst into flower over the top of it, and now the delicate scarlet lanterns swung in the wind and glowed like flame in a sudden burst of sunshine. Each was fire and music, for the outer petals turned up crisply to show the purple bell within, with its clapper swinging low on the long stigma. The grass of Grandmother's garden was vividly green after the rain and there was a second budding of roses by the porch. Across the lane from the low white cottage the great yews in the churchyard were so weighted with darkness that they did not move in the wind, but their bright red berries lit their gloom and the glow of the sun was on their trunks. Hilary's red-brick vicarage was mercifully half hidden by the swaying cherry-trees that grew at the bottom of his garden, but Sally had long ceased to think of it as ugly; it housed Hilary, and the sight of it was almost as reassuring as the sight of Hilary's stout form in its shabby cassock.

Damerosehay, Lavender Cottage, the Vicarage and The Herb of Grace, the old inn on the river where Lucilla's second son George lived with his family, were all Eliot homes and fortresses of strength to Sally.

Awake one stormy winter's night, and a little scared by the fury of wind and water, she had imagined them standing at the four points of the compass, so that whichever way the wind blew it would bring with it the thought of the particular brand of courage which each house stood for. Her own home, so battered at times by the great gales from the sea, was a west-wind house. The men and women who had lived there before the Eliots and whose stories David had told her—Christopher Martin, Aramanthe and old Jeremy— had had the courage of the west wind, the clean uncompromising strength of it.

The Herb of Grace was an east-wind house; not the bitter east wind of winter but the wind that blows out of a clear dawn, sending banners of flame across the sky and the ringing and singing of falling water and bird-song chiming round the world. Ben, Tommy, Caroline, Jerry and José were all growing up at The Herb of Grace, and faced the world with something of the jovial welcome of the house itself, as well as with the laughing valiance of their youth. Come what might they always seemed ready for it at The Herb of Grace.

And Grandmother at Lavender Cottage had now for them all the gentleness, the warmth and comfort, the steady quiet breathing of the south wind that refuses to be ruffled by adversity. And Hilary in his northward-facing cold vicarage was after a lifetime of austerity so disciplined that one could not imagine him breaking beneath anything at all that might occur.

The idea had had the absurdity of all midnight fantasies, but looking now from Lavender Cottage to the Vicarage, and remembering Damerosehay and The Herb of Grace, Sally thought of it again. Strength, gallantry, quietness and discipline, we'll need them all before we've done, she thought, and we'll all need each other, pooling our different sorts of courage, not shutting ourselves up each in his own trouble, like we do now.

David opened the car door and slipped into the seat beside her. He put one hand over hers, that lay clasped in her lap. His hand was warm and hers were cold.

" All right now? " he asked her.

" Yes, I'm all right now."

They sat without moving or speaking for a few moments, and his warmth sent a glow through her cold exhausted body. She sighed contentedly. These were the best moments of marriage, these times when the surface irritations fell away and each gave to the other what the other needed. For she was giving something to him, too, though she did not know what it was. He could have told her. When she had need of him he forgot about himself and the torment of his self-hatred stopped for a moment.

The luxurious grey car slid forward slowly beneath the swaying trees of Big Village. Fairhaven was all one parish but two separate hamlets, Little Village and Big Village. The houses in both were for the most part old and, like all old houses, looked alive. The houses at Little Village were crustacean creatures, confronting the sea wind with hard grey shells, clinging for dear life to the rock on which they were built. The Big Village houses, with cob walls and thatched roofs, grew out of their flower-filled gardens like larger flowers. The winding lane that linked the two ran between tall hedges of wild rose, sloe, blackberry and hawthorn, and deep green fields where black-and-white cows grazed. The country was flat here, and the sky with its masses of hurrying cloud was wide and steep and glorious. David drove very slowly, relaxed in the slowly growing joy of home-coming.

"What were you thinking of, Sally?" he asked. "In a brown study when I came out of Grandmother's."

It was a question he often asked her, because instead of the usual evasion she always gave him a truthful answer, and the thoughts that came out of Sally's mind were usually odd and sweet and unexpected, like toys taken out of a child's playbox.

Flushing a little, for she always found it difficult to tell her brilliant and sophisticated husband about her childish thoughts, unaware as she was that it was partly for love of her childlikeness that he had married her, she told him about the four winds and the four houses. "And I was thinking that we ought not to be all of us so separate from each other," she said. "We ought to find some way of sharing whatever in us can help; and what needs help, too."

She looked at him and saw the muscles of his face tighten. "Is it possible?" he asked harshly. "Courage, yes, but not the other thing. How could we? It is of the essence of it that it is a lonely thing."

"The Thing," he called it. And he was right. Meg had a Thing which she called the black beast, but though she cried in the night because of it, she could never explain to Sally what it was, any more than Sally could tell David about her fear of separation from him, or her fear of pain.

" But there are those who at times can reach a world-consciousness of suffering," David went on. " A man who had been in a concentration camp talked to me about it once. He said that for a moment or two there can come to you, through your own suffering, a consciousness of the suffering of the whole world."

" How horrible ! " said Sally.

" On the contrary, he said that it was only those moments that made it possible to go on."

" We can't share our particular Things, but deep down somewhere they can link us together," said Sally.

" That's the idea."

" But I expect that only great suffering, like that of the man you talked to, would let one in," said Sally. " Not just the little silly things that fortunate people have."

" I think the little things could let us in, too, if we knew the way to let them," said David. " Only we don't know the way. If we did, if we could all of us attain to that sort of world consciousness all the time, instead of only the best of us at rare moments, it might yet save the world."

" From war ? " asked Sally.

" Or through it. What a conversation for a home-coming day ! "

She laughed, and asked him, " Who was that man you talked to ? "

" My new secretary, Sebastian Weber. It was at our first meeting, the only time he ever talked to me. After that he shut up like a clam, and now he only makes the appropriate noises. Good heavens ! Sally, did I phone to Mrs. Wilkes ? "

" Phone to Mrs. Wilkes ? "

" Yes. About Weber."

" About Weber ? What about him ? "

" Sally, didn't I tell you I had asked him down to stay ? He must have come on the twelve-five. Surely I told you ? "

" No, you didn't tell me," said Sally.

He stopped the car abruptly. " What's the matter, Sally ? "

" It's only, a stranger, and I thought it was going to be just us."

" Take your hat off and cry," suggested David. " It's been a long day. Blast Christopher! "

She did what he suggested, her rumpled curly head on his shoulder. She had never been the kind of woman who cried, or he the kind of man who could regard unnecessary tears with toleration, but they had both now accepted the fact that she occasionally became what Meg called " unstuck " when a baby was on the way. It was a fact of nature, like the weather, and like the weather must be accepted.

" Finished? " asked David briskly, when he had had enough of it.

" Yes," said Sally, blowing her nose. " But I think it was too bad of you."

" You didn't see Weber on the boat," said David. " He hid himself away somewhere. If you had seen him you would have realised how necessary it was that he should make contact with Mrs. Wilkes."

" Why? He doesn't drink too much, does he? " asked Sally anxiously.

" Not that I know of. Though I should if I were he, poor devil. But when unsteady, from whatever cause, one always derives a sense of equilibrium from Mrs. Wilkes."

Sally suddenly remembered the concentration camp. " I'm sorry," she said. " I'm glad he is there. But what will he do? You're not working now."

" He's going to translate some German plays for me."

" Do you want German plays translated? "

" No."

Sally laughed. " You'll find a use for them some day. They'll fit in somewhere. And Mr. Weber too. Everything and everyone always does at Damerosehay."

" It's a way old houses have," said David. " Whatever comes into them they draw into place by a species of suction."

" Drive on quickly, David," said Sally. " Meg's waiting."

CHAPTER III

NURSERY tea was drawing to a sticky but comparatively peaceful conclusion when Robin suddenly raised himself in his high chair, knocked over the honey, seized his silver mug and flung it violently across the room. It landed in the middle of the goldfish bowl, which broke. Goldfish, water and the milk that had been at the bottom of the mug flowed in a turgid stream over the nursery floor.

"Yabbit!" yelled Robin, and began to roar again. He had been shouting "Yabbit" throughout the day, and no one knew what he meant by it. Mouse barked. Zelle, after a long day of migraine and Robin's rages, burst into tears. Mrs. Wilkes, appearing upon the threshold, surveyed the scene with resignation. Then her eyes met Meg's and a current of wordless and sympathetic understanding flowed between them. Meg put her unfinished chocolate biscuit in the pocket of her cherry-coloured cotton smock and slid to the floor.

"I'll take Robin and Mouse down to the gate to see if Mummy and Daddy are coming," she said.

"My poppet," said Mrs. Wilkes briefly, lifting the roaring Robin from his high chair.

The endearment was addressed not to Robin, whose behind she smacked good and hard as she set him upon his feet, but to Meg. Sally, Mrs. Wilkes and Meg had quite unconsciously formed an alliance together, its object the peace of Damerosehay. Disinterested women, all three of them, they had the sure instinct of the disinterested as to which portion of a bit of bother each should individually tackle, and wasted no time in argument as to who should do what. The gasping goldfish, the mess on the floor, Zelle's tears and migraine, were now the portion of Mrs. Wilkes, while Meg towed Robin and Mouse into the night nursery and shut the door firmly between Mrs. Wilkes's sphere of action and her own. Mouse, who was becoming hysterical, she put in the laundry basket with the lid down, and Robin she locked in the wardrobe. The while masculine rage boomed and thumped in the wardrobe, and female hysterics rocked the basket back and forth, she sat down cross-legged on the floor and finished her chocolate biscuit. She finished it slowly, because she liked chocolate biscuit, and wiped her fingers daintily upon a diminutive square of pocket handkerchief with a kitten embroidered in the corner. Then she sighed, her small face wearing the slightly worried expression it always wore when Robin was in a temper, and that made her look so absurdly like her god-mother, Aunt Margaret, whose name she bore by David's wish.

In the bringing up of David it had been Margaret who had borne the burden and heat of the day. She had dealt with measles and mumps, explosions of water-pistols, and frogs in the linen cupboard, while Lucilla had had all the beautiful and gentle tasks, such as hearing prayers said and filling Christmas stockings, and had had in consequence a far greater love. David felt a certain compunction now and had made what reparation he could by making Meg Margaret's special child. Yet as Meg grew out of babyhood he was sorry, for it seemed that Margaret's mantle as daughter of Damerosehay was falling upon her. She was far too old for her years, as Margaret had always been, and like Margaret was beginning to show signs of becoming an anxious pilgrim. But Meg, unlike Margaret, had beauty and charm to conjure love about her and the quick wits to use it in the cause of peace.

The turmoil inside the wardrobe subsided quite suddenly, and Meg unlocked the door and looked in. Robin was sitting upon the floor and sobbing heart-brokenly. That was one of the disconcerting things about Robin. He would be an utter devil on and off for an entire day, stamping and roaring, thumping and smashing, no one knew why, and then quite suddenly his rage would turn to a quiet misery which wrung the heart of all beholders; and again no one knew why. Some little thing would start him off—the loss of a toy or a pudding that he did not like—and the small frustration would pass him on to this anger and despair for which no one could find an explanation. Meg perhaps could have done so, but she was too little to explain in words the things which she knew, least of all to herself. If it had been suggested to her that Robin went berserk with rage against the unfamiliar encagement of his spirit within the frustrations of human life, much as a convict who has known the freedom of the world will lose his reason and beat his body against the walls of his cell, she would have shaken her head in bewilderment. And if someone had wondered aloud if he wept because he knew he would never get out until he was an old man, she would have been equally bewildered. Yet she knew it was that. And she knew that once she had dried his tears the only way to comfort him was to put his boots on, take him out of doors and let him run to the edge of the world. If it was pouring with rain, and he had a cold and Zelle would not let her take him out of doors, still she put his boots on—his seven-league boots that would carry him to the edge of the world when his cold was better—and in the contemplation of them he was comforted.

Meg knew the value of symbols, though she could not have told you that she did. Had it not made it easier for her to bear her fear of the Thing that lived in the dark that she called it the black beast? She knew it was not a beast at all really, but because she was not afraid of beasts, not even Farmer Brown's bull, the Thing seemed less terrible when she pictured it to herself as a big black horse; only with wings like a bat; try as she would she could not get rid of those bat-like terrible wings.

" Boots, Robin," she said. " We're going out."

She fetched her wellingtons, and Robin's, and put them side by side in the middle of the night-nursery floor. Then she sat down beside them, spread out the skirts of her cherry smock and made a comfortable lap, in the way she had seen her mother do for the afflicted.   Robin removed his fat wet fists from his eyes, squinted at the boots through his tears, and then stumbled across the room into Meg's lap. She rocked him gently, her thin arms straining round his corpulent person.   He wept with an immense amount of moisture, and the tears cascaded from his screwed-up eyes to roll off his round fat cheeks like marbles.   He was always rosy, but in these times of affliction his face became puce colour, and as crumpled and creased as when he had been born.   Meg took out the handkerchief with the kitten on it and mopped up his tears, but the handkerchief was not quite adequate in size, and smears of the chocolate that she had wiped off her fingers added themselves to the streaks of dust from the wardrobe that had stuck to the honey on his face. Meg sighed and looked worried again.   Her mother and Zelle, and even her father, mopped up with such efficiency, but she was not very good at it yet.

Mummy and Daddy!   In the upset of Robin she had actually forgotten them.   Another of those great waves of joy broke over her head.   It held her still for a moment, her illumined little face buried in Robin's mop of red curls, then she pushed him suddenly over backwards, his legs in the air, and pulled his boots on.   Leaving him prostrate, she reached for her own.   He was all right now, rolling about like a porpoise and chuckling.   He was so circular that once down on the floor he had a certain amount of difficulty in getting to his feet again.   He just rolled and chuckled until somehow or other he came the right way up.

"There!" said Meg, her boots in place.   It was fine and sunny now, and they did not need their mackintoshes, only their wellingtons for the squelchy puddles.   "Quick, Robin!   Mummy and Daddy!"

She grabbed him by the slack of his beech-brown jersey and pulled and he came curly head uppermost, boots down, and strode forth towards the night-nursery door with a grand seven-league motion.   With a final desperate heave Mouse tipped over the laundry basket, spilled herself out and dashed after.   The stairs slowed them down a little, for even in moments of intense excitement Robin could only negotiate them by lowering his right foot first and bringing his left foot to it, and his right leg, which got all the bumps, got very tired and slow before the bottom of the stairs was reached. It would have rested it if he could have lowered the left leg first for a bit, but he couldn't seem to do that, even when Meg showed him how. Mouse was silly on the stairs, too. She was always leaving her back legs behind, and finding herself in the most peculiar difficulties as a result. But Meg was patient. Robin and Mouse had lived in the world for only twenty-four months, while she had been in it for forty-eight months, and that made a great deal of difference.

" We're going to meet Mummy and Daddy," said Meg when they reached the hall.

" Mummy," said Robin. Yes, he knew about Mummy. He'd seen her yesterday.

" And Daddy," said Meg.

" Daddy? " questioned Robin. He was not quite sure about Daddy. The word connoted an idea partly pleasing and partly not. Chocolate came into it, but there was a suggestion of spanking too.

" Yes, Daddy," said Meg firmly, and opened the front door.

Out in the drive, running down it in the sun and the wind, ecstasy took hold of the three of them. Meg was running to Mummy and Daddy, Robin was running to the edge of the world, and Mouse was just running; and running, to Mouse, did not just mean covering the ground with all four legs twinkling so fast they could hardly be seen, it meant tearing round in circles, leaping into the air with ecstatic barks, chasing unseen presences and snorting and scrabbling at rabbit-holes that the human eye was unable to perceive. Running free in the oak-wood like this she was in an Elysium whose glories a mere human was only able to guess at feebly, through the vibrations of joy that pulsated from the soul of Mouse like music from a violin. Not that one could hear anything, except the earthly barks and snorts, but one's being quivered in a delight that was not earthly, as when strings that are well tuned are touched with artistry.

Robin, too, ran in Elysium, for he ran to the edge of the world, and for him the path that lay in any direction from the front door to that place where he took off at the world's end and was free was enchanted country. What he saw, smelt, heard, no one knew, any more than they knew what Mouse saw, smelt and heard, but the eager tugging of his fat hand in the hand that held his and kept him from falling headlong in his haste, the passionate striving of his short legs, the rosy effusion of joy over his whole face, the fling-back of his curly head and his ecstatic chuckles, said that it was good. When he reached the end of the world he tugged his hand free and ran still faster, and to those who watched it seemed that as he ran his body took on a new sort of motion, as though he were indeed flying, not running; until suddenly his wings failed and he fell headlong with a roaring of lamentation that was almost classic in its power and scope.

But Meg at four years old had forgotten that particular Elysium of the very young. Hers was different now, and the best of all. During the last two years she had been coming to know what human love means, not only in terms of warmth and comfort and protection but in terms of differentiated knowing and giving. Mummy and Daddy were no longer just warm bodies and strong arms and kind voices that charmed away fear, they were separate and most precious people who could receive love as well as give it, and be a little known as well as know. When they were away, with no flow of love coming to her from them and no flow of love going back from her again, it was as though the tides failed and the winds dropped and the birds fell silent, and the world was dead like the parched and pallid moon. She ran now among no imaginary joys to no headlong fall of disappointment, but to a reality that could be actually possessed through days and weeks, perhaps for months, a stretch of time to her as immense as eternity itself.

They were through the gate, the sea wind blowing about them and the gulls circling overhead, and before them was the village green that separated Damerosehay from the harbour and Little Village. It was almost too small to be noticed—no more than one diminutive green patch upon the coloured patchwork of the marshes—but to Robin at this moment it seemed a vast green sea stretching away into limitless space. This was the edge of the world. This was where he took off. He wrenched his hand out of Meg's and was away, running over the green turf, although he had not seen, as Meg had, the bonnet of a long grey car coming round the corner and nosing its way between the post office and the harbour wall, like an animal thrusting its head into the burrow that leads to home. Robin, when he took off, was aware of nothing except that the something he had lost when he came to this world was over there, beckoning, and that if he ran hard enough and fast enough and long enough he would find it again.

But that he could never do. With the buckling up beneath him of his inadequate legs, and the failure of the breath in his fat little body, there came also the fear. He was going to fall into the black pit. It would suddenly open just in front of him, a horrible blackness that was interposed between him and the strong safe thing to which he was running. And yet he could not stop his staggering stumbling run. He never could. It was always the same. He came to the brink of the pit and fell headlong into the blackness and the fear.

But today it was suddenly different. Just as his legs began to fail, and the first onslaught of the terror came upon him, he looked up and saw an immense figure striding towards him, a rescuing figure of glorious and victorious power. A man. If only he could get to that man before the black pit opened he would not fall headlong but would be saved. The man was holding out his arms. Robin's knees gave and he stumbled, but he did not fall. He recovered himself and staggered on. Now he was nearly there. He was there. No, he wasn't. The worst had happened. His left wellington had somehow got itself entangled with his right wellington, his legs were twisted up and he was falling.

" Got you! " said a triumphant voice from the sky, and

upon the very brink of the black pit he was lifted and locked into complete safety. " Daddy," he said, without knowing in the least what he meant by the word, and with his eyes tight shut he burrowed and screwed himself into the warm strength that encompassed him. This was the source of his being. This was life. This was the thing towards which he ran.

David was most extraordinarily moved and most deeply honoured. He was used to appreciation, but this highly appreciative scrap of humanity was his own son. He had left a noisy baby and had come home to an appreciative son. He had never had such a welcome. His son. Robin. He detached the limpet-like creature with difficulty from his shoulder and sat him up on his left arm to have a look at him. What a face! Completely circular and very fat, scarlet with exertion, streaked with chocolate and dirt and some sticky substance that was also adhering to his coat. A couple of tears had made tracks through the dirt, and the long golden lashes that fringed the grey-green eyes were clotted together with other tears.

" What was the trouble, old chap? " asked David. For it was obvious that the trouble had passed. Robin was chuckling now, his eyes sparkling with green fire and his tossed curls like flame in the wind. What a glowing fellow! thought David, and the spit image of his father-in-law. Not that he objected to that, because he liked his father-in-law. And there was something of Sally there, too; the warmth was Sally. Nothing of himself that he could see. Nevertheless the creature was his son, bone of his bone and flesh of his flesh. The dirty face was unkissable, but the nape of the neck was moderately clean, and he kissed that. The skin was silky soft and smelt of violet powder, and just above it was a twist of a red curl like a drake's tail. Robin wriggled and chuckled and slid to the ground. " Car," he said, and staggered in his ridiculous boots to the grey monster purring at the roadside.

David saw, to his astonishment, that it was empty. Where was Sally? Where was Mouse? Above all, where was Meg? He had had to greet Robin first, for it had been with a queer feeling of imminent disaster that he had caught up the little figure in the stumbling seven-league boots. His son safely in his arms, the feeling had gone in a flash, but it had left him for a moment or two unconscious of anything except Robin's need of him. While he bundled his son into the car, in a hurry to drive on and find Meg, his mind was busy with his children. Perhaps this scrap here, so unlike himself, would have greater need of him than Meg, so like him that the subtle comfort of her likeness, giving hope to the bitter self-knowledge of his middle life, might give him a greater need of her than she of him. In Meg he saw the child that he might yet become by the grace of God, but in him Robin in years to come must see a man whose greatness of stature in days of danger would be for him both protection and challenge; and that too would come about only by the grace of God.

As he bumped the car up the drive he deplored with sudden impatience the inescapable and impossible demands that his children make upon a man. It would have been more comfortable to have remained a bachelor and wallowed along in the agreeable state of self-deception that had been his before marriage. Fatherhood revealed one's inadequacies in an appalling manner, and his triumphant American tour, putting the final polish upon a fame that few men are able to achieve in their lifetime, had further destroyed his worth to himself in his own eyes. The contrasts between the luxury and adulation and the stark dreadfulness of Shakespeare's thought, between himself and Sebastian Weber, had seemed to batter him backwards and forwards between them and then let him fall into this pit of humiliation.

Near the front door he overtook Sally, breathless and troubled. "Meg hardly got farther than the gate," she said. "The minute she saw Robin running towards you she turned and ran back. I thought I'd overtake her, but I haven't."

"She'll be in the hall," said David.

But Meg was not in the hall or in the nursery. They looked for her and called her, but she did not come.

"Better 'ave a nice cupper tea," said Mrs. Wilkes, shutting Robin firmly in the nursery with a now restored Zelle, lest he get lost, too, and evade bedtime, and shepherding the distracted parents downstairs. "Meg, she's got a good 'ead-piece. Never comes to no 'arm. Mouse is with 'er, too. A cupper tea will do you both good."

"It's late for tea, Mrs. Wilkes," said Sally, sure that tea would choke her unless she first found Meg. "Nearly six o'clock."

"You said as 'ow you'd be 'ome for tea, and tea is ready in the drawing-room according to your orders, Madam," said Mrs. Wilkes.

Sally capitulated instantly. Madam was an ominous word in Mrs. Wilkes's vocabulary. It meant that though Mrs. Wilkes's temper would not be permitted to rear its head, it was nevertheless writhing underfoot.

"I'm sorry we're late," she said apologetically. "We went to see Lady Eliot."

"Too much excitement don't do 'er no good at 'er age," said Mrs. Wilkes. "I put tea in the drawing-room, Sir, not in the garden; not in this weather."

David had thought of looking out through the garden door, just in case Meg were hiding behind the lavender hedge, but was out-manœuvred by Mrs. Wilkes. It was never any good trying to slip round her to a door behind her back. Mr. Wilkes, hemmed in the Wilkes kitchen with a thirst upon him, knew now that it was no good. Mrs. Wilkes, with a forbidden door behind her, and advancing majestically from the strongly consolidated position of her impregnable virtue, could be no more resisted than a tidal wave. Lifted upon the strong current of her determination, her employers were deposited in the drawing-room before they knew it. Shutting them in, she left them and went to fetch the old silver teapot.

"That Mr. Whats-It," she said, returning and setting it

down among the delicate Spode cups on the tray, " 'e's 'ad
'is tea and 'e's settling in real comfortable."

" I meant to ring you up, Mrs. Wilkes," said David.

" The road to 'ell is paved with good intentions," said
Mrs. Wilkes. " Glad to see you 'ome, Sir," she added with
great kindliness. " Real peaky you look. Well, that's to
be expected. We don't none of us get no younger. Now
'ave your tea in comfort. There ain't no call to worry about
Meg."

She left them, and they went on worrying about
Meg.

" You see, whenever you come home you always greet Meg
first," said Sally. " And this time it was Robin. You
shouldn't have done that, David."

" I had a queer feeling the little fellow was in danger."

" Well, so he is when he runs at that pace. He's not a bit
steady on his feet yet. He'd have tumbled headlong if
you hadn't caught him. But you couldn't expect Meg to
understand that."

" She wouldn't be jealous, Sally."

" Not jealous exactly. Hurt and wounded. Thinking
you didn't love her any more."

" She'd never think that," said David, with sudden
energy. And then he smiled to himself, for not even Sally,
he thought, his wife and Meg's mother, quite understood
the closeness of the bond between him and Meg. Sally,
watching his face, smiled too. Yes, she understood, and she
did not mind in the least that David loved his daughter a
little more than he loved his wife. And how absurd of her
to think that Meg might have been jealous, for she herself
wasn't, and she knew that in just one thing Meg took after
her : both of them could love without possessiveness.

David turned the trolley round to face himself instead
of Sally and poured out with sudden energy. " We are
being ridiculous, Sally. Our eldest infant is momentarily
mislaid inside the safety of her own home, and we spoil my
home-coming by fussing like a couple of demented black-
birds when the cat's about. Meg will turn up when she

wants to. Don't sit on the edge of your chair like that, sort of watching for the cat. Sit back and relax."

Sally sat back in the comfortable depths of the shabby old arm-chair, where Lucilla had always sat when she reigned at Damerosehay. Even after five years of married life in this house she found it hard to think of herself as the mistress of it. Always, whatever she was doing, she remembered Lucilla and tried to think and plan and act for the welfare of this house as Lucilla would have done. And if ever, even in thought, she shrank from the primary duty of hospitality, as she had shrunk just now from the thought of Sebastian Weber, she was deeply ashamed. What was Damerosehay for? Through an open window she could see him moving slowly among the flowers and enjoying them. When she had cleared away tea, and David had gone to his study to sort out his mail, she would go out and tell him she was glad he had come.

" You've scarcely altered a thing in this room, Sally," said David gratefully, from the depth of his own chair.

Lucilla had taken only the most personal of her treasures to Lavender Cottage, and the Damerosehay drawing-room was much as it had been, with the same beautiful Sheraton chairs and Persian rugs, and the same Dresden china figures standing on the mantelpiece beneath the great carved overmantel of polished wood. The old chintzes and brocade curtains had given way at last, but Sally had replaced them with new ones as like the old as possible, and kept the room filled with flowers, as Lucilla had always done. On chilly summer days, such as this one, there was still always a log fire, the scent of the flowers mingling with the smell of the burning wood. It was an extremely old-fashioned room, belonging to another century, as old-fashioned as the old silver teapot and the miniatures upon the cream-painted panelled walls. Another wife than his, thought David, would have altered the position of the furniture, and cleared away half the ornaments that took so long to dust, and the flower-bowls that took so long to fill, and made some sort of an effort to put the impress of her own personality on her own room. Yet Sally, in effacing herself, had unaware put her impress very firmly on Damerosehay. The sense of continuity that she had worked for and achieved in her home, with its concomitant assurances of peace and safety, was something that was part of her own nature. There was no variableness in Sally. If her mind moved sometimes with a slowness that occasionally irritated her quick-witted husband, it moved to sound convictions from which it did not move again, and if in friendship she lacked the easy demonstrativeness of her generation, she gave her love, when she did give it, with a dedication that no abuse of it could change or tarnish.

" I like it this way," said Sally. " I like to sit in this room when I am tired, and watch how the light falls on the panelling, and think of the other women who have sat here and watched it fall in just the same way—Aramanthe, Grandmother, and other people. A sort of freshness comes then. I don't know why."

David knew why. A woman loving her home was something that lay deep where the green pastures are. Bombs could not destroy it, though they might destroy the home, and the woman and her children. He felt in sudden desperation for his cigarette case. The States had been riddled with the dread of war and the talk of it, worse even than here, where blinkers were a normal part of the national costume. It had all added to the wretchedness of the time out there. The stench of war, the reek of burning cities that had once been so sickeningly familiar, had been back with him again. It was with him now in this quiet flower-scented room.

He lay back in his chair again and listened to the old clock ticking and the settling of the wood-ash in the grate, and Sally talking softly about Robin's teeth. There was a way, there must be a way, of liberating that freshness of the indestructible and letting it flood over the reek and stench. There must somehow, somewhere, be a way. Just the knowledge that there was a way, even if men were too mad and blind to find it, brought a sense of peace.

" I must clear away tea and see what Mrs. Wilkes is doing
about supper," said Sally. " And then there's Meg and
your Mr. Weber. I must tell him I'm glad he's come."
She tried to keep the weariness out of her voice, but it
escaped at the edges.

David piled the things on the trolley and pulled her to her
feet. They clung to each other for a moment, thankful to
be together again.

" That damn party tomorrow," said David. " Why do
we always have a party on our wedding day? It's an insane
thing to do."

" We do it to please Grandmother," said Sally. " And all
the family like it too."

" Damn the family," groaned David. " Always the
family. Never us."

" Sometimes," said Sally. " Now, at this moment. And
it is always us deep down."

" Five years of it and it's worked," said David.

She was suddenly happy. What if she could not know
him as well as she would like to know him, or be to him all
that she longed to be? She would have to be perfect, and
he too, to achieve a perfect understanding. It was human
imperfection that kept human beings so isolated. It was
crying for the moon to ask for a perfect relationship with
another while one remained what one was. And meanwhile, until one was something different, to say that
one's marriage worked was to count oneself supremely
blessed.

" Five years of you, David," she said softly.

" No other woman would have stuck it," he said,
and laughed and kissed her and went away with that
disconcerting suddenness of his that always hurt her.
For he would vanish so quickly and silently that it
was like a repudiation. As she pushed out the trolley,
her sudden happiness died, and she was back again
with that fear that no growth of which she was capable
in this life would ever bring her to be with him where he
was.

2

David at his study table savagely tore open envelopes while the waves of his shame went over him. " Five years of you," she had said, honouring him.   She did not know what he was.   It was unbearable to think of her knowing, and yet it was unbearable that she should not know.   He wanted her not to know and yet he wanted her to know.   He imagined that the child she was would be harmed if he were to tell her all he knew of himself, and yet to have her loving and honouring a man that he was not was a deception that seemed equally to harm her.   Well, there was nothing he could do about it.   Only endure this darkness in which the one ray of light that shone through it showed him not the man that he had thought himself to be, nor the man that others thought him, but the man that he was.

He got up and pulled off the coat he wore, exchanging it for the shabby old tweed that Mrs. Wilkes had put ready for him in the cupboard.   There was relief in the movement, though he could not so easily tear himself free from the man that he was.   Then he went back to the sorting of his letters.

His study was a small room beyond the dining-room, facing west, which in old days had been called the dump room.   Margaret had done the flowers here, and struggled with her housekeeping accounts.   The dogs' baskets had been kept here, garden chairs and catalogues of seeds.   It was the only room at Damerosehay that had been entirely refurnished and the only room in the house that looked really luxurious, with its deep comfortable arm-chairs, warm fitted carpet, plum-coloured curtains and book-covered walls.   There was a Cézanne over the fire-place and an old French mirror between the book-cases.   The big writing-table and chair looked more comfortable than austere, and the reading-lamps had shades cleverly made of old theatre play-bills.   The one luxury that David had insisted upon when they came to Damerosehay had been electric light, and the one that Sally had insisted on was this room for

David.   He had always liked it, yet coming back to it now,
and remembering the room in which he had first talked with
Sebastian, he felt afraid of its luxury, for it was always these
contrasts that increased his darkness.   He dropped the
letters he held and shut his eyes for a moment, as though
with a hope that that darkness might shut out the other.

A comforting warmth suddenly deposited itself upon his
feet and there was a soft drum-like sound as of a tail thudding
up and down on the carpet.   A small peal of laughter rang
out and was checked, so that against the darkness of his
closed eyes David saw a little fountain of light leap up
and fall in a shower of bright drops all shaped like bells.
He leaned back in his chair.   " Bells and drums," he said
aloud.   " Who can possibly be under the table? "

There was a giggle, instantly suppressed, and the drum
notes increased their tempo while a minor earthquake
heaved upon his feet.

" I've got my eyes shut," he said.   " If someone were to
come out and climb on top of me I shouldn't have an idea
who it was.   I should have to guess."

She was there in a moment, lighter to hold than Robin.
She was not demonstrative and made no attempt to strangle
him with her arms round his neck, as Robin had done.   She
sat most lightly on his knee, but the glowing warmth of her
body, that he could feel through the stuff of her smock,
seemed as much the warmth of love as of life.   Though he
knew it by heart, he touched with his hand the curve of her
head beneath the soft silky hair, and the outline of her cheek.
How little one needed sight to be aware of one's child with
the sort of awareness that is like light flooding all the dark
places of one's being.   Mouse, sensing the change in his
mood, removed herself from his feet and came out from
beneath the table to pounce upon a sunbeam on the floor.
She was not yet of an age to be quite sure if sunbeams could
be picked up and shaken or whether they could not.   Disappointed, she sat down upon the sunbeam and scratched
herself, the little medal she wore on her collar tinkling softly.
Dogs of Damerosehay who were now dead, Pooh Bah and

the Bastard, had worn those medals too, and with that little familiar sound in his ears David knew he was home again.

"You haven't guessed," whispered Meg.

"Mrs. Wilkes?"

"No."

"Mummy?"

"No."

"Robin?"

"No."

"Could it be Meg?"

"Yes! Open your eyes!"

"Who'd have thought it," said David, his face a mask of profound astonishment.

Meg seized the lapels of his coat and swung on them, laughing in delight, her head tipped back as she looked at him and her fair hair falling back from her face. Her usually pale cheeks were rosy with joy and her eyes were slits of mirth. No one could pretend like Daddy. Not even Mummy, though she did her best. Only Daddy of all the people in the world could play the games that Meg wanted to play with complete understanding of his part. There was not a sign on her happy face of the hurt that Sally had feared for her.

"Why did you run away, Meg?"

"Too many people," said Meg.

He remembered that when as a boy he had come home from school he would not go into the drawing-room to greet Grandmother until he could be sure she was alone there. How relationships repeated themselves in life, like a recurring chord in music, and when they were good ones, each striking of the chord seemed to increase its beauty.

"You all right, Meg?" he asked.

"I'm all wight," said Meg.   "Are you all wight?"

"Yes, I'm all right."   And so he was, with Meg there. "I suppose you couldn't kiss me, could you?"

She gave him a kiss that felt like the touch of a butterfly's wing upon his face and then settled herself comfortably in the crook of his arm, her head on his shoulder and her

feet upon the arm of his chair. She had removed her
wellingtons and contemplated the red leather slippers she
had had on inside them with satisfaction.

" They're new," she said. "For you," she added drowsily.
The room was warm and golden with the westering sun, she
was utterly happy and it seemed that she was going to sleep.

David, more or less sleepless for weeks past, roused himself
with a jerk and remembered that he must go and tell Sally
that Meg was safe, but a snore from Mouse, now asleep on
the sunbeam that had refused to be shaken, changed the
current of his thoughts. Sally, coming in five minutes later
to tell David it was Meg's bedtime and still she could not be
found, contemplated the three of them with amusement.

" And yet he says he doesn't want more children," she
thought. " There'll have to be another girl after
Christopher, or whatever will he do when Meg is at boarding-
school?"

She went out, closing the door softly. Outside in the
passage that led to the garden she stood with her hands
pressed to her aching temples and tried to think what she
had to do next. Robin was bathed and in bed and Zelle
comforted, the chicken was in the oven and the vegetables
ready, and Mrs. Wilkes was laying the table and had
promised to stay and wash up, providing they were punctual
in coming to supper. Mr. Weber! He was the next thing.
She didn't look forward to him very much, but she must
try and take him without fear, with no before or after.
When one was well the next thing flowed in so easily and
naturally, but when one was tired to death it sent before it
a wave of nervous apprehension. Would one be able to
manage? Would one make a mess of it? Was it going to
be just the last straw which would break one down completely? Engulfed in this fear, Sally had taught herself to
think of the next thing as though it were the last thing.
Just this one more thing and then no more. If it were the
last thing, then it did not seem too hard to rally one's forces
just once more. Obliteration of the future seemed to lead to
obliteration of the past too, and there could be a sense, she

knew, in which this living for the moment only could be evil. It could be licence, and then the destruction of past and future was a betrayal of both. But when you took the moment in your hands as selflessly as you were able, past and future were not so much destroyed as gathered into it in one perfect whole, and living for it was not destructive but creative. The moment was no longer the last thing but the one thing, and so nothing else mattered and one would not fail.

She opened the garden door and went out into a world which the wind and the rain had swept and cleansed and then left to a happy loneliness. Each flower, each leaf, burning with colour in the streaming light from the west, was held in such a stillness that it seemed alone, and yet by its very loneliness a more integral part of the immensity of light. Sally stood bathed in light and felt herself made new. The loneliness of each leaf and flower was like the loneliness of each next thing. It was all there was, and yet it was a part of a whole whose before and after was the circle of eternity.

CHAPTER IV

I

RESTORED by Mrs. Wilkes's ministrations, Sebastian had explored the garden with growing delight. Like all old gardens, it had many trees and bushes: lilacs, laburnums, guelder roses and strawberry trees, cherry trees, rose trees that must have been there for a hundred years, a magnolia growing against the house, and on the lawn outside the drawing-room window a grand old ilex-tree lifting its islands of darkness against the bright blue sky. There were rosemary bushes and lavender hedges, and the scent of lemon verbena was coming from somewhere. There were still late roses in bloom and a grand show of asters and dahlias in the borders. There was no kitchen garden that he could see but a wall bordered the flower-garden to the west. This wall was almost hidden by a riotous growth of winter honeysuckle, and the jasmine that country folk call mind-your-own-business, but behind a guelder-rose bush he saw a wrought-iron gate in the wall and unlatched it and went inside, leaving it open.

It was not a kitchen garden, but just such a wild enchanted place as in his childhood he had pictured that garden where the sleeping beauty dreamed away a hundred years. One could dream away a hundred years in this place, he thought, untouched by time. It was a continuation of the oak-wood beyond the drive, though the trees must have been thinned out to make this place more of a garden than a wood. Rough grass grew beneath the trees, and the moss-grown path wandered in and out between them. Honeysuckle and traveller's joy, brambles and mind-your-own-business grew everywhere, and there were lavender and rosemary bushes growing in the grass. Yet he could see that the heavenly wildness of the place was a planned wildness, and carefully restrained. Here and there a small flower-bed

66

had been cleared and planted with hardy plants, michaelmas daisies, hollyhocks and Japanese anemones, with plenty of primrose roots about the old trees. There were birds everywhere: tits and chaffinches, whose wings made almost a mist of colour about the silvery branches of the trees, nut-hatches, wrens and robins. A thrush was singing some-where, though it was not the season of song, and he followed the path towards the heart of the garden, from which the singing came.

Here there was a very large oak-tree, gnarled and old, with lichened branches, and the thrush was singing high up on the topmost branch. There was a seat beneath the tree, and the grass all about it was carpeted with the delicate mauve of autumn crocuses. A child's swing hung from one of the branches and lying among the crocuses was a bedraggled toy rabbit, wearing a pink bow, but minus one ear.

Sebastian sat down abruptly upon the seat. Crocuses of just that colour grew in the mountains in his country, and in the garden of his house at the foot of the mountains he had hung a swing for his children from the branches of a tree. The path to the heart of the garden had carried him straight to the heart of his own past, where he did not allow himself to go. "Fool!" he said to himself, fighting the impulse to get up and walk from this garden and from Damerosehay, to get away somewhere else. Somewhere. Anywhere. Yet where? "Fool!" he said again. "Senti-mental fool."

His heart was pounding, yet his mind was groping through darkness to a thread of light swinging there to which he could hold, he thought, if he could reach it. It swung towards him and he caught it and knew what it was. Merely a memory of light, that sanctuary light that had come to him without distress up in his room. If he could have re-membered that, and been glad, the time might come when he would welcome the memory of the swing in the garden. His mind presented this to him as an impossible hypothesis, and yet in these days was anything impossible? He had seen the unendurable endured and had himself endured it. He had seen men match themselves against impossible horror and surmount it; but not slumped on a seat in this attitude of defeatism.

He sat up and found himself regarding the rabbit. It was an engaging creature in spite of its condition, with pleading green glass eyes and a pink lining to its one ear. It must belong to Meg, or to the other child who had been yelling blue murder upstairs. He must take it indoors, or further rain in the night would bring it to a soppy end. He had not handled a child's toy since the days that belonged now to another life, and it took all his resolution to bend down and pick the creature up, and yet once he was holding it he found himself in no nightmare of recollection, but merely thinking that he must find a bit of felt and make another ear. Sawdust was oozing from a split seam, too, and that also must be seen to. Altogether the creature was in a bad way, though obviously much beloved, for repairs had taken place before: there was a patch on the nose, and a new scut made out of a woman's powder puff had been rather clumsily attached in the place of one lost. He leaned back against the tree, in the warm sun that was now shining full upon him through the branches, and turned it over in his nervous oddly-shaped long hands that had once had such skill in making and mending. Other children besides his own had brought him their broken toys, and stood round him in a tense silence while he examined the broken engine or the headless doll and pondered weightily alternative methods of rehabilitation.

He was almost asleep in the warm sun. How well he remembered those children! They were about him now in this children's sanctuary. In the warm silence he was aware of them, breathing hard with anxiety and yet knowing that he would not fail them. He would restore this rabbit to its pristine glory. He held the creature on his knee and his hands were still, for the sun was like a sedative, it was so warm now. Yes, they were here, but not now the children he had known, and not Meg or the yeller upstairs, but other children who had played in this garden. Wraiths, not necessarily of the dead but of vanished childhood. There were two dark-haired boys, one with a thin keen dark face, the other fat and rosy. A plain little girl with freckles on her face. A beautiful boy to whom the fatherhood in him reached out with such strength that he knew he was fatherless. The boy turned and looked at him, and his eyes were Meg's. And another boy quaintly dressed in green who had lived here so long ago that perhaps he had been the first to play in this garden. But of them all it was the fatherless boy who came closest. Sebastian fancied that he could feel him leaning against his knee.

And there was a woman, the mother of them all, wearing an old-fashioned dress with a full and sweeping skirt the colour of the autumn crocuses. Her dark eyes made him welcome, trespassing though he was in the children's special place. Yet when he opened his eyes and looked at her she was wearing a loose lavender-coloured tweed coat and her smiling eyes were tawny.

" I'm afraid I'm trespassing in the children's sanctuary," he said.

" Not only theirs," she answered. " Yours too I hope."

She looked young, he thought, to be the mother of them all. " You have so many children," he said.

She looked puzzled. " Only two," she said. " Though Robin makes enough noise for five. Oh, you've found his rabbit! "

" Is he missing it? "

" He's been yelling all day, and Zelle did not know why."

" I could make a new ear," said Sebastian. " And re-attach the tail. I used to be good with my hands and I think I could still manage an ear and a tail."

" I'm not good at mending things," said Sally apologetically. " Nor is David. We fail them there."

Sebastian suddenly stood up, his hands eloquent with distress. " Mrs. Eliot? Please forgive me. I believe I have been asleep."

" I believe you have," laughed Sally. " I expect you are like my husband. You have bad nights and fall asleep unexpectedly in the day instead."

But Sebastian was still distressed. " I should not be here. You came here to be quiet? "

" No, I came to look for you. The gate was open so I thought I'd find you here."

His distress had communicated itself to her and she flushed, but she straightened her shoulders and said what she had come to say clearly and steadily, like a child saying her piece. " I am so sorry about this morning. David forgot to telephone and so there was no proper welcome for you. I am so glad you have come and I hope you will be happy here."

She was a tall woman and they were of almost the same height. She thought she had never looked into such lightless eyes. There was no kindling from within, and they were sunk so deeply in his ugly bony head that it seemed they could reflect no light from without. His rough grey hair and his clothes looked dusty and his sallow rigid face had a parched look, as though the dry skin were about to crack. She had thought to herself earlier in the day that she had never suffered and did not know the meaning of the word. Nor did she, but she knew now what men and women looked like who had suffered to the limit of endurance. Scorched like a desert. And she had said that she hoped he would be happy. This was a man who could not again be happy in the sense in which she had used the word. All her adult life she had had a sense of shame because she was so fortunate, but it had never been so deep as now. Her flush ran over her whole face and down her white neck, but her eyes did not drop. She still looked at him steadily, and he at her, both aware that though by experience, race and age they were deeply parted, yet something that neither as yet understood had already given them union with each other. Her tawny eyes were like a lion's, he thought. She was a brave woman, and calamity if and when it came would find her ready.

Yet what a child she was now, although the mother of Meg and the yeller, and in some mysterious way of the children of his dream. And of a child that was yet unborn. He suddenly forgot everything else in concern, for her flush had faded and she looked deadly tired as she obeyed the movement of his hands and sat down upon the seat. He sat beside her. What a pity the English cannot talk with their hands, she thought. The language of movement was better than the language of sound, swifter and more sure.

Sebastian's hands, as eloquent as his face was expressionless, lifted and then moved gracefully to his knees and rested there. The movement was very individual, and awakened a memory. As a child she had seen the hands of a great pianist do that, seeking respite while the orchestra lifted and carried the theme they had stated. Respite. If happiness was now beyond his reach, he could at least know respite, and respite, with its lifelong rhythm, can in the awareness of it be called by the name of peace.

"But there must be no before or after," said Sally.

He looked at her with polite astonishment, and she laughed.

"Please forgive me!" she said. "I was thinking of moments of respite. One can't get the most out of them unless one treats them as one treats the next thing: as though it were the only thing. I mean, if you think about the toothache that has just stopped, it so easily becomes the toothache that is going to begin again, and all your peace is lost."

"That's true," said Sebastian, and he laughed too, his harsh croak of laughter the most surprising sound in the children's garden. He felt so at ease with this childlike woman that he half turned on the seat to look at her. She was the most surprising wife for David Eliot, and he could not picture them together. He tried to see her beside her husband in his dressing-room at the theatre, at parties in New York or on board the luxury liner that had brought them home, but he could no more see her there than he could see Eliot in this old house and garden that suited her timeless charm to perfection. Eliot was of his century, and the bright lights and ceaseless movement of hot rooms and tall hard streets made the right setting for his restless brilliance. But the sunshiny warmth, the quiet tempo of mind and body of which he was so gratefully aware in this woman, belonged with Damerosehay to another age than this, and it was in another age that he sat here with her, talking of his meeting with Meg, of the flowers and birds about them and of that light that comes when tracts of land are islanded by the sea.

A bell tolled softly, sounding so deep and far away that it might have been ringing at the bottom of that same sea, and Sally seized the rabbit and jumped up.

" It's supper! " she cried in dismay. " And I've not washed my hands, and I don't expect my husband is even awake yet. When our Mrs. Wilkes is annoyed with us she does not show it much, but one feels it just the same."

As much as her natural serenity was capable of hurrying anyone, Sally hurried Sebastian, the bell tolling once more in patient resignation as they entered the house. A door in the passage opened and a man stumbled out, shabby and untidy, his shoulders hunched and his rumpled hair standing on end. Meg, deeply asleep, was in his arms and a drowsy little dog trotted at his heels. For a moment he stood quite still. His blue eyes were utterly bewildered and his lined and ageing face looked blind and smudged with fatigue. The golden sunset light, streaming through the glass of the garden door full upon him, was merciless, and yet gave him of its magic at the same time, so that in his red-brown tweed coat, with his face reflecting the light and the child in her red frock in his arms, he looked like a glowing oil-painting, a Rembrandt or a Paul Rubens, a splendid bit of warm colour against the dark velvety shadows of the old house. Sebastian, who in these days of returning sanity lived in a world where fantasy, dream and nightmare were so inter-mingled with actual fact that he felt himself to be per-petually disintegrating like a kaleidoscope, toppling from one level of consciousness to another, looked at the picture with an artist's delight. It was so utterly in its place in this old house, so a part of it. Then the little dog yawned, showing quantities of pink tongue, and the man caught the infection and yawned, too, blinking like an owl. Sebastian realised with a shock that he was alive. An elder brother of Mrs. Eliot's? He had her warmth, and judging by the way he held the child, her tenderness too, to a degree that drew Sebastian's thought to him with liking.

"For heaven's sake, David!" implored Sally. "The bell has rung twice. Take Meg to Zelle, and get tidy while you are upstairs. You have no idea what you look like."

The bell rang for the third time, with a deep mournfulness, and Sally ran to the dining-room to comfort Mrs. Wilkes. There was a seat in the passage, and Sebastian sat down upon it. Damerosehay was prolific in seats, and he realised the fact gratefully, for from combined reasons of physical weakness and mental astonishment they were perpetually necessary to him here. If he had been unable to visualise David Eliot at Damerosehay or with his wife, he was even less able to identify him with the man he had just seen. The beginnings of panic invaded him, and he felt all the more panicky because he did not quite know why he was panicky. Did he want to hate? Had his hatred of Eliot become a source of spiritual strength to him, the only one he had now that change of circumstances had taken other hatreds away? Was it a fact that when a man has deliberately stifled the emotion of love in himself he must hate or dry up altogether? Was he now incapable of love? With panic he pushed his panic away. This was no time for self-questioning, for Mrs. Wilkes was waiting.

2

At supper his host appeared once more as the man he knew, and his dislike flowed back again with the ease of acquired habit; but the ease shocked him now.

Years of hard practice had enabled David to erect the required façade with the speed of a conjurer bringing rabbits out of a hat. He was immaculate as ever as he played the host at his own dinner-table, and his conversational patter flowed with ease; though a little brittle tonight, as though a spray of water had turned to tinkling ice. The situation might have been difficult, comprising as it did a stranger sharing a meal with a husband and wife who only wanted to be left alone together, a hostess who was never very ready with small talk and was by now much too tired to think of anything intelligent to say, and the occasional presence of Mrs. Wilkes, moving in and out like a martyred mountain and impregnating the whole atmosphere with the knowledge that owing to her being kept late Wilkes was already at the local. But situations were never difficult when David handled them. Though he was aware of Sebastian's dislike fanning his face like a blast of hot air from a desert, Mrs. Wilkes's patience running down his back like a runnel of cold water, and Sally's weariness of body sapping the strength of his own in the peculiar way that is one of the drawbacks of a happy marriage, his awareness only showed itself in a sharpening of his faculty for entertainment. Sally helped as well as she could, though she hated it when David talked like this. He had talked this way when she had first met him, when he had just come back to the stage after the war and was talking himself into a nervous breakdown. She hoped he was not going to have another. But Sebastian, sustained by good food, found himself entertained. He liked that icy tinkle in a man's talk. It was like rapier play. Behind it the man moved masked, and there was fascination in trying to glimpse the face behind the mask. Yet this was the first time he had been aware of the rapier and the mask with Eliot. Were they there, or did he only fancy it, because he had seen in the passage a man he did not know?

They went into the drawing-room for coffee. The wood-fire was glowing warmly and there were a few shaded lights, and he gave an exclamation of delight at the beauty of the room. He sat down and drank his coffee and watched the light of the flames leaping up over the strange carved over-mantel above the fireplace. It affected him oddly, and he knew that it must have some history. This room seemed the heart of the house, as the children's sanctuary had been of the garden. He was aware once again, as he had been in his room, of the strong tough spirit of the house created by the fortitude of the men and women who had lived here. He looked across the hearth at the two who lived here now, David sitting on the arm of his wife's chair, and was so sharply aware of their love that it was as though a pit opened between the two of them in their proud possession and himself in his stripped loneliness. Battered between such contrasts, he always fell between them into darkness, and he did so now. He got up abruptly and said he was tired and would go to his room.

" Please don't," he said sharply, when David got up to go with him, but his host smiled and insisted. It was getting dark and the switches were not easy to find.

" Sometimes I think that the putting in of electric light was an act of vandalism on my part," said David. " In old days we all went to bed carrying candles." He smiled at the recollection. " Such a procession as it always was, with the candles and the dogs."

" You've lived here long? " Sebastian asked for politeness sake.

" Nearly all my life," said David. " This was my grandmother's home. My parents died in the First World War, and I came to live with her." He paused, as he always did when he accompanied his secretary up a flight of stairs, so that the poor devil could get his breath, and as always his excuse for the pause entirely deceived Sebastian. " That's the cottage in the village where she lives now," he said, looking down over the bannisters at the painting of a house and garden that hung below them in the hall. " You can't see it properly from here, but I think it is rather remarkable. It's sunset. The colour brims the flowers but it does not run over. It's all held charmed and still. Ben painted it. Ben is another grandson who lived here with his brother and sister. There have always been children in this house since the Eliots came, and now we more or less infest the neighbourhood. All descending on us tomorrow for a family party."

Sebastian looked at him in breathless anxiety, and David smiled.

" I shan't ask you to come," he said.   " I wish I need not be present either.   Not that I don't delight in the family, especially Grandmother, but not in the aggregate."

What nonsense he was talking! he thought, as they went slowly on. But he had to keep on saying something, for Sebastian's dislike of him was harder to bear when they were silent. Yet he did not resent it, for it was to him the rationalisation of his hatred of himself. He even found a sort of relief in it. Here at last was a man who had seen through both the masks to what he really was.

They reached Sebastian's room and he switched the light on. He was silent for a moment, looking round with a half-smile at this room where he had slept as a boy and a young man. He did not often come here now, but it seemed that the boy he had been was still in the room, over there by the window, smiling at himself and Sebastian; the eternal child in a man who had not yet needed to put on a mask, and who did not know that when the pleasure and pride he felt in himself and all that he did had parted company with his innocence he himself would become a mask to hide the egoist gone rank and foul within.

David saw that the room still held some of the treasures of his boyhood: Van Gogh's lark, the sea-horse and a good many of his books—books which had meant a good deal to him at one time but which now he had forgotten. He moved towards a book-case. Humbert Wolfe's " Un-celestial City." He remembered lying in bed in this room and reading that on a night of storm that had been a night of crisis in his life, and it had helped to turn him in the direction that he had taken, a direction that had led away from Nadine, whom he might have married, to Sally and Meg and Robin . . . Meg . . . But for that decision there would have been no Meg. He turned cold at the thought. And yet he had almost forgotten that poem now.

And next to it was Gerard Manley Hopkins. After the war, during those sleepless nights when he had worked himself into such ridiculous states of fear, afraid he would kill himself, afraid he would go mad, afraid of this, that and the other which had never happened at all, he had found the sonnets of darkness and had the sense to know that his torments were nothing at all to the mental suffering that other men endured and survived. That had been a bad time, in its different way as bad as this. He had forgotten the sonnets now. Would they help in this? He took the book out and then put it quickly down on the table by the book-case and swung round in apology, for he had entirely forgotten Sebastian.

" I'm sorry," he said, and laughed. " I had forgotten you, Weber. This was my room when I was a boy."

Sebastian, standing by the window, smiled faintly, and David moved towards him. It was that moment of dusk when the world outside a lighted window wraps itself in a cloak of such deep and heavenly blue that the mere gift of sight with which to see it seems in the moment of seeing all one can need. David opened the window, which Mrs. Wilkes's disapproval of night air for the indisposed had firmly closed, and they could see the lights twinkling on the Island and the lights of a ship sailing up the estuary. There was no sound but the faint rustle of the reeds, and the air was fresh. David remembered that night when they had stood together in Sebastian's room high above the noise of a big city, so high that the sound of the night traffic had been hardly louder than the rustle of the reeds. The lights had twinkled then as now and the air had been fresh. Did Sebastian remember? He turned towards him, but the man's face was expressionless. " Good night," he said quickly, and went away. As he closed the door he had the ridiculous thought that he hoped the smiling boy who was still in the room would be kind to the poor devil.

CHAPTER V

I

SEBASTIAN sat down in the chair by the window, and he was conscious of the boy standing close to him, the same boy who had come so near in the dream in the garden and whose identity he had known when Eliot on the stairs had spoken of the children who had lived in this house. It was of a boyish innocence and sensitiveness that he had imagined himself aware in Eliot that night in America; it was that, he supposed, that must have got beneath his defences. He had not been aware of that boy again, and he had hated Eliot not only because of the contrasts but also because he had said so much to a man who was no different from any of the others. Just a little more fortunate, that was all, slightly more arrogant and therefore more cynical. . . . Yet here was the boy.

He gave an impatient exclamation. His mind was once more at its tumbling kaleidoscope tricks, falling from memory to fantasy and back again. Looking across at the lights on the Island, he was back in the room high above the lights of the city, the roar of it far down below, as though in the depths of a canyon. It was a bare room, with very little in it except himself and his poverty and the thesis he was trying to write on the rickety table by the window, by the light of one failing electric bulb that he feared might go out at any moment; and he had not got another to replace it. The thesis was not going at all well, and even while he continued to struggle with it he knew that he would never finish it. How could he expect to, with a crippled mind and crippled hands? There were pits in his once brilliant mind. The dialectic would fall into place easily for a while, and then would come a gap in which he fell and floundered, and when he got out upon the other side, the necessary link between one thought and another would be missing. Concentration gave him an almost constant headache. His hands were slow—not yet recovered from the rheumatism that at one time had made them helpless—and he could not afford a typewriter. Yet if he finished the thesis and acquired the academic post he wanted, what then? He would not be able to hold it. He had had several posts during the last few years and lost them, sooner or later, through illness of mind or body. Yet he went on laboriously writing because only working at something, however futile, kept his hopelessness at bay. Then came one of those pits, worse than usual. He stopped working and it became one with the canyon beneath his window. He looked at it drearily, stretching his cramped fingers, and the miasma of his hopelessness came swirling up out of it, just as it always did out of all the pits. For there were many of them. They lay between every contrast. What he had once been and what he was now. What he had once possessed and the present nothingness. The joys of other men and his own sorrows.

"Come in," he said, for there was a knock on the door.

Afterwards he had wondered what he might have done later that night if that knock had not come just then. At his worst moments up till now he had not contemplated suicide, for he had great fortitude, but it had been an unusually bad moment just before the knock came.

But he said " Come in ", and the door opened and shut and a man came across the room to him. At first he had thought he was a very young man, for he was boyishly slender and moved lightly. And then looking up at him in the dim light he saw that he was not young, and the strained exhaustion of the face touched a chord of sympathy in him. And he liked the warm kindness of the eyes. At that point the bulb went out.

"I haven't another," he said apologetically.

His visitor laughed. "It doesn't matter. There's moonlight and starlight. It's a wonderful evening. Quite enough light to talk by. We have a friend in common, Roger Hamilton. He told me you are usually working late and would not mind if I came along one evening. He comes along often at this time himself, he says."

Sebastian listened attentively to the trivial remarks, spoken by a voice he had heard before, though he could not remember where. It was a wonderful voice. He became conscious of his duties as a host and struggled to get up from his chair, but he had sat so long that his limbs had grown stiff. He was full of rheumatism.

"Don't move," said the man quickly. "I'll find another."

"There isn't another," said Sebastian. "Only a packing-case that I use as an extra table. I'll have that."

But his visitor had found it and pulled it forward. It was not very high, and sitting on it with his hands linked round his knees he looked, in the half-dark, the boy he had seemed when he came in.

"There's nothing to drink, I'm afraid," said Sebastian. "And no cigarettes."

His guest produced his own case, and they sat smoking quietly for a moment or two. Sebastian felt oddly at home with this man, as though he had known him a long time. It seemed that he knew him for the type that is uncorruptible. Not necessarily better than another man, but uncorruptible because unresting as running water and not to be satisfied by any end that can be attained in this life. Whatever his disasters, spiritual or material, they would never either deaden or detain him. Always he would slough them off and go farther, afraid because aware in every part of his being of the unsleeping and unwearied evil, and hounded by his fear to outstrip that too if it were possible. "We are the Pilgrims, master; we shall go always a little farther." However bitter present experience might be, there had never been a time when Sebastian himself had not been convinced, though in late years with only a sort of heavy dullness, that it was possible. Aware of his kinship with his guest, he waited quietly, reluctant to have this moment of understanding iced in and perhaps forgotten under the banality of trivial talk. But it had to come, and the moment passed.

"My name is Eliot. I am an actor in need of a secretary. Mine has deserted me and gone to Hollywood. Hamilton told me about you. He thought you might take pity on me. Temporarily, at any rate, for he tells me you hope to get some teaching post here."

Sebastian understood. Hamilton knew that he would never write that thesis, and was now shifting the responsibility of him on to another man. Hamilton was an old friend who had got him out of the concentration camp in Europe and brought him to America. He had sponsored him here, but was tired of him now. The twinge of bitterness he felt was not very severe, for he knew Hamilton. He had always been of the company of those who believe you can end a thing just as satisfactorily by giving up as by going on. But he was not going to deceive this other man, whom he knew instinctively always went on. He must know what it was that he would have to go on with. He must explain himself once again. He was always explaining himself.

"I think I should be an extraordinarily bad secretary. I have been at times a victim of what nowadays they politely call psychosis. It has passed, but I still find concentration difficult. I can type, of course, but I write and therefore take notes very slowly. Did Hamilton tell you that?"

"Yes, he told me. He also told me you were an excellent linguist, that you knew England, where I shall be returning soon, and had some knowledge of the theatre."

"Anything else?" asked Sebastian sharply.

"Nothing else," said David gently. "Except a little of your war-time experience. Concentration camp and so on. Not more than that. Nothing personal."

Sebastian relaxed. This was a man who would never ask questions. Probably, like every artist, he lived in a world of uniquely personal experience and had discovered the impossibility of opening that world to another. Each man within his own world must work out his own salvation. " Prithee go in. Seek thine own ease." He'd stay courteously outside.

Now Sebastian knew who he was and why he had felt such a sense of kinship with him. Hamilton had taken him to see David Eliot's Lear and it had been for him a deep catharsis. His gratitude to the actor had been great and so had his sympathy for him. He had thought that only a man who had himself endured much mental suffering could portray it with a power at once so delicate and so inexorable. His portrayal of near madness, outlawry and bereavement had been to Sebastian, who had endured them all, like the lancing of a surgeon's knife that lets out poison. There had been no slackening until the thing was done, yet it had been carried through with such consummate gentleness. And now he forgot his own inadequacy, his pride, his dread of strangers. This man was no stranger. Each in his own secret world, they had yet reached down to some meeting-place of common suffering. There was in his mind the image of two lakes, separate from each other, yet down in the cool depths the waters mingled. A little while later he found himself talking to David of the things of which he never spoke; nothing personal, but imprisonment in general and its effect on men. He said how it kept a prisoner sane to realise now and then, if only for a moment or two, that though personal suffering can seem to a man an entirely lonely and isolating thing, a prison within a prison, it is in actual fact the exact opposite. Through it he reaches the only real unity, oneness with the whole of suffering creation.

" I can see that a moment when you feel that can be a moment of liberation," said David. " The self is lost."

" Yet when the moment is gone," said Sebastian, " it is hard to believe it was ever there."

They talked a little longer, and then David got up to go away, and in his good-bye there was a tone of reverence, of gratitude, that Sebastian was unable to account for. It was, he thought, he who had reason to be grateful. He remembered afterwards that he had never said in so many words that he accepted David's offer, but the next day he went to the theatre as a matter of course.

But that was the end of their intimacy. Between them, next day, there was no recognition. Their interview the night before had been like one of those moments of which they had spoken, something so fleetingly possessed that now it seemed almost as though it had never existed. Nothing remained of it but a mutual gratitude. His employer seemed to Sebastian all that he most disliked: a man of genius who had prostituted his art and had become in consequence the usual streamlined product of the success he had worked for. Lear's agonies were no more to him than the means to an end. His kindness seemed to Sebastian mere patronage. He had merely been chucked from one rich man to another, from Hamilton to Eliot; who would no doubt chuck him to a third, as soon as playing the good Samaritan produced the inevitable boredom. And the luxury of the life lived by the streamlined infuriated him almost to a return of madness. It was always the sickening contrasts that aroused his hatred.

And David on his side encountered a pride, a dryness, a bitterness that hurt him so intolerably that his defences went up at once, brassy and sparkling, and he withdrew himself behind them. Yet they went on together. Sebastian worked for David as well as he possibly could, to the last ounce of his strength, and David behind his defences was ceaselessly thoughtful for him. They would have liked to part, yet this striving each for the other held them together in a way that made parting impossible.

2

Sebastian, in his room at Damerosehay, sighed and stirred. That first meeting, that had become dust in his memory, had quickened to life again as though a desert had greened with springing corn. What was that book

Eliot had taken from the book-case and left on the table?
He put on his glasses and picked it up. It opened where
a marker had been placed between the pages. "World-
sorrow." The words caught his eye at once and he read the
sonnet slowly through, and then again, and again.

> No worst, there is none. Pitched past pitch of grief,
> More pangs will, schooled at forepangs, wilder wring.
> Comforter, where, where is your comforting?
> Mary, mother of us, where is your relief?
> My cries heave, herds-long; huddle in a main, a chief
> Woe, world-sorrow; on an age-old anvil wince and sing—
> Then lull, then leave off. Fury had shrieked, " No ling-
> ering! Let me be fell; force I must be brief."
>
> O the mind, mind has mountains; cliffs of fall
> Frightful, sheer, no-man-fathomed. Hold them cheap
> May who ne'er hung there. Nor does long our small
> Durance deal with that steep or deep. Here! creep,
> Wretch, under a comfort serves in a whirlwind; all
> Life death does end and each day dies with sleep.

The desolation of the poem did not drag him down, but
lifted him as though on the upward surge of a wave. Had
he had the power he could have written every word of it as
his own experience. Those cliffs of fall. He'd hung there,
and he knew them well. World-sorrow. It was a matter
for exultation when one man could so cry out for a silent
multitude the sufferings of all. The individual sorrows,
like individual drops of water, enclosed each man in his
own loneliness but the fellowship of the dark wave was a
mighty and glorious thing.

For the moment he read no more, but closed the book.
Then he picked up the marker that had been between the
pages. It was only an old envelope, addressed to David
Eliot, and bearing a date of the year after the war. He
sat looking at it as though it could tell him something. Had
Eliot had a bad war? Probably. Most men had. Had
he read that sonnet, and perhaps others like it, out of a
need to escape from his own loneliness into world sorrow?
Why had he taken that book out of the shelf tonight? Had
he felt the same need again? And these contrasts which

bred such hatred in him. Perhaps they were not as deep as they seemed. Was any man ever as fortunate as he appeared, or as unfortunate as he imagined himself to be? There was no answer to these questions, and Sebastian put the book back in the book-case and went to bed.

CHAPTER VI

I

THE fact that Sebastian was obliged to attend the family party was no one's fault but his own. He had spent the day working indoors, and when the evening came, and he had finished the supper Mrs. Wilkes brought him in his room, the enchantment of the world outside his window pulled him out of doors. He avoided the garden, for the dining-room windows looked upon it, and the Eliot clan were enjoying a festival meal there, but outside in the drive the only window that looked upon him was his own. From his room he had noticed a plank bridge that spanned the narrow stream separating the marshes from the grass-edged drive, and he crossed it, pushed his way through the rushes, and found a small green lawn entirely surrounded by them. In winter it was probably very squelchy, but now, in spite of the rain yesterday, it was dry after a day of sunshine. There was yet another seat here, and he sat upon it gratefully, even while he wondered, why all these seats in a house and garden dedicated to children? The sitting posture is seldom appreciated by the young. The reeds rustled softly and about him grew marsh-flowers whose names he did not know but whose pungent scents he appreciated.

He could see the Island in front of him. It faced the sunset, and its white cliffs caught the glow. The cloudless sky was a cool clear green behind the Island, but overhead it deepened to a blue so glorious that it dazzled the eyes not so much by its brightness as its power. Strange that colour could have such power. A lark had braved it and was singing up there, and two great swans passed overhead with a mighty beating of flame-touched wings. But the lark and the swans had the same power. The small bird, tossing almost unseen now above the music that fell like

brightness from the air, had lifted the souls of men out of
their mortal weariness more surely than any other musician
since the world began. And the passing of the swans was
as powerful as a rolling of drums. They were Apollo's
swans, who according to Socrates sing and rejoice on the
day of their death because they foresee the blessings of
immortal life. Conqueror of the souls of men, conquerors of
time and death; the place of the lark and the swans was
in the depth of the blue that would still be there when the
sky had let fall the stars " even as a fig tree casteth her
untimely figs ".

There was a faint rustling behind him, nearer than that
of the rushes, the murmur of a silk dress, and he got up
and turned round with no sense of annoyance or apprehension but of inevitability, for whoever came had a right
to come and belonged here. A very old woman stood
looking up at the swans and listening to the lark. She had
not seen him, and he thought that perhaps neither her sight
nor her hearing were very good now, for there was a look
of strain upon her face, as though the glory of the sky that
was so clear for him was for her only a rumour. That, he
thought, must be the hard part of old age, that slow relinquishment while still in this world of the power to see and
hear the symbols. " For the eternal things of Him from
the creation of the world are clearly seen in the things
which are made." But when they are no longer clearly
seen, and yet the soul has not passed on beyond them, was
it as though she fell into a sort of nothingness? Or was
the dying rumour of the lark ascending replaced by a new
sort of certainty of things to come? He would like to ask
this old woman. He was sorry for that look of strain upon
her face, and instead of trying to escape he stood quietly
where he was, waiting for her and enjoying the picture that
she made.

She was tall, and the folds of her black dress fell gracefully.
A white rose was tucked in her belt and a white lacy shawl
had been flung over her head and draped her shoulders.
She leaned upon an ebony stick and he saw the flash of

diamonds on her left hand.   She looked like some great lady
of the eighteenth century and seemed as perfectly in place
against the background of Damerosehay as Eliot had looked
yesterday, when Sebastian's fancy had seen him as an oil-
painting glowing against the shadows of the house.   But she
was not a Rubens.   The clear black and white, the stately
dignity, made him think of Holbein's Duchess of Milan.
But the Duchess was a young woman, and this woman was
even older than he had imagined when he had first seen
her.

She turned and saw him, and smiled as though he were
an old friend whom she was pleased but not surprised to
see here.   " I'll have your arm to help me sit on that seat,
Mr. Weber," she said.   " I have difficulty in getting down
when I am up or up when I am down."

He helped her, and they sat down as companionably as
he and Meg had sat together on the other seat in the drive.
She turned and looked at him, neither considering him as a
problem nor pitying him, but simply accepting him and
making him welcome.   Her blue eyes had the same steady
appraising glance as Meg's had, and Eliot's, but in spite of
being a little clouded by great age, they saw much more.
That sense of belonging nowhere, that had troubled him
for so long, suddenly vanished.   He settled himself more
comfortably on the seat.

" That is how I felt when I first came to this house,
before it was mine," she said.

" How did you feel, Lady Eliot? "

" Anchored."

" I have no right to feel that."

" Why not? " she said.   " You have come where you are
needed."

" Who needs me here? " he asked her, gently but yet with
bitterness.

" Now, that is a very silly question," she said, answering
his bitterness with a touch of asperity.   " You should know
better than most men that no great artist writes a note or
word, or makes one stroke of a brush, that is not necessary

to the perfection of the whole. Is God less intelligent than His creatures?" She stopped and smiled at him a little anxiously, her asperity vanishing in childlike uncertainty. "I do not see very well," she said.

"You have great insight," he said. "You knew my sense of exile."

"Oh, yes, that," she said. "When you get old, and must lose your hold upon so much, there are new insights. I meant I was not sure that you were you, after all. But I see now that you are. I heard you play in Paris, between the wars. It was my last holiday abroad before I got too old to want to leave Damerosehay. David was with me."

"You cannot recognise me, Lady Eliot," he said. "It is not possible that I can bear the slightest resemblance, now, to the young man I was then. You recollect my name, perhaps. I did not bother to change it because I did not imagine that anyone would remember it."

"I did not remember the name until I saw you," said Lucilla. "You have changed less than you think you have. You know, however altered we may be by age or illness, there always looks out from us, now and again, the young creature we once were and will be again. And then I never remember any other pianist with hands just like yours, nor with that trick of resting them as you do, one within the other with palms upwards. I looked down upon them, I remember. You played the Waldstein. What an evening of delight you gave us! David and I said that we would never forget, and I have not forgotten."

Sebastian smiled. "He has."

"He was very young then. He will remember again. Something will remind him."

"I sincerely hope not," said Sebastian with vigour. "The young man that I was is dead and buried. Don't resuscitate him, Lady Eliot. Let him rot." Then he saw that the harshness of his tone had hurt her, and he made a gesture of apology. "Forgive me. I am afraid that my manners are a thing of the past."

" Then you should play again," said Lucilla severely. " Music recaptures the past."

" That is why I shall never play again," said Sebastian. " Even if my hands were not stiffened, as they are, I should never play again for that reason."

" How very ridiculous of you! " said Lucilla. " Do you imagine that past happiness is lost? You will come round to it again when the circle is complete, and at the end of it all nothing will be eternally lost except evil."

" So they say," remarked Sebastian grimly. " Meanwhile, for most of us at present, it appears to be the good that is eternally lost."

" How can good be lost if it is remembered? " asked Lucilla. " It can be pain to remember, I know, but it is one of those pains that are incumbent on us, and the pain lessens if one does not shrink from the duty."

" How can it be a duty to remember? " asked Sebastian.

" I think it is all part of the purging," said Lucilla. " That hard deliberate remembering of good leaves no room for the remembrance of evil. That way we hasten the time. Don't you sometimes think, Mr. Weber, that one of the dreadful discoveries that we shall make in the life to come will be the extent to which we have put the clock back, and kept humanity upon the rack, by the mere unwilled thinking of idle moments? "

" The mind has pits," murmured Sebastian. " You have to be in a moderate state of normality to control your mind, Lady Eliot. A haunted mind, a sick mind, or even a mind weakened and bewildered by a sick body, hangs always over a pit of darkness."

He was aware of something very odd happening between them. She remained sitting regally upright beside him for a moment, and then she got up, helping herself with her stick. The rose she was wearing fell out of her belt and lay at his feet. " Let it stay there," she said when he bent to pick it up. " It's where I should be. It's where I am. Old age imagines itself wise and experienced. I'm sure I don't know why. One knows no more about how it feels to be wet through if one sits watching the storm from inside a warm room for one hour or one minute."

He picked up the rose, but it was full blown and the petals fell. Holding them in his hand he got up and faced her. "I am glad that the room from which you have watched the storm has been sheltered," he said. "We need warm people; they distil the sun. And even in a warm room there can be pain. And I think old age is wise. Taught by long watching, you feel your way from the lesser pain to the greater, and bear something of that too, and that is sympathy. The actual storm sometimes blinds the eyes, but sympathy can be very clear-sighted."

Absent-mindedly he put the rose-petals in his pocket, and as they crossed the little bridge together he smiled to himself, thinking how ridiculous their conversation would have sounded to an eavesdropper: almost like an interchange of civilities between two grandees of old Castile. Yet for him it had been a refreshment because in this old lady, as in Mrs. Wilkes, he was aware of a well of quiet; this time the quiet not so much of acceptance as of unshakeable faith.

"I envy you your faith," he said to her.

"It is a special gift to age," she told him. "When the symbols grow dim they are replaced by a new sort of certainty of things to come."

She had answered the question he had asked himself, and he dared to probe her further. "The dead return?" he asked her.

"They are where they always were," said Lucilla. "Only you know it."

"I had wondered," he said.

She was glad of his arm going back to the house, and in the hall they both sat down on the settle, slightly breathless.

"I hope you appreciate the numbers of seats in this house and garden," said Lucilla.

"I do," said Sebastian in heartfelt tones.

"They've been accumulating through the years on my account," she said. "As I've got older and older I've kept wanting to sit down in yet another place, and we've put another seat. Now we've got our breath again perhaps we had better join the others. It sounds as though they've gone to the drawing-room."

"I have been excused from this party, Lady Eliot," said Sebastian formally. "I understand it is a family gathering."

"I would like you to come in for a while," said Lucilla. "I want you to meet my grandson Ben."

Like Cordelia's, her voice was always "soft, gentle and low", and it was markedly so when she intended to get her own way. Sebastian was powerless in the grip of her adamant gentleness, and before he knew what had happened found himself sitting by her in the drawing-room.

2

Sally had vacated the big arm-chair tonight, and Lucilla sat there enthroned by the fire, the glow of it rose and gold in the folds of the silk skirt that was spread about her, the lights on the mantelpiece turning her hair to shining silver. Perhaps enthroned was not quite the right word, for in spite of his own recent subservience, Sebastian was aware of abdication. Yet authority that has not been dethroned but willingly set aside retains power, and he was aware of the whole Eliot clan circling about her like planets about the sun. There appeared to be a great many of them, and the room seemed to him so vibrant with alien life that he felt for a moment or two confused and troubled. Then Mouse deposited herself upon his feet, steadying him, and beside him, smoking a pipe, he found an old gentleman with a bulging clerical waistcoat and a bald head who was just as unfortunate to look at as he was himself, and he felt better in consequence. Beyond the old parson an elderly spinster of the rugged gardening variety, of which he believed no country in Europe except England could produce the perfect type, sat knitting a jumper of a blinding shade of violet. Upon the other side of the hearth was another elderly gentleman, smoking a cigar, good-looking in the

English military manner that Sebastian considered a contradiction in terms, with its combination of weary kindliness and clear-cut hard efficiency.

" My eldest son Hilary, who has been Vicar here for thirty years," Lucilla was murmuring. " My daughter Margaret. My second son, General Eliot."

" Typical English August," General Eliot informed them, smiling kindly at Sebastian through a blue haze of smoke. " Chilly once the evenings draw in."

" One's glad of the fire," Hilary told them all, beaming at Sebastian through thick double-lensed glasses.

Margaret's plain face was irradiated with sudden sweetness as she paused in her knitting, smiled at Sebastian and told him that Mouse was on his feet. The art of conversation, Sebastian decided, was, with a few exceptions such as David Eliot, unknown to the English. Making a mighty effort they told you what you knew already and then relapsed into silence, comfortable or uncomfortable, according to temperament. This one was comfortable, and Sebastian felt suddenly at rest in this circle of tired elderly people. The life that had so confused him had withdrawn now to the outer spaces of the large room, young and restless, and here there was a harbour of placidity with the bulk of Hilary Eliot interposed between him and the disturbance of his peace.

And between him and so much that was disturbing, and more than disturbing, between him and spiritual danger, the powers of darkness, the demons and the ghouls. He had been half turned towards Lucilla, but now he turned towards Hilary, a little startled in spite of his peacefulness. His deep experience of evil in the last decade had given him a correspondingly deep awareness of the bulwarks. He now recognised spiritual power when he met it, but he had not expected to find quite this degree of fighting strength in a man who had been for thirty years vicar of an English country village. Power does not develop without challenge. He had himself been challenged; with poor results, he thought. He was aware of no strength in himself. He had never of his own will surrendered to evil, but he had come to find hatred easier than love, and he had for short periods lost his reason. This man, if he had had his experience, would have done neither. Yet how, in this sanctuary of peace, this Fairhaven, had he met his challenge? Hilary's voice broke in upon him.

"My mother had at one time five sons and six grandsons," he said. "And even now, after two wars, she still has two sons and four grandsons. She is therefore as inured to smoke as a pre-war haddock."

"I don't smoke," said Sebastian.

"That's the disadvantage of a faulty ticker," said Hilary in a husky whisper. "May the merciful heavens preserve me from falling ill of any ailment that separates me from my pipe."

His remark was heard only by Sebastian, and meant only for him. Sebastian laughed. It was impossible to look at Hilary's round and cheerful countenance and not laugh, even though at the same time one did reverence to the discernment of his selflessness. Sebastian wondered to what extent the violence of a man's wrestling with self implied a correspondingly violent attack upon him by the forces of evil. If the war was always upon two fronts, his previous questioning was answered. A man like Hilary Eliot would not have to go to a concentration camp to discover the power of hell. Turning to Hilary, he began to talk lightly and naturally on the subject of tobacco, the unaccustomed ease with which the words came from the surface of his mind telling him how deeply stirred were the depths that reached wordlessly after friendship with him.

"Though you need not pity me," he finished. "I was never much of a smoker."

"Not even a pipe?"

"No, not even a pipe."

"Without a pipe, what do you think about?" asked Hilary. "Some man said once that women knit to give themselves something to think about while they talk. It was meant for a backhander, but he doubtless smoked himself for the same reason. We must employ our minds in some way while we throw dust in the other fellow's eyes."

" I like to speculate as to what is behind the dust," said Sebastian.

" I used to," said Hilary, " but I never got it right. So now I just think about my pipe."

Sebastian took that as a reassurance that he was safe from probing. He did not wish to be safe from Hilary's understanding, for he coveted that. Men could understand each other without asking a single question. And Lady Eliot had asked no questions. He glanced at her, and met her smiling eyes. It was almost impossible to realise that the beautiful old lady upon his right was the mother of the comically plain old man upon his left. Yet how alike they were in their power of sympathy, that he had described as the gift of feeling from a lesser pain to a greater and bearing something of that, too. It was because they took a little of the weight that they could establish intimacy so quickly. Even with Meg he had achieved a quick intimacy. These three—the old lady and the old parson and the little girl—must stand very near the frontier of another world so to transcend the body's power to separate. Though even Meg's father, at that first meeting when David had asked no questions . . .

" Ben, come here a minute," said Lucilla. " I want you to meet Mr. Weber. He will like you."

A lanky, dark-haired young man obeyed Lucilla's gesture and pulled a low chair forward between her and Sebastian.

" What Grandmother means, Sir," said Ben, his pale face flushing a little, " is that I shall like you."

" Allow me to mean what I say, dear," said Lucilla tartly. " And put another log on the fire."

Ben reached a long arm towards the log-basket behind her chair, and Sebastian was aware that his sallowness and lankiness, that had seemed to put him with Margaret among the plain Eliots, combined themselves with David's grace of movement. His voice and hands were David's, and so was the slight look of strain on his sensitive gaunt young face. But his deep-set dark eyes were not Eliot eyes. They were not even English eyes. The English, Sebastian thought, seldom combine gentleness with an almost fanatical ardour; the climate is all against it. English enthusiasts, overcoming the somnolence of the weather, generally do so with a certain violence of eccentricity. Yet, whatever the turbulence of Ben's feelings, his manners would never suffer. He was a thoroughbred. And this well-dressed young man, the finished product of a very expensive education, had flushed at their introduction and called him " Sir " with a humility that he found unexplainable. Lucilla was right. He liked Ben.

Yet they found little to say to each other, and only the kindly interpolations of Lucilla upon one side and Hilary upon the other kept their conversation going. With their help Sebastian was able to discover that Ben had finished with Cambridge and had been lucky enough to pass the difficult examination for entry to the Foreign Office. He was thus exempted from military service, but would not start work for another month. Just now he was at a loose end. " Just ' messing about in boats '," he said.

Sebastian knew and finished the quotation. " ' Believe me, my young friend, there is nothing—absolutely nothing— half so much worth doing as simply messing about in boats '." They both laughed : Ben with delighted surprise.

" At one time I travelled a good deal, and I tried to read all the best-loved children's classics in all the countries I visited," explained Sebastian. " I had an idea that if you read the books they write for their children, you will know something about the soul of a people that you could not know otherwise. Folk-music teaches you a great deal, too, and the little pictures a peasant paints on the walls of his house to beautify it are of more value as evidence than the pictures in the art galleries. I wanted, you see, to under- stand the soul of the people to whom I—for whom I worked." Suddenly Sebastian remembered that picture in the hall. " You will know what I mean about the paintings. You paint yourself."

" Not a great deal, now," said Ben, with a sharp hardening of the voice that made Sebastian wince and Mouse
transfer herself from his feet to Ben's. It also most unexpectedly brought the General to his feet.

" You've not met my wife," he said to Sebastian.

Sebastian could see no reason why he should be detached
from the comfortable circle of the elderly and towed out
among the ebullient young to be introduced to the General's
wife; unless of course he provided a way of escape for the
General, who must be Ben's father, for behind the haze of
his cigar-smoke his anxious eyes had never left the boy's
face. Yet Ben had never once looked at his father.

" My wife," said the General, and Sebastian suddenly
liked him immensely for the pride in his voice. " Nadine,
this is Mr. Weber."

She was certainly a beautiful woman, and he paid immediate homage to her beauty, bowing over her hand after
the fashion of his country, a fashion he thought he had forgotten. She could not be entirely English, surely, or he
would not so have saluted her. It was from her that Ben
had inherited his arresting dark eyes.

" Sit down here," she said. " David is playing card-
games with my children, but there are moments of quiet
when Sally and I can hear each other speak."

He sat beside her on a sofa, with Sally next to them on
the window-seat. The General had been absorbed into
the vortex of noise a little farther off, and he looked more
closely at Ben's mother. He guessed her to be past forty,
for her dark hair was streaked with white at the temples and
her fine pale skin was delicately lined about the eyes. The
oval of her face was flawless and she carried her small head
proudly. She had the figure of a slender and elegant boy,
and her plain black dress, as simple and expensive as it well
could be, had been chosen by a woman who knew how to
make her clothes the foil of a beauty that had been to her
all her life her weapon and her wealth. He could feel the
steel in her, and guessed with what skill she had fought for
what she wanted, and how rich had been her giving when

D

she had won her will. She had the classic beauty, and the mastery of it, that can drive men mad, but there was upon it now a sheath of quietness that reminded him comically of Mrs. Wilkes. Like Mrs. Wilkes, she must have learnt acceptance, and how to be content with what she had. She obviously had much, but that did not lessen the respect he felt for her, for she had the true serenity that stems only from self-denial.

He gazed in astonishment at the crew at the card-table. " My children," she had said, but he found it hard to believe her the mother of so much blatant noise. Of the dark-eyed Ben, yes, but not of all those hooligans.

" It is the twins who seem to be five children each," Sally explained.

A moment of quiet cleared his sight. There were actually only two children : a twin of eleven or so, boy and girl. Though they had a delicate beauty, the thought of gangsters rather than sprites or angels presented itself to his mind on this his first introduction to them. They had peculiarly penetrating voices.

" Jerry and José," said their mother. " Avoid them. Caroline has all the virtues. Ben is the eldest. Tommy comes next."

She spoke with a certain detachment, and he guessed her to be not naturally a maternal woman. Yet her voice warmed at the mention of Tommy. Her best-beloved, thought Sebastian, and had a good look at Tommy. " He'll go far," he said aloud.

Not that he liked Tommy. A more magnificent specimen of young manhood he had never seen ; six splendid feet of vigorous bone and brawn, healthy dark good looks, a head with plenty of brains in it, merry eyes, a fine deep voice and a good rollicking laugh. But what an impervious-looking boy ! It was difficult to think of any sort of battering that would hurt enough to awaken the sleeping soul in him. It amazed Sebastian that he should be his mother's favourite ; unless he was the sublimation of herself. She had had to deny herself what she wanted, but Tommy would not.

Caroline at eighteen, sandy-haired, freckled and small, her head bent anxiously over her cards, was, in spite of her mother's careful dressing, not very noticeable until her father came and stood beside her and touched her cheek with his finger. She looked up then and smiled at him, suddenly so vividly alive that she was beautiful. He withdrew his hand at once and moved on round the table, and she looked down again at her cards. They had thought that no one saw them. A father and his young daughter can have great fun, Sebastian knew, in keeping the depth of their love for each other a delicious secret between themselves.

The little dark Zelle was also there, sparkling with vivacity. She sat between Tommy and David, and they were both seeing to it that she enjoyed herself; Tommy with the effortless good nature of all healthy young animals, and David spilling his more mature charm with equal ease. Yet was he? The man was a fine actor, and he looked mortally tired.

The General had made the round of the table, and there was that in his eye that suggested to Sebastian that he would like to finish his cigar sitting on the sofa beside his wife, gloating with her over their offspring in a state of mutual self-congratulation. Only Sebastian doubted if Nadine Eliot was a gloating woman. She was too serenely detached. But her husband would not notice that. Sebastian was sure he had been all his life too competent a soldier to be now a domestically noticing man. But he was a domestically devoted man and he wanted to sit by his wife. With a murmured apology Sebastian got up and sat beside Sally. He had been aware that she had been watching him while he studied Nadine's children.

"There's not much about us all that you don't know now," she said, smiling at him.

"Indeed I know nothing," he said hastily, his quick hands deprecating the nothing that he knew. "How could I know anything in so short a time?"

"It is not a question of time," said Sally, and her smile

seemed to accuse him of a want of truth which he acknowledged with another quick gesture.

"It might," he said, "be a question of shortness of
time."

He had spoken without knowing what he was going to say,
and he wondered if he was right. Old Lady Eliot's time
was short, and she had told him that the nearness of death
had given her a knowledge of the dead that had not been
hers before. Had it, in his case, brought a deeper knowledge of the living? But perhaps she had that, too. Perhaps the one had preceded the other. Certainly he felt
very near to these people, whom he had not even heard of
a short while ago, and oddly at home in their home. And
for all of them except David Eliot he felt genuine liking—
a thing he had never expected to feel again; and for
David Eliot's wife something that was already deeper than
liking.

Was that what it was? Was that what had brought them
so close to each other in the children's garden? It did not
seem within the bounds of possibility that he could be
capable of love again, but if it was so, there would be no
passion in it, and so no harm. He had not thought such a
thing was possible, after the bereavements he had suffered,
and finding as he did such strength in hatred. But he was
glad to discover it might be possible. It showed that he
was not entirely arid; in him, too, there was a hidden
freshness.

He turned to look at her, liking the green silk dress she
wore, with its full long skirt and full sleeves gathered at the
wrists. She wore no jewels, except a big square-cut emerald
above her wedding ring, but he noticed there were little
festive touches about her. She had washed her hair, so
that it made an angelic brightness about her head, and she
wore gold shoes. A lace handkerchief was tucked in her
belt and she had put on her make-up with care. Tired
though she was, she had done her very best to make it
clear that the anniversary of her wedding day was a great
day for her. Her hands were folded upon some treasure

that lay in her lap. Sebastian looked at her as he would have looked at some picture that he wished never to forget, as though memorising every light and shadow, every curve and plane of colour, intently and yet not with hunger, for though he desired to love and remember, he did not want to possess, with pity because he knew on what short tenure she might hold her earthly joy.

Feeling his eyes upon her, she turned towards him, and for a queer long moment of sheer courage they looked at each other. The compassion in his eyes, a light in profound darkness, filled her with foreboding, but she would not drop her eyes. The childlike trust, the vulnerability that he saw in hers equally appalled him, but he would not look away. She had a feeling that she must reach beyond his compassion to his darkness and dispel it. He thought that he must teach her some way of protecting herself. Though she would have courage in the face of calamity, she might be so deeply wounded that her warmth would drain away. To think of this woman without her warmth was as bad as remembering children's faces when the eyes have lost their light. Yet how could he teach her any art of self-protection when he himself, he imagined, had never learnt any except that of indifference and hatred, and the aridity of hatred was in its turn only another form of suffering?

With a friendly little gesture, Sally opened her hands to show him what she held between them, and the moment enabled them both to look away from each other to her treasure. It was a miniature of her children painted on ivory, and framed in gold and pearls so that she could wear it if she chose, a lovely thing that might have been painted by one of the eighteenth-century masters. It lay in a green leather case that was in itself beautiful, and it must have cost a fortune. The familiar rage took hold of Sebastian, so that he could no longer see the delicate smiling painted faces. A small fortune squandered that a rich woman might wear the counterfeit of healthy living children as a gaud upon her breast, while all over the world other children had died of starvation and neglect, and nothing lay on their mothers' breasts but the dust of their graves.

"That is very beautiful," he heard himself say, though he saw nothing now but the dust that came up into his face like smoke from the pit at his feet.

"David gave it to me," said Sally proudly.

Sebastian was not surprised. Eliot's extravagance had always sickened him. He turned his head blindly towards the card-table where he sat, hating him. The warm liking that he had felt for all these prosperous well-fed people abruptly left him. Even Sally at this moment seemed to him just a rather over-blown woman in a most expensive frock. Yet because he was aware that she wished it, he took the miniature into his hands. His sight cleared suddenly and he saw Meg's fresh little face. It was good of Meg. And good, too, of the glowing boy. Meg and Robin would grow old, but freshness and warmth do not change. He returned the miniature to their mother and turned to look at their father, impelled by the fascination of his dislike. He saw only David's empty chair, and it gave him a queer jolt, as though it were the chair in which Banquo's ghost sat at Macbeth's feast. His mind was confused again and he was conscious of the dust and the chasm at his feet. He said good night to Sally and stepped across it. But unknown to himself he left the room gracefully, bowing to Nadine, to Lucilla and the group by the fire, inheritance and training still bone of his bone.

"That chap was somebody once," General Eliot remarked to the room at large.

"Is now," said Hilary. "I have never felt greater strength in a man."

Margaret opened her mouth to say she had thought he seemed such a weak sort of man, in every way, but, not liking to contradict Hilary, said instead that she thought Mr. Weber was very nice.

"If there is one adjective that I dislike more than another it is 'nice'," said Lucilla, and then was sorry she had spoken so sharply. "Dear Margaret," she added gently.

3

Sebastian went slowly and breathlessly up the stairs, following the grey figure that so uncannily preceded him with an equal slowness. Twilight had invaded the old house, and at first he guessed the grey figure to be a hallucination of his own bewildered mind. Banquo's ghost. The ghost of a murdered man. He was always seeing them, for so many murdered men had been his friends. He followed slowly, and saw the ghost cross the landing and go in through the half-open night-nursery door. He was moving so slowly because he was carrying something with great care. Pausing on the landing to get his breath, Sebastian heard the beginning of the murmured conversation within.

" Daddy."

" Meg."

" What have you got? "

" A sort of little icy pudding, all whipped up. I don't know what Mummy calls it."

" Lemon-snow. Anything else? "

" A bit of the cold fowl we had. It was a dowager and wore an ermine cloak."

" White hen. That's not ermine. It's white sauce with bits of chopped mushroom. Anything else? "

" Greedy pig. What more do you want? "

" A peach."

" It's here. And for heaven's sake, Meg, don't be sick afterwards."

" I'm never sick when it's one of our secret feasts. Did you bring a spoon for you as well as me, or shall we take turns? "

" Take turns. I could only find one clean spoon."

Sebastian's breathlessness increased to such an extent that though he wanted to go on to his own room he could not. He had done the same thing so often himself. It is hard on little girls who are not quite old enough to join the fun downstairs, and yet are kept awake by the noise of it. Elsa

had never been sick either. Bad discipline, but fun.
Fathers and daughters have great fun in keeping the depth
of their love for each other hidden. There was silence in
the night nursery except for the clink of a spoon and the
creak of Meg's little bed as David sat upon it. Then there
was a deep sigh of concentrated appreciation and the murmur
began again.

" Was it a nice party? "

" Not so nice as this one."

" You eat the other cherry, Daddy."

" It's a queer thing, but I don't really like cherries."

" Then shall I eat it? "

" Well, it looks sort of lonely where it is, without the
other one."

" It's not lonely now. Daddy? "

" Yes? "

" Tell about when you were a little boy."

" All right. Comfy? "

" Almost nearly. You're a bit bony, but you can't help
it. Tell about the time when you and your daddy played
cricket out in the street at six in the morning with the cat's-
meat man."

Sebastian moved on down the landing and came again to
the quiet of his own room. He sat down in the chair by
the window and told himself that he should not have left
it, for social contacts did him no good. He felt less
wretchedly ill if he lived as much as possible alone. One's
fellow human beings drained one of strength. Yet was
that quite true? They took and they gave. And could
one be alone, in the lonely sense, at Damerosehay? The
place was a well of peace, but peace is not emptiness.
There is life in it, and life is never impersonal. Even now
he was not lonely, because that boy was here again—the
boy who had played cricket in the street at six in the morning and grown up into the man he hated. Yet whom did
he hate? The actor who had given him the relief of catharsis, or the employer who had been so thoughtful for his
comfort? The father telling stories to his little girl, or the

grey ghost going up the stairs? Was it possible that he hated a mere ghost, the ghost who had been sitting in Banquo's chair when he looked across and saw it empty? A dead man, or a man whose eventual death was so certain that he could be already counted as dead. A man who was being done to death in David Eliot by some terrible adversary; terrible and glorious. The glory smote suddenly upon him so that he winced from the light. Then it was dark again and he was cold and shivering.

"And crazy as a coot," he said, and switching on the reading lamp he reached across to the book-case for a book; just any book. He took one out at random and opened it at random. It was the same book that he had had before, and it opened where it had opened before, and he read another poem.

Not, I'll not, carrion comfort, Despair, not feast on thee;
Not untwist—slack they may be—these last strands of man
In me or, most weary, cry " I can no more ". I can;
Can something, hope, wish day come, not choose not to be.
But ah, but O thou terrible, why wouldst thou rude on me
Thy wring-world right foot rock? lay a lionlimb against me? scan
With darksome devouring eyes my bruisèd bones? and fan,
O in turns of tempest, me heaped there; me frantic to avoid thee and
    flee?

Why? That my chaff might fly; my grain lie, sheer and clear.
Nay in all that toil, that coil, since (seems) I kissed the rod,
Hand rather, my heart lo! lapped strength, stole joy, would laugh,
    chéer.
Cheer whom though? the hero whose heaven-handling flung me, fóot
    tród
Me? or me that fought him? O which one? Is it each one?
That night, that year
Of now done darkness I wretch lay wrestling with (my God!) my God.

If that was it, he had not been so coot-like as he thought. Even a confused mind can feel through its delusions to the truth. Not many men are chosen in this life for that appalling struggle. Most of them experience only a shadow-play of what is to come. If David Eliot were one of the chosen, had the poor devil any idea of what was happening to him? And only at the beginning of it yet. Poor devil! Who could help him? Who had passed that way? Not Sebastian himself, so far as he knew. He remembered the old parson with the pipe and the strength in him. Not quite the same, perhaps, because the experience was never the same in different men, but perhaps a darkness as deep in its own way. He felt a great desire to talk to Hilary Eliot again; though what he would say he had no idea.

Lying in bed a little later, the words of an old prayer that he thought he had forgotten came to him.

" Take, O Lord, from our hearts all jealousy, indignation, wrath, and contention, and whatsoever may injure charity and lessen brotherly love. Have mercy, O Lord, have mercy on those that crave Thy mercy; give grace to them that stand in need thereof; and grant that we may be worthy to enjoy Thy grace, and attain to everlasting life. Amen."

He said the prayer several times to himself, as he sometimes said lines of poetry, merely to drug himself with the beauty of words. Then he found he was really meaning what he said, praying as he would have prayed in the days of his childhood, when, as children do, he had held his parents' faith without question. And a moment before he had been thinking of the Adversary with objective faith. It was as though the years of question, the years of stark unbelief, had vanished and he was back again in his childhood. What had happened to him in this place? At what point had his mind admitted again the possibility of faith? He had said to Lady Eliot that he envied her her faith, yet all the time he had talked to her he had shared it. He had shared the faith of Socrates while he watched the swan. " Everlasting life." He had believed in it again as soon as he had come into this house and felt its tough spirit, made by the endurance of those who had lived here. Endurance was never for nothing. Something enduring came out of it, or it was not endurance. If it took you nowhere, then it was just nonsense, and he had clung to it for too long for him to think it that. The life-line to which the wrecked sailor clings in a raging sea is not nonsense, but, for him, the most important fact of existence, and it would not be there at all if it were not held firmly upon some shore that through the blinding spume he cannot see. The problem for him is simply that of holding on.

The wind had risen and was sighing across the marshes. The moon was up, and the window-curtains, blowing in the wind, were white like the sails of a ship. Half asleep now, the imagery of his thoughts changed, and he thought of the old house as a ship burdened with souls, not a wrecked ship but a ship in full sail, lifting and dipping gently over a sea that was quiet now between the storms. And into this ship, this sanctuary for souls, he had come with his hatred. Abruptly he was awake once more, forcing himself to ask again, of whom? and to give a truthful answer. Of a man who possessed all that he had once possessed—fame and the gifts of fame, wife and home and children—and who like himself might one day lose them. Of a man as extravagant, emotional, egocentric and arrogant for all the world to see as he had once been himself, and as deeply sinful in ways known only to himself and to his God, or even only to his God, as he was now. Of himself, in fact. Of that dying self who, in the eyes of the " terrible ", purging the grain, was only the flying chaff.

O God, the idiocy of jealousy, indignation, wrath and contention. Yet it would be hard to stop hating, when hatred had been the source of his strength for so long. It had been like food to him while he clung to his endurance. It had been life. Without hatred he would feel hideously weak. It might take him a long time to learn to let go of hatred, to learn to endure after some different fashion. " Give grace to them that stand in need thereof." What exactly did Christians mean by grace? Hilary Eliot would know. He was half asleep again, dipping over the quiet sea in the quiet ship, with her burden of souls bound for the country of everlasting life.

CHAPTER VII

I

AFTER an early lunch Meg and Robin were getting ready to go and have tea with Jerry and José at The Herb of Grace. Meg, buttoning her new strap shoes, was in two minds about it. She was a little frightened of Jerry and José, who at eleven years old were so very grown up, so polished and slippery. Older than anyone except Aunty Nadine. Much older than Uncle George, Ben or Caroline, or Jill, who used to be their nanny, who were not grown-up at all. Tommy was not grown-up either, but he had the same hard slippery polish as the twins, and Meg found the same difficulty in adhering to him. Meg liked to join on to people; not in the physical sense, because she was not very fond of endearments, but in the sense of not feeling herself a separate and lonely island in the sea, miles away from the person she was with. She liked to feel there was a causeway between herself and other people, so that they could go backwards and forwards to each other. But there was no causeway between herself and Jerry and José, only sea.

On the other hand, going to The Herb of Grace meant being driven there by Mummy or Daddy in the car. She sat beside the one who was driving, and when they were not attending to hens on the road they attended to her, and that was heaven. To-day Daddy was going to drive them over while Mummy stayed at home and knitted clothes for the new baby. She did not knit very well, and Zelle gave little private cries of distress over the way she sewed the seams up, but she liked making them, and so Zelle did not discourage her. She would sit and knit in the wild garden, as she liked to do when Meg and Robin did not want it, and the children who came sometimes to the wild garden would play around her as though she were their mother. But she

would not know they were there. Meg, coming in unexpectedly early once and running to the wild garden, had
found her there with the children around her and had been
most surprised when she had called out, " Meg, come and
sit with me. I'm all alone." Meg had not argued about
it, because she never argued, but she had thought it most
odd that Mummy should not know about the children.
Because Mr. Weber did. With Meg's and Robin's permission he worked in the wild garden quite a lot, and once
when Meg went to fetch him to lunch he had said, " Here
comes another. That makes six." And Meg, looking
round and counting, had seen that it did. Perhaps he
would point them out to Mummy one day. Meg knew
that he went and sat with her sometimes when she was
knitting in the wild garden. It was Meg's belief that he
was joined on rather firmly to Mummy. They seemed to
go backwards and forwards a good deal.

" Now then, Meg, your bonnet," said Zelle. " The sun
is 'ot."

Zelle spoke the most beautiful English—indeed, much
prettier English than the English do, except just for the
dropping of the h's. Neither she nor Mrs. Wilkes seemed to
possess that particular little bellows in the throat which
enabled the wolf in the story to Huff and to Haw and to
blow the House down.

Meg got up from the floor, where she had been sitting to
button her new shoes, and Zelle tied her sun-bonnet under
her chin. It was blue, and so were Meg's new shoes, and
so was the smocking on her crisp white frock. Zelle was
wearing a white frock too, with small red roses on it,
and her lipstick matched the roses. Her eyes were bright
and sparkling and she had washed her curly dark hair
yesterday, so that it was fluffy and soft about her face.
Meg thought that she looked ravishingly beautiful; and
indeed there was about Zelle to-day an atmosphere of
enchantment, as though she were not living in the usual
world, but in some private fairy tale that enclosed her
like a delicate soap-bubble. One saw her through its

rainbow wall, soft and shining and transformed by its magic.

Robin wore diminutive garments of a delicate shade of elfin green, and did not look his best. Sally imagined that green suited him, and he did look well in the brilliant shouting green of grass after rain, but the fragile colour of his present outfit only made his bulging scarlet cheeks and blazing curls and fat legs look more than ever of the earth earthy. He had put on even more weight since Mr. Weber had found Yabbit and mended him and made him as good as new again. And he had had no screaming fits. He was clasping Yabbit to him at this moment, and Meg had her doll Maria Flinders. Mouse, circling round and round on her beam end, was trying to catch a source of irritation situated in the exact centre of her back. If she took it to Mary, the pampered white pekinese at The Herb of Grace, she knew there would be trouble.

David, waiting for them in the car below, expressed impatience on the horn, and Zelle swung her scarlet leather bag with the long strap over her shoulder, hurried them all out of the night nursery and down the stairs. Robin had got a bit quicker on the stairs lately. He still had to lower the right foot first with a mighty thump, but the left foot came to it with more precision than formerly. Mouse, too, was less muddled about her back legs, and fell on her face less often. In fact, they came down in grand style, watched admiringly by Sally, Sebastian and Mrs. Wilkes, who had issued respectively from the drawing-room, the study and the kitchen to see them off.

This seeing the children off was part of the normal routine of Damerosehay. As soon as the familiar thumping was heard on the stairs, everyone dropped what they were doing and ran to the front door. They did the same when the car was heard returning, hooting at two-second intervals, which it always did from the oak-wood onward if the children happened to be aboard. The children were royalty. They could not leave their kingdom nor return to it without the event being marked by demonstrations of loyalty and esteem.

Sebastian had been delighted to conform to established habit in this matter, and followed Sally and Mrs. Wilkes out to the drive to see the start.

" Come too, Weber," said David suddenly, as he lifted Meg and Mouse and Maria Flinders on to the seat beside him.

" Thank you, no," said Sebastian with alarm, thinking of the twins. " I have a great deal of work to do," he added in one of those careful after-thoughts with which the human race justifies its immediate instinctive reaction to danger. " I am making very little headway with those translations. I am afraid I lack application. I am afraid . . ."

But Mrs. Wilkes had fetched his hat from the hall, and her gently propelling hand was beneath his elbow. " What you lack, Sir, is fresh air," she said firmly. " It's a nice drive to The 'Erb of Grace."

" You must see The Herb of Grace," said Sally. " It is beautiful. It is an old Pilgrim Inn, and there is a wood there by the river. David, don't let him miss the wood."

" No," said David.

Robin, clasping Yabbit, was wriggling close to Zelle on the back seat, so that there should be plenty of room for Mr. Weber. He turned his round red face towards Sebastian and smiled. When Robin smiled, his bulging apple-cheeks bulged yet more, so that his eyes were pushed shut by a roll of fat. His mouth, on the other hand, opened wide, and two bottom teeth came prominently yet attractively into view. Meg turned round on the seat beside David and also smiled at Sebastian. Her small pale face was dim to his view within the blue shade of the bonnet, but he knew she was smiling because of the comfortable warmth within him that was always engendered by a smiling Meg. Mouse, standing up beside Meg, rested her nose between her forepaws on the back of the seat and looked at him pleadingly, while her whiskers vibrated in rhythmical sympathy with the swing of an unseen tail. Mrs. Wilkes applied that adroit lift below the elbow which he had already experienced, and he found himself sitting on the back seat with Robin's small fat red hand laid possessively upon his knee. Good-byes were called and the car purred down the drive. Meg and Mouse still had their backs to the view and their chins on the back of the seat so that the light of their eyes might beam upon him, and Zelle was smiling at him shyly over the top of Robin's flaming head. David turned his profile towards him and said gently that Nadine had the twins under control more often than not and that the wood was called Knyghtwood.

As the car passed under the oak-trees Sebastian realised with astonishment that he had added to the pleasure of all five of them by coming with them to a place that meant a great deal to them. Or at least meant a great deal to David and his wife, and so by inheritance, though they might not know it yet, to Meg and Robin. The Herb of Grace. Knyghtwood. The names attracted him. They seemed to promise just such another small country of enchantment as Damerosehay itself, and even David wished to give him the freedom of it. What did these Eliots see in him that they had so quietly let him into the heart of their life? For that, after a bare fortnight at Damerosehay, was where he felt he was. He had ceased to feel an outsider. There were moments when he felt that the two weeks were two years, and others when they might have been two centuries, so vast was the tract of time that seemed to separate him from the darkness of the time before he came. So vast and so peaceful. Even David's profile no longer had power to irritate. Its perfection was not a thing the man could help. It was turned away from him now, but in his mind's eye he still saw it, and with pleasure. It had the precision of a profile incised upon a silver coin, and the same look of lastingness, as though it were symbolic of that something eternal within the perishing man that was struggling for its freedom.

As the car came from under the oak-trees out into the sunshine of Little Village he was wondering about physical beauty. Was there always some particular thing in the

changing, dying human aspect of every man or woman—
a smile, a lift of the head or look in the eyes—that was
symbolic in that way? If so, to those who loved that man
or woman it should be a memory that would outlast death
and lead to recognition in " the world of light ". That was
a descriptive phrase that Lucilla had taught him, and he
liked it. It was the light of the small world of Damerosehay,
he realised suddenly, the sanctuary light, that was the
symbolic element in its multifarious beauty.

As Mrs. Wilkes had said, it was a nice drive to The Herb
of Grace through the narrow lane that threaded the woods
and green fields of the valley, and then widened and lifted
over the high moorland where the wind sang and the tang
of the sea made each breath of it strong in the body, like a
draught of wine. The fading heather was wine-coloured
on the moors, and the children sang when with the lifting
of the hill they felt the wind, but when they dropped down
to the valleys again their voices fell to a soft bee-hum of
gentle talk. Zelle talked, too, in the valleys, telling Sebastian
about the famous places to which they would soon be coming;
the Hard, the ship-building town by the river where the
sailing-ships of England had once been built, and the
Cistercian Abbey beyond whose pilgrims had been housed
at The Herb of Grace.

" And it is still an inn ? " asked Sebastian.

" And a guest-'ouse," said Zelle. " General and Mrs. Eliot
take ver-r-y special guests, but it feels more like just their
'ome. It is lovely. Pr-r-etty, and so quiet."

Sebastian listened with only half an ear, but he liked her
talk, with the dropped h's and rolling r's. He thought he
had never heard a more musical woman's voice. It lacked
the depth and warmth of Sally's, but the words fell like
a chime of bells, and every note was true. Though she was
not pretty, she had great charm, a sparkling vitality and an
airy, sprightly motherliness such as Titania must have
shown when Bottom's great ears lay flapping on her breast.
But it hurt him to see that tautness on her face and the
sadness of her eyes when she was not laughing.

David said little, but attended to his driving, and Sebastian realised that he drove his high-powered car at great speed but with skill and care. When he did speak it was in answer to the soft little flow of song and conversation that came from within the blue bonnet. Always his head was turned very slightly towards Meg, even when his eyes were on the road. There was never a teasing note in his voice when he answered her, only a charming and serious courtesy. Sebastian realised that Meg was not a child to her father. She was Meg, and in so far as his life was not centred upon himself it was centred upon her, who was a part of himself. Sebastian was suddenly alarmed, and could have shouted to the man to disorientate himself before it was too late. " He that parts us shall bring a brand from heaven and fire us hence like foxes." It was already too late. He had not known, when he had heard David as Lear speak those words, why they had moved him so unbearably. He knew now. It had been fire from heaven that had destroyed his own small daughter. The fires of Hamburg. The walls of flame. And afterwards the dust, the smoke and stench. " Let me not be mad, sweet heavens." He saved himself on the brink of the pit. He could occasionally do that now, though the effort to control his thought seemed to wrench his whole being. Yet he could now, sometimes, control it.

" Yes," he said to Zelle as the car slowed to a standstill, " it is a lovely street."

It was the place they called the Hard, and there was only the one street left now of the once-famous little town. White cottages with casement windows and rose-red steep old roofs. A grass-bordered street, and golden-rod growing against the walls. A view of the river at the bottom and the woods beyond. A few boats rocking at anchor and a white gull flying overhead. For a moment the smoke of Hamburg drifted across, but he pushed it away and saw again the blue and green and gold.

" It is a pity the rest was destroyed," he said, forcing the words politely, and found that David, his arm stretched along the back of the seat behind Meg, was looking at him intently and oddly, almost with fear.

"Only by time," he said quickly. "Not by violence. We had better get on, I think. Someone has had the sense to open the gate. That will have been Ben."

2

The gate led into a narrow lane, and a storm-twisted oak-tree grew beside it. It might have been one of the trees from the oak-wood at Damerosehay, and Sebastian knew they had entered the second Eliot kingdom even before the lane itself made it abundantly clear. For the narrow lane, winding downhill between its grassy banks crowned with gorse, gave the same sense of home-coming as the drive at Damerosehay. It led to a home deeply and deservedly loved, and so many hearts had sung with joy all the length of the lane that there seemed almost a singing in the air, an unheard melody woven into the music that was heard; a robin fluting, Meg singing inside her bonnet, the wind in the gorse, and Zelle laughing. Zelle was gloriously happy, Sebastian realised. Each fresh turn and twist of the lane brought her more deeply into her joy.

The final turn brought to Sebastian, too, what was almost a sense of joy. Upon his right was the wood of which Sally had told him, Knyghtwood, thick and deep and many centuries old. He knew these ancient woods, hung with dark curtains of shadow about pools of light, each tree as much its own world of mystery as a star in the sky, each leaf and flower as transient as a flake of fire, and yet seeming as fast held in the mystery as jewels in a king's cloak. He knew the richness of these woods and the breath of them, pungent and warm. He knew the ancient homeliness, and the safety of them. All his life they had brought him ease.

The orchard on the left looked almost as old, and the lichened apple-trees had grown so much according to their own wild will that their condition would have shocked a trained horticulturist. Yet they bore apples—yellow and red and russet—so many of them that though some had fallen, and made pools of colour in the rough grass below the trees, many were still left glowing above in the sunlight.

At the bottom of the lane was a sheet of light that resolved itself into the same sunlight dancing on the river. The lane seemed to run straight into the light and lose itself there, so that its joy was not ended, but transmuted. He thought that this was more of a world of light even than Damerosehay. There the silver sanctuary light was more diffuse. Here it was golden wine brimming a golden cup held out to the parched by the jovial spirit of the place.

" Comfortable-looking, isn't it? " said David, stopping the car at the bottom of the flight of steps that led up to the garden gate upon their left.

The garden was full of autumn flowers, yellow and red and russet like the apples, and beyond their warmth The Herb of Grace was comfortable indeed. Its stout white-washed walls shone almost golden in the sun, and above them the steep uneven roof was tiled with amber-coloured tiles. The walls were buttressed, so that, though it was a two-storeyed house, it seemed to squat down into its garden with a suggestion of immovable strength, facing Knyghtwood across the way on terms of equal age and lastingness. As he got out of the car, Sebastian saw that at the point where the river and the lane met there was a small fan-shaped beach of jewel-like stones. Over the inn door there was a sign-board with blue flowers painted upon it. Then he noticed nothing else because the door opened and, to his surprise and delight, Hilary limped out and came down the flagged path towards them, his pipe in his mouth, leaning on his stick and beaming at them through his thick glasses. Sebastian had not seen him since that night of their first meeting at Damerosehay. He had not realised that he was lame. He walked as though he had an artificial leg. The First World War, thought Sebastian.

" I'm a shock to you all, I'm afraid," said Hilary. " I'm spending the day. I brought Grandmother over."

There was such an outcry of delight from the children

and Mouse, as they hurled themselves out of the car upon
Hilary, and from Zelle, too, as she stepped out lightly with
gay skirts swinging, that David and Sebastian were silent.
Yet they were attentive only to Hilary, the beauty all about
them for the moment non-existent for them. It was only
when he saw the old boy unexpectedly, David thought, that
he realised his own immense reliance on him; unstable as
he knew himself to be, it was as though he felt sudden firm
ground under his feet. Sebastian thought that if the spirit
of this place had ever existed as a man, he had been in
essentials just such another as Hilary Eliot.

A surge of colour and noise came out of the front door,
its spear-point the high shrill voices and blinding scarlet
sun-suits of the twins. Sebastian's head spun until Hilary's
hand gripped his arm above the elbow and he felt himself
being steered away from it.

"Round this corner there is another bit of garden and
a seat in the sun," said Hilary. "I know nothing worse
than the sudden eruption of a large family *en masse*; unless
it happens to be your own, and even then after a certain
age one can prefer it in its component parts. Sit down.
You look better than when I saw you last. I wish you
smoked."

"It is a pleasure to me that *you* do," said Sebastian
courteously. "It seems a part of your—your——" His
hands moved expressively as he sought for the right word.
"How did Mr. Eliot describe this house just now? Comfortable-looking. Your comfortableness."

"I think the word you really want is corpulence," said
Hilary, his eyes twinkling.

"No. Comfortableness," insisted Sebastian. "And in
the strong sense."

"You mean, not just bed-socks?" asked Hilary.

"Certainly not," said Sebastian. "Comfort in the sense
of a house built on rock. Was mine host of this inn at one
time a priest of your quality?"

Hilary looked startled. "In the days when the Abbey
over there beyond the river was a house of the Cistercian

order, and The Herb of Grace a hostelry for its pilgrims, one of the brothers was always guest-master here," he said. "One of them set his mark very firmly on the place. Ben imagines that he has found out a good deal about him, and has even gone so far as to paint an imaginary portrait of the fellow, showing him as very stout. But I should not presume to say that I was at all like him, apart from the corpulency, which you so kindly describe as comfortable. You are a remarkable man. I know who you are, you know. My mother told me. She thought that you would not mind, and I'll not give you away. I wish that I had the artist's awareness. Myself, I know so little."

Hilary's remarks came quietly between puffs at his pipe, and Sebastian minded none of them.

"The artist's awareness of atmosphere and quality, both in people and places, even when, as in my case, it is perhaps a little intensified by the nearness of death, is not knowledge," he said. "Knowledge is something deeper than that. I think that you have it, though you may not know you have. I suspect that you have fought the last deadly battle with self and know what one knows when that is over."

"It never is in this life," said Hilary; but Sebastian noticed that he did not deny that there had been a fight or that it had been deadly. "While evil still attacks, not even a saint can dare to say, ' I've won '."

"Perhaps that is true," said Sebastian. "But he can say, ' By the grace of God I know what I know '."

"Yes, he can say that," said Hilary. "Even a sinner can say that."

"Is it incommunicable?" asked Sebastian.

"Why ask? You know it is," said Hilary. "Yet if I should attempt to put what I think I know into words, and you were to do it, too, I suspect that the formula would be quite different but the incommunicable knowledge much the same."

"I am not where you think I am. I am not where you are," said Sebastian.

Hilary puffed at his pipe, and his eyes twinkled, but for a moment or two he said nothing. Then he said, " The other day we talked about throwing dust in the other fellow's eyes, and most of the time that is what we all do. Shall we do that now, or shall we try to get behind it? "

" For I should think the first time in my life I should like to try to get behind it," said Sebastian. " That, for me, is a *volte-face*, but I know that I have not long to live, and there are things I should like to speak about."

" You look better," repeated Hilary.

" I am. But all the same, one knows."

" Some do," said Hilary. " I hope I do when my time comes. I should dislike taking a header, so to speak, into eternity. I would rather be like Dante's good mariner, who, ' when he draws near to the harbour lets down his sails, and enters it gently with slight headway on; so we ought to let down the sails of our worldly pursuits, and turn to God with all our understanding and heart, so that we may come to that harbour with all composure and with all peace '."

It was easy to see what had brought the quotation to Hilary's mind. From where they sat on their seat in the sun they looked across the flowers in the garden to the broad shining reaches of the tidal river. Quite close to them a boat rocked at anchor with sails down. It had reached a perfect haven.

" One cannot turn to God unless one finds Him," said Sebastian.

" At your worst hour you found something," said Hilary. " You must have found something, or you could not have come through."

" Nothing," said Sebastian. " Except, at brief moments, just a consciousness of world-suffering."

" Held within it. Supported by it and cleansed by it. And yet at the same time you were taking your infinitesimal share in the bearing up and the redemption," said Hilary. He asked no questions, but stated facts.

" I did not analyse it," said Sebastian.

" You do not analyse Christ," said Hilary quietly. " You find Him. Or perhaps it would be truer to say that He finds you; sometimes without your conscious knowledge. For the Christian, searching hour by hour through the days and nights, the months and years, if the time ever comes when he can say, ' By the grace of God I know what I know ', what he experiences can seem more or less like a conscious finding; but for those who have not chosen to search, but whom yet He has chosen to find, when for a brief moment He speaks to them they call Him by another name: ' Christ, or whatever name is given to the secret kingdom of heaven in which we are and have this shadow of life, that shadow of the grave.' I seem full of quotations to-day. The fact is that you other fellows, you poets and musicians, say these things so much better than the rest of us."

" The kingdom of heaven is a queer name to give to the ' huge debt of pain ' that ' mounts over all the earth '," said Sebastian dryly. " I am quoting now, you notice."

" I noticed," said Hilary. " I also noticed that you used the word debt. It is the right word. Pain and death are owed for sin. Christ paid the debt, and He is the debt, for it was His own life that He put down in payment. We offer His pain and death, and our own within His—of no value apart from His—for the redemption of the world. Forgive me for putting extremely badly what you have probably known all your life."

" Heard all my life," corrected Sebastian. " Heard, but not known. You have to relate information to experience before you can be said to know."

" Do you think now that you and I both know the same incommunicable thing? " asked Hilary.

" I think the occasional shaft of light in my darkness may have pierced its way through from your sun," said Sebastian. " I would not say that anything I have known approaches anywhere near what I believe is called the mystical experience; for that, as I understand it, is a direct apprehension of God by the mind, leading to a process of purging through which the loathsome demon of self in a man is done to death. If that had been so I should have recognised your Christ and He would have made something of me by this time."

" No man can form any judgement as to his own state," said Hilary, smiling.

" I still hate," said Sebastian.

" The last of the chaff," said Hilary. " You use strong words about that substratum of our being which is usually referred to with tender consideration as the lower self."

" I have seen it, corrupted by great evil, at close quarters," said Sebastian grimly.

" You saw it in others? " asked Hilary.

" In others," said Sebastian. " But now, God help me, I am beginning to see it in my own hatred."

" If you hated your persecutors, then there was not much to choose between you. If you hate a man more fortunate than yourself, then you deserve your misfortune. Is that how you feel now? " asked Hilary.

" Not quite as far as that yet," said Sebastian, smiling.

" Getting on," murmured Hilary. " The grain lies sheer and clear. And if it is David whom you imagine you hate, I doubt if the contrasts between you are quite so deep as you imagine. Much like yourself. Much the same temperament. Always in trouble of one sort or the other."

Sebastian smiled. " And now, perhaps, in what seems to him the worst yet."

Hilary took his pipe from his mouth and was still and attentive.

" Merely my fancy, perhaps," said Sebastian.

" What made you fancy it? " asked Hilary gently.

" Merely a feeling I had that the man I hated was a dying man," said Sebastian. " Not in the physical sense, you understand. And then I read a poem I found in my room. You may know it, for you spoke of the chaff and the grain. Merely conjecture, as you see."

" You are probably right," said Hilary soberly.

Sebastian fancied that he felt deep hurt in him. " Forgive it that a stranger——" he murmured.

" No, it is not that," said Hilary quickly. " I am glad that your intuition has convicted me of blindness and dullness. Very good for me. I am troubled because I happen to be fairly comfortable myself at present, and I'll feel the worst sort of hypocrite if I try to tell him about the right and wrong way to endure. That had better be your job."

" Impossible to my ignorance," said Sebastian, smiling. " For myself, I have merely endured because there was nothing else to do."

" That is what he did before," said Hilary. " And broke."

" Had he a bad war? " asked Sebastian.

" A great deal better than most," said Hilary. " But the bombing of other men's homes and children was not the best war service for a man of his type."

Sebastian felt a little dizzy. Hamburg and the walls of flame. Hatred of David and a surge of sympathy for him, deeper than anything he had felt yet, had hold of him together.

" Thought about it too much," said Hilary.

" Yes," said Sebastian. " We do, men of our type. We think about the harm we do until we become monsters in our own eyes. That is good, you'll say; but we think about the monster until he has us circling about him as though he were some hideous little heathen god. If it stops there it can become almost a form of devil-worship, and it is not worship the devil in us needs. But I am wandering from the subject of endurance."

" Not at all," said Hilary. " The right kind of self-knowledge calls for a good deal."

" In your war, the first, how did you endure? " asked Sebastian.

" My war was nothing," said Hilary hastily, " nothing at all compared with yours, or even David's. Yet I had a way, then, that helped with other things later. For there is always the Thing, you know, the hidden Thing, some fear or pain or shame, temptation or bit of self-knowledge that you can never explain to another. . . . And even in those

very few healthy insensitives who do not seem to suffer,
a love of something—of their work, perhaps—that they
would not want to talk about and could not if they would.
For it is the essence of it that it is, humanly speaking, a
lonely thing. . . . Returning to the sensitives, if you just
endure it simply because you must, like a boil on the neck,
or fret yourself to pieces trying to get rid of it, or cadge
sympathy for it, then it can break you.   But if you accept
it as a secret burden borne secretly for the love of Christ, it
can become your hidden treasure.   For it is your point of
contact with Him, your point of contact with that fountain
of refreshment down at the roots of things.   ' Oh Lord,
thou fountain of living waters.'   That fountain of life is
what Christians mean by grace.   That is all.   Nothing
new, for it brings us back to where we were before.   In
those deep green pastures where cool waters are there is no
separation.   Our point of contact with the suffering Christ
is our point of contact with every other suffering man and
woman, and is the source of our life."

" You could put it another way," said Sebastian.   " We
are all the branches of the vine, and the wine runs red for
the cleansing of the world."

" The symbols are endless," agreed Hilary.   " Too many,
perhaps.   They complicate the simplicity of that one act of
secret acceptance and dedication."

They were silent, and then Hilary said, " We have talked
too much of the demon in men.   There is the child, too.
It is an antidote against hatred to think of the child.   The
mask that a man shows to the world hides a frightened child,
and the child hides the demon.   But it is the child who
wins.   The mask drops at death, and the demon is finally
destroyed either in this life or another, but the eternal child
in us lives on."

" Invariably? " asked Sebastian grimly.

" You are right.   I am speaking too confidently," said
Hilary slowly.   " I believe it to be a matter for our
choice."

" The demon might live on and the child die? "

The bright landscape seemed a little shadowed to them both, and Hilary did not answer for a moment.

"That is why the child is afraid," he said at last. "While the outcome is still in question the child is always afraid. I believe that that appalling possibility is the source of all fear."

"All frightened children need the comforting of love," said Sebastian. "To deny it to them is the worst of sins. I see that now."

3

From where they sat they could see Knyghtwood upon the other side of the lane. A flight of steps led up to a green gate that opened into the wood. As they sat in silence, with no more to say for the moment and yet unwilling to break the intimacy that had come between them, they saw a tall young man in grey flannels and a girl in a gay frock with roses on it come up the steps, lift the latch of the gate and go together into the wood. They followed a path through the trees, walking slowly, yet with a buoyancy that seemed almost to diminish the bright sparkle of the sun on the water and the shimmer of the leaves in the wind. The girl's light feet were almost dancing, but the man held her where he wanted her with his hand within her arm. Yet the grace of his movement, too, was almost that of a dancer. She swayed away from him for a moment, seeing a flower she wanted, but with one quick pirouette she had picked it and swung back to him again, and this time his arm was lightly about her shoulders. They moved a little deeper into the green and gold of the wood and looked like the wraiths of lovers in a forgotten story; they drifted farther and were gone. The two who watched, the old man with his bald head and his paunch and the middle-aged man with his bony parched grey face, could not take their eyes from the spot in the wood where they had vanished. Their stiff limbs weighed heavily upon them and the blood seemed sluggish in their veins. They felt a little cold,

though the sun was so hot. They might have stayed there
until they became fossilised had Sebastian not forced himself
to say something.

" It had an almost incredible delicacy," he said gently.

" As though it had never happened before," said Hilary
with gloom.

" For them it has not," said Sebastian. " For them it is
the unbelievable miracle."

" It will need more than a miracle to bring his mother
round," growled Hilary with increasing gloom.

" She is hard to please, this Nadine ? " asked Sebastian.

" She asks conformity of her children," said Hilary.
" Though a less conforming woman than Nadine in her
youth we've never had in the family. George does not
demand it quite so inexorably, though he himself did con-
sistently conform, good fellow that he is.   Tommy conforms,
but not Ben. The eldest seldom does, it seems to me. I
take it they are not so strong physically, these first-born,
and there is a waywardness in them. You agree ? "

" I agree," said Sebastian. " But waywardness in a boy
can become genius in a man. Only the flowering is slow,
and parents are not naturally patient."

" No ? " asked Hilary, surprised.

" The sands run out so fast," explained Sebastian. " They
are afraid they may die before the children have reached a
place of safety."

" A place of safety ? " asked Hilary, incredulous. " Is
there such a thing in this world ? "

" Parents always believe," said Sebastian, " that for their
children, just theirs only, the Almighty will bestir Himself in
a particular way. Their children being, you understand,
quite exceptional."

His voice had a rasping dryness. He has had children
and lost them, thought Hilary. He would have changed
the subject, but Sebastian seemed to want to go on with it.

" Parents think conformity is safer for the children,"
he said. " They do not always realise that genius, suppressed and denied, can twist the whole nature."

Hilary saw now why Sebastian had wanted to pursue the subject of the children. " You might explain that to my sister-in-law," he said dryly.

" I should not presume to encroach upon your office," said Sebastian, smiling.

" If you think that the priest in an English family is by way of being that family's father confessor and adviser, you've got it wrong," said Hilary. " In France, possibly, in England, no. None of my family ever pay the slightest attention to a word I say. Nor do my parishioners either, for that matter. I don't blame them. Though I happen to be the eldest of my family, I'm the exception that proves the rule, for genius missed me over altogether, and one is powerless without a spark of the stuff."

He spoke with humorous resignation, and Sebastian, still smiling, knew he believed what he said. They never know, he thought—they never know what they are and what they do, and that is of the essence of them.

" What you call a genius can make a noise with his fiddle or his powers of oratory," he said, " but it's not the sound that is powerful, but the silence in it. The silent word can be spoken in men's souls just as well, or better, in ways that are silent."

He was not surprised to find that Hilary had remained impervious to his suggestion. He merely looked puzzled, and then indicated with his pipe-stem a second party going towards the wood. A sophisticated white pekinese bustled importantly before the twins in their scarlet sun-suits, both of them gloriously gay and so noisily informative that what they were saying was lost in the row they made saying it. Tommy, whistling piercingly, followed after with Robin bouncing on his back and Meg holding timidly to the forefinger of his right hand. Mouse followed in the rear, looking very miserable.

" Getting the kids out of Mother's way," shouted Tommy good-humouredly to the two poor old blokes in the sunny garden. " Zelle should do it, but she's vanished. Get along, kids. Put a sock in it, Jerry."

" I will say for my nephew Tommy," said Hilary approv-
ingly, " that he loves his mother.   To the extent, mark you,
that at the age of twenty-one he will spend a summer afternoon amusing four little children in a wood just to give her
an hour of rest.   Though he likes children.   He takes a
good deal of care to keep the fact hidden, but I've noticed it,
and upon that and his love of life and work I build my
hopes for the eventual salvation of the soul to which he will
never pay the slightest attention."

But Sebastian was not interested in Tommy's soul.   " Meg
is not happy," he said sharply.

" No more she is," said Hilary, adjusting his glasses.
" Nor Mouse.   Tommy!   Stop!   Mr. Weber has not seen
the wood.   Send Meg back as escort."

" O.K.," shouted Tommy.   " Get along, Meg."

Meg let go of his finger very politely, being careful he
should not see how glad she was to do so, and gave him a
shy sweet smile from inside her bonnet.   He meant to be very
kind to her, she knew, and so did Jerry and José, but she
just did not feel comfortable with them, and there it was.
With Maria Flinders in her arms, and Mouse at her heels,
she climbed the steps into the garden and ran along the
flagged paths between the clumps of michaelmas daisies
and golden rod, and the lavender and rosemary bushes,
until she came to the two elderly gentlemen on the garden
seat.   Beaming at them, she scrambled up and sat herself
down between them with a deep sigh of relief.

" What can she see in us? " wondered Hilary over the
top of Meg's bonnet.   " You would expect her to prefer
Tommy."

" Females of this age have very little eye for personal
beauty," said Sebastian.

" So it seems," said Hilary.   " Mouse, too.   She's on my
feet.   Am I worried about anything? "

" You must have many worries," said Sebastian gently.
" What is the phrase?   The cure of souls."

" I wouldn't lay it down," said Hilary hastily.   " A
parson's job is so profoundly satisfying because it is just

that. We handle eternal stuff, and are the only men who do not lose our jobs at death." He paused. " Except, of course, musicians like yourself. Now, I had not thought of that. A priest at the altar or a great pianist at his piano, both of them lifted up above the people, giving souls to heaven and heaven to souls. Should you say that is why Meg likes us? "

" Daddy," said Meg in a small sad voice.

Another couple were going together to the wood, and they, too, walked with the grace of dancers, well matched in beauty. They were deep in talk, the man's hand in the woman's arm, and Sebastian felt hatred surge up in him again. But nothing to do with himself this time. For Meg's sake. For Sally's sake. What was Nadine to David, that he should take her into the wood where he had once walked with Sally? And who was Nadine, that she this afternoon should be preferred to Meg, to Meg's hurt? He looked across at Hilary and saw that he, too, was watching the tall graceful figures, but placidly, with a merely reminiscent eye. He heard a step behind him and saw the General strolling towards them and he, too, was watching his wife, and in his eye there was not even reminiscence, merely a proprietorship that dismissed David as a mere appendage to a beauty that was all his own. It had passed, Sebastian realised, and Hilary had known, but not Nadine's husband. It had been, but they had denied themselves so completely that now they could go together into the wood. He felt respect for them both, for it must have gone deep; never had he seen a man and woman who walking together with that dancer's grace looked so perfectly the complement each of the other. The green shade of the strange wood took them and they vanished. It was certainly a wood for lovers. No matter how many couples it absorbed they would feel themselves alone in it. He looked down and saw Meg's hand lying on his knee.

" Shall we go into the wood, Meg? " he asked.

" Yes," said Meg, levering herself forward on the seat. She smiled sweetly at him when he had assisted her to reach the ground, and took his hand. She would have preferred to go into the wood with Daddy, but, since she couldn't, she would like next best to show Mr. Weber where the stream was.

"Where is Zelle? Where is Jill?" asked the General, a worried host. "Why must our young be inflicted on Mr. Weber? Or, for that matter, the wood either?"

"All visitors to The Herb of Grace visit the wood," said Hilary firmly. "And I fancy he will experience the one with greater delight in the company of the other. Is that right, Weber?"

"Quite right," said Sebastian, and bowing to the courtesy in George and the discernment in Hilary, he followed the path into the wood with Meg and Mouse and Maria Flinders.

CHAPTER VIII

IN the beautiful kitchen–living-room of The Herb of Grace, Caroline and Jill were getting tea ready while Lucilla sat by the wood fire and alternately watched them and slept a little. The guests who were staying at the inn had taken tea on the river, and Jill's Aunty Rose, who was cook at The Herb of Grace, was out for her half-day, so it was for the family only.

"Though that is enough, in all conscience," said Jill, counting cups. "Thirteen." She paused in consternation. "Thirteen! There now, how unfortunate! That means I'll have to have tea with the rest of you, when I wanted to do my ironing. If I don't, one of you will die before the year is out. There now!"

"It is all right, Jill," said Lucilla soothingly. "Mr. Weber is here. That makes fourteen."

"Daddy says," chimed in Caroline, "that there is nothing in these old superstitions."

"Isn't there, then?" said Jill darkly. "And I don't feel happy even with fourteen, for the Reverend might be sent for to a sick bed."

"Nonsense, Jill," said Caroline strong-mindedly.

"I sympathise with you, Jill," said Lucilla. "Count in Mary and Mouse. Put bowls for them, Caroline."

Laughing, Caroline took from the china cupboard a pink bowl inscribed "Mary" and a green one bearing the legend "Drink, Puppy, Drink", and put them beside the beautiful pale yellow Worcester cups and saucers. "Now everything's all right. Grandmother, I like it when it's just us— you and me and Jill. Everyone else is in the wood."

"The General and the Reverend are in the garden," said Jill, cutting bread-and-butter with the precision of a reaper cutting corn. She had been cutting bread-and-butter for children on and off for twenty years, and had evolved a technique all her own. Lucilla loved to watch her, though the rhythm combined with the warmth of the fire made her sleepy. Jill held the loaf against the bib of her white apron and cut towards it. The process looked most dangerous, but the knife never slipped. It swung out and back with perfect timing, and the slices of bread-and-butter fell to the plates on the table below in a constant even flow, thick for the children to the left, thin for the grown-ups to the right. She counted in a soft sing-song as she cut, to the accompaniment of the ticking of the grandfather clock. Two each for the grown-ups, four each for the children. If they wanted more they couldn't have it, for the fat ration wouldn't stand it. Bread-and-jam for them after that. Jill still counted Ben and Tommy amongst the children, and would do when they were old and bald-headed, for she had been their nurse. " Forty-one, forty-two," she counted. " That's the lot. Her Ladyship is asleep again. Come along, Caroline; time those biscuits of yours came out of the oven."

Caroline was looking out of the window that faced on the garden. Her father and her uncle were sitting together on a seat in the sun. George's hat was tipped over his eyes, and Hilary's mouth was slightly ajar.

" They're asleep, too," laughed Caroline. " The moment they sit down together they fall asleep. You'd think they'd have something to say to each other, wouldn't you? "

" Not two brothers to each other at their time of life," said Jill. " What should they say? "

Now she came to think of it, Caroline didn't know. Being so old, they probably couldn't think of anything to say to each other that they hadn't said before. Yet they were happy together. One could see that by the way they were not minding if one of them woke up first and saw what the other looked like.

" They might as well not be there," she said, turning her back on them and sitting down on the window-seat. " And we are alone together in The Herb of Grace."

Jill smiled at her as she went into the inner kitchen,

where the oven was, and rescued the biscuits. No use expecting any work from Caroline just for the moment, if she had been taken with one of her dreaming fits. She'd come to later and get on with it, for she was naturally domesticated and a good worker. Why the three of them alone in the house gave such pleasure to Caroline, Jill didn't know and didn't enquire. Girls had odd fancies when they were growing up, and it was best to take no notice.

Caroline folded her hands in her lap and was deeply happy. All was so well with her young and healthy body that she was not aware of it. Looking down for a moment, she was conscious only of the wide-spreading rose-pink skirts of a girl who had always lived and worked in this house, and loved it, and always would so live and work and love. And beyond the girl was an older woman in a white apron, and she, too, had always been here, loving the work that she did. And by the fire was the very old woman who did not work any more, but sat with her eyes shut and slept and prayed, but without whose past work and present prayer the other two would have been no good at all. The three of them, who were perhaps not three women at all but one woman getting older, were an inseparable part of The Herb of Grace, and stood there behind the hospitable spirit of the house whose arms spread wide in welcome.

For what is the welcome of the host if behind it there is not the labour of the women? Through the years the three women had lit the fires and spread the sheets, scrubbed the floors and washed the dishes, polished the furniture and baked the bread, tended the children and nursed the sick, comforted the sorrowful and prayed for them. Caroline could never understand how women could dislike looking after a house, especially an old house like this one. Did they never pause sometimes and sit quietly as she was sitting now, and remember the other women and feel their present toil a part of that past toil? A sort of freshness came when one did that, as though the work were a clean wind or a running river that lived for ever to cleanse impurities away. For herself she asked nothing better in life than to stand always behind the master of the house and make it possible for him to welcome all who came.

The master of the house now was Daddy. Perhaps she would not have felt quite the same if he had not been Daddy, for Caroline loved her father deeply. Her whole life at present circled about him. It was because this house was his that she loved and served it with such devotion. She had decided that she would never leave it until the hero of her other day-dream, the magnificent young man who would one day love her to distraction, came to fetch her away to a house even lovelier than The Herb of Grace, where she would be what her mother was here, an adored wife and mother and a hostess of renown, and also what her mother was not, an incomparable housewife.

Though Caroline found it difficult to imagine a lovelier house than this one, or any room that she would love better than this kitchen–living-room. It was the private property of the family, and the guests seldom came to it. There were two kitchens at The Herb of Grace, the inner one where they cooked and washed up, and this one where they lived and ate. It was a beautiful room, stone-floored with white-washed walls. Besides the south window looking across the garden to the river, there was another looking on the stable yard, set open above the pots of geraniums on the sill, and through it came the cooing of doves. Oak beams crossed the ceiling, darkened by age to the same rich colour as the big oak table and the dresser with its willow-patterned china. There were bright rugs on the floor and gay chintz curtains at the windows. Nearly all the year round there was a log fire burning on the wide hearth, with the settle set at right angles to it. Beside the hearth the bread-oven was set in the thickness of the wall, and the spit for roasting the meat was still there, and the hook for the kettle.

Jill had filled the kettle and was hanging it on its hook to boil as Caroline came back from her dream. The fire-light lit up her pale plain face and her usually lustreless tow-coloured hair. Jill at thirty-three was skinnier than ever, and had no beauty to commend her except her clear green eyes and the tender mouth above the strong chin. But her neatness and freshness gave her a sort of beauty. There was never a hair out of place on her small well-shaped head, and her flowered cotton dress and white apron always looked as though they had just come from the wash-tub and the iron; as indeed they generally had, for Jill adored washing and ironing, and was at it for Nadine, Caroline, the twins and herself every spare minute that she had. Caroline never thought of beauty in connection with Jill; she was just Jill, who had been nurse to them all and was now their mainspring at The Herb of Grace. It was difficult to imagine the house without Jill; indeed, it had never occurred to Caroline to try, for apart from the two day-dreams of the three women and the adoring husband, she was not imaginative. She loved beauty and she was creative, but her creativeness found its joy in the shaping of everyday life to a form of comeliness, so that it became not just something that one put up with, but something that was enjoyable and lovely in itself.

Caroline could never understand Ben's impatience with everyday life, as though it were no more than a jumping off place for something else. It was the something else that roused Caroline's impatience because Ben could not seem to find it. He fell between two stools, and she thought he was the most tiresome and discontented young man she had ever come across. Just at present she liked Tommy better, for there was never anything vague about Tommy. He went bald-headed for what he wanted, and always had the sense to want what he could get. And the stuff of everyday life meant a good deal to him. He would have roared with derisive laughter if she had told him that making beds and baking cakes were activities that had for her beautiful shapes like flowers, but he snored in a well-made bed and devoured a well-made cake with equal pleasure and en-thusiasm, while Ben had no idea what he was eating and slept just as badly between smooth linen sheets as he would have done on a mattress on the floor.

To Caroline at present Tommy was certainly the more

satisfactory of the two, though she confessed to herself with shame that she did not much care for either of them, nor for the beautiful gay and blatant twins, though they, too, did great justice to her cooking. She stood a little by herself in the middle of the family, looking neither to right nor left, but directly to her father at the centre. Of her mother, with her cool clear beauty and her cool clear brain, she was a little afraid, though she admired her intensely and hungered for her love. If Nadine was disappointed in her eldest daughter she never showed it, but her gentle kisses and amused tenderness seemed to Caroline to come to her from some way off; while her father had only to touch her cheek with his hand to make her pulses leap as though his life as well as her own was flowing through her body. She felt very near to Grandmother, too, who with Jill and Aunt Margaret had loved her so much when she had been little and lived at Damerosehay, and she was very fond of Uncle Hilary and Sally. Meg and Robin she adored, as she adored all children.

Of David, in spite of the hero-worship she felt for him, she was frankly terrified, as though in some way that she could not understand he constituted a threat to her happiness. Lucilla, seeing her admiration and her fear, could see that subconsciously she knew already that the vital spark that attracts men to women was not in her; she was not likely to marry and have the children she longed for. David just now was a symbol of the magnificent male who would never open the door of her woman's paradise to her anywhere but in her dreams. Lucilla, awake now, but not opening her eyes, and deeply aware of Caroline and all her thoughts, thanked heaven that the child and her father were so infatuated with each other, for at least Caroline would have that much of a man's love in her life. They had a fellow feeling, no doubt, for George had never had the vital spark either. He had married a beautiful wife, but until the last few years had never won from her more than affection and her wifely duty. Lucilla could only hope that Caroline was as slow in the uptake as dear old George, who had never even guessed the identity of the man who had set Nadine on fire as he had never been able to do. It was always better for the frustrated to be slow in the uptake, Lucilla thought. A certain amount of stupidity was nicely insulating.

Her heart ached over Caroline, who at eighteen had not yet discovered how many gaps there were in the personality that had been given her. She still walked in a dream world that endowed her with all the gifts and graces, and had never had a good look at herself, and found, to her misery and shame, that the attributes she most admired were the very ones that were missing. When that happened she would need to have someone there to tell her that it was not only what she had that was important to her, but what was missing; what she did about the gaps would play the larger part in the making or breaking of her soul. Lucilla was sure that there would be someone, for it was her belief that for the children of many prayers—and all her grandchildren were that—the vital moments are always taken care of.

"We don't know what they are, of course," she said, opening her eyes.

"Yes, Milady?" inquired Jill with loving but anxious concern, for really her ladyship did come out with such odd remarks at times that one feared her great age might be telling at last upon the clearness of her mind.

"The moments in life that matter most to us," said Lucilla. "We think something very important—like getting jilted, for instance—and perhaps some little thing that we hardly notice, such as reading a particular paragraph in a book at a particular moment, or something someone says to us, matters much more."

"Grandmother, how could anything matter more than getting jilted?" demanded Caroline. "Except, of course, getting married."

"Getting married can be important," agreed Lucilla. "But not getting married can be just as important, and very often a great deal pleasanter."

"Didn't you like being married, Grandmother?" asked Caroline.

"Not much," confessed Lucilla with perfect truth. Then she smiled at her incredulous, almost outraged granddaughter. "But I like having grandchildren, darling. I have liked being a grandmother better than I have liked anything in my life."

"Then that's important," persisted Caroline.

"No, darling, I don't know that it is," said Lucilla. "I remember I had an idea one day. I was sitting on the beach when I had it. Of course I can't be certain, but I rather think it may have been more important to me than my grandchildren, dearly though I love them."

"What was the idea, Milady?" asked Jill politely.

"Just at the moment I can't recall it," said Lucilla, and went to sleep again.

Jill and Caroline looked at each other.

"We have to remember," said Jill gently, "that her ladyship is now ninety-one."

"She looks lovely asleep, doesn't she?" said Caroline, and they both regarded Lucilla with loving pride.

"Pretty as a picture," agreed Jill. "She's a wonder, that's what she is."

CHAPTER IX

I

"WHAT one dreads with the children," said David, wrinkling his forehead, "is that at the most vital moments one will fail them."

"Probably," said Nadine serenely. "Really, David, the older you get the worse you worry."

"Don't you?" asked David.

"Very little," said Nadine.

"Not even about the children?" he asked.

"A little, of course—one must if one is a mother—but not more than I can help," she said, eyeing his furrowed countenance. "I trust in Providence and cherish what remains of my looks. So should you, David. They matter in your profession. Have you ever considered your looks in connection with the children's school bills?"

"I can always play Caliban," said David bitterly. "I should play him well, too. I'd make a good Iago, a fine Shylock and a superb Angelo. I could play the whole bunch of the monsters and rather enjoy it. A nice change. Men have little pity for whited sepulchres, and quite rightly, but they do not always realise how bitter whitewash tastes in the mouth. Yes, I'd like to play Angelo."

Nadine gave no sign of the slight dizziness that she felt. Angelo? She strolled on serenely, and wondered if she would be able to tackle this. How odd it was, she thought, that David, whom she had once loved with such passion that she would have consigned George and the children to the bottom of the sea if only she could have married him, had now become to her no more than the eldest and the best-loved of those children. Was that true? Yes, it was, for she loved him even more than her beloved Tommy. Nadine in her late middle age was assiduously cultivating truth as well as serenity, even when it shamed her. Yes,

it was true. And the words "no more than" were true
in that context, too, for she was not naturally a maternal
woman. When what she had of a maternal instinct was
strongly called out it was seldom by her own children,
whom she had borne to a man whom at the time of their
birth she had not loved. She had never felt so motherly
even towards Tommy as she had felt towards Annie-Laurie,
the girl who had once lived at The Herb of Grace for a
short while and had had great need of her, and as she now
felt towards David.

How odd it was! she thought. When she had finally
denied her selfish passion for him, setting him free to marry
Sally, she had adopted the ruse of motherliness. She had
made him feel himself relegated to the status of the twins in
her love, and his hurt pride had done the rest. And yet
now the ruse had become truth. That, she remembered,
had always been Lucilla's way. One worked from the outside in. One compelled feeling by action, slowly and laboriously by one act of self-denial after another, instead of allowing feeling to control action. Lucilla had done that, but
she had never expected that she would do it, too. Yet she
had. She felt a deep thankfulness, here in the depths of the
wood where she had once died a sort of death, and received
her soul made new like the soul of a child. And now her
love was made new. She could walk with David in this
wood made for lovers, of all sorts and kinds, and love him
as the dearest of her children, and receive back from him
again, even if he didn't know it, the love of a son.

She looked at him strolling beside her, wretched and
self-engrossed, and in spite of her concern for him she
smiled. No, he didn't know it, for he thought of her very
little these days. But he told her things. He thought of
Lucilla and Sally with a constant watchful tenderness, and
spared them all that he could, but he did not spare her.
Self-centred children never spare their mothers. For he
was a self-centred child. Loving him as she did, she yet
owned to herself that it was generally upon women that
these self-engrossed men unloaded their troubles, for men

are not particularly interested in each other's woes. She did not believe that David had ever made any close friendships with men. It was a pity.

" Do you like Sebastian Weber? " she asked suddenly.

"What's he got to do with Angelo? " asked David. " What irrelevant minds women have! "

She laughed. " No, not really. It's just that a woman cannot explain to a man the process by which her mind has passed from one point to another. It's all much too complicated. David, let's sit down a moment. It is so lovely here."

They had reached the oak-tree that for her was the heart of the wood, her special place where once she had picked the leaves of the herb of grace, and she sat down at its foot. She was playing for time. She had once helped Annie-Laurie here in the wood, but David was another proposition altogether. Angelo? Now, was he who she thought he was? She wished she knew her Shakespeare better. One was always paid out for intellectual laziness.

" David, you are not looking at this wood," she said. " The queer thing about you so-called artistic people is that you are supposed to be so sensitive to beauty, and yet when it is stuck down right under your noses you never seem to notice it."

David laughed and sat down. He realised now that he had always been more absorbed in himself than anything else. He supposed everybody always was, the saints excepted. That was probably the essential difference between a saint and a sinner. As a sinner he was an extreme case, he thought. Yet there had been a time when the momentary switching of attention from himself to an external loveliness had not been much more difficult than the pulling back of curtains in a dark room. The curtains stuck sometimes, but one could do it with a little effort. But now he lived so deeply sunk within himself that it was like living in a pit, and there were no windows, and no light except that one beam that showed him what he was; and that did not come from any beauty of the external

world, but from some terrible beauty that was as yet to
him unknown and nameless. But one must crawl out of
the pit sometimes, even though it meant leaving the light
within, because the reflected light of the external world, as
well, made its rightful claims upon one. But it was the
beam within that was so unspeakably precious, even though
without it the wretchedness of self-loathing would have been
a thing unknown. He had not realised how precious it
was until this moment, and he was intensely grateful for
the knowledge. It made his darkness not only bearable
but almost welcome. Who had told him? Was it Nadine?
In sheer gratitude he set himself to come to Knyghtwood,
where she sat waiting for him.

The hot sun beat through the leaves over their heads and
was warm on his closed eyelids, and under his hand one of
the exposed roots of the old oak was rough and warm and
hard. He moved his hand, and between the roots of the
tree there were dead leaves and acorns, warm and dry.
Behind his back the trunk of the tree had a tough strength,
and the earth beneath him seemed to hold his tired body in
a hard warm hand of everlastingness that was almost vibrant
with power. In the darkness, the silence, the feel of things
was immensely reassuring. The silence was vast, yet just
as he began to fear its vastness it began to fill with small
sounds: the cry of a bird, the scurry of some small beast in
the undergrowth, the rustle of leaves and wings, the gentle
regular breathing of the woman beside him. The little
sounds mounted until the silence was no more than the gold
of the cup that held the wine, and the wine brimmed over,
and the world was so loud with song that he opened his
eyes. But when he looked, the music ebbed away again
and it was colour and light that filled the cup.

The broken blue of the sky, seen between leaves, is something so near that hands held up could receive it like drifting
petals. It even seems to have a scent, fresh beyond that of
any earthly flower. Against it the leaves burn with the
changing colours of the seasons, and the colour of each is its
own gift that can never be repeated. The boles of the

trees are muted, but they have their colour, too, withdrawn a little into the strength of the wood but ready to flash out when the beams of the sun strike through and touch them. When the light pierces and splinters through the leaves, the colours of the mosses and lichens are the loveliest upon earth, and the flash of a jay's wing or a robin's breast can dazzle the eyes. And then, when the eyes close against too much glory, the music of the wood mounts again and is older than time, and sinks, and there is no sound but the cooing of a dove. And then there is a cloud over the sun, and the eyes open to a deep green shade full of coolness and peace.

> " When will you ever, Peace, wild wooddove, shy wings shut,
> Your round me roaming end, and under be my boughs?
> When, when, Peace, will you, Peace? "

For men, not yet, for " Patience plumes to Peace there-after ". Yet in the woods there is a foretaste of it.

Nadine was wearing a green dress, and the pattern of the leaves lay upon it, and upon her hands lying in her lap. Her hands were white and thin, and the blue veins on the wrists showed more than they used to do. David had not noticed before what she was wearing, or how her hands had aged since he had last looked at them with attention. Looking at her hands he could visualise the wings of white in her hair and the lines about her eyes. The woman he had once loved so ardently was growing old, and so was he. Yet they still loved each other in some serene and peaceful fashion that was at home in this deep green shade.

" What were you trying to tell me just then? " he asked her.

" I don't think I said anything," said Nadine.

" You don't need to put it into words in a place like this," he said.

" Then why ask? " she murmured sleepily.

" Just to get it verified," he said.

" I was thinking," she said slowly, " of the Damascus Road. That sounds odd, I know, for a woman who mostly thinks of hats, but one can't live at The Herb of Grace, with the story of Saint Eustace painted on the chapel walls, and

not think of conversion occasionally. So often it seems to
follow a bad break, and then the light pierces. Have you
ever thought about what St. Paul saw when he was blind?
Darkness, of course, but a gleam of the light he had seen
still there showing him its awfulness. Perhaps he was even
sorry when he was dragged out of the darkness back to the
light of the outer world again because he had to leave that
other light. Whatever would Grandmother say if she could
hear me talking like this? It's not my style at all."

" I asked for the verification," said David. " Thank you.
It's unfair, isn't it, that the sinful heathen sometimes have
these visitations vouchsafed to them when the devout have
to go without? "

" If there's been a bad break there's been a bad shock,"
said Nadine. " One thinks, I was so sure of my own
decency, yet I could do this thing. I thought myself so
safely grounded in fidelity, or whatever the particular
virtue may be upon which one prides oneself, that no
temptation could shake me, yet I went down like a rootless
tree. The shock shatters one's self-complacency, and that,
I suppose, gives the light its chance."

" And yet, you know, I was not actually unfaithful," said
David.

" Then why all this talk of Angelo? " asked Nadine.

" Well, nor was he, as it turned out," said David. " But
the credit was another man's, not his. Damned hypocrite!
So am I. Think of it, Nadine. After having loved you,
after five years of happy married life with a trustful child
like Sally, it was only an accident that saved me from what
might have ended in a really bad mess. You didn't know
I was quite such a cad as that? "

She turned her head to say that given the circumstances,
separated from his wife, over-worked and emotionally over-
strained, a man whom women fell for quite mercilessly, a
passing love affair was hardly a matter for such great blame,
but decided suddenly not to insult him with the suggestion.
Even to console him she would not relegate him to the company of those who take their own failings lightly, or argue

that sin which is halted before it becomes disaster is not sin.
Instead she asked, " What sort of accident? "

" A chance meeting with Sebastian Weber," said David.
" It was the contrasts." And then, before he could explain
what he meant, shame and confusion fell upon him. " Good
heavens! Nadine, I must be crackers to talk to you like this.
You of all people."

She laughed. " Why me of all people? I suppose you
think that because half a lifetime ago you fell in love with
me I'll be insulted because you have lately fallen for another
woman? What a dear jackass you are! Sit back. Relax.
He is a disturbing man, that Sebastian Weber. I felt the
contrasts, too. Several of them. One seems to fall into the
pits between them, and it is most uncomfortable, but very
good for one. Look, there's a kingfisher! "

David leaned back against the trunk of the tree, and the
sudden miraculous shaft of blue pierced him.

" There was one the day I met Sally here," he said.
" One of our great days."

" Whatever you do, don't tell her," said Nadine. " You'd
feel much more comfortable, but it would be extremely
selfish. Let her keep her trust in you. You know now
what a cad you are. (Your word, not mine.) Keep the
knowledge as a private hair-shirt."

She was devoured with curiosity to know more about
the woman. Was she tall and dark and soignée? Young
and lovely as she had been once? Or gold and chestnut
like Sally? Or was the creature blonde and blue-eyed, for
a change? That would be a thorough change. French?
American? But the subject was closed now. She would
be devoured with curiosity for the rest of her life, but she'd
never know. It was amazing that he had told her as much.
And amazing that she had spoken as she did, for she was
really not in the least interested in St. Paul. It was this
wood. It always did odd things to one. Gently she began
to talk again about the children.

" We'll fail them at times, of course," she said. " Parents
always do. But when one is really—how shall I put it?—

dedicated to the children, really loving them to the best of one's ability, as you love Meg and Robin, I think the vital moments are taken care of. Not that we know what they are. They come so quietly, and we don't take care of them ourselves, except in holding to that first dedication. How can we when we don't recognise them?"

2

The sun had come out again and she relaxed in its warmth and shut her eyes. David remembered how quiet had been that moment when he had turned in through the doorway that led to Sebastian's room, instead of going on up the street and round the corner to Anne's flat. He had stopped and pulled out his wallet to see if he had that letter he wanted to show her. It was there, and on the back of it he had scribbled the address of the man Hamilton had asked him to take on as his secretary. It was this street, and this house by which he was standing now. He looked up and saw a dim light in a window far above him. Though the traffic roared by he did not hear it. The restless city night was for a moment or two quiet about him, as though it held its breath and looked up as he did at the dimly lighted window. He looked at his watch, and found it was still early. Anne would scarcely have had time to get back from her party. It would not take him five minutes to go up and see that fellow Weber and get the thing settled and off his mind. He met someone who directed him, and when he had gone up several flights of stairs he found Weber's name on the door. He knocked and went in.

He had never felt so near to anyone as he did for a shocked moment or two to the man who welcomed him. Not to Grandmother, to Nadine when he had first loved her, to Sally his wife or Meg. Not even to Anne, whom he had met on the liner coming out, and later loved in that mad and evil fashion that annihilates the past and the future, in the destructive and not the creative sense, and makes only the beloved seem real in a world of wraiths. But this man seemed even more real. He seemed the self upon whom he had lately had no grip, benighted as he had been in a fog of weariness and unreality, feverish with the strain of his love and his genius. He had not been a man at all just lately, only a cracking scorched sort of skin through which the two passions poured their power. But this was his lost self. This was a man. Himself.

They sat down and began to talk, and the feverish fire, the unreality and illusion seemed to drain out of David, and cold and certain knowledge took their place. This man was a great man; not himself, but himself as he might have been. The self that he had thought he was, and upon whom he thought he had lost his grip, did not exist at all; or existed only in an immeasurably distant future, personified for him by the man sitting at the table. The man he actually was he did not as yet know, though he knew with sickening fear that he was going to know him. He knew only this about David Eliot: that he was the husband of Sally and the father of Meg and had not kept faith with either. The eyes of the man talking to him were strangely lightless in his parched face, yet that added to David's consciousness of another pair of eyes looking through them that saw what he was. Sebastian Weber's conscious mind would perhaps not know what he had seen, but presently he would instinctively hate the man whom at the moment he liked extremely.

For they were getting on very well, talking as easily as if they had known each other for a long time, completely in accord in this moment of quietness that seemed to lift them not only above the city's roar but also above all confusion of place and time. The slow cold shame did not affect the working of David's conscious mind, which was clear and steady now as it had not been for many weeks, but the contrasts were shocking. Between this man here that he was and that man there that he might have been. Between the life of comparative ease that lay behind him and the bitter experience that lay behind Sebastian. Between all that he possessed and Sebastian's present dereliction. And he was condemning himself and Sebastian to live with these contrasts for an indefinite future. They would possibly shock Sebastian into deeper dislike, but what did that matter if he himself was shocked into some sort of sanity and knowledge of himself?

He said good-bye quietly and went away and walked straight back to his hotel. He did not see Anne again, but left her to her unhappiness. For unfortunately she had loved him deeply, as women always did if he gave them half a chance. His knowledge of her unhappiness increased his own wretchedness in the weeks that followed. And richly he deserved it, he told himself. If he was ever tempted to think that love welcomed and enjoyed outside marriage is not infidelity if it stops short of the act, he had only to think of Anne's unhappiness to have that argument refuted. The innocent always suffer for the guilty. For if it had been she who started their flirtation it had been he who had submitted to her will and let it develop into passion.

Looking back, he saw now that that moment of quiet in the street had been a moment that had been taken care of; perhaps for Meg's sake, for he did not deserve that it should have been for his own. Perhaps, too, in some way that he did not understand, for Sebastian's sake also. As Nadine had said, one did not know.

3

He fell suddenly and exhaustedly asleep in the sun, but Nadine, once she knew that her example of relaxation had been followed, was wide-eyed and alert again. She slept well at night these days, and did not need these cat-naps in the sun to keep her going. Not that she would have allowed herself to indulge in them even if she had needed them, for she allowed no one to look at her in unguarded moments; not even, if she could help it, George, though, as he insisted on their still sharing the same room, that was not always easy. But, then, George, dear old thing, was such a creature of habit that, having once believed her beautiful, nothing that could happen to her looks would be likely to alter his belief. Nor his love. Her old George was now sixty-two and had never, since the day he married her, looked at another woman with any emotion stronger than a tepid mental acknowledgement of the creature's existence. How unhappy they had been once! And now how happy!

Yes, she was a happy woman. With a shock she realised that until now she had not acknowledged that to herself. Under this very tree, some years ago, she had died a sort of death and been born again. She had let her passion for David fall into dust with the failing breath and dedicated herself to love life as it was held within the walls of her home. " The lover of life sees the flame in our dust and a gift in our breath." But she had not seen it. It had pleased her to walk through her days for a long time with a serene melancholy, wearing her martyr's crown of lilies and roses with an exquisite sad grace that suited her dark pale beauty to perfection, or she would not have worn it so. It had in truth been a martyr's crown for a little while, for it had been a real death that she had died, but she had admired herself for her self-denial, and had not removed the crown when it had become entirely outmoded.

" And I have always prided myself upon my hats," she said to herself. " Dear heaven, I am a foolish woman. I acknowledge it and that hat is in the river. But a happy fool! Most happy. Dear old George. If I had married David I would have had five years of heaven and then he would have fallen in love with another woman. And I'd have known it. He may pull wool over Sally's eyes, but he wouldn't have pulled it over mine. I would have ferreted out the whole thing, and what a row we would have had! I believe I'd have hated him for it. And now I don't hate him. I love him, with all his failings, just as I love Ben and Tommy. Though *they* will never be so unutterably silly. George has brought them up too well. They'll treat their wives as dear old George has treated me."

She did not look at David. Though she had made all possible excuses for him, she found that she was shocked at what he had told her. In another man she would have thought nothing of it, but she had always loved the integrity and austerity which she thought she had seen in him. Had she only imagined them? Was David really just the same as all the rest of the men whom he and she had known in the careless days before the war? She forced herself to turn and look at him. Yes, it was an austere face, clear-cut, a little hard, and deeply worn. Even in sleep, when youth so often reasserts itself, he looked older than he was. And yet, as lives went these days, his had been easier than many. What exactly was this fiery thing called genius? Was it something from beyond this life that could scarcely be held by human personality as it existed in the world? If so, the genius, be he artist or mystic, was vulnerable to the attacks of evil as other men are not, for he was strained and exhausted as other men are not. He would fail in ways unlike himself when, if the fire of genius had not been poured into him, he would have stood firm. But " he is a chosen vessel unto me ". Fire annealed as well as cracked. If the personality did not break in pieces altogether it might finally become something rather glorious. But what a process the annealing must be! She thanked heaven she was an entirely ordinary woman married to an entirely ordinary man, and that her dear old George.

" David, wake up," she said gently. " It's nearly tea-time and I'm the hostess."

He woke up, blinking and stupefied at first, then instantly alert. " You go back," he said. " I'm going a little farther."

She nodded, and he strode off through the trees, and she quickly lost sight of him. They all had their special places in Knyghtwood. David's, she knew, was where he had once met Sally. She did not know where it was, or what he and Sally had said to each other there, but she guessed he was going there now. That was all right, then. " If thou hast broken a vow, tie a knot on it to make it hold together again." He'd keep tryst with Sally there and tie a fresh knot on his marriage vow. " It is spiritual thrift, and no

misbecoming baseness, to piece and join thy neglected
promises with fresh ones. So shall thy vow in effect be not
broken when new mended." Hilary had quoted that from
Thomas Fuller in a sermon lately. Hilary in his old age
was getting rather irritatingly full of quotations from queer
old writers one had never heard of, yet they came in handy
sometimes, for there was no doubt about it that the longer
ago people lived the better sense they seemed to talk.

Like Knyghtwood itself, with its old secrets that it guarded
so carefully until the right moment came and then yielded
with so rich a grace. How she had disliked the country,
and above all this wood, when she had first come to live
here, and now how she loved the country quiet and the
wisdom of the wood! She strolled slowly home, loving the
feel of the floor of the wood beneath the thin soles of her
shoes: moss here, a few crackly twigs now, the akermast,
crunchy and delightful, then, best of all, the trodden bare
earth. Walking slowly and lightly, one's feet caressed the
solid hard ground where all delights are rooted. The trees
seemed strolling by her, rather than she by the trees, and
she greeted politely those whom she knew. For so many
years they had been walking around in this wood, talking
to so many, yet each spring they renewed themselves again
for fresh meetings and greetings. Although she loved
winter in the wood, with the bone-beauty of the bare
branches against the sky and the delicate dove's-breast
colour of the twigs, yet already she was looking forward to
next spring, when the scent of hidden violets would blow
through the aisles of the wood and there would be primroses
growing beside the path and anemones under the thorns.
And the ringing of bird-song and the dapple of sun through
new leaves would make one forget all sorrow and dismay.

She came to the gate of the wood and stood looking across
at her home, strongly built and stoutly rooted in its old
garden that glowed under the hot sun with all the fiery
colours that in winter glowed indoors, on the wide hearths
and on the candle-brackets round the hall. And at George
asleep with his hat over his nose and Hilary asleep with his

hands folded over his stomach, neither of them looking their best but both a picture of placidity, and happy now in this quiet pause that old age sometimes gives men and women between the stresses and conflicts of their working days and the fear and the weariness of their dying and their death. Men had a right to such a pause, she thought, and the harder their sufferings through life the deeper their right, so that they could get their breath to face their end. For always, she supposed, even for the greatest and the best, there must be some terror in death, either at the time of it or in a secret anticipation of it that could be shared with no one else. "Death is a fearful thing." One of the sinners in "Measure for Measure" had said that, not Angelo but the other one, the one she had always sympathised with because he did not want " To be imprisoned in the viewless winds. And blown with restless violence round about the pendent world."

She had her own secret dread of death, born of her own innate frivolity, a dread of finding that when her beauty, her love of pleasure, her gifts of vitality and charm, all fell away from her at last, that it would appear that it had been only for those she had been in life so deeply loved, and that there was nothing else there, nothing at all; not even the child that in her moments of faith she believed God would take in His arms at death to nurse into new life. Nothing at all. Not even the weakest wraith of a child. Of her, nothing left but a handful of dust. It was the sort of fear that one could not speak of to anyone, and it was only very occasionally that it came upon her, as now, in the midst of present joy. She thought abruptly of Sebastian Weber. He looked a dying man. Did he ever feel afraid of death? But perhaps those who had suffered as he had, passed beyond such fears. Perhaps they were the prerogative of the comfortable and the happy, just crumples in the rose-leaves. The fortunate always felt their crumples very acutely, like the Princess and the pea. And a good thing, too, thought Nadine. It gave them some minute share in the pain of the unfortunate.

As she walked across the lane and up the steps to the garden, George woke up. He always did when she came towards him, though her step was so light, as though sleep were a waste of time if she were there. He restored his hat to its proper position and smiled at her, and her fear vanished. In a marriage such as theirs had become these last years there was a tie deeper than the physical one, deeper than that of the shared children, of habit or even affection, a tie most mysterious and unexplainable. She thought suddenly, and for the first time, that it was stronger than death. Each had come to share, now, the something in both of them that would live beyond death, and if in her there was scarcely anything, that which was in him would, wherever he was, in this world or the other, lend strength to her trembling dust at the hour of her death.

Hilary slept on. No woman's step had ever troubled his dreams in the slightest degree.

CHAPTER X

I

TOMMY, whistling cheerfully, Robin bouncing on his back, had come far through the wood, past Brockis Island and the stream in the clearing and farther on still, following the twins and Mary. He walked fast, but the twins, flashes of scarlet among the trees, ran faster, and Mary rolled faster still. She had put on weight with increasing years and was now somewhat spherical in shape, so that when she ran it was like a large white puff-ball rolling over and over. The twins' bare legs and backs and arms had been tanned by the sun to the colour of brown boiled eggs. They were tall and slender, and running now through dappled shade and now through pools of sun, they had today an astonishing unearthly beauty that Tommy could not define. It was not a fairy beauty, for there was nothing diaphanous about it. Tommy had no fears that the twins would vanish into thin air; indeed, the scarlet of their sun-suits seemed almost to shout down the glow of the summer woods. Not heavenly—good Lord, no! thought Tommy, remembering the noisiness of the twins and the devilment of their general behaviour at times. Pagan? Yes, that was the word he wanted. Crowns of poppies and leopard skins and that sort of thing. He could picture them scampering on the outskirts of some bacchanalian feast, painted on a Greek vase, perhaps. How did it go? "What pipes and timbrels? What wild ecstasy?" There was a wild ecstasy in the way they ran in the woods. They liked it here. Jolly little beggars! They were growing like Mother, which was why he liked them and bothered with them.

And yet you wouldn't call Mother's beauty pagan. He couldn't picture Mother in a leopard skin. But he could see her in the sort of austere draperies those old Greeks

153

wore. Classic, that was the word for Mother. He could picture her now, moving on ahead in the wood with that wonderful grace that he adored in her, the thin draperies clinging to her long limbs so that one could see the lines of them through the gauze. She had a wonderful line from the hip-bone to the knee. Her femur was unusually long. Jerry's was, too. And how those kids' muscles did ripple under the skin! Gosh! he was getting quite poetical. Most unsuitable in a surgeon. Poetry and surgery didn't go together at all. It was the wood. Though he was never so barmy about it as the others were, it always affected him oddly, all the same. He always thought of Mother here. He did not suppose he would ever be able to fall in love, because he would never meet a girl who would hold a candle to Mother. But he'd marry, all the same. He'd pick her with an eye for child-bearing, healthy and good-tempered with good wide hips. Pretty and a good cook, too, because though brilliant surgeons had little time to spend at home, they did occasionally have a meal there; and a decorative hostess was necessary to a man who wanted fame. Which he did want. And he'd have it, too. There was nothing to stop him. He'd got the brains and he'd got the guts, and the health and strength. He'd got what it takes, too. And there wasn't a nerve in his body. None of this highly-strung business for him, like those poor fools Ben and David. He was tough, like Robin. He bounced the baby on his back, and a thrill of delight went through him at the feel of the warm compact little body between his shoulders. Funny how the kid adored him. He believed that Robin would go to Land's End and home again on his back and never even whimper or ask to be put down. Stout fellow. He whistled a stave of " Robin Adair ", and Robin chuckled like the last of the bath-water gurgling out of the bath. Tommy had taught him how, and he did not chuckle that way for anyone else.

" Hi, you kids! " yelled Tommy, but the twins and Mary took no notice, and ran on down the narrow path that led into the deepest and most secret part of the wood. It led to the Buckpen, where the old ruined Chapel was, and where Mine Host of The Herb of Grace had once tended the sick animals, and it was their special place.   Tommy let them go, merely shouting after them that if they made him late for tea he'd wallop Jerry's backside good and hard. They vouchsafed no answer, and he stood between the two giant beeches, that leaned together to form an archway over the entrance to the path, and watched them.   The two scarlet figures gleamed brightly against the darkness of the great holly-trees, that grew in the deep and secret part of the wood, and then they were gone.   The white ball that was Mary shone out for a moment, and then that, too, had vanished.

Funny, he thought, how all the family except himself and Father and Caroline had a bit of the wood that was their special place.   Mother had the oak-tree, Ben Brockis Island, the twins the Buckpen and David the place where the stream was.   Crackers, they were.   Even Mother. Good thing for the family that he and Father and Caroline had more sense.   They gave a little ballast to the general Eliot sloppiness.   Perfectly barmy to go sloppy about a wood.   Now that he was here he'd just take the kid down to the place where the golden willows grew.   He liked that place.

He left the path and strode away to the left, where the great oaks and beeches grew so close together that even on a day of summer sunshine there was shadow and mystery, and a breath of pungent coolness from the wet mosses and multi-coloured lichens that patched the bared roots of the trees. This bit of the wood was so old that it felt almost primeval. The trees were so tall that the sighing of them was lifted to an immeasurable height above one's head, and down here at their roots one might have been at the bottom of the green gloom of the sea.

He swung Robin off his back and took him in his arms, ostensibly to keep the briars from scratching his legs, but really because he thought the kid might be a bit scared by the shadows and the silence.   Robin's red curls tickled his

his chin, and his heart knocked hard against the cage of his ribs because of the feel of the little boy's warm body held there. Who was to know? No one, Tommy thanked his stars. A strong man must keep his weakness hidden, and he'd take jolly good care that no one ever knew about this queer passion that he had for small kids. There was no danger, for he was always very offhand with them in public. Perhaps that was why he repelled Meg. He was sorry that Meg did not like him. She was the only kid he knew who didn't. But, she wasn't like a kid. She'd been born a woman, and though women admired his good looks they didn't like his toughness and the way he didn't care a damn about them.

Except Mother. But, then, she was his mother. She'd made his body, with its strength and beauty, out of her own strength and beauty, and for that he worshipped her. "With my body I thee worship." A man said that to his mate, but a son could just as well say it to his mother, who had given him the glory of physical life. Why had people always got to be going on about the soul? Personally he didn't care a damn about the soul. He didn't know if he had one or if he hadn't, and he didn't care. He'd no wish to go drifting around after death with no body, just dressed up in a lot of gas. It was the body that mattered, this splendid bit of form and substance with its symmetry, its intricate mechanism, its beauty, its tough strength. Odd that he should want to be a surgeon and carve it up. But it was not the fact of the carving in itself that appealed to him, it was the caring for the body, the mending of it, the cutting away of detestable evil growths that dared sap its strength and hinder its efficiency. And then surgery made such demands upon one's own body, upon the perfect co-ordination of eye and hand and brain, upon concentration, strength, the control of nerves and muscle. In surgery the body was an instrument in full power and full play, used for the restoration of other instruments to their birthright of enjoyment of this glorious world.

Like a child coming from the primeval darkness of the

womb out to the light of day, he had come through the darkness of the trees to the brightness of the river's brink, where the willows grew. The sun was brilliant on the water and the willows were wands of gold and orange, growing in a semicircle about a little beach of smooth silvery pebbles. The shallow water lapped in here like a faery ocean on a faery shore. Not that the word "faery" would ever occur to Tommy; he just thought this was a good safe place for the kid to paddle, and sitting down on the flat boulder that had been so conveniently placed here at some time by some obliging prehistoric monster, he peeled off Robin's entire outfit, vest and all. Sally and Zelle would have had fits, had they seen, for both disapproved of the entire immersion in cold river-water of the very young, but luckily they had no idea of what Tommy did with Robin when he had him to himself.

"Get 'em tough early," said Tommy to himself, pulling off his own shoes and rolling up his trousers. "Come on, youngster." With Robin in his arms he waded out until he was knee-deep in the sparkling water, and then with his hands beneath the little boy's armpits lowered him down into it up to the neck.

Robin squealed in delight. If anyone else had done the things with him that Tommy did he would have been terrified, but he was never afraid with Tommy. For Tommy's hands gave him the same feeling of complete security as did his father's arms. The same sort of feeling, but not the same sort of security. In David's arms he was in the fortress that is at the beginning and the end, with danger a thing unknown or else finished with for ever, but Tommy's hard hands were a strength that held him in the danger and would not let him go. At this moment he was right up to the neck in the danger, and there was no firm ground under his feet, but the grip of Tommy's hands was like iron, and he gloried in it. Either way, in the fortress or in the hard hands, there was no danger of falling into the black pit, and his squeals turned to shouts of triumph.

" That'll do, youngster," said Tommy, and carried him back to the boulder and dried off his top half with his pocket handkerchief. " Now you paddle while I go to sleep."

This was a figure of speech, for Tommy never went to sleep in the day. But he liked sitting on the flat boulder in the sun, with Robin splashing in the shallows, and remembering the day when he had first found this place and taken a fancy to it. He'd had an odd experience here, one of the queerest things that had ever happened to him; in fact, now he came to think about it, the only queer thing; for queer things did not happen as a general rule to those like himself whose common sense, and mental and physical health, kept them well above the mire of nonsense that engulfed such poor fools as David and Ben.

Searching back to the beginning of things in remote childhood—a soppy sort of thing to do, which he did nowhere else but here—he remembered how as a very small boy he had wanted to be a policeman because he had liked taking the numbers of cars. Numbers had fascinated him, and they still did. They were so definite. Number seven was number seven, the number of perfection, people said, and nothing on earth that anyone did or said could make it number six. But later in his boyhood a visit to a Gilbert and Sullivan opera had informed him that a policeman's life is not a happy one, and meditating on the number of hours put in by members of the Force conducting old ladies across busy streets and picking up drunks, he had been inclined to agree, and had transferred his passionate interest from the collecting of the numbers of cars to the cars themselves.

And then he had discovered the wonder and glory of machinery. If a number is definite, how much more definite is a machine. A number in the abstract is merely an idea; it cannot be grasped, smelt, heard, or set in motion by yourself, like a motor-bike. Oh, ye gods, the joy of Boanerges, his first motor-bike! Oh, the bliss of knowing that if you did this, that or the other, a particular movement, noise or stink would be the result! And no uncertainty about the noise and the stink. *That* noise and no other. *That* stink and no other. And the joy of taking the thing to pieces, of having it disintegrated and at your mercy, and then by the power of your own knowledge and skill putting it together again, giving it life, so to speak, bestowing upon it once more the ability to make the noise and stink that so delighted you. To give life to a machine. To give life. He believed it was the idea of life that had switched him over from wanting to be a motor mechanic to wanting to be a surgeon. For though you might talk about restoring life to a disintegrated motor-bike, you didn't really do it. Stink and noise are not life. It was dead stuff that you handled. But when a surgeon handled a human body the tissues were living, the flesh was warm, the blood spurted hot and red. Life was there—life the eternal, fascinating, baulking mystery. For Tommy, rationalist though he was, was honest with himself. There *was* a mystery. He might in his boyhood have dismissed number seven—the number of perfection—as merely an idea, but the idea had nevertheless haunted him. Perfection. An idea, but yet real. Life. An idea, and yet real. The perfection of life. The phrase embodied precision, strength, warmth, movement—all that he most worshipped. And eternity.

It had been here, sitting on this flat stone, with the golden willows behind him and the sun sparkling on the river, that he had first worshipped eternity.

2

He'd been out on Boanerges and got himself mixed up in an accident. Nothing to do with him. He just came to a cross-roads and found two cars had had a collision. The police were there, and an ambulance, so he was not really needed, but all the same he stopped and did what he could to help. Two people had been killed, one of them a little boy of about four or five. Even then, though he had not

been more than sixteen at the time, he'd loved children.
He helped the driver of the ambulance to lift the dead child
on to the stretcher. It was the first time he had seen death,
and he drove home in a mad rage. He didn't go in to
lunch. He just flung Boanerges into the garage and tramped
off into Knyghtwood. He did not see the wood or know
where he was going. He did not see anything but the scarlet
fire of his rage. That kid not to grow up. Jolly little kid
he'd been, with red curly hair. That kid not to grow up
and have a motor-bike and play rugger, and stand knee-
deep to watch the waves come in. That kid not to know,
as the glorious years came toppling one upon another, the
leaping of fire in one's blood and the strength of one's body
when one rode it like a horse over the hills, and the rain
beat in one's face, and the sun and the wind. That kid to
be defrauded of it all, just be dust in the earth, with the life
drained away. It was damnable! How could one live
in a world where kids got killed like that? Where some
damn fool, who'd been too lazy to get his brakes attended
to, could crush a perfect little body to pulp, under the
summer sun, with the bees humming in the heather and
everything happy and nice one minute and utterly damnable
the next? A world like that did not make sense. Nothing
made sense. Nothing at all.

He was sitting on the flat stone among the golden willows,
and he had no idea how he had got there. He remembered
that the wood had been dark and cool as he came among
the dense old trees and that the coolness had somehow eased
his hot hurt fury. Yet he supposed that he had subconsciously swung away from the deep places of the wood,
for he never liked darkness, and always made instinctively
for the open places and warmth and light. It was light
enough here. The sun was dazzling on the water and the
willows were rods of light. His body soaked up the warmth
and his rage quieted as the strength of the sun took hold of
him. Literally took hold. He could have sworn that
warm hands held him. It was the queerest feeling. Yet
they could not be the hands of the sun, because they held

the sun, too. And the butterfly that had perched on his foot. And each minute creeping thing down there in the grass. Hands of such power that they held the whole universe, of such delicacy that the butterfly was not crushed by their hold. And what they held lived, and what they laid down was no more held in life. Yet it did not matter, because there was no diminution of life. There was not less of life because a sparrow or child fell to the ground. Loss of life was something that could not happen, because life was something entirely whole. Nothing could be taken from it or added to it. It was eternal perfection to be worshipped and adored for as long as one retained consciousness of its beat and glow in one's body. While the hands held him he vowed he would enjoy that beat and glow to the utmost, and cherish the bodies of others, so that they could enjoy it, too; especially the bodies of the children that were so lightly held, so easily laid down.

It did not occur to Tommy that day, or any day, to notice his own concern and wonder where it came from. He did not give to it the name of love, or wonder if his own warm anguish of pity was a faint echo of some tremendous compassion identifiable with the life that held the universe in being, and of which the symbol of the hands had been given to him because it was with his own hands that he would serve his fellow men, and through them his God. He did not think of God at all, but only of life, and though he would always now recognise life as being transcendent as well as immanent, it was in its immanence that he chose to worship it. The artist's gift of wonder had not been vouchsafed to Tommy. As a general rule he wondered about nothing. Only, when he came to this particular place, he would wonder at the way in which his childhood's love of numbers had led him to his manhood's love of life. And in this place he would remember the hands that had held him as men remember their first love, and know they will remember when they have forgotten everything else. For with Tommy, though he did not know it, the

F

experience had been a falling in love. The love of a woman, if it ever came, would in comparison be as the light and warmth of a candle to the light and warmth of the sun.

3

He got up and stretched himself, for time was getting on, and the kids must be carted back to tea. But he was reluctant to leave this place that he liked. To sit here and remember that day, even though he sat broiling in the sun, refreshed him as though he had drunk at a spring of cold water. He felt that way sometimes when he was doing his work and remembering, as he often did, old Æsculapius and surgeons and physicians down the ages who had handed on their wisdom one to the other for the renewing of life in the bodies of men. He grinned, thinking what a study Aunt Margaret's face would be if he were to tell her that dissecting a corpse or watching someone have their insides cut out refreshed him. Only he would not tell her, fun though it would be, because his love of his work was something that he did not seem able to talk about. And to say that he liked work better than anything else would sound quite crackers. Yet it was true. In spite of this place, and Mother and Robin, it was a bit boring being at home, and he was always panting to get back to work. " Like as the hart desireth the waterbrooks." That was a line of some soppy poem. No, it wasn't, it was a psalm, and Uncle Hilary would have a fit if he heard him quoting it in this connection. Good Lord! how crazy one's thoughts were, tumbling out of one's mind like sausages out of a machine. He grabbed Robin and began to dress him, and the little boy was happy in his hands, and did not mind leaving the water when it meant being handled by Tommy.

" Come on, youngster. Honey for tea."

He picked up Robin and strode back through the wood, whistling like a blackbird. The wood was very old, and

that whistling had echoed in its aisles through many centuries. The young men changed, and the tunes they
whistled were not the same in one generation as another,
but the life and the song that the wood held within its own
were eternal.

CHAPTER XI

I

IF the love of a woman would never mean a great deal to Tommy, to Ben just now it meant more than anything had ever meant; except his painting, with which it was so inextricably confused that he could not put paint upon canvas without thinking of Zelle, or see Zelle without wanting to paint her just exactly as he was seeing her at the moment. The gallery of his mind was hung all round with portraits of Zelle in every attitude, mood and frock that she possessed. He understood now why so many paintings labelled " Portrait of the Artist's Wife " are inflicted upon the world. He had deplored them in times past. From now on he would be obliged to regard them with a tolerant eye.

He had only lately discovered the joys of portrait painting, for until now it had been the beauty of earth and of legend that had absorbed him. They had seemed one, even as now the thought of Zelle and the thought of painting were one. The figures of legend had clothed themselves in natural beauty. The familiar spirits of Knyghtwood and The Herb of Grace, the Cistercian lay brother who had been the pilgrims' host at the inn and had fed the wild animals in The Buckpen, and the great white deer who had been with him in the woods and whom the twins called the Person with the Horns, had to his imagination taken form from the natural beauty they haunted. In his picture of the white deer, that hung now in the drawing-room of The Herb of Grace, the body of the deer seemed formed of moonlight and his antlers of the branches of the winter trees, growing in such a manner that they formed a cross in the centre. The shadowy figures of the red deer who fled after him, as men pursue the vision that always eludes them, were clouds that chased the moon, and the picture was full of the wind of their frantic chase. And when he had painted the Brother, the dark wood and the shadows of The Herb of Grace had gone to the forming of the great cruciform figure with arms held out in welcome.

Lucilla had said once that a wood is a foreshadowing of the fact of paradise, and when it lived in spring he agreed with her. The smallest petal of a flower, held in life, took the curve of the hand that held it, as did the earth itself, and the sun and moon. When the petal fell, the curve of life would go out of it. The unseen thrust through into the seen, like a hand into a glove, holding and moulding, revealing the shape of things to come. Always in nature the curve and the cross, life and death; the summer trees with the rich curve of foliage and the winter trees like the antlers of the deer.

And now he was beginning to see the bodies and faces of men and women as he had hitherto seen the natural world. In portrait painting, too, there was the curve and the cross. The Italian masters with their flowing lines had seemed to have their minds and imaginations fulfilled with life. El Greco had seen the rigid lines of death in every face and form. And in this twentieth century the pictures of some of the moderns were as angular and disjointed as the times. Zelle's cheek, when he turned to look at her walking so lightly beside him, had the curve of a flower-petal, and her whole body the flowing lines of Leonardo da Vinci's Virgin with St. Anne. Sebastian Weber, as day by day life loosened its hold upon him, looked more and more of an El Greco.

And just as the figures of legend had to his imagination clothed themselves in natural beauty, so now he saw the spirits of men wearing material form, as the white deer had worn the moonlight and the Brother the strength of wood and the darkness of shadow, moulding it from within. One felt an eavesdropper sometimes, painting a face. You knew things you were not supposed to know. But Sally's father, John Adair the portrait painter, who had taught him all he knew about painting, had said that did not matter

provided you held your tongue. You need not feel guilty.
Did you feel guilty when after an hour spent in painting a
tree you found yourself a little nearer to the animating,
sustaining spirit of immortal life? You felt humbled, perhaps slightly scared, but not ashamed, for you knew yourself
possessed of a knowledge that was intended for you. And as
with trees, so with men when you painted them. You felt
your way into union with, and some infinitesimal knowledge
of, a microcosm of the same spirit. Polluted, as a pool of
water can be polluted, but possessing within itself the possibility of a clarity beyond belief. It was upon that you
fixed your mind when you painted a portrait, so much so
that sometimes you painted a face not as it was now, but as
it would be in five years time, when the soul of the man or
woman you painted had moved a little nearer to her possible
perfection. " Have you ever had it happen the other way
on? " Ben had once asked John Adair, and the painter had
replied grimly, " Only once, thank God. And then it
wasn't evil that I painted into that face so much as fear.
I believe the knowledge of the possibility of damnation,
even the unconscious knowledge, to be the source of all
fear."

Now that the faces of men and women had become his
study it astonished him to find how often he caught a look
of fear on a face. He was constantly afraid himself, but
he had imagined he was abnormal in that way, and had
not realised how deeply fear was woven into the fabric of
human personality. He had little fear of physical danger,
but he was afraid of decisions, of responsibility, of hurting
those he loved, and he could see that John Adair was quite
right, for in each case his fear could be traced back to the
fear of wrong-doing. And he could see that it might be
the same with the physical fears. The shrinking of the
nerves from noise, from darkness, from the supernatural,
from pain, all had their roots in the fear of physical death,
a change which to his mind was not so dreadful in itself as
being the image and symbol of the second death.

The ubiquity and depth of fear that he saw shocked him,

revealing as they did the depth of that darkness of which men were afraid. It was a relief to look in a face in which he did not see fear. Only once or twice had he seen a shadow of it in Grandmother's face, never in Hilary's. Though Hilary's humility would never think it of himself, Ben supposed he had reached a level of being in which there could hardly be the possibility of loss. Yet one never saw fear in Tommy's face either. But, then, Tommy, at the other end of the scale, had no belief in his own soul, and you cannot fear the loss of what you don't believe in. And he had no imagination to bring what he had not yet experienced into the realm of possibility, and no nerves to shrink from it if he had. Yet he did not envy Tommy either the self-confidence of his fearlessness or the definiteness of his machines. Deeply aware though Tommy might be of the glory of life, Ben did not think he ever felt the thrilling inwardness of things. It was fear and uncertainty that admitted one to that. It was the fear of loss that made the artist cry out for the invisible beauty of a flower in the sun, that he might capture the rumour of the one in the other before the transient thing fell to the ground. And the probability of failure kept alive in one that sense of personal nothingness that seemed to call out in otherness such a depth of glory. One could sink one's nothingness in the otherness and come back refreshed.

" It's odd how when you're in love it can all come to a focus in one person," he said to Zelle. Only he did not call her Zelle, but by her own name of Heloise.

"What all comes to a focus in me?" asked Zelle. They were walking quickly now, for Ben wanted to get to Brockis Island, his special place, and show it to her. His hand no longer held her, but sometimes the rough tweed of his coat touched her bare arm as they swung along under the trees, and she thrilled at the light touch, longing for Brockis Island and the kisses he would give her there. It was strange to be longing for a man's kisses, because for much of her hard young life she had been warding them off. But, then, Ben's odd, delicate, fastidious love-making was no more

like other men's than he himself was like any other man she
had known or imagined. No, that was not quite true, for
in the worst of the bad days she had comforted herself with
an imagined impossible lover not unlike Ben. The fantasy
lover had been wonderful to look at, of course, which Ben
was not, but he had been gentle as Ben was and he had
loved in her some suffering thing, hidden in some place of
deep peace within her, that had nothing to do with her
being a woman, and nothing to do with those dark fires
that lit up when men wanted her who were not gentle, and
that made her so terrified both of herself and them.

"What do you mean, Ben? " she asked again.

"When I try to paint it isn't only the shape and colour
that I like," said Ben, " it's the something that you don't
see creating the shape and colour from within. And
possessing it from without, too, like the invisible air that
holds us. It's hard to explain. And why the dickens do
I use such a milk-and-white word as ' like '? Worship
would be better. ' With my body I thee worship ', the
man says in the marriage service. You seem all the beauty
of the world that I worship, and the invisibility that makes
it visible, focused in just one being whom I can love and
serve mortally and immortally with all the powers of my
body and my soul."

Zelle was not sure that she knew quite what he was
talking about; and she was not sure that he was as sure as
he thought he was. Compared to her he was a child in
experience and knew things chiefly by intuition. She was
the opposite. Her intuition had consisted in an almost
desperate conviction that a woman's experience should not
be like this, and that in the face of all impossibility one day
hers would not be. Somehow or other she had gone on
believing that it would not be, and had kept that something
hidden like a child within her, inviolate against that day.

As she walked with this impossible young lover of hers
in this faery wood that could not be true (and yet he was
here beside her, and yet the trees of her paradise arched
over her head) she felt almost dizzy with thankfulness.

There had been times when the hidden child in her had seemed asleep and the fires had not frightened, but excited her madly, waking up something else that was deeply hidden in her, some primeval woman who lived licentiously for the moment only, so that she had wanted to plunge into them and lose the self that suffered so and be done with it for ever. And there had been other times when to refuse men what they wanted had seemed cruelty, like refusing a cup of water to a thirsty child. And other times when the fires had died down to a warm glow that allured with a promise of desperately needed comfort. Yet always the deep instinct of self-preservation, not of the body but of the self that suffered, had conquered against every temptation to oblivion or unlawful comfort. Always fear had returned in time to save her, so that now she could walk lightly under these trees, beside this impossible boy who so deeply satisfied all her passionate maternity, and feel more of laughter than of shame when he said that he worshipped her. And feel glad, too, of her hard experience. He might need it, so unprepared did he seem to her for life in the world as she knew it; he might need it as much as she needed his intuition.

"I've never learned to see the 'idden beauty in things," she said humbly. " I've never even learned to see the outward beauty. I've never done anything but just scramble along. You'll 'ave to teach me. I 'ardly know even 'ow to be'ave."

The collapse of her h's, tumbling away so fast out of her lovely lilting speech, was suddenly Ben's undoing, and he could scarcely wait for Brockis Island. They were nearly there. He took her hand and they ran along the sun-dappled path to the fallen tree-trunk that spanned the amber stream, and crossed it, quick and sure-footed as wild creatures of the woods.

2

They pushed their way through the loosestrife and bog-myrtle on the farther side, and came through the break in the rampart of thorn and crab-apple trees to the hidden depth of peace that lay inside. For that was how it appeared to Zelle as she looked round at the small perfect green lawn, roofed with branches, cool and fresh, fragrant with the scent of the bog-myrtle and silent with the silence of the deep woods in one of those midsummer pauses when the birds and the winds are still. This place had the same quiet as the deep peace within her where her suffering self lay hidden. Only just now that self did not suffer. There was nothing but joy to feel in this green shade that was so unbelievably lovely that it couldn't be true.

Then she was in Ben's arms and being kissed with a thoroughness not met before in Ben. Yet still there was the gentleness that she loved. She could yield herself to it, her whole body pliant in his arms, without any sense of fear, and laughing with amused delight.

"Why do you always laugh when I kiss you?" asked Ben, holding her away from him and looking down at her. He loved to see her like this, with the laughter banishing the taut look that was usually stretched like a mask across her face, and the sadness of her eyes that was so disquieting. There was nothing demanding in his eager look, only a delight in her and adoration of her that made her feel queen as well as woman, crowned as well as loved in this enchanted island that suddenly seemed her throne as well as her hiding-place. Outwardly she would seem to rule this man through their life together, but secretly he would be her refuge, though no one but themselves would know it. A love that is worth anything has its secrets, she thought, and they are fun to keep.

"I think I laugh because the unexpected is always some-'ow funny," she said. "I thought it was only in dreams and story-books that men and women love this way. But, look, it 'as happened."

He picked her up and carried her to a fallen tree-trunk and sat beside her. Facing them was an old thorn-tree, and between the roots of it was the entrance to a badger's holt. They sat watching it, both of them oddly stirred.

There was a home inside there, warm and intimate. " The brockis," said Ben softly. " Do you know him? He's stripey, with one of those fascinating *retroussé* noses, rather like yours."

" You Eliot men! " complained Zelle. " Do you always compare the women you love to wild animals? I've 'eard Monsieur Eliot telling Sally she looked like a lioness. That lovely Sally! It's an insult."

" Not at all," said Ben. " What's lovelier than a lioness? Or a brockis either. Black and white, he is. Beautiful markings. I'll tell you you look like a shy violet, if you'd rather, perjuring myself though I should be." He paused, and spoke again with a slight trace of exasperation. " Though maybe there's some truth in that simile, too. Heloise, why can't we have this out in the open? I hate holes and corners."

" Is this an 'ole and corner? " she flashed back at him. " This beautiful 'idden place? "

" No, no, no," he said, and swung round and took her face between his hands. He hated it when anger suddenly flamed up between them like this, as it did sometimes just when they were at their happiest. " There must always be the secret places of love, but why should love itself be secret? I want to tell the whole world that I love you, and you won't even let me tell Mother."

Least of all his mother, she thought. She might lose him that way. He adored his mother, and she had no illusions as to what Nadine would think of her as wife for her eldest son. Or the General either. The daughter of a murdered Jew and a secret service agent, who had been left alone to look after herself as best she could from her teens upwards, and was now nursery governess to their great-niece. Not at all the sort of daughter-in-law they would have hoped for or expected. These English might say they were democratic, and pride themselves upon their broad-minded tolerance, but she was shrewd, and she had noticed that the family pride of the English gentry died hard in them. At heart they were still deeply intolerant, whatever they might say, and Ben was not strong in character, and almost morbidly conscientious. He was vacillating and perpetually un-decided as to which way duty lay. He had already, after torturing months of indecision, relegated his painting to the status of a hobby and chosen the Civil Service as a career, under pressure of what his parents told him was his duty. And he cared for his painting only a little less than he cared for her. Tommy, of course, would have let the whole world go to blazes before he would have given up his own will, even for Nadine. But then Tommy, if he ever loved at all, would love suitably and in keeping with the English aristocratic tradition.

"Wait," she said, her flash of anger dying at the touch of his hands. "Never force things to 'appen, Ben, but wait and let what 'appens show you the way. I've learnt that. The spring comes slowly. The way will open out for us if we wait and are patient. You've never learnt patience, but I 'ave. Patience, *mon Dieu*! I've learnt it!"

He took her hands and held them tightly. The laughter had gone out of her face, and her eyes were sombre. He thought of the little that she had told him about her life. Her French mother had married against the wishes of her family, distinguished scientist though her husband was. But they had been very happy, and the little Heloise had been as loved by her parents, and as loving, as was Meg. The war had caught them on a visit to Poland, and her father had been murdered there, and his wife and daughter had seen him die. Somehow, through the chaos of those days, they had struggled back to France, and France had fallen. Penniless now, and filled with hatred, Heloise's mother had worked for the Maquis through much of the occupation. Then the Nazis had got her and she had died, and Heloise at seventeen years old had carried on where her mother had left off. She had hoped she would die, too, and so she had lived, as those do who hope for death. After the war she had done a great many things, and gradually life had come to seem to her not so bad after all, for she was healthy and still young. Then she had thought she would like to come to England to perfect her English. She was a clever girl, and she might have got a good teaching post, but she chose instead the care of little children. For she adored children. It was the child in Ben, so much in need of looking after, that had made her fall in love with him the moment she had set eyes on him. . . . But that she had not told him, and never would, for she was a supremely tactful woman. She was four years older than he was, and that, too, was a matter that she would never obtrude upon his attention.

" Forgive me," he said. " No, I'm not patient. There has been nothing to teach me patience. What have I ever suffered, compared with you? I'll go slow."

She pressed home her advantage. " You didn't go slow when you chose the F.O.," she said, and still holding his hands she bent forward and kissed him, so that he should not be too much hurt by what she said.

" I dithered for months," he said drearily.

" Dithered, yes; but that's not the same as going slow. Dithering is just going round in a circle, and giving in just the same at the end, as you might have done at the beginning. When you go slow you go patiently on, not round. And you get there, Ben. You get there."

" At the F.O. it won't take me too long to make a home for you," said Ben. " As a painter it might have been years before I'd been making enough to keep a wife."

" Do you think I want a comfortable 'ome at the cost of your integrity? " said Zelle hotly. " I'd rather be very poor with you, or wait years before I married you, than commit murder."

" Murder? " asked Ben, shocked.

" Yes, murder," flashed Zelle. " If I kill the artist in you, demanding a comfortable 'ome, that will be murder. And if you kill 'im, just to please your parents or marry me quickly, that will be suicide. Oh yes, it will, Ben. That is, if you mean by integrity what I mean. What *do* you mean? "

" Constancy in service to my own vision," said Ben

slowly. " My vision may not be the same as another man's, but if I serve his instead of mine I've lost my integrity. I see that that's a sort of murder. The vision and the man who might have served it are both killed. I don't know if I've quite understood what the Bible means by the sin against the Holy Ghost, but in my own mind I think of it as believing that I have seen the truth and believing that I know how I must serve it, and then deliberately doing the other thing. But I don't see what that's got to do with the F.O."

" Everything," said Zelle. " You've 'ad your vision; something within creating shape and colour, you said. You tried to explain to me, though I don't think I understood very well, and per'aps you did not either. But there is something you 'ave seen. Could you serve it as a Civil Servant? "

" Yes," said Ben obstinately. " All honest work serves it."

" Work isn't honest unless it's done by honest men," said Zelle. " Are you being honest when you deny you are a painter? For you do that when you were made one and won't be one. First you lie and then you kill."

" You're making the most enormous mountain out of a very small molehill," groaned Ben. " And I'm a rotten painter, anyway. If I were a genius it would be a different thing altogether."

" No, it wouldn't," said Zelle. " The question is, are you a painter or aren't you. Are you? "

" Yes," groaned Ben.

" Darling, don't let's talk about it any more," said Zelle. " I 'ad to say it once. I 'ad to tell you 'ow I feel. Now let's talk about the brockis."

But Ben could find nothing more to say about the brockis. What she had said had been so like what John Adair had said when he had talked to him once. Only John Adair had expressed himself with less concern for Ben's feelings. That argument, and others that had taken place during the months of dithering, came jostling so vividly into Ben's memory that Zelle and Brockis Island lost outline and reality.

3

"Damn fool," said John Adair, his red beard bristling with fury. "Rotten painter, are you? So you are. Rotten. So am I. So are most of us. The point is we *are* painters. Sit on your behind filling in forms at the F.O. if you want to. It's your affair, not mine. They'll pay you well. Your mother will be pleased. Pretty woman, your mother. I fell in love with her once, but I soon got over it. I never fell permanently in love with anything except painting. I had that much sense. No mothers or wives could ever take my mind off it for more than five minutes. What's that? Paint as a hobby? You young fool. If you say that again I'll knock you down. You remind me of a maiden aunt of mine. She painted roses in oils on velvet tea-cosies. Very pretty, they were. Well, it's a free country, as far as murder goes. Nothing to prevent you hitting the other fellow on the head with an umbrella if you want to. Murder Ben the painter if you wish. Rotten fellow, as you said. Well, I won't say any more, except that if you go to the F.O. I'll never speak to you again, and if you choose the paint I won't lift a finger to help you. You'll start from scratch, as I did. I don't say I won't lend you my old easel with the woodworm in it, and look at your work now and again and tell you how damn bad it is. And should you do a good bit of work, which isn't likely, I might talk about it, as I would about any young chap's work that appealed to me, but that's all I'll do. I won't use my influence to help you, and I won't lend you money. I didn't become the rich man I am (or would be, but for this damned income tax) by lending money to young fools. Let 'em starve, I say. Do 'em good. Now get out and think it over."

At that point Ben went to Lucilla for help, but she would not help. "No, darling," she said. "You must decide. I've advised people too much in the past. I've imposed my will on them too much. I don't do it any more. . . . At least," she added, striving, as always in these days, after absolute truth, " I try not to do it any more."

And always there had been the pressure of his parents' deep anxiety. In a changing anxious world they wanted to see their sons safely settled in careers of financial and social security. They knew nothing at all about painters and their life, but they were quite sure struggling young artists could be certain of neither. They didn't know where their next penny was coming from and they consorted quite often with very odd people. Knowing Ben's weakness of health and of will, Nadine and George were worried to death. A life of financial uncertainty would bring back his asthma. Noisy parties in airless studios, drinking and smoking to all hours, would bring back his tendency to lung trouble. The very odd people would undermine his morals. He'd marry the wrong sort of girl. Meals at irregular hours would upset his digestion. From the moment of Ben's birth George had set his heart on his eldest son following him into his old regiment, and it had nearly broken his heart when Ben refused categorically to go into the army. But the Civil Service was the profession of a gentleman, according to George, and art was not. Of course when fellows painted the royal family and became royal academicians like John Adair, that was another story. But there was no likelihood of Ben being asked to paint the Queen, so far as George knew. George thought Ben's paintings were very pretty, but he couldn't see the promise of that much eminence in them. Nadine said that even if there had been, Ben would never live to attain it. At this point, one day, she broke down and cried, and Ben, holding her in his arms and trying to comfort her, realised with a shock that this was the first time in his life that he'd seen his mother cry.

" See what you've done to your mother," said George.

It wasn't as though they were asking him to give up his painting altogether, Nadine and George both said pathetically, when Nadine was feeling a little better. He could paint as much as he liked over the week-ends. They liked him to paint. His sketches were very pretty and his portraits and miniatures charming, and the anatomy in his allegorical works had improved a great deal lately. But they didn't want him to make it his profession. At least, not at present. Of course in years to come, if he should really turn out to be a genius, the whole matter could be reconsidered again. But at present surely it wasn't too much to ask that he should at least give the F.O. a trial. Didn't Ben feel he owed something to his parents? Couldn't he do just this one thing to please them? And Ben said he would. Later he wavered again, but Nadine cried again, and he came back once more to the beginning of the circle.

"Thank heaven surgery is considered the profession of a gentleman," was Tommy's private comment to Ben. "But what rot it is! Poor old Pop, how he dates! Almost antediluvian. Kipling and so on. And Mother the same. She's a damn pretty woman, and she dresses well, and that makes her look less prehistoric than Pop, but in point of fact there's not much to choose between them. To all intents and purposes both of them might have been dead for years. It's odd how soon people date. David's starting to date now. Have you noticed?"

Ben said miserably that he hadn't. He longed for David, who had never confined his acting to week-ends, but David was in America.

"Badly," said Tommy. "And as for his acting, it's positively ham. It makes me squirm. I don't know how it is he still rakes in the dough. But look, Ben, I'm like Mother and Pop in this. Painting's all very well as a recreation, but it's a pretty poor show as a life's work unless you happen to be a genius, which, old boy, speaking quite frankly, I don't think you are. The painters one knows are so wet. They just drool around with locks of hair falling over their eyes. Of course if you're a commercial kind of chap you can make a bit by it, like old Adair, but you're not that sort. Not forceful. You're more the wet sort. Or at least you will be if you don't look out. You need to counteract the tendency. Better try the F.O. Don't take my remarks to heart, old boy. They are all for your own good."

Hilary, appealed to, was not much more helpful than Lucilla. " I know nothing about painting," he said. " I don't even know if your work is good or if it isn't. And even if I did know I should hesitate to advise you. The older I get the more chary do I become of giving advice, especially upon the matter of vocation, which lies between a man and his God. A true vocation is inspired, and if you deliberately refuse it, even for such good motives as love of parents and so on, you run the risk of spiritual disaster. There is a sin against the Holy Ghost which is not forgiven either in this world or the next, and the refusal of inspiration is a part of it. As to whether painting is your vocation, I don't know. Only you know. And if you don't know, it's your business to find out."

" But how? " groaned Ben.

" For a start, leave off allowing your female relatives to make up your mind for you upon all the trivial matters of your life. Make up your own mind as to which tooth-paste you prefer. Try to get a little practice in decisive-ness, indecisive fellow that you are. And in this non-trivial matter, go slow. The movement of events sometimes shows one the will of God. But once you honestly believe you've seen it, nothing in earth or hell should deflect you from it."

But in the end it was Nadine who made up his mind for him. She came to his room one night, when he had gone up early with a headache, and sat on the edge of his bed, beautiful and slim in the moonlight. She slipped her cool fingers over his forehead and up into his hair, as she had so often done when he was a child and was ill. As a mother she had never been very free with her caresses, and for that reason they were doubly precious to her children. They all adored her, but her aloofness had never made it easy for them to tell her that they did. Ben, especially, had always longed for her to know how much he loved her. He saw now the anxiety in her face and a look in her eyes that he had never seen there before: the look that he'd seen in Sally's eyes once when Meg had mumps. He had had no idea, until that moment, that his cool, reserved mother ever felt like that about him. He sat up in bed suddenly and flung his arms round her. When he had done that as a small boy she had laughed and gently withdrawn herself from the bear-like hugs she did not much appreciate, but she did not withdraw now. She yielded to him as Heloise did, pliant and lovely, her cheek against his, more as a woman to a man than a mother to her son. In the moonlight she seemed as young as Heloise. It was thrilling to be a man and have a woman yield to him like this. His sense of his own power roused all the chivalry of his unselfish nature. He would have died for her at that moment, so surely to please her he could just try the blasted F.O. for a few years. It was not a denial of vocation (if painting was his vocation), only a postponement of it.

"Mother, I'll do what you and Father want," he whispered. "I mean, I'll try the F.O. for a bit."

She did not speak, but sighed out her relief and turned her face with her lips against his cheek. They had never loved each other so much, and with this compromise (and compromise was always as the breath of life to the gentleness in him that tried so hard to please everyone all round) he was extremely happy for a short while. Until the nagging demon of indecision woke up in him again.

And now here was Heloise underlining what John Adair had said, and what Hilary had said. But he had promised his mother. How could he go back on that?

4

"You've not spoken a word for ten minutes," said Heloise. "Not a word about the brockis. I don't believe there's any brockis. That's just a rabbit-'ole, and the brockis is an imaginary person, like Pan."

He found he was still holding her hands and she was laughing at him as she talked, helping him to come back again to the island and the summer afternoon in the faery

wood. Men were like this when much of their life was lived
creatively among the images of memory or imagination.
They would be suddenly away, re-living what they had
done, building castles in Spain of what they might do,
following byways of thought that led them to the queerest
places of speculation or fantasy or fear, and then forming
out of it all the stuff of their pictures or their poems, the
shadows and the lights that made their playing of great
music always different from that of another man. Her
father had been like that, and many of his friends whom she
had known in after-years. And a young Jewish writer who
had loved her, and now Ben. How could anyone imagine
Ben would be of the slightest use in the Foreign Office?
Promotion comes only to a man who can keep his mind
forever on the job, and if Ben ever learnt to do that he
would paint no more pictures.

" Pan's not imaginary," said Ben. " At least, not in this
wood. The twins used to see him when they were little.
They called him the Person with the Hoofs. And once or
twice I could have sworn I'd heard the sound of his pipes
here. Shrill and sweet and terrifying, far away and very
near at the same time."

" Like you these last ten minutes," said Zelle. " Where
were you, Ben? "

" Nowhere interesting," said Ben drearily. " Only going
round and round again."

" We're not 'appy now, like we were when we first came
'ere," said Zelle. " That's wrong, and an insult to the
wood. Come on, Ben, we'll walk and be 'appy again.
Woods like this one are so old that the tops of the trees 'old
up the sun and moon and stars like candles, and the roots
go down to where the freshness is. ' There lives the dearest
freshness deep down things.' I read that in an English
poem once. Come on. There's a bird that pipes like
Pan, and another that laughs, but they flute and laugh so
quietly."

" A nuthatch and a yaffingale," said Ben. " The birds
are not very noisy now, but in the spring they sing so loudly

that you can't hear yourself think in the wood for the row they make."

They had left the island by another little bridge and were walking quickly through the bit of the wood that lay beyond. There was no regular path here, only the suggestion of one made by the feet of the Eliots as they walked from Ben's place to David's place, the clearing where the stream was, and where the bog-myrtle grew robed in silver light. If one saw a kingfisher in Knyghtwood one most often saw it here, yet, though he would have liked Zelle to see a kingfisher, Ben swung away from the clearing, with a vague feeling that it was not his place and that he might disturb another pair of lovers there. He struck deep into the wood, to the right, with Zelle merry beside him. She had so resolutely brought back their joy that it had banished time and place, and they were the immortal lovers who had lived and loved under the trees in Eden's garden in the beginning of the world, and would live and love in all lovers until its end. They possessed the end in the sun and moon and stars above them and the beginning in the freshness of the green shade. Zelle's laughter and talk fell like a chime of bells, making faint echoes that rang farther and farther away, until they were absorbed into the deep places of the woods. The nuthatch blew once on his pipe and the yaffingale laughed, and the silence flowed in again where the lovers had been.

CHAPTER XII

I

" THAT'S a pretty one," said Meg, and picked it out of the stream and handed it to Sebastian where he sat comfortably beside her upon a moss-grown stone. He had heard Zelle's laughter, but he had not looked round, because he realised that in this wood each pair of lovers lived in their own fool's paradise and were careful not to trespass in that of another pair. Fool's paradise? Was that the correct description? Correct in the sense of being transitory, for they would all have to come out of this wood at the call of that disrupting thing the English tea-hour, the most idiotic institution that even the English had invented yet. But incorrect in the sense that their happiness here was self-deception. This happiness that he was experiencing with Meg was no self-deception. It was more completely real than anything that had happened to him for a long time.

" Experience " the wood, Hilary had said, not just enjoy it. He'd been right. Enjoy was too shallow a word for the experience of renewal that was his at this moment. " A strain of the earth's sweet being in the beginning in Eden garden." He had now read many more of the poems in the book in his room, and lines from them kept recurring to him like phrases of music. Hilary had been speaking of the place of contact where the freshness springs up, a fountain of living water, but he had not said that this wood was the symbol of it. But it was so to Sebastian. He would never, as long as he lived, think of the place of contact without thinking of this wood. A wood for lovers. A place for the contact of one soul with another. A wood for lovers in the deepest of all senses because a place for the deepest contact of all, for the soul with her eternal lover. He imagined that Hilary would say that that could be in greater or lesser degree an unceasing contact, if the search of the soul was unceasing, but the realisation of it came most readily in places where the symbols were. What was this state of rest and peace in which he was held? Was it prayer, the kind of prayer that is called consolation?

"It's a very pretty stone," he said to Meg. "It's veined like a wood-violet, and coloured like one, too."

He had spread his handkerchief on his bony knees, and it was slowly filling with the treasures Meg fished out of the stream.

"But now it isn't," said Meg, looking at it. "It's gone grey. When they're in the water they are all bright, like Mummy's necklaces, but when I take them out they aren't the same."

"They need the freshness of the water to bring out the colour," explained Sebastian. "But they *are* the same. The wood-violet colour is still in the stone, though you don't see it now. When we go home we'll put all the pebbles in a bowl of cold water, and they'll be alive and beautiful again."

"That's all right, then," said Meg. "Here's another one. It's pink. We did come a long way, didn't we? I've only come here twice before, with Daddy, and both times we had the push-cart that shuts up for bits of the way."

They had certainly come what was for them a long way, and Sebastian marvelled that his insubordinate heart and her short legs had stood the strain as well as they had. They still had to get back, of course, but sufficient unto the day. It amazed him that Meg had come so unerringly to a place where she had been only twice before. He imagined that the place of the fresh stream and the gleaming pebbles, and the bog-myrtles dressed in silver light, had some particular significance in the lives of her father and mother. Children inherited their parents' memories, both good and fearful. He remembered how his small daughter had once described to him a dream she had had. She had been walking in moonlight and shadow up a moss-grown path with nut-trees arching over it, and at the end of the path the trees had framed a patch of sky blazing with stars, like a door opening into space. It had been the path where he and Christiana had had their greatest moment together.

Or what had seemed to them their greatest moment. For how could one tell, as the moments flowed in and one held them and then relinquished them, which were great and which were not? That moment of good honest down-right human passion, both of them at the peak of triumph, strength and beauty, had seemed a great moment, yet per-haps that other moment, when he had looked down at the smoking rubble that hid her burnt-out body, had been greater. For all he knew, she had been nearer to him then, even though he had felt nothing—not even grief or rage, but only that absence of all feeling which in its emptiness can be more horrible than either. Her love for him might have been filling that apparent emptiness, for all he knew, and have been driven out when the rage came later; such unreasoning rage that he would have imperilled what felt to him like the last remnants of his sanity if only he could have got his hands on the throat of the man who had caused her death. Reason would have told him that no one man, but many, had caused it, but in his murderous rage he had not listened to reason. One man alone had become real to him: her murderer, whom his hatred could not reach.

" Here's another," said Meg.

Out of the smoking pit her little face rose up and smiled at him. With a sense of shock and desecration he put out a hand to grab hold of her, lest she tumble back into it. Unaware of her peril, she put the pebble into his hand.

" A green one," she said.

But, of course, for her there was no peril. She was not his child, and his memories had no power to hurt her. He thanked heaven his own children had been conceived in the days of his happiness, and whatever nightmares had haunted them before they died had had no origin in any experience of his. But David Eliot could not say that. Sebastian looked a little anxiously at Meg's small upturned face and

wondered if any shape of fear ever lay in wait for her in
the dark places of her dreams, or in the shadowy corners of
the old house when she went upstairs to bed.   Some Thing?
Bat-winged, perhaps, like the planes that had brought death
and destruction to women and children in the war.   God
help me, he thought, to what thoughts am I giving free
passage in this place of refreshment?   In the presence of
this child? He had fallen from prayer. The unwilled
thinking of idle moments, Lucilla had said, could help to
keep humanity upon the rack. Yes, it was evil. The
perpetual remembrance of past misery was sin in him, after
all these years, and now that he possessed the power to push
it away. He called upon all the strength he had, and the
pit closed, and in its place was a scene like an illustration in
a nursery picture-book, all clear line and pure bright colour
and simplicity and mirth.

The doll Maria Flinders was sitting on a stone beside the
stream. She was an amiable jointed creature who could
hold a desired position with ease. She was fishing, apparently, for a long stick with a piece of grass attached projected
from beneath her person. Not being able to hold it in
hands that were permanently star-fish shape, she sat on it.
Her frock was bright magenta and there was a magenta
bow in her flaxen hair. The expression of her podgy pink
face was peacefully and statically seraphic, like that of so
many fishermen, and like them she gave one a delightful
sensation of permanence in a changing world, as though
rooted where she was until the day of judgement. Only
the rear elevation of Mouse, violently agitated, was visible.
The front elevation was snorting and snuffling beneath a
bog-myrtle bush. There was Something There; only
Mouse knew that. Meg was bending absorbed over the
stream. Her blue sun-bonnet had fallen backwards, and
the sunlight gleamed on her silvery fair head. Her crisp
white frock stuck out horizontally in the most absurd way
when she bent down, and her back view, when she turned
round in this position, was enchanting. Her new blue
shoes were not what they had been, but they were still

blue, and her usually pale face was rosy with exertion. The little stream was a ribbon of pure light. Pads of bright moss on the stones, a company of toadstools in liveries of dove-colour, orange and pale buff, a brilliant scarlet moss-cup on a lichened stick, the doll's dress, were all sharp notes of colour in the general gaiety, but not challenging enough to take one's attention from the glowing life of the child. One could have warmed oneself at it.

"Meg," said Sebastian.

She came to him at once, and this time she did not bring him the stone she was holding, but dropped it. He had spoken her name as a lover might, and she had responded with the instant warm giving of herself that she had inherited from Sally. She stood in front of him and beamed up at him while he held her lightly between his hands. The bodies of small children were almost incredibly warm and alive. He did not quite know why he had called her or what he wanted of her. Perhaps it was simply this warmth and assurance of life in the long-drawn-out cold ending of it all. But, whatever it was, she had given it to him and he was satisfied.

"Is it tea-time?" asked Meg.

He looked at his watch and saw that it was. He sighed. How early in life these English became the slaves of their tea hour! He tied up Meg's pebbles in his pocket handkerchief and stood up stiffly, stretching his cramped limbs. Mouse, English to the backbone in spite of Scottish ancestry, backed out from beneath the bog-myrtle bush and cavorted round them, barking impatiently. She always had a piece of bread-and-butter for tea, and tea in the slop-bowl. Meg took Sebastian's hand, and they left the clearing talking softly to each other, as lovers do. Maria Flinders remained sitting on her fishing-rod, gazing beatifically into space.

2

David also stretched his cramped limbs and came out from behind the largest bog-myrtle bush, farther up-stream. He strolled down the clearing and sat where Sebastian had sat, on the large flat rock. He gazed with distaste at Maria Flinders. He had always disliked the woman. All that pink. And that seraphic expression was entirely bogus. If you looked fixedly at it, it turned into a most unpleasant smirk. The creature knew he had been eavesdropping. But he had not meant to. He had been farther into the wood and, coming back again, had found them here in his special place, where he had wanted to be. Meg, of course, had a right to be here, but not Weber. What had it got to do with Weber? Why should Weber take possession both of his child and of his special place? He was damned if he was going to be turned out of here by Weber, he had said to himself. He would simply sit down here and wait till they'd gone. So he had sat down behind the bog-myrtle, his back against a boulder, and fumed.

But in five minutes it was himself he was fuming at. Great heaven, what childishness! And what detestable childishness, too! Knyghtwood was not private property, though to hear the Eliots talk anyone would think they owned the entire place. Weber had as much right in it as anybody. More right, for he was one of the disinherited who inherit the earth. What did it feel like to be stripped of everything? There could be joy in it, they said—that joy of spiritual inheritance that through the grace of God could flow into the emptiness of material loss. In vulgar parlance, what you lost on the swings you could gain on the roundabouts. But the experience of loss, of whatever kind, must be pretty frightful—a sort of darkness through which you would have to struggle with no certainty that you would ever arrive at the roundabouts. He turned away quickly from the thought of it, and watched Meg.

She was enjoying herself, utterly absorbed in taking pebbles out of the stream and carrying them along to poor old Weber. And he was not sure that Weber was not as absorbed as she was. He suspected that to both of them each pebble was one of the wonders of the world, in which they saw beauties that he would not see, if Meg were to show them to him. They neither of them owned anything, of course, Meg because she had not yet clutched and Weber because he had let go. He imagined that the absorption of a child and the prayer of a man who was truly great had much in common, and they much in common, and that he was looking at both. Which he had no right to do, being what he was. Ashamed of himself he shut his eyes and wished Weber did not dislike him so much. Not for his sake, for he still saw Weber's dislike as a rationalisation of his own hatred of himself, and found relief in it, but for the fellow's own sake. It was a smudge on the character of a man whom he was coming more and more to reverence and almost love. He knew that love was a word that should be used with caution, but his gratitude to this man, whose light, shining so infinitely above him that night, had saved him from disaster, was so profound that he believed it had almost earned the name of love.

He must have slept again, for he was visited by a dream-memory of one of the nightmares that used to torment him after the war; for quite a long time after the war, because it had not left him until Meg had been born. Then, until now, it had entirely vanished. He would be riding through the air at night on the back of a most horrible Thing, a devilish Thing with wings like a bat and a filthy body that stained his hands when he touched it. But he had to touch it, because if he had not held on he would have hurtled through space to destruction. Yet it was difficult to find hand-hold on the Thing, because its body was infested with parasites—worm-like creatures whose touch filled him with shuddering revulsion. Yet, sickened though he was, he had to be one with this Thing that was carrying him through the night because he had become the instrument of its evil will. There was no escape. The stars were like flowers about him in the clear sky, but as he passed them they shrivelled up and burned away. The stars could escape, but not he. As his horror grew, the Thing slackened speed and began to circle lower and lower. There was a city below them, and a terrible sight was given him whereby

he was able to see inside the houses. He saw children in
bed, their faces rosy with sleep, and their mothers sitting
beside shaded lamps, reading or sewing peacefully. He saw
hospitals and the sick lying quietly in the narrow beds. He
looked down on them all as a messenger of heaven might
have looked, in pity and love, and lifted his hands from the
filthy Thing because he wanted now to fall from it and go
to them in pity and love. But the minute his hands were
empty they were filled, for the worm-like things crawled
into them. In horror he shook his hands, to be free of
them, and they fell from his hands upon the city below and
destroyed it. He heard the scream of the children and the
sick, and he saw the flames, and the smoke of the burning
city came up and choked him. And then he fell from the
back of the Thing into a pit of darkness. He went on
falling and falling, and he longed to reach the bottom so
that he could have his back broken and be finished with
the Thing for ever. But when he reached the bottom he
merely woke up, shaking and drenched with sweat, and
found he was in his room at Damerosehay and the war
was over. But the night was not over, for he would hear
the cuckoo clock strike one or two, and know that he would
have to get through it as best he could, remembering the
fires of Hamburg and knowing himself the sole man responsible. He was not, of course, but such is the power of the
small hours to distort the judgement, that he would not
know he was not until the dawn came and he heard the
sea-birds fluting in the marshes.

But the awakening now was not to darkness, but to the
silvery peace of his special place in Knyghtwood, and to the
sound not of the clock striking, but of a voice saying gently,
" Meg." The dream memory of the nightmare had not
gripped him as the nightmare itself used to do. Though
he was trembling when he woke, he shook himself free of it
quickly, and could even think what a ridiculous childish
nightmare it was. Yet in the moment of waking the figure
of Weber seemed curiously near to him, as though the man
was standing by him. He almost spoke to him, and then

he saw that Weber was still sitting on the flat rock, and that it was he who had said "Meg." He saw Meg drop her pebble and go to him, and though he was horribly jealous, he nevertheless fixed his eyes balefully upon a lady-bird crawling up a stalk of grass beside him, so as not to pry upon the two lovers down below. He had a feeling that Weber had called Meg to him that the fact of her might keep at bay the thoughts he did not want, just as the fact of her had banished the last of the nightmares from her father's mind, almost as though the new-born baby had lifted the Thing right off him and taken it upon herself. Staring at the lady-bird, he heard Mouse barking, and then the two of them murmuring softly to each other as lovers do, though the subject-matter of their talk seemed only the relative merits of honey and strawberry jam, and then they went away.

Sitting on the rock, looking with distaste at Maria Flinders, David was suddenly reminded of Anne. It was the fair hair and the smirk. Anne had not smirked exactly, for he could never have loved a smirking woman, but she had smiled as a woman smiles who knows her own power. And no wonder, for her snow-queen blonde loveliness, combined with her sparkling vitality, had been the most bewitching enchantment he had ever met. And she had had the wit to use both to get what she wanted, and she had wanted David desperately, but not the strength of character to want the same thing long. . . . Any more than he had. . . . It was the first time David had owned that to himself, for, while it lasted, their passion had seemed to have the quality of eternity in it, like bad illness, and, as with illness, now it was over it astonished him that he could ever have thought it would not cease.

Passion, like illness, was of the body only. He and Anne had had a motor smash together in America and had been lucky to escape with their lives. He tried to imagine what it would have been like to have been suddenly flung together into the grey dimness of the life beyond. For a grey dimness it would have seemed to them, utterly rooted in the life of the body as both of them had been. For there was so little that such as he and she could have taken with them when they died. Stripped of everything that belongs to this world, practically nothing. On his side, only a single-minded devotion to his art and, growing out of it, a hard and aching hunger for a beauty that would have blinded him and burned him to nothing had he seen it only distantly and far away. For at that time this shame of self-loathing had not fully come to him. Now he had that. Perhaps that was something. On her side, he did not know. He had known next to nothing about her, he realised now. They would have been like the dead lovers in Flecker's terrible poem, two desolate wraiths blown away by the wind.

He got up from his stone and picked up Maria Flinders from hers. It was a temptation to put the creature face downwards in the stream and leave her there, but Meg was attached to her and it was incumbent upon him to carry her home. To spend the next five years looking at Maria Flinders (for Meg was faithful in love) and being reminded of Anne was just a small penance that he must pay for his own unfaithfulness. He sat down again with Maria in the crook of his arm, for he was afraid to be separated from her lest he should forget her.

Looking down the lovely length of his special place, to where the river was a sheet of light at the bottom of the clearing, he could not see her, but her angularities stuck into him, and for a moment or two the three women seemed present with him here, Nadine, Anne and Sally. Nadine. That was all right now. How ridiculous that they could have loved as they had and now be so serene in affection! Anne. Soon for her it would be over, and for him no more than an abiding shame. But Sally. That was different. That might be for ever, if one chose it so. Already his quiet love for her had stood firm beneath the turmoil of his love for Anne. It had been extraordinary to come home and find his marriage just what it had always been. He had not expected that. But, then, though he was not single-minded in love, she was, and upon her constancy their life together was grounded. But he could be if he chose. He had worked at his art, sweated at it, disciplined himself for it, denied himself for it. He could do the same with his marriage. That something beyond life that he ached for was present in life. One could worship it, and in some minute sense possess it, in a three-fold discipline of love and work and shame; for that particular discipline was one of the trinities that must not be divided. A kingfisher flashed across the clearing, cutting the light like a sword. That had happened on the day when he and Sally had met each other here. He could see Sally's face now, amazed and almost stunned as she looked at him. And she had told him afterwards that he had looked the same. He had not understood their amazement then, but he did now. They had seen each in the other not only a mortal lover but, under God and if they chose it so, the instruments of each other's immortality. She had chosen already. He, who until now had sought in her chiefly his own comfort, chose now. " I will," he said, and took out his handkerchief and tied a knot in it; why, he had no idea. " Sally," he said, " Sally," and heard her voice replying, " What were you seeing? " She had asked him that before, here in this place, and he had said then, " A kingfisher. A heavenly bird." Now he said, " A sword," and knew that he had cut himself off for ever from every woman except Sally.

" What we ought to be seeing," she had said after that, " are the twins and Mary. I brought them for a walk, and now I've lost them."

3

He blinked in utter bewilderment, and found that it was Tommy standing beside him, with Robin on his back. " Did you say you'd lost the twins? " he asked vaguely.

" I've been saying so for the last five minutes," complained Tommy bitterly, " and all you did was tie a knot in your handkerchief. I always did suspect you of being more or less crackers. That's proved it. Those blasted twins!

I've shouted myself hoarse. Take this kid of yours and
cart him home. I'd better go a bit farther. Mother will
make a stink of a row if I turn up without the twins. Here's
the kid."

He shed Robin and Yabbit at David's feet and was gone,
trampling away through the undergrowth like a young
heifer. And what, wondered David, had he been doing
with Robin? Even to his inexperienced eye his son's small
shirt seemed buttoned wrong. And where was Zelle? He
believed he paid her a handsome sum to keep her eye on
his children, but her eye appeared to be upon neither this
afternoon. He felt extremely irritable. He had been so
shaken by shame and resolve that he was tired out, and
exhaustion always made him feel like a cat with its fur
stroked the wrong way. And the sight of Yabbit did nothing
to improve his temper, for the fact that Maria Flinders had
reminded him of Anne made him now see a likeness to himself in Yabbit. The creature, rehabilitated by Sebastian,
had a pleasing enough exterior, elegantly masculine in
shape and tailoring, but there was a suggestion of effeminacy
in the genteel pink-lined ears, and the pleading look in the
eyes was bogus. Yabbit had nothing to plead about. No
stuffed rabbit ever had a more comfortable home. Stuffed
rabbit. There lay the rub. For that elegance of outline,
that gentility and pathos, enclosed nothing but sawdust.
Burst Yabbit and there would be nothing there at all but
dusty stuff drifting on the wind and a deflated outer garment
of grubby flannel. Façades. That was what he and Yabbit
were. And behind the façades only wraiths like the dead
lovers in Flecker's play. Nothing.

He got up quickly, suddenly ashamed of his shame. He
had been more or less absorbed in it the entire afternoon.
As things now were with him, he must carry his shame until
the end of life, but such absorption was merely another
form of the self-engrossment of which he was so ashamed.
He had no business to be nothing. He *was* something. He
was Sally's lover and husband and the father of her children.
He could start from there.

G

" Come on, Robin," he said. " There's honey for tea."

Robin had sat down backwards in the stream and was extremely wet. Whatever Tommy had been doing with him, he had at least kept his clothes dry, David thought with compunction.

" Cawwy me," said Robin.

" You must walk a bit to dry off," said David. " Come on." Holding Maria Flinders and Yabbit in one arm, he held out his other hand to Robin. " Come *on*, Robin."

Robin removed himself instantly from the stream, for he vaguely remembered that that irritable note in his father's voice preceded a slapping if not attended to. He took his father's hand and smiled at him, his cheeks bulging up and pushing his eyes shut, his two bottom teeth extremely prominent. His cheeks were scarlet with his exertions in the stream, and his hand, though wet, felt in David's warm and fat as a minute muffin just out of the oven. They walked slowly through the wood, for though Robin could run fast until he fell, his walking pace was that of a tortoise. Running to the end of the world, he forgot himself, but walking he felt as top-heavy as a peony on an inadequate stalk. After a bit he didn't like it. He sagged at the knees and his tummy ached.

" *Cawwy* me," he insisted.

David sighed and heaved him up on his arm, for he had never learned the trick of bouncing him on his back and remaining upright, as Tommy did. Robin smiled across at the occupants of his father's other arm.

" Mwya Finders and Yabbit," he said.

" Three of you," groaned David. " Where on earth is Zelle ? "

" Wiv Ben," said Robin. He had early acquired the habit of knowing where people were. Like all Personages, he liked to know the whereabouts of the royal entourage.

" Is she, indeed ? " said David, and fell into thought that was unconnected with himself for the first time that afternoon. Ben and Zelle. What would Nadine say to that? She was not exactly a humble woman, and for her children, extensions of herself, her ambitions soared. She had accepted obscurity for herself with a good grace, but she would not for her children, if she could help it. David did not doubt that in her present imaginings (for he supposed that even in Nadine's well-ordered existence the usual ridiculous day-dream masquerade was somewhere firmly battened down) Ben guided the destinies of nations as Foreign Secretary, with the assistance of a wealthy well-born wife. Zelle was neither. She would fight Zelle, as she had already fought Ben's painting. David sighed and frowned worriedly. It had distressed him to come back from America and find Ben pledged to the F.O. A worse Civil Servant he couldn't imagine, or a finer artist. But everything had seemed settled, and he had been afraid to interfere between Ben and his parents. Father and mother and child. That was another of the trinities with which one must not interfere. He looked at Robin, whose top-heavy sleepy head was now lolling against his shoulder, and it seemed to him that Sally walked beside them. The puppets on his other arm, Anne and the David Eliot who had imagined that he loved her, were merely puppets.

"Heavens, Robin, you weigh a ton!" he groaned, but Robin, too, had a tendency to self-absorption, and his concern with his weight was only lest it should be put down.

"Cawwy!" he commanded sleepily.

There was a short cut from the clearing to the green gate, and David had taken it. It was with profound relief that he saw the strong walls of The Herb of Grace shining through the trees, and with greater relief that a few moments later he saw Zelle running down the path to meet him at the blue gate.

"Do you ever carry this child any distance?" he asked, as he transferred Robin, Maria Flinders and Yabbit from his arms to hers. "If so, don't. You'll get a rupture."

"'E can perfectly well walk a little distance," said Zelle.

"Not if he doesn't want to," said David.

"You must be fir-r-r-m," said Zelle with a touch of severity.

Stretching his cramped limbs, David looked down at her. There was gentleness in his eyes, but something, too, of judgement, or of summing up, and she flushed. She braced herself, the child held on her hip with strong and lovely ease, and looked him bravely in the eyes. " It is I who should 'ave been looking after Meg and Robin this afternoon," she said. " I am sorry. I went for a walk with Ben."

" That was nice for Ben," said David with a touch of sarcasm. He had seen little of Zelle, and when they had been together he had just endeavoured to be kind without noticing her very much. The great man patronising his children's nursery governess. This being kind to those who in the bad old days had been called one's dependants, how detestable it was; no more than a flung coin, costing nothing, and undeserving of the name of kindness. " Charity suffereth long and is kind." If charity and kindness did not hold on, one on each side, to suffering and patience, they both turned at once into patronage. What a frightful thing! For the first time he looked attentively at Zelle, and liked the way in which, though her flush deepened, she did not shrink from his scrutiny. Her curly hair had been pushed back from her broad wise forehead (probably by Ben, he thought) and he saw how deeply scored it was by lines of anxiety and concentration, lines that had no business to be there at her age, and behind their sparkling vitality her eyes were somehow sombre. She'd obviously been through something. Most of the vivid lipstick she usually wore had been removed from her mouth (probably also by Ben), and for the first time he noticed its strength, and the determination of her pointed chin. She's not pretty, he thought, but she's got what it takes. He knew her already to be sensible and tender, for he had a keen eye for anything that concerned Meg, and that much he had been careful to verify in Meg's governess, but the strength and courage in her took him by surprise.

" That's all right, Zelle," he said. " And I repeat—it was nice for Ben." There was no sarcasm in his tone now, but real sincerity, and an undercurrent of meaning which for a moment or two she did not understand. Her lips parted in surprise and she looked at him as keenly as he had been looking at her. Then she turned and fell into step beside him as they walked together up the flagged path. Her heart leaped with joy, but David's sank. Good Lord! now I've let myself in for something, he groaned within him. He would say for patronage that it did not involve one in any bother.

CHAPTER XIII

I

ROUSED to fresh devotion to duty by David's unexpected alliance, Zelle was at the blue gate to relieve Sebastian of Meg when they arrived by the longer way round ten minutes later. And this time Ben came with her.

" We are late? " asked Sebastian anxiously. " This English tea hour. I know its importance."

" No," comforted Zelle, who knew how he felt about the English tea. " It's not till five at The 'Erb of Grace. And at Damerosehay we 'ad lunch early, you remember, so that there should be no danger 'ere. Come, Meg, mignon. You must wash your 'ands."

" I had a nice time," said Meg.

She was not as self-absorbed as Robin, but she did think it was important that she should enjoy herself. It seemed to her that the beautiful world about her demanded enjoyment. She could feel the grass enjoying her when she ran over it, and she liked to feel its pleasure, so it was only fair that she should enjoy the grass.

" And Mouse has had a nice time," said Meg, as Zelle led her up the path. " And Maria Flinders is still having it. I left her behind fishing. We must fetch her after tea. I did not want to stop her nice time."

" She did not catch anything and she got tired of it," said Zelle. " So Daddy brought 'er 'ome."

" I hope *you* had a nice time, Sir," said Ben shyly.

" Excellent," said Sebastian. " And you? "

Ben smiled and said nothing. Sebastian was aware of distress as well as exaltation in him. He had not forgotten how swelling and immense were the emotions of youth. They came riding in like huge breakers, climbing the sky, and as they curved and broke in thunder and beauty, they seemed the whole ocean to the breathless swimmer. It was only when he looked back from the deep water far ahead, the arch of the sky revealed again, that he saw them as ripples creaming on the sand. They said youth was always obsessed by the importance of its own affairs. No wonder, when they filled the sky like that.

"You've not been here before, have you, Sir?" asked Ben. "I'd like to show it to you. I can show you the hall and the drawing-room while tea is coming in. And the Chapel after tea, for it's upstairs."

Sebastian smiled at the *naïveté*. David, too, would have thought of a session upon a chair between a period of activity and a journey upstairs, but he did these things so adroitly that Sebastian had only just discovered that he did do them. Ben's consideration as a host was less practised, but it had the same intuition, and was the more delightful in him in that the waves were even now breaking over his head. In another twenty years, Sebastian thought, he would have become an extremely unselfish man, even more so than his cousin. Sebastian was beginning to admit that side by side with David's egotism there existed a certain selflessness. Or perhaps that was putting it too strongly. Perhaps it would be truer to say that David had headed his egotism for the loss of it, as a man shooting the rapids deliberately steers his boat for the sickening fall that is just ahead of him.

"You are very like your cousin," he said, as they walked up the paved path to the front door.

"Like David?"

"Yes."

Ben flushed with pleasure. "I only wish I were," he said. "He's a great chap. And he's succeeded."

"Is that so important?" asked Sebastian drily.

"I don't mean in that sort of way," said Ben hastily. "I mean, he's done the job he wanted to do as well as he could do it."

Sebastian noted the sudden hardening in Ben's voice, but he only said, "Now I can see the old signboard. What are the blue flowers?"

"Rue, the Herb of Grace," said Ben. "The garden rue is yellow, but the wild rue is blue. It used to grow in these parts, but you hardly ever find it now. It's an astringent herb that's supposed to be good for clearing the sight—both sorts. Country people used to apply it for rheum and drink it to foresee the future. In our family we say it's the symbol of single-mindedness."

"A very good symbol," said Sebastian. "But I don't think I care for these hyphenated words of your complicated language. I prefer the single word integrity. The meaning, I think, is much the same?" He felt Ben stiffen beside him and went on easily, "But you've already expressed my meaning in describing your cousin. He's done the job he wanted to do as well as he could do it. You couldn't describe the integrity of the artist better. To others, perhaps, there seems a certain ruthlessness (or astringency) about the clear sight of the artist who has got rid of the rheum and foreseen the future. He sees his job and his goal of perfection, and to hell with what gets in the light."

There was a sudden quiet but steely anger in his tone that astounded Ben. Sebastian had impressed him enormously, but, troubled as he was about his own affairs, he had not analysed the respect he felt for him. He had vaguely thought it the shamed admiration which the fortunate feel for those who have suffered ordeals which they are not at all sure they could have survived themselves. But now the sudden flash of the steel was so fierce that he felt transfixed by it. And in anger, too. He had thought the man liked him, but Sebastian's anger was hot in his body. He had thought of the poor chap as a broken man, but there was nothing broken about this steel, or the anger either. You can't break steel, nor fire. He opened the door, and as he waited courteously to let Sebastian pass in first, he dropped his eyes, that he might not see the contempt in Sebastian's. Then he was ashamed. He had accepted the thrust of the steel with an instant sense that this was justice. He must accept the contempt, too. Flushing to the roots of his hair, he forced himself to look at Sebastian. But there was nothing in the man's sombre lightless eyes but great kindness, and the gentleness of his face seemed almost to belie the anger. Yet the anger had been there, for the steel was still in Ben, stiffening him.

" Who told you? " he asked.

" I don't think anyone in particular," said Sebastian. " Just a word here and there. The way in which you have all so generously made me one of the family has made me know more about you all than perhaps I ought to know." He paused a moment, passing his hand across his eyes, wondering if that was quite the truth, for living now as he was in the shadow of death, any slightest dishonesty revolted him. Though why did the Psalmist talk of the shadow of death? To him it was all light; a terrible light. Even now, coming towards him like the rays of a rising sun, it showed him sin where he had not known there was sin. He wondered how the soul endured it when the last of the dark places had been searched out and shown to her. Possibly adoration of the unspeakable beauty of the light helped one to endure the shame. But he must let that ambiguous statement pass, for he could not talk to this very young man about the clairvoyance of death. He took his hand from his eyes and saw the hall of The Herb of Grace, into which they had passed. " This is—this is—no one told me," he said.

Ben was thankful for the astonishment that had made Sebastian suddenly forget all about him. He could stand beside him in the shadows and recover himself. The conversation had been of the briefest, and he supposed it had taken them only a few minutes to walk up the path and in at the door, yet it had seemed years. And nothing that John Adair, or Heloise, had said to him had shaken him like this. No, not shaken him, stiffened him, for he knew now what he had to do.

Sebastian stood still, and was royally welcomed by the great glowing personality that informed the house. Almost he could have said the man shouted aloud, only there was no sound in the stillness except the ticking of the clock. The welcome was so personal that they might have been old

friends. It seemed to come from two places at once: from
the fullness of light beyond the horizon and from the house,
too. What a giant you must have been upon this earth,
thought Sebastian, and what a giant you are now beyond it.
To leave your mark upon this house so strongly, and to shout
to me like that among the stars. Velvety shadows filled the
dark oak-panelled hall, and the staircase rose up steeply and
then divided, sweeping to right and left, so that it was
cruciform in shape. It seemed to Sebastian that the giant
stood there " with his arms outstretch'd, as he would fly ".
Aware of Ben's waiting presence, he struggled for speech.
" This place is dedicated," he said. " Damerosehay is a
great house, but this is greater."

" It was a Pilgrims' Inn for the Abbey," said Ben.
" ' Maison Dieu.' Perhaps you didn't notice, but that's
written on the old signboard. ' Herb of Grace ' above the
flowers and ' Maison Dieu ' below."

Details were slowly revealing themselves to Sebastian.
An alcove in the panelling above the branching of the staircase with a small stone figure of a deer enshrined in it.
Old oak posts beautifully carved with birds and beasts. A
wide fireplace and deep windows. Splashes of bright
colour in the shadows, made by curtains and cushions,
pictures and china and gleams of brass. And over there
to the left, the bar. He turned hastily to Ben. " You said
you'd show me the drawing-room," he said. He did not
want to have ash-trays and glasses and brass spittoons, sport-
ing prints and spotted china dogs brought to his notice.
He did not want to watch the debris of the picnic of man's
mortality spreading itself like a scum upon the surface of
what he had seen and obscuring it. More and more in
these days the paraphernalia required by bodies irritated
him. Especially that required by well-to-do bodies. All
those glasses of every sort and shape, that would soon be
stained with the disgusting dregs of every sort and kind of
drink. And all those ash-trays that would soon be loaded
with the revolting remains of so many cigarettes. What
did they want with it all? Just one of those drinks, just the

stub end of one cigarette, would have been like bread to
the starving to men he had known. Anger flared in him, and
then hatred, and he was caught in the toils again, the chaff
boiling up around him. He had exhausted himself, steeling
the boy with his own strength, and it was always when he
was most tired that the evil of his hatred attacked most
savagely. Struggling with himself, he turned his back on
the debris and looked at the clear face of the young man
who was still so much more of a child than he had any idea
of, so much more at the beginning of it all than he could
possibly know, and pity purged him of some of the hatred.

" There's the integrity of Everyman, as well as of the
artist, though inclusive of his," he said gently to Ben.
" One can express it in fewer words. Perfection of soul.
What's in the way *is* hell."

Ben smiled politely, if a little anxiously, and opened
the drawing-room door. Deeply though he reverenced
Sebastian, he did think he was a little odd. And he was
looking very peculiar just now, a queer grey colour, and
completely crackers. He suddenly found the idea of family
tea in the kitchen most attractive.

Sebastian, with his demon still not quite subdued, tried
to be only dimly aware of the beautiful drawing-room,
furnished with that expensive austerity of only a few things,
but those the loveliest and the best. He did not want to
think how much Nadine Eliot had paid for those curtains of
old brocade, nor the old glass upon the mantelpiece. Nor
the beautiful Chippendale chair upon which he had most
thankfully sat down. He suspected her of being a most
extravagant woman, but he did not want to hate. Such a
short while ago the emotion of hate had seemed such a
source of strength. The first night at Damerosehay he had
wondered if, when a man became incapable of love, he must
hate or dry up altogether. What utter nonsense! He had
panicked, he remembered, and refused to face the meaning
of his panic. Hilary had said all fear had its roots in the
fear of damnation. No wonder he had panicked. His
hatred a source of strength? What an infamous lie! It was

not the source of his strength, but the particular demon who had been appointed at this particular moment by the father of lies in a last effort to drag his soul into the pit. And he was not incapable of love. He loved. He loved Meg and her mother. He loved Lucilla. He loved the old house of Damerosehay, the marshes and the sea. He loved, already, this house and the spirit of it, and the young man who was pulling the curtains farther back from the window that faced the sunlit river, so that the light might flood in and show him the beauty of the room more clearly. He loved the beauty of it. The curtains were pale green, lined with peach colour. He and his wife had chosen curtains much like them for their house in the mountains. Lately he had been trying to follow Lucilla's advice in the matter of memory, and now he deliberately tried to remember those curtains.

Suddenly subterranean laughter filled his soul and he smiled, for he had remembered that they had been extremely expensive. He wondered how many of the poor devils of struggling musicians, whom he and Christiana had delighted to entertain in their house when they could, had hated him for the luxury of it? How irrational were men in their sin, and how often the tongues of demons must be in their cheeks. Though perhaps not, for evil was irrational, too. His own demon, for instance, had suddenly let go, unable to reason that now was the time to hold on. He had choked and fallen into Sebastian's subterranean laughter. He'd return, for demons, though irrational, had a perseverance that men would do well to imitate. But meanwhile, his arms laid along the arms of his chair, Sebastian relaxed in a sudden blessed peace, and a happiness such as he had never expected to feel again. It was never too late for a new upspringing of that fountain of freshness that Hilary had called the grace of God. The miracle had happened. He could love.

" This is one of the loveliest rooms I have ever seen," he said. " And I mean that in the literal sense of the word. It is a room to be loved."

Ben, who had been perturbed by the long silence and

stillness of the man in the chair, looked round at him and smiled. The old chap was looking more normal now, a better colour and not so crackers. In fact not crackers at all. He had never seen a man look so at peace.

"Mother is an expert on old furniture and antiques and so on," said Ben. "She's got a flair for picking up beautiful things for next to nothing. She made the curtains, and the chair-covers."

"Madame, my apologies," murmured Sebastian to himself, and his penitent glance moved round the room, paying homage to Nadine's bargains. It was halted by the picture that hung over the mantelpiece, a water-colour of a herd of red deer galloping through a village street in the moonlight, with one white deer leading them. "You painted that," he said quickly.

"Years ago," said Ben apologetically. "Before I'd learned anything. Not what could be called one of Mother's bargains."

"I have not much knowledge of painting," said Sebastian humbly and gently, as he put on his glasses to look at the picture, "only of music. But I recognise the same quality that I noticed in your water-colour of Lady Eliot's cottage and garden at sunset. You know the one I mean, in the hall at Damerosehay. It is a painting of stillness, as this of movement. I don't know how to describe the quality, but I think I should just call it the quality of awareness. 'A running that could not be seen of skipping beasts.' In this, the running of the red deer, and the white, is seen, and you make me aware of the other."

Ben could find nothing to say. His gratitude for the steeling strength, and now for this gentleness of understanding, choked him.

Sebastian went on with a cheerful change of tone, "Is it landscape that chiefly holds you captive now?"

"Just now, portraits," said Ben.

"Oils?" asked Sebastian.

"For men and women, yes," said Ben. "Developed character is a tough sort of thing, and you get the strength of it in oils. For children, miniatures. Not that I'm very good at them yet, but they suit children. You get the delicacy, the littleness, and colour is so fresh and clear on ivory."

" Did you paint Mrs. Eliot's miniature of Meg and Robin ? " ejaculated Sebastian.

" Yes," said Ben humbly. " It's rotten, I know, but David wanted it for Sally."

" I might have known," said Sebastian. " The awareness is there. It is a painting of eternal youth as well as of those particular children. But—forgive me—it is so extraordinarily good."

" I stayed with David in town one vac. and had lessons," said Ben. " He arranged it for me. John Adair, who taught me all I know otherwise, would have nothing to do with it." He grinned as he remembered John Adair's rage. " He asked me why I didn't go to a pastry-cook's and learn how to stick cherries on iced queen cakes."

Sebastian remembered how the thought of the extravagant sum David had paid to some fashionable miniature painter had infuriated him. " Sir, my apologies," he murmured to himself.

A second door opened, and Caroline stood shyly smiling at them. " I do hate to interrupt," she said, " but we've been waiting tea for ages, and now we've just started."

Sebastian hurried towards her, his hands conveying a distress that was momentarily too deep for adequate verbal expression. " My apologies ! " was all he could say.

Until now Caroline had felt scared by Sebastian, for his shabbiness and breathlessness had seemed to cast a shadow across her bright world, but now she suddenly liked him. Such concern over meal-time punctuality touched her. Though her patience gave no sign, a leathery fluffy omelette and cold scones tore her very heart. No one knew what she suffered when her works of art were kept waiting and turned cold and deflated.

" It's all right," she said hastily, slipping her hand in Sebastian's arm. It was not her habit to take the arm of more or less strange men, and she did it quite unconsciously, to reassure him. " There's nothing to sit down. I mean, I didn't make scones today, only biscuits. But Grandmother said if Ben had been talking about himself all this time you'd need your tea by now."

She flashed a sisterly glance at Ben as she tenderly piloted Sebastian towards sustenance, but Ben only grinned, and Sebastian saw with relief that in spite of his native humility he had not yet outgrown his youthful conviction that the topic of himself was interesting. That was good. The young needed to hold themselves and others to that belief until they were well established in the following of vocation. Then the sooner they were disillusioned the better.

They had passed from the drawing-room into a small passage-room panelled in dark oak. It seemed full of books and bones. A most unpleasing skeleton hung from a hook on the wall. Its skull had dropped a little sideways, as though it hung on a gallows. It was a sight so unexpected that a tremor went through Sebastian's body. After all that he had seen, such things had no power to shock his mind, but his body knew how soon he would abandon it, and, quite independently of Sebastian himself, it shivered a little. The two young things, not understanding how detached the spirit of a man can be from his body, were full of contrition. Caroline gave a motherly cry of distress and tightened her hold upon Sebastian's arm.

" Confound Tommy ! " ejaculated Ben. " He always leaves Horace about."

Sebastian noticed that below the dominant note of Tommy's occupation the little room kept a memory of the activities of others. Horace's toe-bones appeared to be executing some sort of ghoulish dance upon the cover of a sewing-machine, and odd bones were piled on top of an overturned work-basket in the corner of the room. The canvas cover of a painter's camp-stool had given way beneath a pile of surgical textbooks, and a beautiful water-colour of Brockis Island was obliterated behind Horace's back. Observing it, anger flamed in Ben's face.

" Simply takes Horace," he growled.   " Never asks."

" Horace is yours? " asked Sebastian.

" Had him for years," said Ben.   " John Adair gave him
to me."

" For your birthday, too," mourned Caroline.   Though
she liked Tommy better than Ben, her sympathy was now with
Ben.   He respected other people's property.   If he had the
misfortune to knock over her work-basket he always turned
it right way up again.

Sebastian felt for his glasses and put them on once more,
that he might admire Horace the better, but he did it with
care, so as not to disturb Caroline's hand in his arm.   He
liked the feel of her firm young fingers there.   So strong
was the current of her sympathy that it had quieted the shaking of his body.   He thought, with no envy but merely as
one ageing man congratulating another, that her father was
fortunate.   Her charm was that of her youth only.   With all
her gentleness and sympathy, she lacked the beauty and
vitality that would capture the attention of young men.
Only the discernment of the elderly would appreciate her.
From such a state of affairs fathers frequently benefited.

" I have seldom seen a finer skeleton," he said seriously.

" All the same, it's a waste of time to look at Horace,"
said Caroline.   " With tea waiting, I mean.   Tommy will
be walking the hospitals soon, and then he won't get home
much."   She sighed with naïve satisfaction and added with
further satisfaction, " And I don't suppose Ben will either,
from the F.O."

" I'm not going to the F.O.," said Ben softly but decidedly
from behind them.

Caroline looked back at him over her shoulder, startled and
dismayed, but she had already opened the farther door into the
kitchen, and the noise of Eliots at tea flowed out and over them.

2

The tea was so vocal, even though Tommy and the twins
and Mary had not yet reappeared, because George had dis-

agreed with David about something and David could be hot in argument, Robin was noisy, Mouse had a barking fit, and Hilary was enjoying Zelle's vivacity. But Lucilla did not allow the family noise to distress herself and Sebastian. Though the others sat round the large table, she remained enthroned in her chair, a small table before her, and made him sit by her on the cushioned window-seat.

"Let them all sit round a dinner-table for tea if they want to," she said. "It's done these days, I know. Either that or one of those dreadful trolleys. Either is equally uncivilised. To have one meal in the day when leaning both elbows on the table, and holding your cup in both hands while you argue, is not physically possible, taught manners. Of course I know you can't lean elbows on a trolley, but the thing rattles so. And then the dog gets underneath and heaves it up. And it reminds me of the thing the dentist has with instruments on it to probe you with. I have always disliked probing of any sort or kind."

"As we are now, with this little table and this silver teapot to ourselves, I am reminded of the afternoon tea of the old days in England," said Sebastian gently.

"Did you know England in the old days?" asked Lucilla.

"Yes, I knew her well in the years between the wars," he said.

"Those weren't the old days," said Lucilla. "Already, then, manners were decaying and noise increasing. I mean the days when you could drive through London in a victoria and smell the wet lilac in the gardens. I don't know how it is, but lilac always looks and smells dry and dusty these days, or else it's beaten to pieces in downpours. It's never shining and fragrant in sunshine after a spring shower, like it used to be."

"It's the weather that's all wrong these days," said Sebastian, smiling at her. "In the old days spring was spring and summer was summer, winter was winter and be-haved accordingly. Now the seasons are in as great con-fusion as the world, with spring warmth in December and snow in May. It never did that in the old days."

"You're laughing at me," said Lucilla, without pique.

"No, no!" declared Sebastian, in dismay at the mere idea.

"You may not have realised it, but you were," said Lucilla. "With indulgent affection for me, I'm glad to say, just as my children do. I know the look in the eyes. I am so glad you can laugh at me now. When you first came you were like Queen Victoria."

"Queen Victoria?" ejaculated Sebastian.

"You were not amused," said Lucilla. "Did you ever see Queen Victoria?"

"No, Lady Eliot, I can't say I did," said Sebastian, and this time he laughed outright. "You see, I was not born when she died."

Lucilla looked at him. "You are laughing, but I am not," she said. "You should be thankful I am not the sort of woman who cries, or the arithmetic I am doing would have me weeping. It is not as one of my children that I should be thinking of you, but as one of the grandchildren."

"Provided you count me among your family that's all that matters," he said, his usually hard, dry voice suddenly warm with the delight of the fact that he could love her, a fact that gave him much greater delight than the fact that she could care for him. With his amusement a spark of brightness struggling for existence in his usually lightless eyes, he looked round and saw the burning curiosity in hers only partly veiled by their compassion. He hastened to relieve the curiosity. "I am forty-eight," he said.

"You look sixty," she said. "I didn't probe, did I?"

"You never probe," he said. "None of you do. I am in peace among you all, and at Damerosehay. To leave you will be infinite distress."

"Then why do it?" asked Lucilla. "Were you thinking of leaving us?"

"Mr. Eliot's secretaries come and go. I can hardly have the good fortune to stay here till I die, can I?" he asked her, smiling.

" It depends how long you take about dying," said Lucilla.
" Are you wanting to die ? " she continued serenely.

" Yes," said Sebastian. " I should like to be finished
with it now."

" So should I," confided Lucilla. " Though I don't say
so to the children, for they would be hurt by my wanting to
leave them.   Except to my son Hilary, of course, who agrees
with me that I can love them just as well there as here, if
not better, and that it's natural that at ninety-one I should
have got very tired of dressing and undressing my body.
Because, you know, at ninety-one that's about all one does. By
the time you've got rested from dressing it's time to undress."

" You're not speaking the strict truth, are you ? " said
Sebastian quickly.

" No," said Lucilla, after a moment's pause.   " I am not.
I am fond of dressing and undressing, for I like clothes.
And that's not all I do. I pray. I take trips in Hilary's
car on fine days like today. I worry. I talk a great deal,
and very sententiously, as you well know. Thank you for
reminding me."

" Ah, but I was not reminding you," he said in distress.
" I was grateful for all you said to me that evening among
the rushes. I spoke without thinking. It was just that——"

" I know," said Lucilla. " As one comes near to death
strict truth seems to matter more and more. It's the awful
justice that waits for us that makes us feel that way. I said
I wanted to die. I do almost always, but not quite always.
Sometimes I feel the terror of death. The soul shrinks from
justice and the body from dissolution."

" That's justice, too," said Sebastian. " What else does
this body deserve ? It has been the garment of our selfishness."

" Yes," said Lucilla. " But I have looked sometimes at
the bodies of those I love and thought I saw an immortal
stamp upon them."

" So have I," said Sebastian. " A look or a smile.
Something. But the stamp is not the wax. Yet it's good to
get the stamp by heart, for it will make the new body of

selflessness recognisable." He paused and smiled. "I talk as if I know. How can I know? We know nothing. It's just an idea that came to me this afternoon."

"How did it come?" asked Lucilla.

"Something about your grandson's profile gave me the idea."

"David's?"

"Yes."

"Of all of them, David is my dearest," said Lucilla. "So I'm glad you—I hesitate to use the word and I don't use it lightly—love him."

Sebastian was silent, but it was with no sense of insincerity that he held his tongue. He did not examine his silence. He was not ready for that. Instead he changed the subject.

"Who is that quiet-faced woman who is pouring out tea?" he asked.

"Jill. She was the family nanny for years, and even after the twins is still the most serene woman I know."

"She is not serene just now," said Sebastian. "She appears to be counting beads, and the sum we add up to disturbs her."

"So she is," said Lucilla, and then she laughed. "Poor Jill! She believes all the superstitions, and without Tommy and the twins we are thirteen at a meal."

"I make it twelve," said Sebastian, after a pause.

"It shocks me that you should consider Mouse negligible," said Lucilla.

"I don't," cried Sebastian. "But she's under the table. On Jill's feet, I expect. It was a mere oversight."

Jill's eyes came to rest upon Lucilla and widened in distress, until Lucilla smiled at her.

"There now," said Lucilla. "She sees I don't mind."

"But it might be me," said Sebastian with almost a jealous note in his voice.

"It might," agreed Lucilla. "But I am, after all, forty-three years older than you." She laughed. "Now don't let's be jealous over such an absurdly small matter.

For what does it matter which of us goes first? What matters is that pulling up our anchors together like this we have become good friends. Except to Hilary, I have talked to no one for years as I have talked to you. . . . I think I hear Tommy and the twins safely home. And Mary."

Sebastian wondered why she said " I think " when there was no doubt at all that she heard Tommy and the twins, and Mary. Tommy set foot within his home much as Hercules must once have done, his footfall giving rhythmic stress to the thunder of his voice. The twins' voices were high and sweet, but today the sweetness was more than usually piercing. Though not more so than Mary's bark. But this time he did not accuse Lucilla of insincerity. The fault lay in the non-committal habit of mind of the English, who never dared use their fairly flexible language in any but the most gingerly fashion. " Not half-bad," they would say. It had taken him a long time to discover that they intended appreciation by the phrase. Conversation continued desultorily in the kitchen while a herd of elephants moved about upstairs, various articles of furniture being flung to the floor by the wind of their passing. A hissing sound, as of innumerable serpents in great anger, took Sebastian by surprise until he realised that taps had been turned on to their fullest capacity for purposes of cleansing. Then the herd moved downstairs by what was apparently another staircase—judging by the noise, a stone one—and entered the kitchen by another door. Though " enter," that musical and gracious word, was again an understatement. Sebastian could think of no word to describe the arrival of Tommy and the twins in a state of hunger.

" They'd been to the Buckpen and got in a filthy mess in the stream," explained Tommy, reaching for the loaf, for he disdained cut bread-and-butter as being always inadequate to his needs. " In one place it's all ooze at the bottom, and that duckweed stuff. They've washed. Jam, please. I've done nothing about Mary."

Mary had a low under-carriage, and the beautiful silky-white fur on her stomach was clotted together with sticky

mud. Duckweed adhered to her slender legs. The silvery
foam of her tail, the soft whiteness of her back and her
delicate little head rose above the black slime like Venus
from the waves. She stood imperiously upon the hearthrug,
her pugnacious whiskered countenance turned towards her
mistress, and demanded attention.

Nadine, leaving a cup of tea to get cold, knelt before
her little dog and ministered to her with a towel and soft
endearments. It astonished Sebastian to see her proud
beauty so prostrated and enslaved. He could not picture
her kneeling so to remove wet socks from her children's feet
when they'd been small. She would have sat royally
enthroned, he thought, and lifted the children to her lap.
There is a royalty, either of dynasty or temperament, that
can be humbled only by dogs and their Maker, who perhaps
made them in part for that purpose. Mouse, one speculative
eye and a quivering nose showing from beneath the table-
cloth, watched in awe. She had her underneath rubbed
with a towel herself on occasions, but not like that. She
had not yet reduced her branch of the Eliot family to such
complete subservience as she now beheld, but, then, she had
had not had the time. She was only two and Mary was
six. She took a lesson. She withdrew her speculative eye
and vanished from sight again. Under the table she looked
round at the various pairs of feet, and sniffed. But Jill being
now comforted, she could not smell distress of any kind. She
curled herself round in a soft grey button and placed her
tail over her nose. She thought that, undisturbed by the
loud crying of distracting smells, she would now meditate
quietly upon the glory she had seen.

Sebastian was meditating upon the twins. Until now
they had seemed to spin before his eyes in an almost solid
ball of noise, colour and speed, and his own shrinking from
their impact had increased the confusion he felt at the sight
of them. But now, apart from champing jaws and the rise
and fall of hands that moved from plate to mouth and back
again in a way that reminded him of the movements of small
birds, they were still, and he realised that they were unusually

beautiful children. Though obviously as physically strong
as young ponies, they were delicately made, with small
bones and a thin wiriness that would one day become their
mother's slim elegance. Their dark hair curled only a little.
José's lay over her small beautifully shaped head in soft
rings, and Jerry's, cut shorter, crisped above his fawn's ears.
Their grey eyes were bright and needle sharp, their skin so
clear and satin-smooth that it still caught and reflected
the light, like the skin of very small children, as Meg's did.
They were exactly alike, except that Jerry had more colour
in his face than José. But she had no less vitality. The air
about them seemed almost to sparkle with it, and with the
love they had for each other, the sparkle seeming to Sebastian
to make a circle of light about them, a small circle within
the larger one of family love. Now that he was himself so
miraculously able to love again he was quick to notice the
love between others. Their conscious absorption in food
was not so great as their unconscious absorption in each other.
Without looking at her, Jerry knew when José wanted the
milk, reached rudely across Caroline for the jug and banged
it down before his twin so that the milk slopped over.

"Jerry!" thundered George. "Look what you're
doing!"

"Many apologies," said Jerry, his sparkling eyes glancing
round the table with a wicked insolence that no one could
take personally because his tone dripped honey until it
dropped into the vernacular. "Wot cheer, folks. I do be
a dummle." He mopped up the milk with a very dirty
handkerchief, sneezed explosively and wiped his nose on the
back of his hand.

"Jerry!" said Nadine sharply.

"It wasn't me," said Jerry. "I was being Wilkes. Well,
folks, look see, I do be to 'ave caught a tarble cold in this
'ere clulbery weather."

"Serve you right," said Ben hotly.

"That's enough, Jerry," said Jill.

Jerry sneezed again, and this time his elbow sent the milk-
jug flying.

" Apologise to your mother," said George, the veins on his forehead swelling with anger.

" Sorry, Mother," said Jerry with no contrition whatever, and sneezed a third time as loudly as he possibly could.

José did not look at him, but her right hand and his left disappeared instantaneously beneath the table, his reappearing immediately with a dainty little handkerchief with red daisies on it. Upon this he blew his nose with that same loud trumpet-blast which punctuated Mr. Wilkes's conversation at the local.

" Young toad! " said Tommy very quietly to Jerry. " You needn't think you're going to get away with it. I'm only waiting till we're finished. I told you in the wood what would happen if you made me late for tea, and after speaking to Mother like that you'll get the best I can do."

For just a moment Jerry stopped eating. For the same fraction of time an apprehensive stillness held José. Sebastian did not actually see them lean together, but for that same moment he seemed to see them as one child. He had not been able to picture them in Knyghtwood, but he could now. Knyghtwood was their true home.

With the promise of justice the little storm was allowed to blow over, and he turned his attention to Tommy. In spite of all appearances to the contrary, was he, too, at home there? One could not tell, but he noticed that Tommy, while taking not the slightest notice of Robin, who sat beside him with mouth ajar, was practising some sleight of hand whereby the cherries in the piece of cake in front of him, though not seen to move, were nevertheless disappearing one by one. He liked Tommy the better for it. The burgeoning of spring was fresh and cool. Looking down, it surprised him to see his hands as brown and dry as ever, like dead wood. He had almost expected to find himself bursting into leaf.

" I apologise for my younger grandchildren," said Lucilla. " I don't know why it is, but it seems impossible to teach manners to the modern child. We all try, but it can't be done. Robin will be just as bad in a few years' time."

"Meg?" asked Sebastian with a smile.

"Meg," said Lucilla, making music of the little name. "Meg's not a modern child. Scarcely even a child. Nor was David at her age. Nor his father before him. Don't you think that in each generation there is some special person who is a candle lighted for the rest?"

"Yes, I do think so," said Sebastian, but he could never speak the name of his son Josef.

"'Light me a candle,'" quoted Lucilla. "Maurice died in a burning of pain. He bore it, and so did I. Something of the sort must happen to David, and I hope I am as willing as he will be. For Meg, though I shan't see it, I can't bear it, and I'm not willing." Her soft old voice stopped abruptly.

"You can and you will be," said Sebastian lightly. "Anxiety for your children is your Thing."

"Now whatever do you mean by that?" asked Lucilla, curiosity getting the better of her sudden spasm of shrinking.

"Ask your son Hilary," said Sebastian.

Their friendship, that had come so suddenly, and which they deepened now with a sense of urgency whenever they could, as though there was so much to say quickly before this particular mode of intimacy was taken from them, kept them where they were together, as though enclosed in the same sort of circle of light as held Jerry and José. But now tea was over and the two small circles dissolved and the larger one of the family enclosed them all.

"I'm going to show the Chapel to Mr. Weber," said Ben.

"No, you aren't; José and I are," shouted Jerry. "It's our Chapel. We found it."

"You'll show no one anything, Jerry, till you've had what's coming to you," said Tommy darkly.

"You won't show the Chapel to Mr. Weber," said David. "The noise you make would destroy his powers of appreciation."

José's beautiful eyes met Sebastian's and were full of pleading. If Tommy's dark purpose were postponed he might forget about it. That had been known to happen.

"If Ben will forgive me," said Sebastian unexpectedly, "I should like to be shown the Chapel by Jerry and José."

3

They were instantly beside him, standing sword-straight as their mother did. They were tall children, and their heads nearly reached to his shoulder.

"It's this way, sir," said Jerry. "Through the other kitchen." His wickedness had suddenly fallen from him and his modernity receded. His grave courtesy was charming, and in his scarlet sun-suit he looked like a boy from another age than this. He might have set on the grass among the scarlet anemones, in an Athenian spring, and heard Socrates talk, or run over the Sicilian hills when the sun was drawing up the hot scent of the mignonette. José's eyes were soft with gratitude as she smiled at Sebastian. Her face had an unexpected maturity when she smiled. In protecting Jerry from the consequences of his actions, motherhood had begun for her already.

"Your blazers are hanging on the back of the kitchen door, Jerry and José," said Jill. "Put them on before you go into the Chapel."

"Why?" demanded Jerry.

"It's not right to go into the Chapel with only sun-suits on," said Jill firmly. "Not nice at all. Your mother doesn't think it's right." She eyed Nadine with respectful firmness, and Nadine said meekly, "Jill's quite right." Nadine was not a meek woman, but Jill, who was, had, like all good nannies, considered the training of the mother as important as that of the children. Without a well-trained mother it is not possible to train the children. From her first day with Nadine and the twins Jill had begun as she meant to go on, but she had been more successful with Nadine than the twins.

" Rats! " said Jerry contemptuously, and opened the door into the further kitchen.

His tone had made Sebastian fear that the tide of modernity was coming in again, but with the door shut, and the three of them alone together in the further kitchen, he was conscious once more of the warm wind of the golden age blowing over the flowers in the grass. It is always so with normal children of eleven or so, he remembered. At one moment they are loudly self-assertive, proclaiming their rights and staking their claim in this new age in which they must fulfil themselves, and at another time there breathes from them the fresh sweet air of all the innocent and timeless beginnings. It is the timelessness of beginnings that makes their freshness, he thought. To begin again is to be born again and also to have some foretaste of the end. Down in the depths where the eternal freshness eternally springs there is no time, and creation and fulfilment are one thing.

Bringing his thoughts back to the kitchen, he realised that though they were just as much a tumbling kaleidoscope as ever, the fragments fell into pleasing patterns more often now.

" It is a beautiful kitchen," he said, looking round at the shining pots and pans, the huge scrubbed kitchen table, the gay china on the dresser, and the view of the orchard seen between the scarlet curtains at the window. The back door, set wide today, opened into a porch almost as large as a little room, with seats in it, and outside doves strutted on the cobbles of the yard.

" It's nice and bright," agreed José.

But it was the stout strength of the kitchen that had impressed Sebastian. This room had known for generations the meaning of hard work. Backs had ached here, carrying pails of water from the well, loads of wood, heavy baskets of apples and pumpkins. Women had worked early and late, washing and ironing, baking their bread and brewing their wines, worked until they had hardly had a leg to stand on. Men had dropped asleep on the settle by the fire, worn out after a long day driving the plough or cutting the corn. He was aware of past labour much as Caroline was, only in her day-dream there were no backaches, no sense of the driving obstinate force that seemed to make this room a physical power house. How surprised those men and women would have been if they had known how the stored-up energy of their bodies revitalised his own now that theirs were dust.

In the corner of the room an opened small door showed a turret staircase winding away into dimness. " It's this way and it isn't far," said José. " Not the whole way upstairs."

Two school blazers hung on the other open door, and Sebastian wordlessly indicated them with a gesture of the head and a movement of the hands which, though courteous, had authority.

" Rot," said Jerry, but without conviction.

" Would you like us to wear them? " asked José politely.

" I think that I should like you to," said Sebastian.

" O.K.," said Jerry cheerfully, and fetched them. He liked this bloke. José did, too, he knew, because she was being polite, and she was only polite to people whom she liked. She was not polite very often. She had been sent away from her first school because she had not liked the headmistress or the staff, or any of the girls. She did not like women at all, except her mother and grandmother and Jill. She now went to a co-education school with Jerry, where she liked Jerry and the headmaster, so things were better. And now she liked Sebastian, and put on her blazer with such a beautiful meekness that he had seldom felt more complimented. It was with compunction that he remembered how he had tried to avoid Jerry and José, and with horror that he remembered how a short while ago he had wanted to strike the mouth of a smiling child. Hilary had talked cheerfully about the last of the chaff. What would he have thought of such hatred of the innocent? Hatred of the haters was bad enough, a wind blowing upon flame, but hatred of the innocent was murder most foul. He had never felt so ashamed of himself.

The narrow turret stairs only allowed of ascent in single file. José went first, and Jerry brought up the rear. José went up with deliberation. "Because," she said, "though it's only twelve steps, I always take old people up very slowly. Jerry, don't hustle behind Mr. Weber."

"I wasn't hustling," said Jerry. "I was only jigging."

"Then don't jig," said José. "Put one foot on the step and bring the other slowly to it, the way Robin comes downstairs."

She did not need to do that herself. She ascended slowly and gracefully, like a tall young angel going up Jacob's ladder. Her blazer was cerulean blue. Sebastian would have been content to watch her for quite a long time, even at the cost of a stone for a pillow. Well, he had that. Shame is a hard pillow, and he would lay his head upon it every night now until he died.

José stopped at a small arched doorway and looked round at him. "It used to be a store cupboard," she said. "But one day Jerry and I pulled a bit of the wallpaper off and there were paintings underneath. And then Ben and David and old Beaver (that's Sally's father) pulled it all off, and cleaned the walls, and it was a Chapel with what they call frescoes all round."

"Sixteenth century, and painted by the old monk who was Mine Host here then," said Jerry, pleased to air his knowledge. "So Ben says," he added. "But the way he works things out never makes sense to me."

"It wouldn't," said José, opening the door. "You can't make sense unless you have it, Tommy says. Don't fall over the step, Mr. Weber. And don't let it take you too much by surprise."

"The chairs were put there for people to be struck crackers on," said Jerry.

Sebastian sat on the nearest chair.

The small room was octagonal in shape, with narrow lancet windows. There was a plain oak table for an altar, with branched candlesticks upon it and pots full of summer flowers, and all round the walls the artist had painted the

story of St. Eustace. Only it was not that wood outside
Rome where the great noble went hunting that was painted
on the walls, but one of the deep old woods of England.   The
flowers and trees, the birds and beasts upon the wall, were
those of Knyghtwood, the lovers' wood.   Each had been
painted with a passionate delight in the unity of its creation,
and yet not one of the creatures—and Sebastian's mind used
the word creature in the sense of a created thing—but was
subordinated to the whole creation.   Each, though a world
in itself, lay as humbly in its place as Jacob had when he lay
with his head on his stone looking up to heaven.   Only
these had no stone, for they had reached their perfection.
Bright and gay, they made each its patch of beauty in its
place, and yet, though stillness held them, their colours
seemed all fused together in the white light of the figure of the
great stag over the altar, its branching antlers twisting
themselves into the form of a crucifix held in a thorn tree.
Eustace, with his dogs and his hunting-horn, rode through
the wood, royally dressed, like the twins, in scarlet and
sky-blue. But he was not perfected. He had only just
reined in his galloping horse, and the whole group, man
and horse and dogs, was tense and quivering with checked
speed.   Eustace, one arm raised to shield his eyes from the
blinding light, leaned from his saddle as though he were
about to fling himself out of it.   In another moment he would
be kneeling before the white stag, waiting for the words that
all men find they know by heart the moment they are
spoken. "Why dost thou attempt to injure me? I am
Jesus Christ."

How Europe loved the story! Sebastian wondered how
many representations of it he had seen, sublimely pictured
in great churches at Canterbury, Abbeville and Paris,
humbly pictured in the carvings and paintings of peasant
craftsmen in Bavaria and Austria. He had had a wooden
box on his study table in the house in the mountains, with a
crude picture of the stag and the kneeling man painted upon
it by a man in the village. Reading music, correcting a score,
he had often picked it up and held it in his hands, amused

by the crudity and yet touched by the devotion of the kneeling figure. The children had loved to play with the box, and he had told them the story a hundred times. Yet he had never seen it portrayed as movingly as here.

Or else he had not until now reached the point in his own journey through the wood when he heard the words spoken to himself. He did now. He saw every thought of hatred that had ever formed in his mind as an arrow in the body of that stag, and saw the body quivering. Yet the worse the pain the more brilliantly the light shone. Though it was day in the wood, it was night behind the stag, and as with the flight of each arrow the darkness deepened, so the light increased. No wonder Saul of Tarsus had been blinded by it. Eustace the hunter had galloped all day in the wood, and when at last the chase was over and the creature turned at bay, it was seen to be one with the Creator and Redeemer of all creatures. Men defaced in the creatures the beauty and love they longed for and did not know what they were doing. It was the most dreadful fact in the world, and to know it at last not with the mind only, but with this piercing personal knowledge, was neither pleasant nor easy. Why was the knowledge so long in coming and yet so familiar when it came? That was another of the mysteries. There were so many mysteries, and yet they were all one mystery. He put his head in his hands and abandoned himself to it. That was all he could do. He might be entirely cleansed of hatred while he yet lived in this world, or he might not. He could not know. Cleansed of it at last he must be, now that he knew what he knew. Meanwhile the silence comforted him, and time so old " it hath forgot itself " washed with oblivion over his head.

The twins, sitting behind Sebastian at the back of the Chapel, were in no way disturbed by the time he was taking coming round from being struck. They were used to showing visitors the Chapel, and used to the oddness of their behaviour when shown it. There were, of course, degrees of struckness. Some were only mildly struck, some so mildly that they had got over it before they knew they had

been. Others were bad cases. Mr. Weber was the worst
case they had seen yet, but that was only to be expected
because he was a foreigner, and foreigners always seemed to
take what they took a great deal worse than the English took
it.   There were several foreigners at their school, and they
were observant children. The smooth marble hardness
which they shared with Tommy was due not to lack of
observation, but to not worrying about what they observed.
It slid off them.   So now Mr. Weber slid off them, and they
were pleased to find that there were bull's-eyes in José's
blazer pocket.   They had thought they had finished the
ration, and it was a pleasure to find themselves mistaken.
José wrenched the bull's-eyes off the lining of the pocket,
removed from them the traces of fishing-bait that had been in
her pocket before the bull's-eyes, and they sucked happily.

They were always happy in the Chapel.   When they had
first come to live at The Herb of Grace, and the Chapel had
been only the storeroom, they had known it was the most
important part of the house.   It was right deep in, just as the
Buckpen in Knyghtwood was right deep in.   José thought
sometimes that if the kitchen below made one feel like a car
that's just been filled up with petrol, the Chapel made one
feel like the same car coming out of the garage into air and
light.   Coming from one to the other, first you felt you could
go, and then you felt there was somewhere to go to.   She
had peculiar ideas sometimes, but did not mention them to
anybody.   She was sure no one else in the family had peculiar
ideas.   She was unique, she feared, but she did not worry
about it.

Sebastian was recalled to consciousness of his whereabouts
by a penetrating smell of peppermint.   For how long had he
been absent, he wondered?   An hour or five minutes?   He
turned round in his chair and looked anxiously at the twins,
but with cheeks pleasantly distended and legs swinging
happily, it seemed that for them, too, time had forgotten
itself.   With their round bright eyes narrowed to sleepy
slits, and that distension across the cheekbones caused by a
peppermint in each cheek, they had now a distinctly

Mongolian appearance. They might have been lamas in the making. Undoubtedly young celestials of some sort.

" Shall we go now? " he asked them humbly. " I am in your hands, of course, but I think that it may be getting late."

Their eyes returned to the normal shape and they crunched loudly, the Mongolian appearance slipping from their faces as they did so.

" If you like," said José when she could speak. " I did hear people calling, but Jerry and I don't usually bother when people call. It wastes our time."

Sebastian got up quickly. " Then we must go," he said. " Not to go when people call wastes their time, surely."

" We don't let that worry us," said Jerry. " They should mind their own business."

Sebastian led the way out hastily. The crunching, and the turn the conversation had taken, seemed to him equally unsuitable to the Chapel. He did not even look back as he shut the door behind him, for had he done so the glory on the walls might have seemed to him no more than rather crudely painted medieval frescoes. He wanted now to leave the wood quickly with the treasure he believed he had found in it, for if the wood ceased to be a wood, the treasure might seem to cease to be a treasure. Only seem, for he had it.

4

They went downstairs, and found it was long past Meg's bed-time, and the hour when Lucilla had promised Margaret she would be home.

" What does it matter? " said Lucilla placidly. " Margaret will fuss; but, then, she likes to fuss. Sally won't, for I understand that Mrs. Wilkes is with her. I am so glad, Mr. Weber, that you have met Mrs. Wilkes."

Sebastian smiled, accepted her rebuke and tried to calm the agitation he was now feeling. The surge of colour and noise that was a family departure rose like a wave, but this time he was not breasting it, but being lifted by it, and was deposited in the car before he knew where he was. Speeding up the lane, he discovered that both children were behind with Zelle and he was sitting beside David. He settled back in his seat with a movement of relaxation that so surprised David that he looked round at him in astonishment, and met the smile of an equal. He looked straight in front of him again with an absurdly pounding heart. That sense of equality between two men was one of the treasures of life. Bitterness could not live with it, nor envy, nor patronage. He, too, settled back in his seat, and Sebastian realised, to his relief, that David was not going to let loose upon him the brilliance of his conversation. They were going to drive back in pure silence, enjoying the view.

5

" Hilary," said Lucilla to her eldest son as they followed in the vicarage car, " this has been an eventful day."

" Has it? " said Hilary. " I hadn't noticed anything particular about it."

" You don't notice much, dear," said Lucilla.

" Don't I? " asked Hilary. " I notice when you are looking particularly beautiful. It's what I've noticed particularly about today."

" Don't be so idiotic, Hilary! " said Lucilla with irritation. " I am ninety-one and you are seventy-two, and we should be thought ridiculous if some of the remarks you make at times were overheard by others."

" They never are," said Hilary. " It's that hat. It's a new one."

Lucilla gazed at him in astonishment, for it was. " I won't say again, dear, that you don't notice things," she said. " I believe you do, only you won't own to it."

" I always think that perhaps I've noticed wrong," said Hilary.

" I never think that," said Lucilla. " I'm always quite sure I've noticed right. But, then, I'm afraid I'm not even now, at ninety-one, after all my struggling, what you'd call a really humble woman. What should you say you'd noticed today? "

" A look of resolution about Ben, as though he'd decided to stand on his own feet. A look of emergence about Sebastian Weber. A something about Tommy that has made me like him better than I did. A look about David, as though he were beginning to see what an ass he is."

" Hilary, how dare you! " flashed Lucilla.

Hilary laughed. " And, oh yes, I think you'll soon have to persuade Nadine that Ben's marriage to that sensible girl Zelle will be of the very greatest assistance to his artistic career."

" Now, Hilary, there you are being quite silly," said Lucilla. " I've never known Ben take the slightest interest in girls."

" A man must begin sometime," said Hilary.

" You never did," said Lucilla.

" You ruined me for other women," said Hilary, and put his free arm along the back of her seat.

" Have it your own way, then, dear," said Lucilla. " I'm only glad there's no one here to see."

6

" Glad to see 'em come," said George, once more in the bosom of his immediate family only. " And glad to see 'em go."

" *Now*, then, Jerry, you come along indoors," said Tommy.

Nadine and José went hastily round the corner of the house together, to absorb themselves in picking flowers. Ben went to mess about with a boat. George and Caroline found themselves alone on the steps, looking across to Knyghtwood. The sunlight lay level now, and there seemed to be a thousand candles lighted in the wood. George looked at it, and then absorbed himself in lighting his pipe. He blew out the match and looked at Caroline.

" Shall we take a stroll, Elf? "

That had been his name for her when she was small.
He only used it now when they were alone together. She
laughed and tucked her hand into his arm. He thought how
slim and strong her fingers were. They strolled across the
lane together and went into the wood. The rest of the family
thought they had no special place, but as a matter of fact
they had.

CHAPTER XIV

WHEN it was Meg's bedtime, and no one had come home yet, Mrs. Wilkes took off her apron, set her great bulk patiently in motion and went out to the secret garden, where Sally was sitting with her knitting.

" Don't worry, ducks," she advised. " I will say for Mr. Eliot 'e drives careful with the children. 'E 'as 'is faults—all men 'as—but I will say for 'im 'e's a good father. All ain't."

" Sit down, Mrs. Wilkes," said Sally, indicating the basket-chair that had been put ready beside her, waiting for David when he should come back again.

Mrs. Wilkes sat. It was an undertaking. When she was at last down in the chair, with her hands resting on her knees, a sigh escaped her, a sigh so small that it might have been breathed by Meg as she dropped off to sleep, so weary and yet so satisfied that it might have been that of a released soul escaping into paradise. It shocked Sally, and she dropped a stitch. Did Mrs. Wilkes never sit down? To eat, of course, but that was no rest to a woman whose mind during the first course was with the pudding in the oven, and during the second course was already shrinking from the thought of washing up. Never like this, in a hidden garden with sun and shade playing about her, in a stillness with no sound to break it but the distant murmur of a quiet sea.

Though Mrs. Wilkes was not what most people would have called a beautiful woman, she did not look out of place in David's chair in the lovely garden. She had her own beauty, of endurance and rock-like patience, and it suited the old garden that had been so patient through so many winters. Looking up at the leaf-heavy branches over her head, moving now as peacefully as the sea, Sally remembered them stark and bare, bending and lashing in a gale. The wind might seem cruel, but, twisting and bending them, it kept them elastic and supple for the spring. Static though she looked just now, there was somehow an astonishing suggestion of suppleness about Mrs. Wilkes. David's graceful length, flung back possessively in his own chair in his own garden, would have looked as though flung there for life until his restlessness up-ended him again. Mrs. Wilkes, never restless, nevertheless sat upright, staking no claim even on rest, in complete readiness to do something else at any moment should it be required of her.

" What's for supper, ducks? " she asked.

" Nothing that needs cooking," said Sally firmly. " The tinned chicken soup that Mr. Eliot brought from America. That tinned stew that Mr. Eliot brought from America. The tinned fruit salad that Mr. Eliot brought from America."

" 'E's a good 'usband," said Mrs. Wilkes in a sudden rush of gratitude. " So far as we knows," she added, for she did not believe in having too rash a confidence in the goodness of human nature, especially masculine human nature.

" A perfect husband," said Sally softly, and dropped another stitch.

" Now, that you *can't* say, ducks," said Mrs. Wilkes. " And didn't ought to say. Indeed, to my mind it's tempting providence for a woman to boast about 'er man until she 's buried 'im. For getting on in life don't make 'em settle down to be'ave theirselves, like it do a woman. There's Wilkes, now, turned sixty and making eyes at that hussy at the Rising Sun over to Radford. ' Wilkes,' I says to 'im, ' if you was to take a look at yourself in the glass now and again you wouldn't act so silly.' 'And me that knitting, ducks. That's two stitches dropped."

Sally handed over the knitting and leaned back in her chair, pushing her heavy hair back from her forehead with both hands. Under it Mrs. Wilkes's observant eye could see the beads of sweat on her forehead. She had lost her pretty colour.

" Not much longer now, ducks," she said bracingly.

" I wish I could have Christopher at home," said Sally.

" 'Ave 'im at 'ome," said Mrs. Wilkes.

" My babies are so difficult," said Sally. " Dr. Barnes
says that he wants me always to have them in hospital."

" Easier for 'im," said Mrs. Wilkes drily. " Just across
the road from 'is place."

" And Mr. Eliot doesn't worry about me so much if I'm
in hospital," said Sally.

" That's natural," said Mrs. Wilkes. " 'E don't know it's
'appening till it's 'appened. But worry don't kill a man.
Does most on 'em a power o' good."

" I think I mightn't be so frightened if I had them at
home," murmured Sally. " Somehow one is never so afraid
of things in one's own home." She was leaning back in her
chair with her eyes shut, relaxed in that happy sense of
security that Mrs. Wilkes's presence (when Mrs. Wilkes was
not annoyed) always gave her. She scarcely realised that
she had spoken until Mrs. Wilkes said in astonishment,
" Frightened, ducks? "

"Weren't you ever frightened, Mrs. Wilkes? " asked
Sally.

" No," said Mrs. Wilkes. " 'Tis nature."

" So are thunderstorms," said Sally. " And dying."

" I'd 'ave given you credit for more sense than to be
a-feared of a thunderstorm," said Mrs. Wilkes. " And as for
dying, what's to be is to be, and I 'aven't seen one yet that
wasn't glad of it when the time came." Then she looked at
Sally and said slowly, voicing at last a thought that had
long lain unexpressed in her mind, " Seemingly folks must
always be in trouble or they ain't easy in their minds. The
poor, they've their worries ready made for 'em, an' don't
'ave to go worryin' around to find somethink to worry over,
but folks like you and Mr. Eliot, you 'ave to find somethink.
What 'e's worryin' over I couldn't say, I'm sure, but 'e's
lost weight considerable. And as for you, ducks, if you
didn't 'ave the little dears, well, that would be somethink
to worry about an' no mistake. It ain't easy to 'old a man
without children. A man don't like to die without 'e leaves
a living son be'ind 'im. 'E ain't beaten then. Think a lot
of theirselves, men do."

" So do women," said Sally. " I think, as a general rule, that men have more humility than women."

Mrs. Wilkes snorted slightly. She did not belong to the school of thought that believes in allowing points to the enemy. Gladly though she cared for the comfort of the men dependent on her for it, yet they were still to her, obscurely, the enemy. Whenever, painfully spelling out the difficult words in the Wilkes family Bible, she came upon the command, " Love your enemies," she thought immediately, and with deep tenderness, of Wilkes. She did not analyse the paradox of her love and her enmity; though she could never read how God made Eve from Adam's rib without having to smother a feeling that the Lord should have known better. Asking for trouble, it was, for it almost gave the fellow the right to knock her about. Yet she got her own back, for his son, without whom he did not want to die, came from her body. Getting your own back made you feel very tender-like. Poor old Wilkes!

" I'm ashamed of being afraid, Mrs. Wilkes," said Sally.

" And I'm surprised at it," agreed Mrs. Wilkes.

" But not so ashamed of that as of something else," said Sally, and she sat up and the colour flowed over her blanched face.

Mrs. Wilkes stopped knitting in an ecstasy of curiosity. " What, ducks? "

" Of being the sort of person who has to find something to worry about—when you are not."

Sally lay back in her chair, and exquisite relief came to her. She had got it out. Her life-long sorrow for profound good fortune was expressed at last, on behalf of all women who had much to all women who had little. Mrs. Wilkes, mastering her disappointment, thought out Sally's statement. It took her a long time, but she did it, and, having done it, her native shrewdness carried her farther. " The Lord has let you make amends, ducks," she said.

This time it was Sally who did not understand. " How? " she asked.

"With the fear," said Mrs. Wilkes. "Thunderstorms even. Well, I never!"

A flash of insight gave Sally the understanding of herself that she had been feeling for on the day that David had come home. Her shame had been so deep it had been prayer, and pain and the fear of it had been the answer. For a moment of complete acceptance she suddenly and most deeply rejoiced in them. Such rejoicing could not last, or they would not last, but the acceptance could.

"I'll have Christopher at home," she said. "Not to escape being afraid, for perhaps I'll be just as afraid, but so that I can be with you, Mrs. Wilkes."

She wanted to feel closer to Mrs. Wilkes. Going through this together, they would reach down to the common experience of all women everywhere. There was a queer sort of wonder in the thought.

Mrs. Wilkes glowed. She mistrusted that hospital at Radford more than words could say. Proper death-trap it was. "I've lost count of the babies I've brought into this world, ducks," she said. "And never lost one."

"We'll have to have the district nurse, too," said Sally. "It's not allowed now without."

"She's a good girl," said Mrs. Wilkes. "Does what I tell 'er. Dr. Barnes, too, 'e knows me. But with any luck they'll both arrive too late."

"Mr. Eliot won't like it," said Sally.

"It's not 'im what's 'avin' the baby," said Mrs. Wilkes.

"No, but I like to do what he likes me to do," said Sally.

"That's where you make your mistake, ducks," said Mrs. Wilkes. "Plain selfishness, that is. No argument, that's what you like. But a bit 'o plain speakin' now and again can 'old a man. Once let a man think 'e can do no wrong and 'e'll do it."

"And so will a woman," Sally reminded her.

Mrs. Wilkes snorted again. In war, self-criticism by the weaker side is no aid to victory.

Sally was silent, her thoughts drifting back to where they

had been before Mrs. Wilkes come out to her, to that place in Knyghtwood where the stream ran over the bright stones among the bog-myrtle bushes. She would never forget the day when, walking alone through the wood, she had found David there, and, deceived by the dazzling light, had seen him not as himself, but as a huntsman on a white horse, seeing what she could not see, intent upon some search that she could not understand. Alone here she had remembered it so vividly that it had been like re-living the experience again. And now, remembering the remembering, she thought that " deceived " was the wrong word. Perhaps the light had not deceived her, but shown her something beyond the outward facts of place and person that was truer than either. Knyghtwood and David, the leaves and branches and water of a wood and the flesh of a man, were not eternal, but the huntsman and his habitation were. How dear was this earth, its beauty the rumour of a habitation that could not be seen, and how dear the body of the man whose touch and look and word could tell her so little of what he really was. Yet it was the rumour that mattered. It was the so little that mattered. It was the moments of light that mattered; though afterwards one might wonder if one had only imagined them.

Had it happened that the so little that she knew of David had been with her in the garden before Mrs. Wilkes came? They had seemed to be here together, enclosed in a moment of quietness. It had been like that when they stood before Hilary to be married. She had been shaking so much when her father, grimly determined, marched her up the aisle, that he had whispered savagely into his red beard, " Pull yourself together, girl, can't you?" And then David, standing beside her, had touched her hand lightly, and she had stopped shaking and stood with him in a quietness that had put everyone else at a vast distance. That to her had seemed the moment of their marriage. When later he had made his vows, they had seemed a rather wordy reiteration of something he had already said. She had felt that touch again, and yet it had not been on her body that she had felt it. All imagination, perhaps, and yet she had never felt so close to him, or so willing to know so little about him. What mattered between them was not her knowledge of him, but their quietness. Mrs. Wilkes was wrong about plain speaking. It might hold Wilkes, but it wouldn't hold David. You couldn't lay down laws about marriage, because no one marriage was like any other, any more than one person was like another. Each was a world in itself, folded about its particular treasure. That horrible anonymous letter, telling her of David's love for a woman in America, had caused her almost unbelievable misery. But she had told no one, burnt it promptly and accepted the fact that successful people had many such letters from those who had been embittered by misfortune. And she had accepted, too, the fact that she could never know if the accusation was true or false. For she would never ask David. To let questions and arguments break in upon their marriage would be to destroy their particular treasure of quietness.

"There's the car, ducks," said Mrs. Wilkes, heaving herself to her feet. "I'll get Mr. Weber a cupper tea and see 'e 'as a nice lay down."

"I don't believe he really likes tea, Mrs. Wilkes," suggested Sally. "I think he likes coffee better."

"Too 'eavy on the stomach," said Mrs. Wilkes firmly. "And 'e likes what I give 'im. . . . 'E'd better," she added darkly as she set herself patiently in motion.

Sally smiled. Watching her exit from the garden, she could guess what peace Sebastian found in complete subservience to Mrs. Wilkes. When you were too tired to know which end of yourself you were standing on, it was heaven to be told just exactly what you had to do next.

David, Zelle and the children came into the garden, and there was pandemonium for a while, and then Zelle took the children to bed. David dropped into Mrs. Wilkes's chair and lay there smoking as though he never meant to move again. Sally's heart beat hard with her longing to ask him if while he had been in Knyghtwood he had made a vow. But she did not ask him. One did not try to prove the reality of the moments of light. That, in its lesser degree, would be like tempting God. They sat together, and talked a little of trivial things, and listened to the breathing of the sea for longer than they knew, until the supper-bell rang.

" Damn," said David.

But Sally was immediately on her feet, remembering the red-haired hussy over at Radford. " Mrs. Wilkes must get back to Mr. Wilkes," she said firmly. " Get up, David."

He got up and stood beside her and gently touched her hand. She did not know she was crying until she tasted the salt on her lips. They both immediately forgot the supper-bell. David patiently threw away his cigarette and put his hand in her arm.

" Unstuck again," he said. " Just Christopher? "

" No," she said. " It was just that I was thinking that between us it always seems to be little things that matter most. It means more to me when you touch me like that than when you kiss me. When we were first married, when you used to make love to me, it did not always seem very real."

David was silent. She was quite right. He had tried very hard, in the early days, to give his young wife the sort of love to which he thought she had the right, but it had not always been very real. What was real? His passion for Anne had seemed very real at the time, but now it had vanished like mist drawn up by the sun. The only real thing about it now was the shame it had left behind. He remembered he had said to Lucilla that he felt he possessed of Sally and Meg only the part of them that belonged to this world. That was no one's fault but his own. All his life he had let himself be caught and battered by the whirlwind and the storm, and the stillness of eternity was not in either.

" You're not vexed, David, are you? " asked Sally. " Why I should cry over such a small thing as you touching my hand I can't imagine."

He tightened his hold on her arm. " Because it wasn't a small thing," he said. " I mean, it was one of those still, small things that matter. Passions and emotions and successes, what a noise they all make! What's war but the noise of broken promises? And then just death and misery and a foul stink." He pulled himself up. "I'm sorry, Sally. What's my talk most of the time but the same sort of noisy selfishness? I could cut my tongue out sometimes after some of the things I've said. I wish I could cut out of my life some of the things I've done. Come on, darling, let's go in. I am wandering from the point. I have forgotten now what it was."

"That you touched my hand," said Sally, as they went slowly through the garden, breathing in the freshness of the dusk. "David," she said breathlessly as he shut the gate by the guelder rose bush, "would you mind very much if I had this baby at Damerosehay?"

"I think it would be a very suitable place," said David unexpectedly. "Have him in Grandmother's four-poster. And when the horrid business is over you can lie there in state, dressed in lace and whatnot, like a medieval queen, and the infant can be bathed in the big silver rose-bowl from downstairs."

"Don't be ridiculous," said Sally.

"I'm not being ridiculous," said David. "This is going to be a very important baby."

"More dear than Meg and Robin?" wondered Sally.

"Not more dear," said David. "Not such a candle lit for the family as Meg is and will be, but more important."

"Do you mean Christopher is going to be a great man?" asked Sally, holding like a child to his arm in her wonder.

"Something tells me he will startle the world," David teased her. "You are calling him after Christopher Martin, aren't you? He was a great man, though he lacked opportunity to startle the world. Our Christopher will do that for him."

"David, I believe you are looking forward to this baby," said Sally.

"Of course I am," David lied glibly. "Though, mind you, Sally, this must be the last."

" One more little girl," pleaded Sally. " For you when Meg goes to school."

" Oh, Lord! " groaned David. " Don't let's think of that until you have quite forgotten having Christopher."

Sally smiled and said nothing. Men always thought that women forgot about the pain of child-birth. Even Christ had thought that they did. And no woman ever undeceived them.

Mrs. Wilkes, in a state of self-control, appeared at the garden door and rang the bell again.

" Did you ring before, Mrs. Wilkes? " asked Sally anxiously.

" I did, Madam," said Mrs. Wilkes. " And you 'eard it, too, or you'd still be where you was."

CHAPTER XV

I

IT was already October, and the leaves were turning. The nut-trees that bordered one side of Lavender Cottage garden were pale gold and the virginia creeper was on fire all over the little house. It was mellow and warm, much warmer that it had been in August, and Lucilla one Saturday morning was sitting on the lawn, swathed in rugs and shawls against an autumn chill that existed only in Margaret's imagination. She was much too hot, but, for fear of hurting Margaret's feelings, would be able to remove nothing until Margaret went down the village to the Shop to buy the mouse-trap and the slug-death. There was only one shop in Big Village, and it sold nearly everything.

"There's nothing else you want, Mother?" asked Margaret from an open window behind her.

"I don't think I actually *want* either a mouse-trap or slug-death, dear," said Lucilla, striving for accuracy. "But you said they were needed. A house and garden always seem to need so much to which one is not personally attracted." Then she racked her brains, for the longer Margaret was away the more freedom she would have from hotting-up like a compost heap in this blazing sun. "I think I do want some sweets for the children, and some little gold safety-pins and a five-shilling book of stamps."

"Stamps?" said Margaret. "That means the post-office, and I'll have to go right down to Little Village."

"Would you mind, dear?" asked Lucilla. "It's a lovely morning for a walk. And you could look in at Damerose-hay and see how Sally and Mr. Weber and all of them are."

"You'll be alone so long," said Margaret anxiously.

Alone. It was a state for which Lucilla sometimes panted even as the hart for the water-brooks, for she found Margaret's anxious love almost as suffocating as too many

239

shawls, but she had not been so well lately, and Margaret did not permit her to achieve it if she could help it. Lucilla chose her words with the utmost care, for it is not easy to combine getting your own way with perfect charity and absolute rectitude. To say she wanted to be alone would hurt Margaret. To say she was sure Hilary would be looking in this morning was not the strict truth.

" I like it when you come back and tell me things," she said.

" There's plenty to tell after just going to the Shop," said Margaret. And she spoke the truth, for Mrs. Enticknapp at the Shop had many most enjoyable ailments and wonderful descriptive powers.

" But not about Damerosehay," said Lucilla.

" I could ring up," said Margaret.

" So unsatisfactory," said Lucilla. " You don't *see* how they are, only hear how they want you to think they are."

" It's not right for you to be alone so long," said Margaret.

" It's bad for me to worry," said Lucilla.

" I'll go to Damerosehay this afternoon, when Mrs. Digley is here," said Margaret. " She can sit with you while she cleans the silver. Now I come to think of it, I can get the mouse-trap and slug-death then too, and I need not go out at all this morning. I'll put the pudding in the oven and then come out with you. I won't be five minutes."

" You are so thoughtful, dear," said Lucilla gently.

Five minutes. She had five minutes. But it would have been fifteen if Margaret had gone to the Shop. Well, it was her own fault. Striving, in her greed, for a little more, she had lost the little she might have had. She tried to make an act of acceptance ; of this hotting-up like a compost heap under too many shawls, of not being allowed to be alone, of being too much loved, of being ninety-one, of not getting her own way. She made it and loosened the shawls a little, so that some air could blow in. Then she tightened them again, for to admit air was not perfectly to accept the compost heap. In the few minutes that remained to her she would try to make of her discomfort what Jacob must have made of his when he laid his head on a stone for a pillow. It should be her resting-place while she made a Jacob's ladder of the beauty about her. The attempt to do this was one of her favourite recreations now, as it must have been of Saint Augustine. " Our soul riseth out of its mortal weariness unto Thee, helped upward by the things Thou hast made." She could take them one by one, each a rung in the ladder, and mount. At least she *could*, and Saint Augustine doubtless did, but unfortunately human interruption or the deflection of her own wandering thoughts invariably prevented her from doing much more than meaning to mount. Resolutely she decided to regard the asters and michaelmas daisies in the border with that profound astonishment and deep thankfulness that would lift her soul upon the first rung.

She remembered that she had always liked all the different kinds of daisies the best of all the flowers. The lilies and roses of martyrdom were all very well for those great ones who were willing to pay the price of the crown. Personally, she was not quite sure that she was, and had always retired before them with a modest grace. They were glorious flowers, but their scent was a bit heady and strong for the groundlings. But the scents of camomile daisies and field marguerites, michaelmas daisies, asters and hardy garden chrysanthemums, and, best of all, of the small daisies in the grass when the sun was hot upon them, were all refreshing pungent homely scents that reminded her of the good and honest daily living of the country life about her. She could not see the flowers in the borders very well but memory supplied what her failing sight denied her, reminding her how sturdily the michaelmas daisies grew, nothing limp about them, and how small were the individual stars that massed their perfect small worlds together to make the glory of each firmament.

Meg had always called the stars " daisies in the sky ", rather than candles, as her father had done. David as a child had always been intensely concerned with light, sunlight and moonlight and candle-light, and had dreaded darkness; he still liked bright lights and hated sitting in the dark. Meg did not seem to have this adoration of light. For her as yet it was not the light in itself that she loved but what it showed her. The love of the light would come later, and meanwhile she loved what it showed her as David had never been able to do. Perhaps if he had he would have been less centred upon himself and the way would not now stretch before him quite so stonily.

Now where had she got to? Not upon the first rung at all, only to David and Meg and worrying about the family, as usual. The gate clicked and Hilary came in, his pipe in his mouth and crumpled sheets of paper sticking untidily out of his pocket. He did sometimes come and sit with her while he prepared his Sunday sermons, and she sighed with relief at the sight of him, for Margaret would now go out and she could be alone or not just as she wished. For Hilary, preparing his sermons, did not speak unless he had to, and she could take off all her shawls (she had forgotten now that she had made an act of acceptance of being too hot) without him noticing and plunge herself in meditation up to the neck without his being in the least affronted. He would not even be aware of what she was doing. Or so she thought.

" Tell Margaret," she said to him.

" I've seen him," came Margaret's voice. " Since he's here, I'll go to the Shop."

" And on to Damerosehay," said Lucilla firmly.

" Are you worried about them there? " asked Hilary, lowering his bulk carefully into the chair beside Lucilla.

" Sally and Mr. Weber are for some reason in my mind," said Lucilla. " And it would be nice," she added, raising her voice, " if Meg and Robin could come and have tea with me this afternoon."

" I'll suggest it," said Margaret, coming out of the house.

" Command it," said Hilary.

" Very well," said Margaret meekly, and departed carrying a basket and wearing a very battered felt hat.

" Such a dreadful hat of dear Margaret's! " mourned Lucilla.

" Very good women always wear hats like that," said Hilary cheerfully.   " It's almost a uniform hat."

" I'm surprised at your noticing, dear," said Lucilla.

" I always notice uniforms," said Hilary.   " They interest me."

" Should you say I was a very good woman? " asked Lucilla.

" I don't know, Mother," said Hilary.   " The evidence of your hats is all against it, but no one can judge of the spiritual state of another."

" I'm very worried about David's spiritual state," said Lucilla.

" Are you? " asked Hilary.   " I'm not. Would you mind, Mother, if I got these sermons by heart? It's Saturday and I'm a bit late with them."

" I don't want to say anything, dear," said Lucilla.   " I was so glad when I saw you coming to talk to me, because then I knew I was sure of a silent morning. I like to meditate."

Hilary polished his glasses and absorbed himself in his crumpled papers.

" I do think it's disgraceful that after all these years as a priest you still have to learn your sermons by heart," said Lucilla.   " Other clergy whom one knows rely upon notes and the inspiration of the moment."

" And look how they go on," said Hilary, laying down his sermon.   " My parishioners know they can rely on me for fifteen minutes in the morning and twenty in the evening, and not a moment longer. Then they know exactly at what time they will be home to put the Sunday tart in the oven, or the macaroni cheese, if it's Evensong. That's why they come to church. What are you meditating *on*, Mother? "

" The beauty of nature," said Lucilla.   " Trying to let it lift me up out of my mortal weariness to where refreshment is and strength unfailing, like Saint Augustine said."

" Did he? " said Hilary.   " I didn't know you read Saint Augustine."

" You told me to," said Lucilla.   " After Maurice died."

" I'd forgotten," said Hilary.   " It is so very long ago," he added slowly.

" That shows you are not really old yet, Hilary.   If you were it would seem like yesterday."

" Why did I want you to read Saint Augustine? " wondered Hilary.   " Because of the window at Ostia, I expect. Did it help you at all? "

" Not in the least," said Lucilla.   " Nothing that people give you to help you ever does help you.   At least, not at the time.   It's generally the unexpected that helps.   With me, then, it was the shadow of a bird's wing on a blind.   Such a little thing, but perhaps God thought it more suited to my intelligence at the moment than Saint Augustine.   You've always over-rated my intelligence.   God never has."

" Should you be taking all those shawls off? " asked Hilary unexpectedly.

" Yes, I should," said Lucilla with asperity.   " And if you had been attending to your sermon, instead of talking to me when I want to meditate, you wouldn't have seen what I was doing."

Hilary re-lit his pipe and returned to his sermon.   Lucilla decided it was no good thinking any more about the michaelmas daisies, because somehow they brought her round to worrying about David, and she lifted her eyes a little higher, to the glory of the nut trees.   The poets compared spring to childhood, but the colours of spring had not the simplicity of those of autumn, and the noisy and complicated exuberance of spring was more that of a young man in his prime than of a child.   But the sunny quietness of this day was very like Meg, and the pale gold of those leaves against the blue of the sky made her think of David's hair and eyes when he had been little.

" Why are you not worried about his spiritual state? " she asked Hilary.

"Whose?" asked Hilary, detaching his mind with difficulty.

"Don't be so vague, dear," said Lucilla. "You ought to concentrate more. Surely you remember who we were talking about?"

"Saint Augustine," said Hilary. "And if ever there was a man about whose spiritual state I do not feel called upon to worry, it's Saint Augustine."

"Saint Augustine was simply by the way," said Lucilla. "It's David we are really talking about. He's not himself, Hilary, and if you're not worried you ought to be."

"He's a new self since he came back from the States," agreed Hilary. "Or at least there seems a new self emerging. A vast improvement on the old one, too—not nearly such an ass. *What* an ass he must have been out there!"

"I don't follow your reasoning, Hilary," said Lucilla coldly.

"There's nothing like being really disastrously silly to draw your attention to how silly you are," explained Hilary. "Without a disaster in that way one doesn't always notice it. There is a paradox, Mother, that ought to be grasped by all female progenitors of the worrying sort. When your descendants appear to be in a state of complete well-being, all glorious and glossy with it, that's the time to worry."

"Then I'm not to worry about David?" asked Lucilla.

"Certainly not. Leave him to Weber."

"If that's what you are doing, then it's very lazy of you," said Lucilla. "The souls of the family should be your special charge."

"It's all I can do to get a couple of sermons by heart per week," said Hilary.

"Even as a little boy you couldn't concentrate," said Lucilla, and bringing her lovely hands softly together she looked up, with a studied superiority of concentration, at the high white clouds that were passing quickly along some current of the upper air that down here was no more than a cool breath. When she was momentarily at peace her hands folded of themselves into a shape that was somehow the very pattern of serenity, but the moment she was agitated they fell apart and the pattern was broken.   Hilary, spending as he did so many hours each week sitting beside her, had learned to watch her hands.   When he was working he was never so oblivious of her as she thought he was.   After only a few moments her hands fell apart again.

" Yes, Mother? " asked Hilary, laying down his sermon.

" There's a cloud there just like the flying white deer that leads the herd in Ben's picture," she said.

" Is there? " said Hilary.   " Which one? "

" That one," said Lucilla.

" I can't say that I see the resemblance," said Hilary. " And nor would you if you were not worrying about Ben. Now why in the world are you worried about Ben? "

" All this trouble at The Herb of Grace," mourned Lucilla. " All these wearing arguments between Ben and his parents. Just like it was before."

" It's not in the least like it was before," said Hilary. " Last time it was Ben who was worn down.   This time it is he who is doing the wearing.   I didn't know he had it in him.   An excellent state of affairs."

" He'll have to do his military service if he isn't going to the Foreign Office," said Lucilla.   " And he isn't strong enough."

" Quite strong enough," said Hilary.   " Be the making of him and keep Zelle with Meg and Robin a few years longer."

" That love affair exists only in your imagination, dear," said Lucilla.   " I always seem to be aware of what is in the minds of the children, and I have not been made aware of Ben's love for Zelle."

" Even your awareness can fail sometimes," said Hilary. " I may be wrong, of course, but if I'm right Ben and Zelle are both the type that knows how to wait.   And I'm glad of it.   Sally, as well as the children, needs Zelle."

" I can't look at those marigolds without thinking of Sally's hair," said Lucilla.   " I've never known her so ill before a baby.   I'm sure she's going to die."

Hilary smoothed out the crumpled pages of his sermon,

folded it and put it deep in his pocket. He sometimes thought what a merciful thing it was that his rheumatism so often kept him awake at night. In the small hours he could accomplish so many things which somehow or other he could never find time to do during the day. Lucilla's hands had now not only fallen apart, but were pulling restlessly at the fringe of the one shawl that still remained over her knees.

" And as for not going to hospital," she went on, " I never heard such madness. I can't imagine what Dr. Barnes can be thinking of to allow it. Nor David. I've told them what I think. Both of them. Several times. Sally, too. I can't imagine what's come over her to be so obstinate. She's changed lately, has my dear Sally. She used to be such a sweet and biddable child."

" Now look here, Mother," said Hilary. " I have always understood that you came to Lavender Cottage for the purpose of laying down the reins of family government."

" So I did, dear," said Lucilla. " So I have. I never interfere unless it's absolutely necessary. I never ask questions now, not even of David. And I don't give advice any more, even when Ben asks for it. But when it's a question of Sally losing her precious life——"

" Which she won't do if allowed to have her own way," interrupted Hilary. " Getting her own way relaxes a woman's mind, I've noticed. Of course I'm not knowledge-able in these things, but surely relaxation of the mind must influence the abdominal muscles."

" Hilary! " ejaculated Lucilla.

" Sally is, as you say, a sweet and biddable child," Hilary went on, unabashed, " but even a worm will turn, and I give Barnes credit for recognising the moment. Don't worry, Mother. I understood you to say, when you came to Lavender Cottage, that you were abandoning worry so as to live in peace and make your soul."

" Yes, I did say that," acknowledged Lucilla. " To make my soul. What did I mean by it? "

" I've no idea," said Hilary.

"But it's a phrase people often use, dear," said Lucilla. "You must have heard it a hundred times."

"I have," said Hilary. "And a hundred times I have wondered what they meant by it. I've heard of people making bootlaces, rock buns and atom bombs, but I've never heard of anyone yet making a soul. Just like their darned cheek to think they can."

"It seems to me I might just as well have stayed at Damerosehay," said Lucilla.

"Worrying being the breath of life to you, just as well," said Hilary. "Indeed, better. There's more to worry about there. I mean, apart from the family, which can be worried about anywhere, there are more feet of pipe to burst and acreage of roof to leak and so on. You'd much more scope there."

"Hilary, you are most unkind," said Lucilla pathetically. "I don't *like* worrying. Instead of being the breath of life to me, it's the thing in life that I find hardest to bear. The Thing. Now what did Mr. Weber say about the Thing?"

"I've no idea," said Hilary.

"Hilary, you must try as you get old not to run certain phrases to death. One does. Mr. Weber said anxiety for my children was my Thing and I was to ask you what he meant."

"Now why put it on me?" complained Hilary.

"Why not?" retorted Lucilla. "Your salary is paid to you, Hilary, for the sole purpose of consoling troublesome old ladies. And, of course, attending the village whist drives."

"Leaving you out of it, Mother, there's always some Thing to prevent me doing my real work," grumbled Hilary. "There always has been, ever since I became a priest. I've never been a priest yet."

"You surprise me," said Lucilla. "I was present at your ordination. I could even tell you what hat I wore."

"I'm sure you could," said Hilary. "What I couldn't tell you is when I have ever had one consecutive hour of uninterrupted mental prayer since that day ; barring the last thing at night, the middle of the night, or the first thing in the morning, when my physical infirmities and the devil see to it that I'm never at my best. And I vowed myself to prayer upon that day."

" Why didn't you go into a monastery? " inquired Lucilla.

" I was thinking of it when the first war broke out," said Hilary. " And then it seemed right to be a chaplain. And afterwards, if you remember, I was enjoying delicate health, and they wouldn't have me."

" Who wouldn't have you? " asked Lucilla sharply.

" The Order with whom I endeavoured to seek refuge from a life-sentence to whist-drives, bazaars, socials, outings, and all the rest of the hydra-headed monster."

" You never told me," said Lucilla slowly, trying to keep the hurt chill out of her voice. She had always thought that her children had no secrets from her. Sometimes, it seemed, they had. And why hadn't he tried again later? If it had been for her sake, then the blow to her pride would be intolerable. She had always imagined that it was she who sacrificed herself for her children, not they for her. " But later, when you were better, and sea air wasn't so necessary, couldn't you have tried again? " she asked.

" I could," said Hilary. " But somehow I didn't."

" I think I know why you didn't," said Lucilla, putting it to the test. " I'd lost two sons in the war, George was in India, and I relied upon you at every turn. I did not know it at the time. I believe I have always leaned my entire weight upon you, Hilary, though I have not realised it until now. I expect the rest of the family do, too, and don't know it either."

" We are not talking about what I wanted to talk about," said Hilary.

" What did you want to talk about? " she asked, and she managed to speak evenly and calmly, even though she felt exactly like a bombed building when the dust begins to settle. She had not realised until now that her pride was such an integral part of her.

" I wanted to have a good grouse about my Thing," said Hilary.

" Do grouse, dear," said Lucilla. " I'd love it. I haven't heard you grouse since you were a small boy. It will be like the old nursery days. You told me everything then."

" No, Mother," said Hilary. " I never told you about the hyena with several heads who lived in the night-nursery cupboard behind the cistern. It came out at night and sat on the foot of my bed and made the most distracting noises when I was trying to say my prayers."

" No wonder you said them so badly ! " ejaculated Lucilla. " I used to hear you say them, and I was always scolding you for the way you stumbled and stuttered. How ridiculous children are ! Why didn't you tell me about the hyena ? "

" Because I thought to draw your attention to it would be to draw its attention to you. You might have turned round and spoken to it, and then it would have bitten your head off. I was very fond of you as a small boy."

" Really, Hilary," said Lucilla, " I don't know whether to laugh or to cry. And now the Thing still interrupts your prayers. My poor Hilary ! "

" Not that I really mind now," said Hilary. " I'm only grousing for the pleasure of it, like Mr. Enticknapp. My monster is as valued a possession as a pedigree dog. I take it about on a lead, so to speak. Mother, I am talking the most ridiculous nonsense."

" I'm used to it, dear," said Lucilla, and there was now a resilient note in her voice that Hilary noted with relief and delight. The dust of her shattered pride had settled and she was rising above it.

" In the war I disliked the after-effects of wounds and gas intensely," said Hilary. " When you are burned, and can't get your breath, and are afraid you are going blind, it is impossible to pray. And then one day, with great difficulty, I suddenly put into practice and knew as truth what of course I had always known theoretically, that if pain is offered to God as prayer, then pain and prayer are synonymous. A sort of substitution takes place that is like the old story of

Beauty and the Beast. The utterly abominable Thing that prevents your prayer becomes your prayer. And you know what prayer is, Mother. It's all of a piece, the prayer of a mystic or of a child, adoration or intercession, it's all the same thing; whether you feel it or not, it is union with God in the deep places where the fountains are. Once you have managed the wrenching effort of substitution, the abominable Thing, while remaining utterly detestable for yourself, becomes the channel of grace for others, and so the dearest treasure that you have. And if it happens to be a secret treasure—something that you need not speak about to another—then that's all the better. Somehow the secrecy of it increases its value."

"You put it better than I could do," said Lucilla gently. "I did feel after that way of prayer in the war, but I did not try hard enough, and when the war was over I fell away. But I recognise what you say as a truth that I know."

"Of course," said Hilary. "I do not think that anyone who has experienced disaster is not in some way aware of one of the fundamental paradoxes of our existence. Only we don't live in a perpetual state of disaster, and it doesn't occur to us to apply the paradox to the worries and frustrations and irritations among which we do perpetually live. We lack the humility."

"Well, really," said Lucilla, "if I couldn't put up with my everyday worries and aches and pains without having to regard them as prayer I should feel myself a poor sort of coward."

"As I said," remarked Hilary drily, "we lack the humility. One feels ridiculous, as you don't feel ridiculous when it is some disaster. But it's not just the way you look at it, it's a deliberate and costly action of the will. It can be a real wrenching of the soul. Yet the more you practise it, the fresher and greener grows your life. And it's the same with joy as with disaster and Things; lifted up with that same hard effort, even the earthly joys are points of contact, and have the freshness of eternity in them."

Lucilla suddenly remembered something that David had

said of his lack of joy in the joys of family and home. He
felt that he had them in the earthly sense only because he
could not find his way to the roots. She had known then
that he had said something that was of importance to her.

" It's like plants," she said. " The thrust upwards means
a corresponding growth of root down. Sun and water. I
believe I am beginning to learn to accept, Hilary, but I see
now that acceptance is only the first step. If I can't stop
worrying (and anguish for the children is part of motherhood,
Hilary—one can't get rid of it), at least I'll worry in a
different way."

" You know how peace comes after effort," said Hilary.
" Well, after that particular effort there comes a particular
sort of peace. Sometimes you're conscious of it, sometimes
not. More often not. But it's there just the same, and is the
peace in which God makes your soul."

Lucilla pondered and then laughed. " *Touché*," she said.

" Should I go on with my other sermon now? " inquired
Hilary tentatively, his hand moving towards his pocket.

" Certainly, dear," said Lucilla. " I've enjoyed my
private sermon very much. You've an excellent pulpit
manner. Now I'll digest it. The sermon, I mean."

They were quiet, and Lucilla tried very hard to deal in
the correct manner with a nagging worry about George. It
was true, as she had said, that Sally and Sebastian were very
much in her mind, but she did not feel that her concern with
them was necessarily a concern with disaster, and they were
only in her mind. But George was in her soul, and had been
since six o'clock in the morning. Of course it was a very
suitable place for him to be, for he was her child, and she
had no premonition of anything being wrong, only she had
never before felt like this about him. There was nothing in
it, of course, and she had been able to forget about it by
remembering other worries. But she always came back to it
again. And with George so near, Maurice felt almost at a
distance, and that was worrying, too. She must lift the
whole thing up and then her roots would go down and life
be green and fresh. She tried, but nothing happened at all.

THE HEART OF THE FAMILY

She didn't feel any wrenching of her soul and she didn't feel
any freshness; merely worry. She looked almost with
irritation at Hilary. The humility of the saints tended to
make them forget that sinners could not do what they could
do; not without years of practice and ninety-one was a bit
late to start.

"It's no good, Hilary," she said. "I can't concentrate.
I'm worried about George."

"What's the matter with George?" asked Hilary, putting
down his sermon.

"Nothing, so far as I know," said Lucilla.

"Shall I ring up?" asked Hilary.

"No, dear. Nadine usually answers the phone, and it
annoys her when I ring up for nothing. She doesn't say so,
but I can tell it by the sweetness of her voice."

"I'll ring up to-night if we don't hear or see anything of
them," said Hilary. "You mustn't go to bed worrying."

"I shall be worrying anyhow," said Lucilla, smiling at him.
"Worrying because at my age it is too late to learn to worry
right."

"You don't imagine we stop learning when we die, do
you?" asked Hilary.

"No, dear, but I did hope we stopped worrying."

"You're not going to worry any more," said Hilary
decidedly. "Either in this world or the next. It's very
wrong, and you should be ashamed of yourself for giving way
to such wickedness at your age."

"Now if you'd said that at the beginning we needn't have
had this conversation at all," said Lucilla. "If worry is a
sin, it can't be my Thing."

"Oh, yes, it can," said Hilary. "Your besetting sin can
very well be your Thing."

"But sin can't be offered as prayer," objected Lucilla.

"Wrestling with it can," said Hilary. "Do you know,
Mother, I think I really must get this sermon by heart. This
afternoon it's the Sunday-school outing to the Fun Fair at
Radford. And after tea there's an expert on the beetle
coming——"

" Beetle? " interrupted Lucilla. " What beetle? "

" The one that's destroying the church roof."

" Nobody told me! " ejaculated Lucilla. " Why wasn't I told? You children never tell me anything. I suppose you think I'll worry. But my poor Hilary! That will mean hundreds of pounds. Where's it coming from? "

" I've no idea," said Hilary. " And after supper there's a whist drive. So I think, Mother, if you don't mind——"

" I won't say another word," said Lucilla. " What a nuisance I've been, and what a comfort it is to think you've been offering up the nuisance I am as prayer for me . . . Have you? " she asked with sudden suspicion.

" Yes," said Hilary. " But not in the crude way that you imagine. What I offered up was joy that this morning's interruption took the form of a woman I adore. After tea it will be the beetle."

" So nice to be preferred to a beetle," murmured Lucilla, and did not speak again.

CHAPTER XVI

I

SEBASTIAN was stretched luxuriously and happily in a long chair under the ilex tree. A fortnight ago he had been taken ill with an unusually bad heart attack, and could not move from the chair in his room where the pain had flung him to find his tablets, but what he could reach was the bell, and being at the moment in a state of mental confusion as to which part of his life he was in, he rang it imperiously for Anna, who had been Christiana's Austrian maid in the house in the mountains. Mrs. Wilkes appeared, and darkness came down upon the expression of unholy joy that spread slowly over her countenance. She had suspected this, as a mother suspects her little boy of stealing jam, but try as she might she had never been able to catch him in the act. Now she had. A sense of having given great pleasure sustained Sebastian through the worst attack he had ever had, and through the humiliation of being kept in bed when it was over, and beneath the irritable reproaches of Dr. Barnes.

"Why have I not been attending you for months past?" demanded Dr. Barnes, cooling the irascibility that was a part of his temperament at the open window in Sebastian's room, where the air from the marshes was sweet and fresh. "Heaven knows I am in the house often enough being fussed to death by Eliot over this dratted baby. The commotion that's made over babies these days. My mother had ten and never turned a hair until she died of the tenth. Why have you not consulted me before?"

"The intricacies of the National Health Service," said Sebastian weakly. "I felt I could not struggle with it. In America there is no such monster."

"Perfectly simple once you understand it," said Dr. Barnes. "Why didn't Eliot insist?"

255

"He wished it," said Sebastian. "Mrs. Eliot also, and Lady Eliot and the Vicar, they all asked me to see you. But I said I was better, which I was, that I had my tablets and that there was nothing you could do for me. Nor is there."

"That's true," conceded Dr. Barnes. "But you are an interesting case. The various afflictions of the last ten years have left after effects which are unusual. When you are up again we'll have a few X-rays."

"What for?" demanded Sebastian, and Dr. Barnes noticed a sudden and remarkable addition of strength to his voice. Where the man got his strength from he could not imagine. How he carried on with a normal life at all he had no idea. If he had been able to reach his tablets this last time, probably no one would have known a thing about it. Men became inured to affliction, of course, but even so it was incomprehensible and slightly mysterious. Now and then one met these people whose source of strength seemed unknown even to themselves.

"Just for purposes of verification," he said.

"In other words, just to satisfy your curiosity," said Sebastian. "No, thank you. All I require of you, doctor, is that now we have made each other's acquaintance you should keep your eye on me and tell me when I should remove myself from Damerosehay. I imagine I have some while yet, but I do not wish to incommode my friends here."

He spoke with a dignity, almost with a royalty, that made Dr. Barnes smile beneath his bristling white moustache and yet very nearly riled him at the same time, for the fellow was young enough to be his son. And who was he, anyway? But one could not be seriously riled by a man so ill, nor fail to pay homage to his courage. It was odd how much and yet how little the dying seemed to know about themselves. This chap knew his number was up, but seemed to have no idea it might be next week.

"Where would you go?" he asked.

"To London," said Sebastian dreamily. "I have something saved; enough to keep me for a short while. I used to be very fond of London." Dr. Barnes saw that he was back in a London of the past. His mind was sometimes as clear as it could be and sometimes confused. He smiled and said nothing, for he would never tell Sebastian to leave Damerosehay. About that he had a private agreement with Eliot, who, though intensely irritating in many ways, was a good-hearted chap on the whole.

Sebastian had enjoyed his days in bed, but he was enjoying even more his days in the long chair under the ilex tree in the golden October warmth. The struggle to lead a normal life had just lately nearly defeated him, and the mere cessation of effort was in itself a sort of heaven. While he had been ill Mrs. Wilkes had entirely owned him, and the rest of the family had been let into his room only on sufferance, but now Mrs. Wilkes was busy in the house and he lived much in the society of Sally and Meg. With the baby imminent, Mrs. Wilkes had taken the unprecedented step of importing Wilkes's sister Emma to look after Wilkes and her sons and was living in, to her vast enjoyment. What effect this first parting of their married life would have upon Wilkes she had no idea, but Emma had a grumbling temper and a heavy hand with pastry, and Wilkes might quite possibly miss her. That he should seek comfort with the red-haired hussy over to Radford was only to be expected, but the hussy had a sharp tongue from all accounts, and a further acquaintance with it might do Wilkes no harm either. So Mrs. Wilkes took a cheerful view, and was giving the house a good clean before starting on the baby. Sally, at liberty, sat beside Sebastian and knitted, if she thought he looked lonely, while Meg read to them the adventures of Flopsy, Mopsy, Cottontail and Peter, the Tailor of Gloucester and Mrs. Tiggy Winkle. Meg could not read very well yet, so she mostly held the book upside down and relied upon her excellent memory. Robin was kept out of the way by Zelle because of the noise he made.

David, when Sebastian was alone, would sometimes appear and ask him, almost shyly, how he was, and talk gently for five minutes about the international situation, and then immediately go away again with a humble sadness that grieved Sebastian. He would have liked to ask him to stay so that he could take hold of the new relationship that had come into being between them, since that silent drive back from the Hard, and wrest it into some sort of shape, but he had not got the strength. Later he must and would. He realised now, from the manner of David's withdrawals, that he must always have been aware of his hatred and suffered it with patience. How could he ever have thought him arrogant? The arrogance was chiefly a defensive system of earthworks. He had erected the same in his time. Stuck up in the public eye, to be stared at by the public and excoriated by the critics, one did. No truly arrogant man could have continued quietly and steadily to like a man who hated him; liking would have turned to resentment sooner or later. But that David had done that he was also now aware. At their first meeting he had been struck by the warm kindness in David's eyes and, looking back, he realised that that look had never chilled. " There's not much about us all that you don't know," Sally had said to him on the evening of the family party, but with David either his intuition had entirely failed or else his hatred had had its roots in something he did not understand yet, and perhaps would never understand. That did not matter. What did matter was that he should make it clear to his friend that the hatred had passed. That he must do as and when he could.

Meanwhile there was Sally, and he remembered the longing he had had that she should be less vulnerable, that she should learn how to arm herself against possible disaster. Yet he felt now that as his hatred was passing, so was her defencelessness. There was a new maturity in her. Her friendliness had been like that of a shy child, glowing yet hesitant, now it was outgoing, as though some barrier had been pushed away.

" How much longer, if Christopher is punctual? " he asked her. The freedom with which he spoke to her in these days would have startled his punctiliousness a short while ago. Now he was as unaware of it as she was. They said what came into their minds as two people do who have lived together all their lives.

"Only a fortnight if he is punctual, but of course he won't be. Boys generally keep you waiting. It's girls who are in such a hurry to be born. At least, that's what Mrs. Wilkes says."

"Is there more eagerness for life in women?" wondered Sebastian. "I think perhaps there is. They generally live longer, as though they felt life to be more desirable than men do. Perhaps that is as it should be, since they are the bearers of life."

"I want children more than David does," said Sally. "Once he had one daughter and one son, that was all he wanted. It was I who wanted Christopher, in spite of being so afraid."

"Afraid?" asked Sebastian sharply.

Sally dropped her knitting into her lap. "How odd!" she said. "I have never told anyone except Mrs. Wilkes about being afraid, and now I have told you."

"Why should it be odd to tell me?" asked Sebastian.

"Because to own up to you, of all people, that I am a coward about a little pain should make me squirm with shame." She stopped and laughed. "No wonder you are smiling. To be laughed at for my fears is what I deserve."

He had smiled because she had spoken like a little girl of twelve. The new maturity had vanished; or rather it had parted like the petals of a flower to show the child she would always be at its heart.

"It was not at your fear that I smiled," he said, "but at that queer English word squirm. Meg uses it frequently. Does it derive from worm?"

"Not that I know of," she said, with a high seriousness worthy of Meg. "It is spelt differently. David could tell you."

"It's not a matter in which I thirst for correct information," said Sebastian. "But I should like to know, I should like to know very much, why you should feel shame in telling me that you carry the burden of fear."

" If you were carrying half a pound of apples in a bag on your back, and you met Atlas, wouldn't you be ashamed to tell him that your back ached? " asked Sally. " But yet, you know, I don't feel ashamed now. A month ago I would, but not now."

" Well, that's good," said Sebastian. " You are less proud, perhaps."

" Am I a proud woman? " she asked.

" No, on the whole you are a humble woman, but only the perfected are without a taint of pride."

" Yes, I was proud," owned Sally. " I felt humiliated, after I was married, to find I was terrified of what most women take as a matter of course. It destroyed quite a lot of my good opinion of myself. I wasn't what I thought I was, you see."

" Yes, I see," said Sebastian gravely, but his eyes twinkled.

" Please forgive me," said Sally. " I ought not to talk about myself so much."

" Yes, you ought," said Sebastian. " Because I want to know about you, and you like to please me. And now you have accepted yourself, you no longer mind revealing yourself. Is that it? "

" Not to you and Mrs. Wilkes," said Sally. " I'm glad to. Of course I couldn't to anyone else. It would never do to tell David, and you can never show fear before children, can you? "

" Certainly not," said Sebastian. " Fear is always a thing that must be secretly carried. What, besides pain, are you afraid of? "

" Of losing David."

" Why should you lose him? "

" Because I can't share his experience. I never shall. He will live always a little farther on. I shall never catch up."

" That doesn't matter in marriage," said Sebastian gently. " Watching you together, I should say that what he wants of you just now is not understanding, but peace. And you will catch up with him one day; if not here, then in that world where we shall not need to look for peace because it will be as the very air we breathe."

"I know that sometimes," said Sally. "I mean about the peace. It is always when we are quiet together that we are happiest."

"Do you fear other things?"

"I fear pain for the children, but nothing else in life as it is now. I am so fortunate."

"You may not always be so fortunate, and as life goes on I expect you will be very afraid indeed. Don't mind if you are. How ridiculous that sounds!"

"I know what you mean," said Sally. "I won't mind. I don't now. I expect one's particular thing is always the thing that is right for oneself, and one can be glad about it even if one does not see why. But with mine I do see why. I asked for it."

"Asked for it?"

"I have a shame that is a good shame," said Sally. "I was born with it, and so it's not to my credit, and I can say that it is good. I am ashamed of good fortune. The shame goes so deep it is like prayer, and it's been answered. Something that less fortunate women make little of is allowed with me to cut deep so that I can be nearer to them. Perhaps later on other things will cut deep in the same way. I can be glad of that, can't I?"

"You will always have that gladness," said Sebastian. "Gladness is a strong armour as well as a bright one. You will be safe with it. And so will I."

"Do you mean you feel glad, too?" asked Sally in amazement, for she remembered how she had been sure he could not again be happy. "You don't mean you feel happy, do you?"

"Not in the way that most people use the word, perhaps," said Sebastian. "The kind of gladness you will feel when in future things cut deep is not what they mean by happiness. My gladness is a sort of deepening of the respite we talked about once. The moments of light are lasting longer, so that the dark times are getting squeezed out between them. Nowadays it is nearly all respite."

She remembered how she had seen his compassion for her, which she had not understood because she had seen no reason for it, as a light in profound darkness, and how she had wished she could banish his darkness. She acknowledged humbly to herself that whoever had done that, it was not she.

"Which I owe to you," said Sebastian. "Why shouldn't I tell you? It can't hurt you. I love you very much; so much that I have come to love all whom you love. The respite I needed was from hatred, and that way I have nearly achieved it."

Sally's astonishment was so vast that it completely swallowed her for a few moments. When she had climbed out of it sufficiently to get her breath she found herself saying quietly, "That is a wonderful way to love me. Generally when a man loves a married woman there is jealousy, and then in the end that means not more of love, but less."

"You can love as I do when you are coming to the end of your life, and have nothing you want to possess through love except an increase of the power of love," said Sebastian. "You have given me that. Did you mind me telling you?"

"Not in the least," said Sally matter-of-factly. "I am glad you did. I love you, too."

It was Sebastian's turn to be swallowed by amazement. "That is so astonishing that it is almost unbelievable," he said at last. "How did you manage it?"

Sally's knitting was now on the grass, and she had turned in her chair to face him, her elbows on its arm and her chin in her hands. Her face was that of a child trying seriously but happily to do a difficult sum. His heart had been beating wildly, but now her matter-of-factness took hold of him, too, and he felt quieted.

"I didn't manage it," she said. "It just happened in the way right things do happen. It was just that there was an empty place at Damerosehay, and in my life and in all our lives, and you just walked into it. Now we are completed. Is it any wonder that we all love you?"

"I still don't understand," said Sebastian. "What sort of empty place?"

"I know what I mean, but I don't know how to put it into words," said Sally.

"You must try, please," said Sebastian.

"It is so dreadfully difficult," said Sally.

"Try," insisted Sebastian.

"There isn't a single one of us who has been broken in any way," said Sally. "Grandmother is old, and David hasn't got a happy nature, and I am afraid, and Ben never knows what to do for the best, and I expect all the others think themselves hardly used in one way or the other. But there is not one of us who has been crucified."

"What are you daring to say?" asked Sebastian in a tone of sharp horror.

"That's what I don't quite know," said Sally. "I don't quite understand myself what I am saying. I think it is that we all needed to have you and to say, this is what it costs. You can't ever really begin faintly to love God until you have said that."

"Stop, Sally, I beg of you," said Sebastian, out of the midst of a whirling of shame and confusion that had set him down finally in the hall of Damerosehay on the day of his arrival, wondering why God demanded the continued existence in time and space of such disconnected items of rubbish as himself. His thoughts then had had a bitterness that had been almost sacrilege, and now most deeply he repented of it. "Stop, Sally," he said.

"I had stopped," said Sally. "And don't ask me any more questions, for I don't think my answers are at all good for you. For your body, I mean. . . . And, Sebastian, the way I love you doesn't make any difference to the way I love David."

The sudden sweet childishness of her change of tone added laughter to Sebastian's whirling emotions, but steadied him at the same time. "Of course not," he said. "Nor does my love for you affect my love for Christiana, my wife."

"Christiana," said Sally slowly. "I like that name."

" I don't want to tell you about my life before I came here," said Sebastian.   " Do you mind? "

" You wouldn't want to tell any of us," said Sally, " for there isn't one of us who could possibly even begin to understand; except perhaps David."

" Why David? " asked Sebastian sharply.

" He does sometimes understand things you wouldn't expect him to," said Sally.   " I think it may be something to do with being an actor.   On the stage actors have sometimes to become people much bigger than themselves. . . . Sebastian, here's Aunt Margaret! "

It was as well, thought Sebastian, getting up and bowing to Margaret, for it brought it easily to its ending.

" Aunt Margaret, come and sit down," said Sally.   " Have you been here long? "

" Not long, dear.   David has been showing me the herbaceous border," said Margaret, subsiding into the chair that David put for her.   " We did not want to disturb you and Mr. Weber while you were talking.   You seemed so absorbed.   How are you, Mr. Weber?   And you, Sally? Mother wanted me to find out.   She said she had you both in her mind together."

2

As well Grandmother might, thought David, and found himself, to his great surprise, back at the herbaceous border, squatting on his heels and pulling up weeds.   After a few moments of savage onslaught he looked over his shoulder and saw Sebastian going slowly and perhaps a little unsteadily towards the secret garden, leaving Sally and Margaret together.   It was his duty, he knew, to go after him and make sure that what he had said to Sally, and she to him, had done him no harm, but he did not do his duty. He could not even go on with the weeding, for it did not exhaust him sufficiently.   He fetched a spade from the toolhouse and went round to the kitchen garden at the back of the house to dig potatoes.   He dug till he had deflected his

rage from Sally and Sebastian to himself. What right had
he to be so suddenly and madly jealous? Couldn't Sally
and Sebastian be friends, even intimate friends, without his
flying off the handle? What about himself and Nadine?
Even if they were something more, lovers of a sort, he still
had no right to his rage; for what about himself and Anne?
Well, why not own it, they *were* lovers of a sort; he had the
evidence of his own eyes for that. But what sort? Not his
and Anne's sort. Digging more slowly, and using all the
power of his imagination, he endeavoured to put Sebastian
in his place and Sally in Anne's. But he couldn't do it.
The niches in which he tried to fit them were far too small for
them. Then he tried the other way round, and the little
puppet figures of himself and Anne, Yabbit and Maria
Flinders, dwindled and cowered down in the large and airy
spaces that were filled by Sebastian's integrity and Sally's
loyalty. The past held Sebastian, and her marriage held
Sally. They had merely leaned from their strongholds to
love each other as men and women may whose destiny, in
perfection of beatitude, is just such an interchange as he
had seen.

What had she given him? A respect for himself that he
had lost? Too much disaster could do that to a man, could
at the moment of his greatest value make him see himself as
so much trash when it was merely the unessentials of body
and fortune that were broken. What had he given her?
Perhaps a greater sense of proportion to steady her among the
many dumb fears of a woman's life. Women moved mysteri-
ously among their fears, that were perhaps known to each
other, but not comforted by each other. It was with men
that women found comfort for their fear, though seldom to a
man that they would tell it. He was always wishing that
Sally would tell him more. Well, he could not tell her much.
The load of the things that he could not tell was heavy to
carry. And serve him right. He flung down his spade,
lifted his coat from the lilac bush where he had hung it and
put it on.

" If you don't change that shirt, sir, before you puts your

coat on," said Mrs. Wilkes from the kitchen window, " you'll be sorry for it. All of a lather you must be. And we don't want them potatoes neither. There's plenty indoors."

" I can't be bothered to change," said David.

" Lumbago for certain," said Mrs. Wilkes. " Your death of cold it wouldn't surprise me. And just with master Christopher expected and all. If there's trouble in the 'ouse already, trust a man to give more." Her attention was distracted by Zelle's entry into the kitchen. " If it's the children you're wanting, ducks, I've no idea. Vanished since their milk."

" I want to give them their lunch early so that they can rest after," said Zelle. " Lady Eliot wants us to take them over for tea."

" Perhaps they are in the secret garden, Zelle," said David, as she came out into the kitchen garden with her arms full of small wet garments to hang on the line. " I'll go and see."

Zelle smiled at him as she pegged out poppy-coloured smocks and sky-blue pyjamas on the line. She knew even better than he the value of what he had done for her lately. Several times he had taken her and the children over to The Herb of Grace and with great skill had somehow landed Meg and Robin with Jill, and seen to it that Nadine and George became aware of her existence. Under his able stage management they had done so, and she had used her wits while they did it. She had sat beside George through lunch one day and captivated him. She had helped Nadine cut out a frock for Caroline, and had made her apple-jelly for her. There had been other things, too. David had been very kind and very clever. And he had taken the trouble to get to know her himself, too; as Heloise the woman, not just Zelle. Her quick eye had not been able to help noticing that he liked himself taking all this trouble and being so kind, tired and preoccupied as he was; but that did not alter the kindness and the trouble.

" Thank you," she said, and meant very much by what she said.

As he opened the gate by the guelder-rose bush, David remembered that Sebastian had gone into the secret garden. Well, his despicable rage was over. He could meet him now with gratitude for whatever invisible good the fact of him at Damerosehay had given Sally. As he closed the gate behind him, a spray of winter honeysuckle, the dew still on it, touched his face. The sudden breath of scent took him by surprise, the coolness of the dew, the perfect trumpets of pale yellow flowers against the glossy green leaves. The fact of it suddenly filled his whole consciousness, blotting out all other facts. He stood looking at it, every one of his senses absorbed by it, until it seemed there was nothing to look at in all the world but just those green leaves and pale flowers, nothing to breathe but the scent of it, nothing to feel but the cool dew on the leaves. Yet the sight of it, the scent and feel, were the least part of its value, even as his body that saw and felt and breathed was no great thing. It had its reality of invisible good, as he is, but though it was a gift to him, he in his ignorance could not even guess at what it was. His consciousness, that had narrowed to such a pin point, widened slowly to an awareness of an ocean surface of form and colour and movement; the grey faces of men who suffered, the rosy faces of children, women's pearly fairness or blotched unsightliness, the grace of bodies and their degradation, flowers and birds' wings and the beautiful pelts of beasts, sunlight on the water and the flames of burning cities; all just an appearance of invisible good or evil that lived in the depths and could not be seen. Yet not in the still depths, only just below the surface where the flow of interchange was unresting and unceasing. One took and gave unendingly, and could not know what one took or what one gave, because one did not know what one was, or who or what it was that gave. One was tossed upon this surface of appearance, and could know nothing of the meaning of it, until one had passed through the fear and agony of its total loss.

He went quickly through the garden, and found Sebastian sitting on the seat with the children, making a jenny wren out of Robin's plasticine. He had already, in the time it had taken David to subdue his rage, made a swallow and a bust of Yabbit. Stiff though they were, there was very little that he could not make with his hands. And what extraordinary hands he had! thought David, standing in front of the little group and watching. His own hands, that could not even write half a page of a letter in a manner that could be read, had hidden in shame inside his pockets. Sebastian's hands were ugly, too long and completely wooden looking, with the veins knotted like cords, but, watching them, David was intensely aware of great creative power expressed by them, a power that was in itself an expression of an even greater good that had nothing to do with the man. A terrible power. A terrible good. They touched him, and he felt fear. Only once before had the appearance of a man's hands moved him in this way, and then the fear had come accompanied by the glory of sound. Yet the sound in itself had been nothing apart from the silence it had yielded to the silence of his own spirit. He groped after the memory, but he could not get hold of it.

The jenny wren was finished, and Meg jumped up and clapped her hands in delight. Robin beat the hot fat cushions on his palms together, too, making a sticky adhesive sort of sound, and David clapped quickly and lightly. To the noise of applause Sebastian rose and bowed to left and right. His hands parted in a gesture of humble appreciation, inimitably graceful, and then he clasped them as he bowed once more. He sat down again, smiling impersonally yet charmingly at his audience, and then his hands fell on his knees, one within the other with palms uppermost. Memory stirred again in David, more sharply than before.

"Run along in to Zelle, kids," he said. "She wants to give you lunch early. You are to have tea with Grandmother."

"Gwanny," said Robin, and grabbing the bust of Yabbit he trundled off. He liked his great-grandmother.

Meg hesitated, touching the jenny wren with the tip of her finger and looking up at Sebastian. She wanted it very badly but she thought perhaps he wanted it more. She flushed a delicate pink and said to him gently, " Would you like the little jenny? "

" No, Meg," said Sebastian. " I made it for you."

" Daddy, would you like the jenny? " she asked anxiously.

" No, Meg," said David. " It's your jenny."

" Really and truly? " asked Meg.

" Yes, really and truly."

Her lips parted in a seraphic smile and she took it tenderly into her keeping, folding both hands about it so that it should not fly away.

" The swallow, too," said Sebastian.

But Meg shook her head firmly about the swallow. " For Daddy," she said.

" Certainly," agreed Sebastian. " Its migratory habits make it a suitably symbolic gift for your father."

" It has folded wings," said Meg. She had not understood what Sebastian had said. She was merely pointing out the beauties of the bird.

David, sitting on the bench beside Sebastian, looked down at the swallow lying in his hands. " The spirit of man . . . has folded wings." The words sang in his mind, and he remembered the day years ago when he had caught the blue bird here in this garden. He remembered it tossing up into the air, and the sound of the singing. The seed of his faith, such as it was, had been sown in him then. Faith in the reality of immortal life. All music sounds its affirmation, from bird-song to the thunder of the Waldstein. . . . Suddenly he remembered. . . . " Run away, Meg," he said.

Meg ran a little way and then stopped, came back and stood between Sebastian's knees. " Good-bye," she said, and with her hands still holding her bird she lifted her face to be kissed.

" Good-bye, Meg," said Sebastian, and holding her clasped hands almost ceremoniously in his own, he kissed her gravely. Meg did not as a rule like being kissed, and Sebastian was the least demonstrative of mortals. Their salutation left David shaken, and brought to his mind the old grave word viaticum, in its sense of supplies for a journey. Meg ran off again, without looking at her father, and Sebastian sat in contented silence. He did not know what he had given the child— the freedom from pain that he might have had in his last moments, perhaps, to give her lifelong freedom from some shape of fear that haunted her—but he knew that the urgency of his wish to give, at whatever present or future cost, had had a selflessness that had been counted to him as prayer and had been answered. Like Sally's shame. But he would not know what he had been allowed to give Meg, for in this world of appearance he would not see her again.

"What an unutterable ass I am!" said David.

"Particularly at this moment?" asked Sebastian drily.

"No," said David. "Throughout. I heard you play the Waldstein in Paris years ago, between the wars. I did not think I could ever forget your name or you, yet I did."

"But you did not forget the Waldstein," said Sebastian.

"No. As you played it then it was a great affirmation of terrible good."

"You were young, then, to be aware of the terror of good."

"I don't imagine I was aware of it very often," said David, smiling. "In my impervious youth I had a magnificent conceit of myself."

"And not now, of course," stated Sebastian in his most completely dry-as-dust manner. In their early days together David had often wondered uncomfortably if his secretary was mocking him. Now he no longer cared if he was. When the doubt came he laughed himself.

"Now, too, at times," he agreed with amusement. "Only I'm not impervious."

"A most painful state of affairs," said Sebastian sympathetically, and got up, for Mrs. Wilkes could be heard in the distance ringing the bell for lunch. They walked slowly through the garden, and at the gate he paused. "Will you be at liberty after supper tonight?" he asked. "After your wife has gone to bed?"

"Yes," said David, surprised. "But surely you'll go to bed early yourself?"

"Not tonight," said Sebastian. "I have never told you anything about myself, and after your great kindness to me it is in my mind that I should like to do so."

"But why should you?" asked David. "You don't want to."

"Yes, I do," said Sebastian. "I find it difficult to explain to you why. I have done you a great injustice, and I should like to make reparation. There is only one thing which it is in my power to surrender to you, and that is my reserve, which I have hugged to myself very much in the same way as a miser hugs his gold." He smiled at the mixture of distress and apprehension on David's face. "I know it sounds a poor sort of gift, and one which you may not wish to receive."

"But I do," said David stoutly. "Even if there is terror for me in your gift, if it is your gold it will be good."

CHAPTER XVII

I

ZELLE had cleared away the tea and was washing up
the cups and saucers in the kitchen while Lucilla and
Meg played spillikins together. Margaret, in the deep
arm-chair, was perforce resting for once because Robin was
on her lap, stolidly and absorbedly turning over and over
in his fat hands a glass bowl with a snowstorm inside it that
Margaret had had when she was a child. Should he tire of
the snowstorm, and of the little man and the red house
upon which the snow fell, there was beside them on the table
a seashell that sounded like the sea when you held it against
your ear, that Lucilla had had when she was a little girl, and
down on the floor was his father's Noah's ark. But he would
not tire of the snowstorm under an hour and a half. Of all
the toys at Lavender Cottage, it was the one that most completely stilled his restlessness and silenced his noise. To him
it was the most fascinating thing in the universe.

But hardly more fascinating than was Robin himself to
Margaret, as she lay back contemplating the bulge of his
cheek and the drake's-tail twist of a red curl at the back of his
neck; or Meg to Lucilla as she watched the lights and
shadows passing over the child's absorbed face, and her small
deft hands lifting the slithers of pale ivory without a tremor
from their nest. Meg was best at spillikins because, though
Lucilla had been an adept in her time, she did not now see
enough to play well, and her hand shook, but it was not
because she always won that Meg loved the game, but
because it had belonged to Lucilla's mother when she was a
little girl.

"Wasn't your Mummy any bigger than me when her
Daddy gave her the spillikins?" asked Meg.

"A little bigger," said Lucilla. "She had them for her
sixth birthday."

Meg knew this perfectly well, for she asked the same question every time they played together, but the question and answer gave her such untold satisfaction that she had to ask, and be told, every time.

" My great-grandmother," she murmured.

" No, darling," said Lucilla. " I'm that. Your great-great-grandmother."

Meg sighed in ecstasy. Unconsciously, both to her and to Robin, that was the fascination of the beautiful and unfamiliar toys at Lavender Cottage. They had belonged to old, old people, their father, their great-uncles and their great-aunt, their great-grandmother, and back beyond them to people older still—people so old that they were now in heaven with Abraham and Elijah, when those old people had been little children. But the toys weren't old. The snowstorm was perennially young, and so was the seashell that sounded like the sea. And the spillikins were more beautiful than ever, for the ivory took on a deeper and lovelier colour with every year that passed, though the little girl who had had them on her sixth birthday was now with Elijah. The whole mystery of time and eternity breathed like a perfume from the fragile toys. Grandmother kept the spillikins in an old cedarwood box, and for the rest of her life Meg would never smell cedarwood without thinking of Elijah.

For Meg's religious ideas at this time had been formed more by Mrs. Wilkes than by her mother, and Mrs. Wilkes leaned more to the Old Testament than the New. Sally told Meg shyly and beautifully about the Baby in the manger and little lambs carried in the arms of the Good Shepherd, and Meg listened courteously, but was not as yet very deeply impressed, but Mrs. Wilkes's dramatic accounts of the adventures of the Old Testament heroes sent her trembling to her bed and were quite unforgettable.

" And up to 'eaven 'e went," Mrs. Wilkes would say of Elijah, " with such a clanging and a banging of that fiery chariot that you could 'ave 'eard it from 'ere to Radford. And all the angels shouted, ducks, and all the archangels blew their trumpets till the sky split right across to let 'im in. Like a thunderstorm it was, ducks. Somethink awful."

And then Mrs. Wilkes would fling her apron over her head and herself back in the kitchen chair to demonstrate the awfulness of the noise and light. And that was the way people went to heaven. To Meg it was wondrous strange and deliciously alarming that such happenings could engulf a little girl who had once played spillikins.

" Did Elijah play spillikins, Grandmother? " she asked Lucilla.

" Yes, darling," said Lucilla.

" Really, Mother! " protested Margaret.

" They tell me it's a very old game, Margaret," said Lucilla mildly. " One of the oldest. I expect Elijah played it as a little boy with bits of bone. I expect he played it with his Granny."

" Did Daddy play spillikins with you when he was little? " asked Meg.

" Yes, darling," said Lucilla. " He played it very well. He always beat me, as you do."

" Did his Daddy play it with you when he was a little boy? " asked Meg.

" Yes, darling. He played well, too, but he didn't always beat me because when your grandfather was a little boy I wasn't so very old myself."

Meg laid down the last spillikin, that made her victor, and folded her hands in her lap while she considered the mysteries that surrounded her. " Maurice," she said, gravely and sweetly, as though he were beside her. Of the two little boys, he was the most real to her because she had never seen him as a man, and because Lucilla often spoke to her of the way he came in and out. It was as a little boy that she thought of his coming in and out, even though she knew he had been a man when he first went to heaven in his fiery chariot.

" Does his fiery chariot make much noise? " she asked.

" When, darling? " asked Lucilla.

" When he drives down from heaven to see you," said Meg.

Margaret picked up Robin, snowstorm and all, and went out to see how Zelle was getting on in the kitchen. It gave her the shivers when Lucilla and Meg started these conversations. She didn't approve of them, either. Meg had far too much imagination as it was, without Lucilla inflaming it with all her ridiculous ideas. They didn't want another genius in the family. David was more than enough.

When she had gone a crystal stillness held Lucilla and Meg. They were within their own world, as the little man and the house and the snowstorm were within theirs.

"No noise at all, darling," said Lucilla. "Indeed, I don't think people really go backwards and forwards from earth to heaven in real fiery chariots."

"Mrs. Wilkes and the Bible say they do," said Meg.

Lucilla was humbly silent, while magnificent words sounded like trumpets in her mind. "I saw as it were the appearance of fire, and it had brightness round about. As the appearance of the bow that is in the cloud in the day of rain, so was the appearance of the likeness of the glory of the Lord. And when I saw it I fell upon my face." But how could she explain to Meg the meaning of the word appearance? She had not yet seen the necessity for symbols. For her the picture of a rose was a rose, cool to touch and sweet to smell. For a little while longer she would be conscious only of the unity.

"They come and go, as sunbeams do," was all Lucilla could think of to say. "You could call a sunbeam a fiery chariot, couldn't you? It's warm and bright, and when it finds a chink in a curtain it runs into a room quicker than anything I can think of. But it doesn't make any noise."

Meg gave a small sigh, for she could not understand, and then the sigh was lost in a cry of welcome, and light broke over her face. Looking round, Lucilla was not surprised to see Hilary standing beside them. They had not heard him come. They never did hear anything when their own world enclosed them. Yet it was not until he, too, entered their world and made himself at home there that they felt the unity of it to be complete. The man, the woman and the child. Whatever the actual relationship between them, there was no more satisfactory combination. Hilary sat down, lit his pipe and smoked placidly while Lucilla and Meg put the spillikins back in their cedarwood box. The walls of their special world continued about them for a moment or two, as though Hilary deliberately held them there, and then they had gone. For a brief moment Lucilla thought she heard the distant thunder of waves on the shore, as she heard it on stormy nights, and then she dismissed the idea as nonsense. It was a windless day.

"Have you seen the man about the beetle?" she asked Hilary.

"He's in the church now," said Hilary. "Looking at the roof by himself. He'll ring up later and tell me what he thinks. He's not staying now, for I have Nadine with me. She's what she calls ' doing her face ' in the bathroom, and then she'll come over."

Lucilla took a deep breath. "Meg, darling," she said, "go and find Aunt Margaret and Robin. I expect they are in the kitchen with Zelle." Meg ran off obediently and she turned to Hilary. "What is it, Hilary? George?"

"It's just that the old boy has appendicitis," said Hilary, still placidly smoking. "He's not felt the thing for some time, it seems, but did not start to take himself seriously until six o'clock this morning. He's in Radford Hospital, and they'll operate this evening. Nadine had just come from the hospital. She couldn't bring herself to telephone. There's nothing to worry about, but she thought she'd come and tell us herself."

"There's everything to worry about," said Lucilla steadily. "Appendicitis can be nothing, or very bad indeed. And I don't doubt there's something else wrong with him, too, that you're not telling me about, as you didn't tell me about the beetle until you had to. It must all be very serious if Nadine had to do her face after telling you."

"I've never known her cry before," said Hilary. "I didn't know she could cry."

A terrible coldness stiffened Lucilla. "Oh yes. She

cries when she is seriously thwarted, or when her own care-lessness as wife or mother is brought home to her. She cultivates serenity for the sake of her looks, and does not notice when they are not well."

"Well, you and I did not notice anything wrong with old George either," said Hilary, equably.

"I have thought for a long time that he was not well," said Lucilla. "I have never disliked any woman as I dislike Nadine Eliot."

"Mother!" said Hilary sharply, for the ice in her tone seemed to him to have lowered the temperature of the room by several degrees. It was that terrible coldness of the absence of all love. Though he had noticed Sebastian's dis-like of David, it had not disturbed him at all, for he had felt it to be, in some way that he did not understand, impersonal, and something that would pass when Sebastian himself understood it. That was often the way with the hot hatreds of men. But the cold hatreds of women were much worse, for they had their roots so often in the anguish of despoiled motherhood. But to find hatred in Lucilla was to him as dreadful as it was unexpected. He had been deeply grieved for his brother, grieved because of the anxiety for Lucilla and Nadine and the children, but he had felt no such sharp pang as he felt now. "Mother!" he said again, and got up and stood in front of her. "You are talking nonsense. At the beginning you disliked her, and you had reason, but not now. Not for many years. You have loved her as the good daughter that she is for many years."

"So I said, and so I believed," said Lucilla. "Extra-ordinary, isn't it, how utterly one can deceive oneself?"

He looked at her and saw her eyes like blue ice in her white face. She sat as though she were a block of stone, and her hands when he bent to touch them were cold.

"Don't let her come in here," said Lucilla.

"Of course she must come in here," said Hilary sternly. "She is crossing the road now. Mother, this is worse than George's danger, worse than his death, if that should come. Mother, I do not recognise you."

" Possibly not," said Lucilla harshly. " I thought myself a very sweet old lady. So did you. We were both quite mistaken." She looked up and saw her daughter-in-law's tall figure swaying gracefully across the lawn. " I won't have Nadine in here, Hilary."

" You will," said Hilary.

" I can't do it," said Lucilla.

" You can," said Hilary. " You've been acting for most of your life. Supposedly sweet women always do. Put on one more act, Mother, and play it for all you are worth. Win this, and you've won."

The rocklike coldness went out of Lucilla and her mind, that had seemed to be ice and lead together, began to work again, so that her body shook with the stress of the thoughts that were tumbling through it. George, my son. George. I hate Nadine for all the misery she caused him. I've never forgiven her. I never will. Hilary does not really like women at all. So he knows how I used to act and act and act. Until just lately. Women must. He doesn't understand that. Or does he? Just once more. What did he mean by win this, and you've won? She's here. How I hate her!

" Nadine, my darling! " she said, and looked up at her daughter-in-law with every appearance of tremulous affection. Hilary could have laughed if he had not been so miserable. But Nadine stood like a tall and graceful boy before Lucilla, and made no attempt to kiss her. She had repaired the damage done by her burst of tears extremely well and she looked very lacquered, very beautiful and very hard. But her usually serene eyes were so wild that Lucilla's heart missed a beat with alarm.

" I'm sorry, Mother," said Nadine. " I deserve this, but you don't."

" My dear, I'm not interested in your deserts, or mine," said Lucilla disgustedly. " I'm only interested in George. Sit down, for heaven's sake, and tell me the truth about him."

The sudden normality of her tone reassured Hilary. The

dangerous corner was turned. He slipped thankfully out of the room and went to the kitchen.

" I am wondering how Mrs. Eliot will manage," he said to Zelle when he had told her and Margaret the news, and Margaret was crying a little in a perfectly ordinary manner and trying to find her pocket handkerchief. Thank heaven there were never any dangerous or unexpected corners with Margaret. If in years to come he had to have her to live with him, he would at least always know where he was. " There's a new lot of guests just arrived, Jill is on her holiday and Caroline has 'flu. Ben's there, of course, but I don't imagine he's at all domesticated."

" I am," said Zelle, and looked at Hilary. In spite of his anxiety there was a gleam of amusement in his eyes. She suddenly dimpled and her whole face was alight in so entrancing a manner that his heart lifted. For a moment the joy in her eyes seemed to counterbalance the anguish he had seen in Nadine's, and a sense of equation steadied him. Even though his heart sank again almost at once, his mind recognised that it was so. Human beings are not divided, and the joy of one woman was in very truth the justification of another's sorrow.

" But what about Meg and Robin? " he asked. " Could Margaret look after them here? Could you, Margaret, if Zelle goes to help Nadine? Do you think you could manage? "

Margaret blew her nose and put away her handkerchief. " Can I manage? " she asked indignantly and delightedly. "The children I've managed in my day! Zelle, you'd better go straight back with Mrs. Eliot, now at once. Mrs. Wilkes can come along with what I need for the children. I'll ring up David. Zelle, do they still have rusks for supper? "

Hilary went out and closed the kitchen door on the spate of it all. He could never make up his mind if women like Margaret actually enjoyed the welter of arrangements that always accompany disaster, or whether they formed lifebelts around themselves with it. For himself, arrangements were part of his Thing. He limped down the passage, ungainly and awkward, conscious of an intolerable heaviness of which

he was ashamed.   He had gathered from Nadine that George
was in great danger.   Well, of what?   Danger was a ridiculous word to use in this connection.   In danger of everlasting life.   Of everlasting life.   Of life.   The phrases
repeated themselves in his mind, and would have brought
him great comfort had George been another man's brother,
or even had he been less attached to him.   He went out into
the garden and smoked his pipe until Nadine joined him.

"Grandmother's wonderful," said Nadine.   "So calm,
and so loving to me.   How can she love me?   I'd hate a
woman who treated Ben or Tommy as I treated George when
I was young.   I'd murder her, I think.   Hilary, will you
come down to the hospital later on?"

"Wouldn't you rather just have Ben with you while
you're waiting?" asked Hilary.

"No, I wouldn't," said Nadine.   "When I'm pleased
with myself, Hilary, there's something about you which
makes me feel slightly uncomfortable, and I wonder if I
really like you, but when it's the other way on I find you
comfortable and I like you immensely.   Now you'd better go
back to Grandmother.   What's Zelle doing sitting in my car?"

"Whether you want her or not, take her along," commanded Hilary, and detached himself with thankfulness.
Women like Nadine, unlike women like Margaret, buoyed
themselves up not with arrangements but with the reactions
of their own emotions.   Of the two, he preferred women like
Margaret.   But it was himself whom he disliked as he went
indoors to Lucilla.   Never could he set himself to the priestly
task of assisting and comforting afflicted women (other than
Lucilla and Meg) without thinking what a pity it was that
the good God ever made them.

2

Zelle was sitting at the wheel.   "I am coming 'ome with
you, Madame.   I will explain as I drive," she said.   She
always called Nadine "Madame", and Nadine liked the
crisp deference of her tone when she did so.

" You can drive? " Nadine asked in surprise.

" Your car is the same make as Mr. Eliot's, and I can drive that," said Zelle.

" I haven't much time," said Nadine.   " I must get home and arrange about things there, and then get back to the hospital with Ben."

" I can drive fast," said Zelle.

She drove fast and skilfully, and at first in silence.   Nadine shut her eyes and had some respite.   Nothing to think of now for twenty minutes.   Zelle was in charge for twenty minutes.   The speed of the car soothed her, and the burden of her anxiety for George, and of the remembrance of all the failures of her married life, pressed less intolerably.   They were nearly at the Hard before Zelle began to explain her presence.

" Madame, I will stay at The 'Erb of Grace until your anxiety is over," she said.   " Meg and Robin will be at Lavender Cottage.   They are always good there, with the strange old toys they love.   They will comfort Lady Eliot, and it will be quieter, too, for their mother if they are there. You need 'ave no distress for your 'ome or your guests. Auntie Rose and I, we like each other.   Caroline and I also. I will look after 'er while she is ill.   I know 'ow she loves 'er father.   I will do all as you would wish."

Her quiet, confident tones were without arrogance.   She knew that her hard experience had made her an extremely competent young woman, and she was unselfishly glad of the fact.   She had her own axe to grind, of course, and acknow-ledged it.   This was her chance to make Nadine, who, thanks to David, liked her already, do more than like her, and she meant to take it.   But she wanted to help, too.   She wanted to be with Ben.   She was very fond of George and she sympathised with Nadine with an intensity which she had the selflessness to keep to herself.   It could be a relief to oneself to express one's feelings, but that was no reason for unloading them upon someone who had enough of their own already.

Nadine was not accustomed to being managed, for she was

herself a managing woman, but for once in her life she found herself glad to be taken in hand. " The guests are a Mr. and Mrs. Withers," she said. " Elderly. She has her breakfast in bed. There's a delicate son with a diet, and Auntie Rose has a boil and is a bit difficult about diets just now."

" If it's sieving, I'll do it," said Zelle.

" Yes, it is," said Nadine. " Even the chickens sieved. And there's a Colonel Armstrong who is one of those strict vegetarians. Caroline was 101 last night, and she'll probably be more this evening from being in such a state over her father. The kitchen sink has stopped up, and Mary went rabbiting and caught her foot in a trap. If there is a big disaster in a house there always seem to be little ones, too."

" I'll see to the little ones," said Zelle, and brought the car to a standstill outside the green gate.

Nadine had not realised they were home already. Usually she savoured to the full the loveliness of the way to The Herb of Grace, passing from one familiar beauty to another and coming gradually to the warm old stronghold and the river full of light. But now she was suddenly there, blinking stupidly at the stout buttressed walls and the flower-filled garden, at the small ripples washing the moon-shaped beach and the cat sunning itself on the wall. It was all so familiar, yet none of it seemed to have substance. The front door opened and Ben came out, but he did not seem alive. Apart from George, her home had for her no reality at all. She had not known it before. If she lost him would she live till the end of her days alone in a world of painted cardboard where even her children would seem puppets on strings? Fear such as she had never known took hold of her, a completely selfish fear for herself alone, a fear that was akin to the fear of death. She turned quickly to the girl beside her, not knowing what she was doing, and found herself looking into the face of a woman whom she did not immediately recognise, a woman much older than she was, with a knowledge of life and death profoundly deeper than her own, and yet not scorning her fear but entirely compassionate and understanding.

" I do not know your name," she said.

" Heloise," said Zelle, managing to sound the H with the utmost difficulty.

Nadine smiled, aware once more that Zelle was young in years. But she would never forget the maturity of her compassion. Then Ben was opening the door of the car and he was flesh and blood again. She touched his cheek and went quickly indoors to see Caroline, upstairs with Auntie Rose. When she came down again Ben was making coffee and Zelle was unstopping the sink.

" It's the wrong way round," said Ben to his mother, " but I'm simply no good with sinks."

" You must learn 'ow," said Zelle gently but firmly. " Get me the spanner from the car."

Ben got it, and he and Nadine drank their coffee standing, and watched Zelle with the spanner. Her efficiency was so reassuring that Nadine sat down to finish her cup.

" You, too, Ben," advised Zelle. " I know one feels more useful if one is uncomfortable, but it is not really so."

Ben smiled at her and sat. When they had been alone together, Zelle had neither kissed him nor condoled with him. She had given him one quick appraising look and tackled the sink. But under her crisp matter-of-fact talk, her quick movements, he was aware of the warm current of her love and of her pride in him. For one glance had told her that he was managing this all right, that he had managed the whole difficult day well and competently, though he was not naturally competent. How odd it must seem to her, he thought, that he should have come to maturity and known no real testing. And even this bit of anxiety, what was it compared to her testing times? She had no idea, really, what he was made of. How courageous was love, he thought, that could give itself so unreservedly to it knew not what.

He smiled at her quickly again and turned to his mother, wondering about her and his father, as he had been wondering at odd moments all through the day. What did they feel about each other, after all these years of marriage, all

these children and all these ups and downs? One lived
with one's parents and yet one did not really know much
about them. Their life together was something from which
even their children were shut out. "Look after your
mother," George had said to his eldest son that morning,
and had had nothing else to say. Even Caroline had seemed
to vanish from his mind. His mother, Ben thought, beneath
all the complications of her whole complicated nature, had
achieved now at rock bottom the same simplicity of feeling.
Perhaps as love deepened it became progressively more
simple. He and Heloise were only at the beginning, and
love seemed a mystery that in its exploration would not be
simple. Hard, perhaps, and difficult, but not simple. Yet
for survival there must be this root of simplicity, and they
must find it as his father and mother had done.

"We must go, Ben," said Nadine. "I'll just fetch my
coat."

He found himself out in the garden, waiting for his
mother at the green gate, with Heloise beside him. The sun
was low and had lighted candles in the wood. They stood
shoulder to shoulder and he had taken her hand and was
holding it firmly while they watched the sunset. But neither
of them was thinking now of the other, or of the sunset, but
strongly, and with pure intention, of George, and without
knowing it they had achieved a union with each other deeper
than any that had come to pass before.

It was so that Nadine found them as she came out of the
front door, and preoccupied as she was, she could not do
other than see them with an almost desperate clarity. A
man and woman clearly outlined against the sunset, so close
to each other that they looked one figure carved out of strong
dark stone, immovable and not to be divided. They looked
to the distance, not at each other, and it was the confidence
of that forward look as much as their seeming indivisibility
that for a moment tore at her heart, so that she put up her
hand against the jamb of the door to steady herself. Poor
children, she thought, poor confident children! What a
way they will have to travel before it's that way with them,

if it ever is! And even then their bodies can be parted and the body that lives will ache for ever.

Her flash of vision was gone in a moment. She dabbed angrily at her starting tears with her handkerchief and was scarcely aware of either of them as she went down the garden path and got in the car. Yet as Ben pressed the self-starter she leaned forward and without in the least knowing what she did gave Heloise the same kiss as she had just given Caroline, the kiss of a completely distracted but most affectionate mother.

CHAPTER XVIII

SOME hours later Sebastian sat in one of the cushioned window-seats in the drawing-room at Damerosehay, looking out at the moonlit garden and marvelling at its amazing beauty. He had put out the lights in the room and was aware of it behind him as a shadowed place with which he seemed to have no more concern. It was the garden that held him fascinated. The moonlight was so bright that he could see each tree, each clump of flowers, more distinctly than he had seen them in the day, when the misty autumn heat had merged colour and form into a blur of loveliness that he had found confusing. But there was no confusion here. Mystery, far deeper than by day, but no confusion. That moonlit country out there had meaning. Each tree, each gleaming white chrysanthemum, had its own meaning and was yielding it to him. He did not know what the meaning was, any more than he understood the meaning of himself, but he possessed it as an integral part of his own being. A sentence of farewell that he had read somewhere occurred to him. " Until we meet in the meaning of the world." Only he dropped the preposition because the words did not carry him forward to some distant future, but described the joy of his present state. He did not understand yet because he looked into the meaning only from the threshold. Though he had no further concern with the shadowed world, yet he was not quite free of it. But the meaning was there, and he was a part of it and possessed it.

The ilex tree just outside the windows was a towering presence, and the stars seemed alight in its highest branches. Though he did not know it, he was sitting on the same window-seat where Lucilla had sat more than thirty years ago, when she first came to Damerosehay, and where she had fallen asleep and dreamed of paradise. He did not know it, but he began to think of her and to hope that she was not lying awake in too great anxiety. He feared that she was. The more he thought of her, the more certain he became that she suffered. He wished he could send her some of his peace. He wished it intensely, and went on wishing it. No, not some of his peace, for that was a niggardly way of giving, but the whole of it. Yes, the whole of it. He owed her so much and he had nothing else to give. He longed with all the power of his being to give this one and only thing that he possessed just now, and abandoned himself and his longing to the will of God.

He felt a momentary joy in the abandonment, yet as the peace began to drain away from him the joy went, too. The garden darkened and the shadowed room took hold of him. A great fatigue was eating away his peace. He had been prepared for the loss of it, but not for the fact that something else must take its place, not for the substitution of this ghastly fatigue. He knew to what it was leading him, and he felt great fear as the moment drew nearer when the meaning would have gone from the garden and the last of the peace from his soul. He knew it was still within his power to halt the moment and bring back the peace, but he did not do it. For Lucilla's sake he did not do it. Instead he strengthened his wish until it became not only longing but a willed intention, and of his own choice the utter exhaustion of all his powers and the bitterness of death took hold of him together.

It was the meaninglessness that made the bitterness. Behind him in the shadows his past life lay like a heap of dust and rubble, mistakes and sins and failures all piled together there, all achievement turned to nothingness, the misery of irreparable loss lying over it all like a pall of smoke. Such an eternity of pain, and all to no purpose. All of it leading to nothing but this exhaustion, this dread of death and fear of extinction. In his ignorance he had thought he would welcome death, he who had never tasted the fear of it until now. He did not know how long he endured the fear, for time as he had hitherto understood it had also lost all meaning. Each moment of it seemed a century, and yet when the centuries had gone by the striking of the clock in the hall told him that only an hour had passed since David after supper had gone up to Sally's room, and he had come in here and switched out the lights to watch the rising moon.

The old clock was like a friendly voice calling him out of a nightmare.   He was still here, in the world of Damerosehay. The bitterness of death had washed over him, but it had not taken him away.   He sat for a long time in a state of nothingness, exhausted but nothing else.   Perhaps it had been merely illusion, a phantom of his confused mind, and the lost peace, too, only illusion.   Nothing was real now except the exhaustion of his body, a cold sickness of exhaustion that brought upon him a new sort of fear—the ridiculous childish fear that he would not be able to get himself off this windowseat, across the room and up the stairs to bed.   And he could not be ill now—on this particular evening, of all evenings—with General Eliot seriously ill, Sally's baby already on the way, Mrs. Wilkes preoccupied and David distracted.   Death no longer mattered.   The meaning, if any, of the world no longer mattered.   Nothing mattered but that he should refrain from making a nuisance of himself.

He heard light footsteps running down the stairs and David came into the room.   He supposed he must have spoken, for he heard David's voice answering from a great distance, " She's asleep now.   Everything all right so far.   It won't be for a long time yet.   Barnes has gone back to the hospital to see how they're getting on there.   What a turmoil all at once!   I'm sorry.   Aren't you cold, Weber?   Let's light the fire and have a drink.   Do you mind the lights? The moonlight is glorious, but so damn cold.   Come over here and get warm."

The distant voice seemed to come nearer and clearer, staccato and edgy with worry, catching Sebastian's attention away from his own distress.   David switched on the two reading lamps by the arm-chairs and bent to light the fire. Sebastian's problem contracted a little.   It was not upstairs that he had to get himself, but to the arm-chair by the fire. He got there while David's back was turned, and then in another moment his host's old brandy was a reviving fire in his body, and his panic receded.

"It was good of you to wait up, and I'm ready," said David gently.

Sebastian's mind groped in confusion. Was he waiting up? He had not intended to. He had only meant to watch the moonlight for a moment, and then had come those phantasms of life and death and held him where he was. For what was David ready?

"That is, if you're not too tired," said David, "and would still like to tell me."

With horror Sebastian remembered. He had asked David if he might tonight talk about himself. He had thought by doing so to make reparation. What madness! How, by torturing himself and embarrassing David, could he atone for his injustice? Well, he was delivered from his madness, for this night of anxiety was no time for such a thing.

"Not tonight," he said.

"Why not tonight?" asked David, smiling.

"You've enough on your mind."

"Actually, so little," said David humbly. "Only the usual things, death and birth, and those made as easy as the comforts of the fortunate can make them. And George may not die, and according to Barnes Sally most certainly will not. And if there is another trouble I shall see that, too, in better proportion when I have heard what you have to tell me."

There was appeal in his voice. He now wanted that which earlier in the day he had not wanted. Perhaps he was right, thought Sebastian. Perhaps he himself had been right when he had felt that he must surrender to David the only thing he had to surrender. "Prithee, go in, seek thine own ease." He would have liked to say that to David now, pushing him back into his own comfortable world, but impossible though it was to share one's experience with another, perhaps there were times when it was right to try. He was not capable of intuition now, but he had been this morning. It might be that only by such a surrender would

K

he be able to convince David that his hatred had passed.
And that, he remembered, he had decided he must do,
where and when he could. For all he knew, this was his
last chance. But the words he wanted would not come to his
confused mind, and if they had come he knew he had not the
strength to utter them. At least, that was what he thought
he knew, but what did he know? Nothing. And he himself, in this abysmal hour, was nothing. If the nothingness
that he was must still do this thing, then something other
than himself must form his nothingness to thought and
speech. To it he surrendered himself, and presently began
speaking slowly and quietly, with many pauses but no real
break in his narrative.

" There is so little to tell, really," he said. " So little that
I wonder that I have, until now, been unable to speak of it.
After so many years, too. Time is supposed to heal. I do
not know why it has not done so in my case. The fault must
have been in myself. Perhaps in the rigidity of my grief
and hatred I would not humble myself to be healed.

" You have remembered that recital in Paris, and so you
know what my life was like before the war. Much like your
own now. I had a measure of success. I worked hard, but
the rewards were great. I married. My wife was a singer,
a German whom I met at her home in Hamburg between the
wars. The marriage of two artists is not always happy, but
ours was as perfect as marriage can be. We had three
children, two boys and a girl. We would have called ourselves entirely fortunate had it not been that I hated the
regime in Germany, and she resented my hatred. But, as
artists, politics pressed less heavily upon us than upon many
others. We travelled a great deal, and our country home in
my native Austria was very remote.

" Just before the war I became ill and was threatened with
tuberculosis. We went to our mountain home, and were
there when the war broke out. Mercifully bad health put
active service out of the question for me, and I was glad, for
even had I not been a pacifist, which I was and am, I could
not have fought for a way of life I hated. I continued my

work in Austria, in Sweden and Finland, but I would not
give any more recitals in Germany, and when Christiana
went each year with the children to visit her parents in
Hamburg I did not go with her. I did not wish her to go,
and in spite of our love a bitterness came between us because
she would not discontinue her visits. She had a great
devotion to her parents, whose youngest child she was, and a
great devotion to her country, unchanging in its verity. You
know what I mean by the verity of one's country, that country of our birth whose ground beneath our feet, whose airs
and verdure, keep faith with the strength and wisdom of
what is past and are unpolluted by the passing corruption
of the present. I should have understood her better, but I
was more cosmopolitan than she. I was at home in many
countries as she never was. If I had let her go in the early
years with a better grace, she would not have withstood me
so violently when in that year of the great fire-bomb raid I
refused to let her go to her parents' golden wedding. It was
chiefly because of the danger of the times that I refused, but
partly also because there was no sympathy between her
parents and myself. They were whole-hearted supporters
of the regime and disliked my pacifism. Because of it they
had opposed our marriage. I disliked them and was jealous
of her devotion to them. I have always had intensely strong
likes and dislikes; until adversity left me for a while with the
power of love dried up in me."

Sebastian had continued speaking fairly easily, though
sometimes breathlessly. David had smoked at first, moving
a little occasionally, but now he stubbed out his cigarette
and sat perfectly still. Sebastian was vaguely conscious of
something unnatural in his stillness, but his whole being was
so focused upon this thing that must be given, so gathered
into this form of thought and speech to which he had been
shaped that he might give it, that his mind could make no
comment upon it. But he could not go on. Some vague
horror seemed to be between them, like the pit of contrast
into which he had so often fallen.

David knew it was not contrast now, it was likeness. In

their past lives one particular thing had represented to both of them the peak of misery, and it was the same thing. David knew what it was, and with every moment that passed the silence grew more terrible to him. He heard footsteps overhead, distant because in this old strongly-built house one did not hear things very easily, and knew that Sally had awakened to pain and that Mrs. Wilkes was looking after her. But he could not move and go to Sally. By this time tomorrow night Christopher would have come and he would have three children, two boys and a girl. But they could not sit here in silence. He must say something. He must get them through it.

" She took the children," he said, making a statement rather than asking a question, and his voice was ugly, a voice that Sebastian would not have recognised had he been attentive to it. He had not even been told that Sebastian's wife had won that battle with her husband, but he knew that she had. He seemed to know her, passionate, strong-willed, with no sense of danger, devoted to her husband, but even more resentful of his pacifism and his antagonism to her parents than he realised.

" She took the two youngest," said Sebastian. " Her father was ill at the time, and she thought he would not see his grandchildren again, or her either, if she did not go and take them. Josef, our eldest child, was not well and he had to stay with me. I still had Josef after the others had died in the flames of Hamburg. I went to Hamburg and saw the smoking rubble of the house, and so I knew how they had died."

There was another long silence, and this time David could not break it. He knew now the chief reason why Sebastian hated him. To what extent, at some deep level of existence, the experience of one man is subconsciously known to another, he had no idea, but he did not suppose it possible for a man to be in the presence of the murderer of his children and not be emotionally aware of it. For David always thought of himself as being the only man who had dropped bombs on Hamburg on the night of the fire-bomb raid. In his nightmare he had always been alone in that dark sky. Only one man had done it.

"I'll tell the rest as quickly as I can," said Sebastian. "You have some rough idea, I expect, of the suffering and confusion in Eastern Europe both before the Allied victory and after it. I need not describe it. At one time Josef and I were in a refugee camp in Eastern Germany; for we had been in Germany, staying with friends of mine, when the Russians overran the country. There were many children in that camp, with not enough to eat and little help or comfort for them when they fell ill. It is wonderful how patient children are when they suffer and how tenacious some of them can be of life. You think the small spectre must die, and yet he lives. After a time that camp was closed, and those of us who were of Austrian birth were put on a train and sent to Vienna, to be sorted out and dealt with there. It was bitter winter weather and there were delays on the journey, owing to the snow and the breaking down of the engine and so on. We were on that train for four days and nights without food or water. We were packed like sardines. The cold was indescribable. A few went mad. Some died. Josef died. When they emptied us out of the train at Vienna, and pulled Josef out of my arms, I imagined that I was sane, but I suppose that I was not, because in the next camp where they put me I attacked and injured one of the Russian guards because I imagined he had murdered Josef. I might have killed him if another guard had not put a bullet through me. After that, when I came out of hospital, the Russians put me in a concentration camp. When I at last came out our friend Hamilton rescued me and got me to America, where in the intervals of jobs of work I put in a good deal of time in hospitals for various forms of mental and physical disaster.

"The rest you know. You have listened very patiently. Why I imagined that I must tell you this, as a gift that I owed you, I do not now feel very sure. My recitation must have been an ordeal that you would have been glad to be spared. But with no foreknowledge that I should benefit

myself, telling you has been a release almost equal to
the catharsis that you gave me when I watched your
Lear."

It was perfectly true. Relaxed in his chair, Sebastian felt
a sense of immense relief. He felt ill, but not so ill as he had
felt earlier. His mind was clear and even receptive. He was
able to realise now that David's ordeal was not over, and was
worse than he knew. He was aware of an agony of indecision in him and then of a decision made.

" Would it help you if I were to tell you why you hate
me? " asked David. " There are obvious reasons, of course,
but for a man of your quality they do not account for the
intensity of your dislike. It must puzzle and distress you.
You may be less distressed if you know the reason."

" I do not dislike you now," said Sebastian gently. " But
I should like to know the reason for what is past."

" I was a bomber pilot in that raid on Hamburg," said
David.

For a few minutes Sebastian felt nothing at all but a sense
of calamitous shock. Then his mind slowly awoke to the
knowledge of darkness. The mind has pits, and he clung
above the abyss and swung there. The one man whom he
had for so long and so intensely hated. The man so like
himself that he might have been himself. It might have
been he who had dropped bombs on Hamburg, murdering
his own wife and children. It was he. The darkness was
like the darkness of his prison days that had been lit only by
that light of oneness. World suffering. Who was suffering
most at this moment, himself or David? Had he killed
David's children, or David his? He did not feel very sure,
but it was not important since they were together in what
they suffered, caught in this lunatic age that was not of their
making. Or had they made it? While one of them har-
boured one thought of hatred, hugged to himself one moment of self-indulgence, they were not guiltless of the misery
of these times. Mutual guilt locked them together, as well
as mutual sorrow. For one man to hate another in such a
situation was sheer madness. Wicked though the times

might be, never in the history of the world had one man's life been so interwoven with that of another. What men felt to be the meaningless writhing of the whole interlocked surface of human affairs was a sort of mockery of what union might be; of what it was down in the depths where the selfless had union with each other and their God. A mockery and a signpost at the same time.

"What shall we do?" asked David.

Sebastian looked up and saw him standing by the fire. His eyes were those of a bewildered child, and he had spoken like a child.

"Do?" asked Sebastian, startled.

"If I have judged your silence rightly, you will not want to stay on in this house," said David. "I should not have told you. It was difficult to know what to do."

Sebastian realised that he had been silent for much longer than he knew. The mind has pits. But he was no longer swinging over the abyss. There was ground under his feet and an extraordinary increase of strength in his body. He sat up and took a grip upon himself. They were in country that was dangerous for David. The nearness of birth and death had brought them to a borderland where he was at home, but not David.

"Do?" he said again. "Have some common sense. Put another log on that fire. Sit down and light another cigarette. What you have told me has certainly given me the explanation that I wanted, but it's done a great deal more than that. It has not only explained my dislike, but transformed it into the exact opposite. I expect that's always the way when half-knowledge becomes true understanding. Half-knowledge is the breeding ground for error. I doubt if you can separate true understanding from love."

"I don't think I know what you are talking about," said David. He had obeyed Sebastian's commands and looked himself again, though tired and confused.

"It is extremely difficult to put it into words," said Sebastian. "Not long ago Lady Eliot said to me, 'I am glad you love David.' Women can say these things without embarrassment. At the time I had no answer to make to that. But the old have prevision."

" I have taken in the sense of what you say," said David slowly. " The egocentric are not capable either of much hatred or of much love, but as far as I am capable of either, I feel them both at this moment. It is myself whom I hate."

" In that case half-knowledge has bred error in you, too," said Sebastian. " Men of your type, and my type, should never fight a war. We see too far for sanity but not far enough for understanding. If your wife and children had been killed in one of the raids on London, you would have seen that as the work of one man only. I don't doubt you saw the bombing of Hamburg as the work of one man only, and that yourself. You saw far enough to recognise instinctively the oneness of men in their guilt. I was able at one time to see the oneness of men in their pain. Neither of us saw far enough to see the oneness of the guilt and the pain. But there is such a union. Men have a union with each other which makes them in very truth one man, each of them members of one body. You cannot divide your hatred and love between yourself and me when there is no division between us."

David moved restlessly. " All the same, in the one body there is division between the hand and the foot," he said. " The hand can be white and shapely and the foot dark and ugly with disease." He stopped, struggling for words, and Sebastian waited patiently. " The undivided being is in pain because of the deformity, sees it and is in grief. When that bright beam of seeing touches the darkness, then the darkness sees itself for what it is. Self-hatred is torment then, but what else is possible? "

" I have been harping on unity," said Sebastian, " but there are divisions that must be harped on, too. If a sick man identified himself with his cancer he would lose his reason. Instead he offers himself to the surgeon's knife— that beam of light you spoke of—in faith and hope."

" Many of us are responsible for our sickness," said David grimly.

"Certainly," said Sebastian. "And so for the sickness of the world. If we seek our own healing, it is also for the healing of the world." His voice, even and quiet, changed suddenly to a queer note of panic. "But, my God, the cost of it! The fear of the knife and of the pain."

"Why are you afraid?" asked David. "For you, it is almost over."

"In this world, yes," said Sebastian. "Perhaps it was your fear I shared just then. But there's a way to endure that makes it bearable."

"What?" asked David.

"You know," said Sebastian.

"Yes, after tonight, I know," said David. "That piercing light—increasingly to love it. Already, a little, I think I've welcomed it. And we are not alone. The same for us all. The same light."

"You feel alone," said Sebastian. "That's the essence of it."

"Yet you know that what you feel is not the truth," said David. "And it's the knowledge that matters."

"You're lucky, for you start with it," said Sebastian. "I endured in ignorance. I had heard, but I did not know."

"Yet it's the same in the end," said David.

"Yes," said Sebastian. "But it's a bitter journey when knowledge comes so late."

"That's another mystery," said David. "Why early for one and late for another?"

"I couldn't tell you," said Sebastian.

"All part of it, perhaps," said David. "You endure without conscious knowledge up to the point when you can do so no longer. For my weakness, that point has come early. To your strength it came late."

"I don't know," said Sebastian.

David looked at him and got up. "It's late," he said. "And it's been the most exhausting day. I'll come up with you."

"You will be sitting up alone?" asked Sebastian. "Would you rather be alone? I could stay."

" You could not," said David, smiling. " And if I can't be with Sally, I'd rather be alone. Not that I ever feel alone here. When you have lived almost all your life in the same house it becomes good company. And so do all the people who lived here. I'll give you an arm up out of that chair."

" I wish I knew about them," said Sebastian. " I have been very much aware of their fortitude."

" I'll tell you about them as we go upstairs," said David. " Christopher Martin, Aramanthe and Jeremy. The Eliots. And now you."

" I have not lived here," said Sebastian.

" You have," said David. " If you'd only been here a week, you'd still have lived at Damerosehay. You know what I mean. In the future the discerning will be just as aware of you as you are aware of Christopher Martin. He was a sailor whose ship was wrecked on the marshes a hundred years ago. That overmantel was made out of some of the ship's carving. And you know that old cornfield that you pass on the road through the marshes, not the one on the inland side of the lane that is sown and reaped each year, but the one in the marsh? The ship had a cargo of grain and that queer tough corn has sprung up every year since the ship was wrecked there."

" ' Except a grain of wheat fall into the ground and die '," Sebastian remembered. There were so many kinds of death, and probably the one he had chosen tonight was one of the easiest. But it would not be unproductive. Though he knew nothing else about it, he was sure of that. He heard not a word more about Christopher Martin, Aramanthe and Jeremy, though he did hear the music of David's voice telling their story. He did not suppose that David imagined he was listening. The story was merely a ruse to disguise the fact that he was more or less carrying him upstairs.

Yet at his own door he straightened himself and spoke with astonishing vigour. " I am very glad," he said, " that I saw your Lear. Yet it's not Lear who speaks the most perfect line in the play; that command that one remembers. Good night."

David found himself looking at a door that had been quietly closed in his face. He put out his hand to turn the handle and go in, for he wanted to help Sebastian to bed and do all he could for him. Looking after himself might be just the last thing that would be too much. But the door seemed to face him with a blank refusal.

" O, let him pass ! he hates him much that would upon the rack of this tough world stretch him out longer."

His hand fell from the door and he turned away.

CHAPTER XIX

I

LUCILLA that evening went to bed even earlier than Meg and Robin, and when Margaret had bathed them they had their milk and rusks in her room, sitting in two little chairs at a small table set before the crackling fire of wood and fir-cones, that had been lit for the occasion in the basket grate, and she lay against her piled-up pillows and watched them. She had been expecting an evening of anxiety, thinking of her dear old George, but, contrary to her expectations, she was enjoying the children. She knew it was completely shocking that she should be able to enjoy anything when George was so critically ill that there was no sort of certainty that he would be alive tomorrow, but she was not shocked. She had lived so long that she was well aware that these moments of respite were a normal part of anxiety or grief. They were like the periods of cessation of pain that came in childbirth, when one fell exhaustedly asleep and then woke again to more pain. She had learned to welcome them and make the most of them, even if they came at quite unsuitable moments, for they did not last long.

She did not often see the children after their baths, and the sight enchanted her; they were so downy, so rosy, so sweet-smelling and roundabout. Even Meg looked fat in a bunchy blue dressing-gown over rose-pink pyjamas, with her hair very smooth and shining after its brushing, her cheeks flushed with the warmth of the fire and distended with rusk. Mouse, asleep in front of the fire, had buttoned herself up into a round ball, with her tail over her nose. Robin, fat at any time, looked completely circular in a scarlet dressing-gown that had once belonged to Jerry. It gaped between the buttons, Jerry having been a slim child, much in the fashion of Mrs. Wilkes's jumpers. His cheeks were as scarlet as the dressing-gown and his riotous damp curls shone like burnished copper. He absorbed his milk with loud noises, taking both hands to it, his head tipped back and his mug over his nose. He had kicked off his bedroom shoes and his toes wriggled with pleasure. When he had finished he emerged, panting with the effort, and smiled at his great-grandmother, his dimples and his two teeth engagingly prominent. Then he reached for a teaspoon and scooped up the sugar at the bottom of his mug, but there wasn't as much of it as there might have been. " More," he commanded, and Meg handed him her mug to be similarly dealt with. Margaret, entering at this moment, Lucilla drew attention to the episode with a movement of her head.

" So fortunate," she said, " that Christopher should be of the sex he is. Another Lord of Creation in the nursery will do His Highness no harm."

" He's started," said Margaret. " Mrs. Wilkes has just rung up."

" Already! " ejaculated Lucilla. " What a hurry he's in! How is my darling Sally? "

" Very placid," said Margaret. " Mrs. Wilkes says she likes being in her own home."

Lucilla had no comment to make upon this, for her views were already well known to her daughter. Instead she said, " How safe the room looks, Margaret."

Margaret looked round the dainty little room, fire-lit and curtained with flowering chintz against the evening chill. With its four-poster, flounced dressing-table, bow-fronted chest of drawers, and religious pictures of lost sheep and angels with lilies that Lucilla had had since childhood, it did not seem to belong to this unsafe world at all. And neither did Lucilla, sitting up in bed with a square of old lace draped over her white hair. And neither did the children, lapped in a security of rosy warmth that appeared inviolable and eternal because the room was four-square and the curtains were drawn and outside was the deep quiet of the country. Margaret sighed, aware of illusion, and seemed to see the little room like a coloured ball spinning alone through the vast night, gallant but no bigger than a drop of dew shaken off the petal of a flower. She was not used to such fancies, and it gave her what Lucilla's old maid Ellen used to call " a turn ". Well, but it was like that. And so were they all. The mystery that surrounded one's small span of life was at times quite terrible to bear.

" Let them come, Margaret," said Lucilla. " And let them go. With equal quietness."

" Who, Mother? " asked Margaret, startled.

" Moments like these."

" I thought you meant—people," said Margaret. " Those who are born and those who die."

" Well, so I might have done," said Lucilla. " We should not hold possessively to either. Though I doubt, Margaret, if I practise what I preach. Have these children said their prayers? "

" No," said Margaret. " Hearing the children say their prayers has always been your prerogative."

She spoke without bitterness, yet Lucilla felt reproached. For so many years they had worked together for the children, the grandchildren and now the great-grandchildren, and Margaret had been like the foundation of the house, not remembered unless deliberately thought about, while she had been like the decorative bits that would have made a poor showing but for the hidden strength below.

" Margaret," she said, " looking back when we are old, I wonder if we really know whom we've loved best through our lives? "

" Surely we do," said Margaret. " With you it's been Maurice and David."

" So I've always imagined," said Lucilla. " But now I'm not sure. I believe when I am dying I shall only think of you."

Margaret went white and then went scarlet. She clasped her knobbly hands together in a most ungainly manner as she fought for words.

" Don't bother with them," said Lucilla. " You've never been any good at them. You've never really been any good at anything, Margaret, except laying yourself down as a foundation stone. Now take away the children's dirty mugs and plates and get my Bengers ready, and then come back with it and take them to bed. Then you'll have to feed the dog. I'll want a hot bottle later, and you'll have the stove to see to and the breakfast to lay ready for the morning. I'll have mine in bed, of course. You will have to wait up because Hilary will be ringing up about George, but you can get on with the mending while you wait. I don't know what time you'll get to bed, and I shall probably get you up with indigestion in the night, and so will the children, and possibly the dog. I know I reproach you sometimes with doing unnecessary work, but that's only because I know how much there is that is necessary. I won't go on, Margaret, because I'm getting breathless, but I'm sure you know what I mean."

Margaret took the children's tray and fled precipitately, Mouse waking up to follow her.

" Mouse is very fond of Aunt Margaret," said Meg.

" Providence saw fit to bestow more sense on dogs than men," said Lucilla. " I've always thought it a pity, but one must not question the ways of providence."

" What does providence mean? " asked Meg.

" Good management," said Lucilla. " It's also a name we give to God when His management is not what ours would have been under the circumstances. Don't listen to me, darling. I talk nonsense at this time of night. Kneel down, both of you, and let me hear you say your prayers."

Meg knelt down instantly, folded her hands, as always, upon the second button of her dressing-gown counting from the top, and shut her eyes. Robin flopped to the floor with a deep sigh, sat back on his heels and scratched his head. Meg was naturally pious but Robin was not.

Lucilla regarded him severely. " Kneel right up, Robin," she commanded sharply.

Meg opened her eyes to defend him. " He's so young, Grandmother," she said. " He doesn't know any words yet."

" Words are unnecessary in prayer," said Lucilla.   " Reverence is.   Kneel *up*, Robin.   Shut your eyes and fold your hands.   If you don't I won't give you a sugared almond."

" Two? " cajoled Robin.

" One," said Lucilla.

" Two," said Robin, and rolled over on his back with his legs in the air.

Lucilla began to feel very tired, but for the sake of the child's immortal soul she could not be beaten.   " One," she said.   " And if you don't do as you're told I'll telephone for Daddy to come and spank you in the morning."

Robin knew Daddy's spankings.   He'd had one yesterday. He knelt up, clasped his hands on his stomach (the third button counting down), bent his head and shut his eyes. His long lashes lay gently on his flushed cheeks, casting an entrancing shadow, and one red curl flopped over his forehead. Lucilla was sure that a sweeter picture of piety was not to be seen even in heaven.   Meg began to pray very quickly, while it lasted, leaving out the middle verses of " Loving Shepherd " and concentrating on the first and last.   She and Mummy had decided that that was best on Robin's wicked evenings.

" Amen," she said.

" 'Men," said Robin, scrambling to his feet.   " Shoogar mond? "

Lucilla reached for her black velvet bag and took out a silver box.   For an incredible number of years this same box had contained sugared almonds for the grandchildren, and she had hardly been able to bear it when during the war they became unobtainable.   She was a conservative born and bred, but she would say for the Labour government that under its ægis sugared almonds had come back upon the market.   She took out a mauve one for Meg and a pink one for Robin, and they sat on her bed sucking and smiling at her, until Margaret was heard coming upstairs with the Bengers.

" Good night, my darlings," said Lucilla.   " I am very sorry for all those poor old ladies who have no great-grandchildren."

2

But when Margaret, too, had said good night, after bringing her a very carefully edited telephone message from Hilary
which did not deceive her in the least, her room no longer
gave her a sense of safety.   That happy time had passed, as
in the rhythm of things she had known it would, and the
birth-pangs were on her again.   Her fire had not quite
gone out, and Margaret had lit a nightlight for her, but that
seemed to make no difference to the darkness and the cold.
They came from the mystery of things, and the consolations
that fear devises, light and warmth, and painted images of
the mystery that translate its awfulness into terms of merely
human comfort and love, were no protection at all against it.
It was one of those nights when she feared death, feared it
so much that the sweat came out on her forehead and her
hands and feet were cold.   She had never been so afraid, so
wrung.

But, then, not for years had death been so near; not near
to her, though soon it would be near, but to a son of hers who
would die tonight.   She knew that her son would die.   It
would be George, for Hilary and George were the only sons
left to her, and Hilary was well.   It must be George.   No
one knew what mothers suffered when their sons died.
No one knew.   It was having the child going out into the
darkness without you, and you not knowing what would
happen to him there.   It was the wrong way round.   One
should be there oneself with arms held out to welcome the
child and make the first strangeness bearable.   Arms?   One
wouldn't have arms.   She tried to remember Maurice, and
the enfolding of his spirit that she felt so often, but she
couldn't remember very well because since George's danger,
Maurice had not been with her.   Or she hadn't felt him
with her.   Perhaps she was too desperately welded to George
and his suffering body to be able to be aware of a bodiless
son. Perhaps the presence of Maurice had been mere
illusion. Wishful thinking. The creations of one's fancy
could have more reality than flesh and blood if one willed it

so. Perhaps the mystery was no mystery, but just darkness and nothing else. Perhaps she would never see any of her sons again.

" The consolations of religion." She had a number of the material ones here in this room, and she looked round at them desperately, but they gave her no help. There was a picture of Christ healing the sick, but the face of the Christ, kindly and sentimental, had nothing whatever to do with the darkness and the cold. And the sick, though they had crutches and a nice clean bandage here and there, looked remarkably healthy. Not one of them looked as George must be looking at this moment. Even her crucifix did not help her. The figure was so tidy and the face so composed and peaceful. Maurice had looked neither tidy nor peaceful during the hours before he died. Such consolations were nothing but a mockery. But she was a religious woman, wasn't she? She could remember two conversations she had had with Sebastian Weber when she had held forth in such a manner that she might have been all the pretty angels in her pictures rolled into one. And he had borne with her. He had even loved her. She clung for a moment or two to the thought of him. He had more true religion than she and so had Hilary. They were her sons (yes, Sebastian, too, a son of her spirit though not of her body), and so much younger than she, yet they knew so much more.

What would Hilary think she should do now? Couldn't she pray for her son who must die? She had learned to pray in the war, but she had been younger and stronger then, and had not been so paralysed by fear that her confused thoughts could frame no words. She had scarcely known, in those days, what it was to be afraid, and she had been able to do things then, and offer them, and now she could not. Her fear changed imperceptibly and became fear for herself. What if she should live on and on, as some old people did, losing the power of thought and speech as well as action and becoming a sort of nothingness? A moth flew into the night-light, and it flickered and went out. Such a little thing, but it seemed to put the final touch to her misery. She began to

cry, a thing she had not done for years, and she seemed to
go on crying and being afraid of being nothingness for hours
and hours.

"Well, what of it? Would it matter?"

She did not know if she had fallen asleep or if she hadn't.
She thought at first that Hilary was with her and speaking
to her, but the room was so dark, with the nightlight out and
the fire fallen almost to ash, that she could not see. And
then she thought that she *was* Hilary, years ago, after he had
lost a leg and been gassed in France, lying in bed in a state of
deadly fear, not of death but of life. A young man facing
the possibility of blindness and a crippled body, uselessness
and dependence, throughout a lifetime, and so paralysed by
fear and weakness that he could not even pray; might never
pray again if he lost his reason and became just nothingness under the pressure of it all. And prayer, for him, was
life.

"What of it? Would it matter?"

It was not Hilary speaking to her, but to himself. She
was not one with him now, she had gradually become
separate again, as she had become separate when his body
had been taken from hers after his birth, but in dream or in
reality her soul had been within his for a while, as his body
had once been within hers, and she had shared his experience.
This morning in the garden he had not said much about his
fear, he had been too intent upon trying to tell her about
what he called " the agonising effort of substitution." She
had not understood very well. She understood better now.
Of course it was agonising, for at its highest level it meant
complete acceptance not only of such small ups and downs as
she had hitherto accepted, playing at acceptance as though
it were a sort of game, but of a thing that seemed unbearable,
for you could not substitute what you had not taken entirely
to you.

Waking or sleeping, she did not know which, she passed
into a wider place that held not Hilary only, but all her
sons. The two who had died in the first war, Maurice and
Roger, were here, and her son Stephen, whom she had

seemed to know less well than the others, and who had died not long after the second war, broken by the deaths of his two sons in Norway and Greece. And George was here, too, her son whom she believed to be dying at this moment. And David, and Stephen's two sons. And, worst of all, Ben and Tommy and Jerry, and little Robin become a man. They were all here, and time did not exist because it was for every one of them the hour of his dereliction. She was the mother of them all, and had she not given them life they would not have suffered in the wars. Their agony, far worse than her own fear, was not to be borne. It was intolerable that even the mercy of time should be stripped away, so that pain that had ended was here in the room with her, and pain that had not yet begun. If it had been possible for her prayer to reach both backwards and forwards in the time that had vanished, and hold and comfort each of her sons in his dereliction, she would have accepted her own, even the whole misery of nothingness that extreme old age can bring, with final and entire willingness. What of it? she would have said, and taken it entirely to her.

" And I do," she said aloud. Waking or sleeping she heard herself speak, meant what she said and willed it. It was as though she were lifting up a great weight from the ground, struggling as she had never struggled before and never would again. " I do. It is my prayer." With a flash of knowledge she knew what she had not known before—that prayer has nothing to do with time. Her prayer at this moment was lifted as high above time as was the body of her sons upon the cross upon the wall.

For though her fire was no more than a faint glow of rosy ash, she could dimly see her crucifix, and it was no longer the comfortless wood-and-plaster image that had nothing to do with the mystery, but was the mystery itself. It was the body of her sons that hung there. She could not see very clearly, but she knew that, and recognised the fact with no shock or horror, but a profound and grave satisfaction. For the salvation of the world. And she was the mother of such sons. It was a matter of immense yet humble pride to her, as it must be to Mary, whose prayer also was lifted above time, and as it would be to Nadine, when she had become truly a mother. Nadine? Was it possible that she had once thought she hated Nadine? What nonsense! She might as well hate herself. All mothers were one mother in the motherhood of Mary.

The figure glowed, and she wished she could see the face. If she could see the face, whose would it be? She did not try to see, for she felt herself unworthy, but just as she shut her eyes that she might not see, she knew it was Sebastian's. Immense peace flowed to her from the knowledge. She did not ask how or why, for such peace did not live with questions. The clock downstairs began to strike and she began drowsily to count the strokes. It must be six in the morning by this time, she thought, for the hours of her misery had been many. But it was only twelve. She was too drowsy and peaceful to be astonished. She merely turned her head on her pillow and went to sleep.

3

She was awakened by Hilary bringing her breakfast tray, and being by now restored to normality by the deepest and most healing sleep she ever remembered, she was immediately intensely annoyed.

"What *are* you doing, Hilary?" she demanded. "Margaret should bring my tray. I will not be seen even by my own sons in déshabille. Put it down on the chest of drawers. Draw the curtains. Go away without looking at me and return in ten minutes."

Hilary did exactly as he was told. Lucilla had everything for the beautifying of herself put ready to her hand, and when he returned in ten minutes she was her most charming self. She had also remembered a little of last night and she was ashamed. She had accepted the full humiliation of old age and death, and her loss of temper was unforgivable. What she would be looking like by the time Hilary had finished looking at her she did not know. That was part of it. He would probably not notice, but David would. She asked for his forgiveness.

"What for?" asked Hilary.

"I was feeling a little irritable, dear."

"You can't feel more irritable than I do," said Hilary. "I had scarcely crawled into bed last night before it was time to get up again and say Mass. And as for those sermons, I still have not got them by heart."

"Have you had breakfast, dear?" asked Lucilla.

"No, I haven't," said Hilary. "I had to come and tell you the news."

Lucilla had now remembered all of last night, and she gathered her courage to hear the news she knew already. "George," she said.

"Pulling round remarkably well," said Hilary. "I rang up before I came over. No one thought he would, but he has. Not out of the wood yet, of course, but there's every hope. . . . Are you all right, Mother?"

"Quite all right," said Lucilla. "I only want a cup of tea. What was the good of putting the tray over there on the chest of drawers? Bring it here and pour yourself a cup, too. I see Margaret's put one for you. Where's Margaret?"

"Feeding those pestiferous children," said Hilary. "Robin has tantrums and Meg is starting a cold. Mother, are you quite sure you're all right? You wouldn't like your sal volatile or your eau-de-Cologne or whatever it is you take?"

"Quite all right, dear," said Lucilla. "It was just the shock."

"What shock?"

"My dear old George pulling round. In the night I knew he was dying. At least, I knew one of you would die last night, and who could it be but George?"

Hilary looked at her, and his irritation vanished. His face took on what Lucilla called his professional look, composed and concentrated.

"You drink your tea, Mother," he said quietly. "I'll be back in a moment."

He went downstairs, and Lucilla heard the sharp click of the telephone receiver being lifted in the hall, but she could not hear his conversation. He was back in a few minutes, saying cheerfully, " No anxiety about Sally. No baby yet, but no need to worry."

" Sebastian? " asked Lucilla. " If it is he, I am not too selfish to be glad."

" Yes," said Hilary. " He and David sat up late talking, so it would have been in the early hours of the morning. He did not call anyone, so he gave no trouble to anyone. That would have pleased him. He could not have taken his departure more courteously."

" There's one thing to be said for being ninety-one," said Lucilla. " No good-byes can be for long. You'll feel this, Hilary. Have a cup of tea at once."

Hilary smiled as he obeyed. Nevertheless, the tea was what he wanted. Heat, he thought, there's nothing like it. All the best symbols have to do with light and fire and warmth.

" So will David," continued Lucilla. " So will we all. What was it about that man, Hilary? "

" What is it about anyone? " asked Hilary. " Nothing in them that you can describe. Just their special quality. What they will be coming to you like the air of another country, and coming more and more freshly as the soul approximates to her true worth."

" So few do in this world," said Lucilla. " For most of us the journey is still before us when we die. Hilary, I was very terrified last night."

" One is sometimes," said Hilary. " But I'm sorry. I don't like you to be terrified."

" I had the most peculiar night," said Lucilla. " Terrible at first, and I couldn't pray, but I tried to do as you told me, and after that, round about midnight, everything was all right and I went to sleep. Do you think it was all a dream, or was it real? "

" I've no idea," said Hilary.

" Hilary! " ejaculated Lucilla in annoyance.

"Well, you haven't given me much information as to how everything was all right," said Hilary.

"But I can't, Hilary. It's impossible to describe what happened."

"I expect it is," said Hilary quietly.

"But visions are real, aren't they?" asked Lucilla pathetically. "One doesn't just make them up?"

"I don't know a thing about visions," said Hilary. "I never have them."

"But you ought to, Hilary," said Lucilla. "You're such a good man."

"I doubt it," said Hilary. "Anyway, I don't have visions. My approach is sacramental, not mystical. I've no imagination."

"But did I imagine my vision?" asked Lucilla.

Women, thought Hilary, for he was abominably tired. He had not, like Lucilla, slept since midnight. But he tried to pull himself together. "I've no idea, Mother," he said gently. "But does it matter? What matters is that you prayed, really prayed, perhaps more selflessly than you have done before, were comforted and slept."

"But if only I could know that my heavenly comfort *was* heavenly comfort, and not just imagination," said Lucilla despairingly. "Hilary, if only I could *know*!"

"Why couldn't it be both?" asked Hilary. "If God has given you imagination, isn't it very probable that He will speak to you through it? If you are starving, Mother, you give thanks for a good meal, and don't enquire if it came from the attic or the basement. If your store-room is in the attic it came from both."

"I see," said Lucilla. "And I *was* starving."

"So am I," said Hilary.

"Darling!" cried Lucilla. "And there's nothing on this tray but my scrap of toast. There are biscuits in the cupboard behind you. How peculiar human beings are! Our friend is dead, and we go on talking and eating as though it hadn't happened."

"There was a rightness in his death that makes it seem

entirely natural," said Hilary. "And so we go on being
entirely natural. The death of the young rends us, for it is
not natural. At least, we don't feel it so. I think George's
death would have rent us, for he did not seem ready, and his
children need him. But Sebastian had finished. The last
of the chaff had gone. That courteous departure was fitting
and right."

"And it's fitting that a soul should go from Damerose-
hay and a soul should come to it on the same day," said
Lucilla. "But, all the same, I wish he had seen
Christopher."

CHAPTER XX

I

"WELL, that's safely over," said Dr. Barnes, imbibing David's sherry and stretching out his long and weary legs in profound relief. "What's the time now? Seven o'clock. As usual, it was a long hard labour, but she weathered it better than usual. A fine baby. You can go up when you like."

"Thank you very much," said David with difficulty, for even his lips seemed stiff with exhaustion, and a glass of sherry on top of no sleep had made him slightly light-headed.

"What for?" snapped Dr. Barnes, irritable now as well as weary. "Only doing my work."

"The Eliots have kept you at it pretty ceaselessly these last thirty-six hours," said David. "If you'd had Sally in hospital, only a corridor would have separated her from old George—I mean—who do I mean?"

"I know who you mean," said Dr. Barnes. "You're entirely fuddled. Why didn't you go to bed last night? No point in staying up."

"There was Sally," said David. "And Weber."

Dr. Barnes drew in his legs, opened his half-closed eyes and was suddenly as alert as he had been before he had sunk into his comfortable chair. "Weber?" he asked. "What about him?"

"We talked late," said David.

"What insanity!" said Dr. Barnes. "Was he exhausted afterwards?"

"Yes," said David.

"Did Mrs. Wilkes, or Nurse What's-her-name, or you yourself, help him to bed?"

"No," said David.

"Or go in during the night to see how he was?"

" No."

" If you had done either of those things," said Dr. Barnes, " it is possible that he would not have died." His tone was drily professional and yet challenging as he lit one of his host's cigarettes, fanned away the smoke and looked at him. The challenge revived David, and he met the look steadily. There was contempt in the doctor's eyes.

" Did you ever read Lear? " David asked quietly.

" At school, I suppose," said Dr. Barnes. " What's that got to do with it? "

A smile came into David's eyes, but it did not reach his lips. He looked profoundly sad, the doctor thought, but the shame that should have been in his face was not there. " If you'll excuse me," he said, " I'll go up to my wife."

2

Sally was already drowning in sleep when David kissed her. " A very important baby," she whispered, lifting her eyelids as though leaden weights pressed upon them. " The silver rose-bowl. Tomorrow."

" You can come in, sir," said Mrs. Wilkes, standing flushed and dishevelled but triumphant in the door of the adjoining room, " and take a peep. Come quiet, now."

With a feeling of deadly lethargy David went into the dressing-room. His mind was divided between thankfulness that Sally's ordeal was over and desolation because Sebastian had died. Had he lived, after reaching such understanding, their friendship would have lasted through their lives. As it was, in spite of Sally and the children, in spite of so many things, the loneliness of the journey appalled him. Yet he meant to take it. Looking down upon Sebastian's face, so grimly satisfied in death, he had pledged himself to take it. " I have a journey, sir, shortly to go." He had half-started so many times, turned back completely many times. He would not again. If he did not hold on this time his way would never again converge upon Sebastian's.

" 'Ere you are, sir," said Mrs. Wilkes, approaching him with a white bundle.

David recalled himself to where he was and blinked stupidly at the bundle. When greeting his children for the first time he could never summon up the enthusiasm proper to the occasion. Just at first it was difficult not to dislike them for the time they'd given Sally; until they started to wail in that unbearably reproachful manner which to his morbid way of thinking put the whole blame for everything, the sorrows of their own adult lives included, upon himself. And they were so ugly. Meg had been puny and yellow, like a minute Chinese hobgoblin. Robin had been scarlet as a boiled lobster and bald as an egg. Both had looked a hundred years old, wizened and intolerably wise. But it had to be got through.

" He's all right, Mrs. Wilkes? " he asked cheerfully.

" Finest child I ever delivered," triumphed Mrs. Wilkes. " Tipped the scales at eight and two ounces. 'E's all right, bless 'im, barring 'e's a girl. . . . There now, sir, you'd better sit down. Tired right out, you must be, wot with one thing *and* another. Sit down in that chair and you shall 'ave 'er, the ducks. Asleep, she is. Nursing the child ain't wot's considered right these days, but that Nurse What's-it, she's downstairs making 'erself a cupper tea and wot the eye don't see the 'eart don't grieve for."

" Does Mrs. Eliot know he's a girl? " asked David weakly.

" Yes, sir. She don't take it to 'eart. Just said, ' Never mind. I'll 'ave Christopher next time '."

David groaned within himself and sat in the chair indicated by Mrs. Wilkes. She gave him his daughter and went out of the room (tactful, delightful, unprofessional woman that she was) shutting the door behind her. David braced himself, parted the folds of the shawl and looked down upon a face like a flower. Slowly the baby opened her eyes and looked at him. He maintained for ever afterwards, against great scepticism, that for a full three minutes her great violet eyes were not unfocused, but looked straight into his. All his exhaustion and lethargy left him as he gazed down into those astonishing eyes. He would not love another child as he loved Meg, that was not possible; but it was to this child, his daughter Christiana, that he would hand on whatever had been given to him of the genius that delights and enlightens the darkness of the world. He could not wake Sally to exult with him, but through the open door he could see her bright head on the pillow, and the golden light streaming into the room. The sky was flecked all over with gold clouds like feathers, as though wings protected the world. Sunset or sunrise, he had forgotten now which it was. The old house seemed to hold them both, and to hold, too, a welling up of freshness, as though it renewed its youth in the youth of this marvellous child.